PENGUIN BOOKS

Black Rabbit Hall

Black Rabbit Hall

EVE CHASE

PENGUIN BOOKS

PENGUIN BOOKS

UK | USA | Canada | Ireland | Australia
India | New Zealand | South Africa

Penguin Books is part of the Penguin Random House group of companies
whose addresses can be found at global.penguinrandomhouse.com.

First published by Michael Joseph 2015
Published in Penguin Books 2016
001

Text copyright © Eve Chase, 2015

The moral right of the author has been asserted

Printed in Great Britain by Clays Ltd, St Ives plc

A CIP catalogue record for this book is available from the British Library

ISBN: 978–1–405–93890–7

www.greenpenguin.co.uk

For Oscar, Jago and Alice

I held him wise, and when he talked to me
Of snakes and birds, and which God loved the best,
I thought his knowledge marked the boundary
Where men grew blind, though angels knew the rest.

If he said Hush! I tried to hold my breath;
Wherever he said Come! I stepped in faith.

Brother and Sister, George Eliot

Prologue

I feel safe on the cliff ledge, safer than in the house anyway. A few feet from the coast path, it's a twenty-minute scramble from the edge of the estate, far enough from Black Rabbit Hall's watching windows, a secret place. I hover on the cliff above it for a moment or two, wind snapping my dress against my legs, soles of my feet tingling, then lower myself carefully, gripping the clumps of grass, sea roaring in my ears. (Best not to look down.) One small heart-stop drop and I'm perching right on the edge of sky.

Jump too wide, it's all over. I wouldn't do it. But it occurs to me that I like the fact I could. That I have some control over my destiny today.

Pressed against the cliff wall, I finally catch my breath. So much frantic searching: woods, rooms, endless stairs. Heels rubbed raw in too-small plimsolls. And I still haven't found them. Where *are* they? Shading my eyes from the sky dazzle with my hand, I scan the bottle-green cliff tops on the other side of the cove. Deserted. Only cattle in the fields.

I inch down then, spine against the rock, and hitch up my dress, brazenly, so that air tunnels through my bare bent legs.

Still at last, I can't outrun the events of the day any

1

longer. Even the sound of the waves on the rocks makes my slapped cheek sting afresh. I blink and there is the house, silhouetted on the inside of my eyelids. So I try to keep my eyes open and let my mind loose in the vast pink sky, where the sun and moon hang like a question and an answer. I forget that I am meant to be searching. That minutes move faster than clouds at dusk. I think only of my own escape.

I don't know how long I sit there, my thoughts pierced by a huge black bird diving over the cliff, so close its talons might catch in my hair. I instinctively duck in its wing draught, nose meeting the cool skin of my knees. And when I look up my gaze is no longer on the sky but flotsam bobbing on the high tide swell below.

No, not flotsam. Something more alive. A dolphin? Or those jellyfish that have been washing up in our cove all week, like a lost cargo of grey glass bowls? Maybe. I lean forward, dipping my face over the edge to get a better view, hair blowing wildly, heart beating a little faster, starting to sense something terrible shifting just below the shimmering blue surface, not quite seeing it. Not yet.

One

Lorna, over three decades later

It is one of those journeys. The closer they get to their destination, the harder it is to imagine that they'll ever actually arrive. There is always another bend in the road, a judder to the dead end of a farm track. And it is getting late, too late. Warm summer rain is drumming on the roof of the car.

'I say we cut our losses and head back to the B-and-B.' Jon cranes over the steering-wheel to get a better view of the road liquefying behind the windscreen. 'Grab a pint and plan a wedding somewhere within the M25. What do you reckon?'

Lorna draws a house with her fingertip in the condensation on the window. Roof. Chimney. Squiggle of smoke. 'Don't think so, darling.'

'Somewhere with a sunny micro-climate, perhaps?'

'Ha. Funny.' Despite the disappointments of the day so far – none of the wedding venues has lived up to expectation, too much overpriced chintz – Lorna is quite happy. There is something exhilarating about driving through this wild weather with the man she is to marry, just the two of them cocooned in their wheezing little red Fiat. When they're old and grey they'll remember this journey, she thinks. Being young and in love and in a car in the rain.

'Great.' Jon frowns at a looming dark shape in the mirror. 'All I need now is a massive bloody tractor up my backside.' He stops at a crossroads where various signs, bent by the wind, point in directions that bear little relation to the angle of the corresponding roads. 'Now where?'

'Are we lost?' she teases, enjoying the idea.

'The satnav is lost. We seem to have gone off grid. Only in your beloved Cornwall.'

Lorna smiles. Jon's is a boyish, uncomplicated grumpiness, one that will evaporate with the first sign of the house, or a cold beer. He doesn't internalize things, like she does, or make obstacles symbolic of other stuff.

'Right.' He nods at the map on Lorna's lap, which is scattered with biscuit crumbs and folded haphazardly. 'How are your map-reading skills coming along, sweetheart?'

'Well . . .' She scrabbles the map open, bouncing the crumbs off to join the empty water bottles rolling on the sandy car floor. 'According to my rough cartological calculations, we're currently driving through the Atlantic.'

Jon huffs back in his seat, stretches out his legs, too long for the small car. 'Brilliant.'

Lorna leans over, strokes his thigh where muscle fades the denim. She knows he's tired of driving down unfamiliar roads in the rain, touring wedding venues, this one, furthest away, hardest to find, saved for last. They would be on the Amalfi coast, if she hadn't insisted that they come to Cornwall instead. If Jon's patience is wearing thin, she can hardly blame him.

Jon proposed back at Christmas, months ago, pine needles crunching beneath his bended knee. For a long time, that was enough. She loved being engaged, that state of blissful suspension: they belonged to each other but they still woke up every morning and chose to be together. She worried about jinxing that easy happiness. Anyway, there was no mad rush. They had all the time in the world.

Then they didn't. When Lorna's mother died unexpectedly in May, grief punched her back to earth and the wedding suddenly felt inescapably, brutally urgent. Her mother's death was a reminder not to wait. Not to put things on hold or forget that a black date is circled on everyone's calendar, flipping ever closer. Disorienting but also oddly life-affirming, it made her want to grab life in her fists, totter through the litter of Bethnal Green Road on a drizzly Sunday morning in her lucky red heels. This morning she wiggled herself into a sunshine-yellow vintage sixties sundress. If she can't wear it now, when?

Jon changes gears, yawns. 'What's the place called again, Lorna?'

'Pencraw,' she says brightly, trying to keep his spirits up, mindful that if it were up to Jon they'd simply stuff his large, sprawling family into a marquee in his parents' Essex garden and be done with it. Then they'd move down the road, near his adoring sisters – swapping their tiny city flat for a suburban house with a lawn sprinkler – so his mother, Lorraine, could help with all the babies that would swiftly follow. Thankfully, it is not up to Jon. 'Pencraw Hall.'

He runs a hand through his corn-coloured hair, sun-bleached almost white at the tips. 'One more shot?'

She beams back. She loves this man.

'To hell with it, let's go this way. We've got a one in four

chance of getting it right. Hopefully we'll shake the tractor.' He presses his foot hard on the gas.

They don't shake it.

The rain continues to fall. The windscreen is mashed
with cow-parsley petals, pushed into snowy drifts by the
squeaking wipers. Lorna's heart beats a little faster beneath
the crisp cotton of her dress.

Even though she can't see much beyond the rivulets of
rain running down the window, she knows that the wooded
valleys, river creeks and deserted little coves of the Roseland Peninsula lie beyond the glass, and she can sense them
already, hulking out there in the mist. She remembers
being on these roads as a kid – they visited Cornwall most
summers – and how the sea air would rush through the
wound-down window, blowing away the last trapped bits
of grimy Greater London, and the stitch of tension on her
mother's face.

An anxious woman, her mother suffered from insomnia
all her life: the seaside seemed to be the only place she
could sleep. When Lorna was little, she wondered if the
Cornish air swirled with strange sleepy fumes, like the
poppy field in *The Wizard of Oz*. Now a small voice in her
head cannot help wondering if it swirls with family secrets.
But she decides to keep this thought to herself.

'Are you sure this old pile actually exists, Lorna?' Jon's
arms are straight and stiff at the wheel, eyes reddening with
strain.

'It exists.' She pulls up her long, dark hair, twisting it
into a topknot. A few strands escape, fringing her pale
neck. She feels the heat of his glance: he loves her neck,
the soft baby skin just below her ear.

'Remind me again.' His eyes return to the road. 'Some old manor house you visited with your mum while on holiday down here?'

'That's right.' She nods enthusiastically.

'Your mum enjoyed a stately, I know that.' He frowns up at the mirror. The rain is falling in undulating silver sheets now. 'But how can you be sure it's this one?'

'Pencraw Hall popped up on some online wedding directory. I recognized it straight away.' Already so many things have faded – the hyacinth notes of her mother's favourite perfume, the exact click of her tongue as she searched for her reading glasses – but in the last few weeks other memories, long forgotten, seemingly random, have come into unexpected bright focus. And this is one of them. 'Mum pointing up at this big old house. The look of awe in her eyes. It sort of stuck with me.' She swivels the diamond engagement ring on her finger, remembering other things too. A pink-striped paper bag of fudge heavy in her hand. A river. 'Yes, I'm almost certain it's the same house.'

'*Almost?*' Jon shakes his head, laughs, one of his big belly laughs that rumble against his ribs. 'God, I must love you.'

They drive in companionable silence for a moment, Jon thoughtful. 'Last day tomorrow, sweetheart.'

'I know.' She sighs, not relishing the thought of returning to the hot, crowded city.

'If you wanted to do something non-wedding-related?' His voice is disarmingly soft.

She smiles, puzzled. 'Sure. What sort of thing?'

'Well, I thought if there was anywhere of . . . significance you wanted to visit?' The words fall awkwardly.

He clears his throat, seeks her dark eyes in the driver's mirror.

Lorna won't meet his gaze. Her fingers are loosening her hair so that it swishes down, hiding the flush of her cheeks. 'Not really,' she mumbles. 'I just want to see Pencraw.'

Jon sighs, changes gear, lets the subject go. Lorna wipes the scribble of a house off the clouded window and peers through the cleared porthole, nose to the cold glass, looping in her own thoughts.

'So. The reviews?' he asks.

She hesitates. 'Well, there aren't any reviews. Not exactly.'

He raises an eyebrow.

'But I did phone and speak to a real live human being, the lady of the house's personal assistant or something. A woman called Endellion.'

'What sort of a name is that?'

'Cornish.'

'Are you going to use that as an excuse for everything?'

'Yeah, yeah.' Lorna laughs, slides her feet out of her silver flip-flops and rests them on the hard grey plastic of the glove compartment, pleased by the tan marks and that her pale pink nail varnish hasn't chipped. 'She explained that it's a private house. First year it's been hired out. So no reviews. But nothing dodgy, promise.'

He smiles. 'You can be such a sucker sometimes.'

'And you can be so bloody cynical, my darling.'

'Realistic, realistic.' He glances into his mirror, eyes hardening. 'Jesus.'

'What?'

'That tractor. Too close. Too big.'

Lorna tenses in her seat, twists a strand of hair around her finger. The tractor does look menacingly large for this narrow road, which is more like a tunnel now, sealed by steep verges of solid rock and a roof of interlocked tree canopies. She grounds her feet on the floor of the car.

'We're going to stop at the next field gate and see if we can manage a U-turn,' Jon says, after a few more tight minutes.

'Oh, come on . . .'

'It's dangerous, Lorna.'

'But –'

'If it's any consolation, the house is sure to be like all the others, some B-and-B chancing it. A dodgy conference centre. And if it's any good we won't be able to afford it.'

'No. I've got a *feeling* about this house.' She tightens the coil of hair, pinking her fingertip. 'A hunch.'

'You and your hunches.'

'You were a hunch.' She puts a hand on his knee just as the sinews of his muscles contract and his foot slams down on the brake.

It all seems to happen at once: the squeal of rubber, the skid to the left, the dark form leaping across the road into the bushes. Then terrible stillness. A clatter of rain on the roof.

'Lorna, are you okay?' He touches her cheek with the back of his hand.

'Yeah, yeah. I'm fine.' She runs her tongue around the inside of her mouth, tastes the metal of blood. 'What happened?'

'A deer. Pretty sure just a deer.'

'Oh, thank God. Not a person.'

He whistles beneath his breath. 'Close call. Sure you're okay?'

A rapping on the driver's door. The knuckles are hairy, the skin raw red. The tractor driver is a dripping mountain of orange anorak.

Jon winds down the window apprehensively. 'Sorry for the hard braking, mate.'

'Bloody deer.' A man's face, as battered as the landscape itself, veers up to the window. He peers over Jon's shoulder and fixes his dull stare on Lorna. It is a stare that suggests he doesn't come across many petite thirty-two-year-old brunettes wearing yellow sundresses. A stare that suggests he doesn't come across many women at all.

Lorna tries to smile at him but her mouth feels twitchy at the corners. She might burst into tears instead. It hits her how close they've just come to catastrophe. It seems all the more unbelievable because they are on holiday. She's always felt immortal on holiday, especially with Jon, who is protective, secretly rather sensible and built like a hammer.

'They get in through gaps in the hedging. Caused a crash only last month.' The man blows a gust of stale breath into the small confines of the car. 'Two mangled a few yards from this spot. Damn creatures out of control.'

Jon turns to Lorna. 'Someone's trying to tell us something. Can we call it a day?'

She feels the tremor in his fingers, knows she can't push him further. 'Okay.'

'Don't look like that. We'll come back another time.'

They won't, she knows it. They live too far away. Their lives are too busy. They work too hard. When they get back Jon's family building firm is due for a long project, some swanky new penthouses in Bow, while the first day of the September school term rears ever closer for her. No, it's all too difficult. They won't come back. And Cornwall is impractical. It's expensive. It asks too much of their guests. It asks too much of Jon. Her dad. Her sister. Everyone is only indulging her because they feel sorry for her losing Mum. She's not silly.

'You don't see much traffic on this road. Where you folks going?' asks the tractor driver, scratching his bull neck. 'You certainly picked the day for it.'

'Trying to find some old house.' Jon reaches into the glove compartment for a sugar fix to steady his hands. He finds an ancient sticky mint, half unwrapped. 'Pencraw Hall?'

'Oh.' The man's face withdraws into the cave of his hood.

Sensing recognition, Lorna sits more upright in her seat. 'You know it?'

A brisk nod. 'Black Rabbit Hall.'

'Oh, no, sorry, we're looking for a Pencraw Hall.'

'Locals call it Black Rabbit Hall.'

'Black Rabbit Hall.' Lorna rolls it around her tongue. She likes it. She likes the name. 'So it's near?'

'You're practically on its drive.'

Lorna turns to beam at Jon, near-death crash forgotten.

'One more turn off this lane – last chance to leave – that takes you into the farmland, what's left of it. Another half-mile or so before you hit the estate proper. You'll see the signpost. Well, I say you'll see it. Buried in the bushes. You'll need to keep a look-out.' He stares at Lorna again.

'Funny place. Why do you want to go there? If you don't mind me asking.'

'Well . . .' Lorna takes a breath, ready to launch into the back story.

'We're checking it out as a wedding venue,' Jon says, before she has a chance. 'Well, we were.'

'Weddings?' The man's eyes bug. 'I'll be damned.' He glances from Lorna to Jon and back again. 'Look, you seem like a nice enough couple. Not from round here, are you?'

'London,' they mutter in unison.

The man nods as if this explains everything. He puts one hand on the rolled-down window, his fingers creating a fat glove of condensation on the glass. 'If you ask me, Black Rabbit's not the place for a wedding.'

'Oh. Why not?' asks Lorna, spirits sinking again, wishing him away.

The man frowns, looks unsure how much to tell them. 'It's not in any fit state for one thing. The weather gnaws away at houses around here unless you throw money at them. No one's thrown nothing at that house for years.' He wets his cracked lips with his tongue. 'Word is there are hydrangeas growing through the ballroom floor, all sorts of funny things going on.'

'Oh . . . I love that.'

Jon rolls his eyes, trying not to laugh. 'Please don't encourage her.'

'I'd better get back on the road.' The tractor driver looks bemused. 'You two, take care, eh?'

They watch him stamp away, listen to the thuds as he climbs the serrated metal steps to the cab of the tractor. Lorna doesn't know what to think.

Jon does. 'Hold tight! Look out for Bambi. I'm going to reverse down to the crossroads. We're going back to civilization and a nice cold beer. And not a moment too soon.'

Lorna presses her hand on his arm, enough pressure to show him she means it. 'It'd be ridiculous to turn back now. You know it would.'

'You heard what the guy said.'

'We need to see it for ourselves, if only to discount it, Jon.'

He shakes his head. 'I'm not feeling it.'

'You and your feelings,' she says, imitating his earlier comment, trying to make him laugh. 'Come on. It's the one venue I'm desperate to see.'

He beat boxes the wheel with his thumbs, considers his position. 'You'll owe me.'

She bends over the handbrake, crushes her mouth against the warm bristle of his jaw. He smells of sex and digestive biscuits. 'And what's not to like about that?'

A few moments later, the little red Fiat turns off the road, then rolls like a drop of blood down the wet green drive, the canopy of trees locking tight behind them.

Two

Momma was lucky not to have been more seriously hurt in
the crash. That's what everyone says. If her taxi had skid-
ded another inch to the right, they'd have smashed the
Bond Street bollard front on, rather than just clipping it.
Momma got banged about anyway, flying across the black
cab with her shopping bags, only saving her face from the
glass with her bent-backward hand. Her new fancy hats
were not damaged. The taxi driver let her off the fare. Still,
not lucky exactly.

Ten days later, she's still got a custard-yellow bruise on
her kneecap, a sprained wrist in a splint. She has to sit, sit,
sit on a Saturday morning, rather than play tennis in
Regent's Park or chase my little sister around the garden.

Right now she is sitting in the turquoise chair by the
parlour window, her stockinged leg planked on the footstool, staring at the black umbrellas wheeling about the
square below. Her eyes have gone distant. She says it's the
painkillers. But I can tell Momma is dreaming of being
back at Black Rabbit Hall, or her old family farm in Maine,
somewhere remote and wild where she can ride her horses
in peace. But Maine is too far away. And Black Rabbit Hall
feels even further.

'Can I bring you some more tea, ma'am?' asks Nette,

respectfully averting her gaze from the startling bruise on Momma's leg.

Nette is the new – three months new – help. She has a lisp – impersonation is irresistible – and has moved from an old-fashioned household in Eaton Square, 'where they're still pretending it's 1930,' Momma says. I think Nette prefers it here. I would.

'Or another cushion?'

'No, thank you, Nette. You're so thoughtful. But I'm quite comfortable, and have drunk so much tea in the last few days that I fear another cup might send me quite over the edge.' Momma smiles, revealing the gap between her two front teeth that makes her smile seem so much bigger than anyone else's. She can stick a match in it. 'And, Nette, please feel free to call me Mrs Alton or, indeed, Nancy. No need to be formal here, I promise.'

'Yes, ma –' Nette catches herself, smiles shyly. She picks up the empty teacup and half-eaten Battenberg and slips them soundlessly on to the shining silver tray. Boris beats his tail, gives her his best doggy eyes. Although she's not meant to give the dog treats – Boris is a fatty, a glutton, and once demolished a pound of butter in one sitting then vomited it up on the stairs – I know Nette feeds him in the kitchen when no one's looking. I like her for this.

'Come here, you,' Momma says to me, once Nette's gone. She pulls up the piano stool beside her, pats it.

I sit down and lay my head on her lap, inhaling her skin tang through the lettuce-green silk of her dress. She strokes my hair. And I feel like both her confidante and her baby and that I could stay here forever, or at least until lunch. Not that her lap will be mine for long: there are too many of us – me, Barney, Kitty, Daddy, my twin Toby, when he's back from boarding school. Sometimes it feels like there isn't enough of her to go round.

'Your leg looks like a root vegetable, Momma.'

'Why, thank you, honey!'

'Your other leg is still nice, though,' I say quickly, glancing down at it, long, slim, foot stretched, pointing like a ballerina's, the second toe intriguingly longer than the first, punching out beneath the raised stocking seam.

'One pretty leg is enough. And the other looks a lot worse than it is, really.' She wraps a strand of my hair around her finger so that it looks like one of the tasselled red silk ropes that tie back the curtains. We sit like that for a while, the carriage clock ticking, London rumbling outside. 'A penny for your thoughts?'

'Grandma Esme says you could have been killed.' I can't stop thinking about the crash. The black bollard waiting for the black taxi. The screech of brakes. The hat boxes flying into the air. Things you can't imagine ever happening, happening. 'It makes me feel . . . I don't know.'

She smiles, bends over me, the tips of her copper hair tickling my cheeks. I can smell her Pond's face cream. 'It'll take a lot more than a cab on Bruton Street to kill me. New England genes, honey.'

I stare at her swollen leg again, look away quickly, wishing I hadn't. The bruise is making me feel really strange. Nothing bad normally happens to Momma. She doesn't get flu. Or headaches. Or the thing that Mrs Hollywell, Matilda's mum, has that means she must go back to bed after lunch most days and sometimes can't get up at all. On the upside, if this is the bad thing that was going to happen to Momma then I guess it's not that bad. At least it's out of the way.

'Please don't worry about me, Amber.' She smooths my forehead with the pad of her thumb. 'The young must never worry about their parents, you know? Worrying is a mother's job. Your time will come for all that.'

I frown at the floor, unable to join the dots between being fourteen years old and becoming a wife and mother myself. What happens to your twin when you marry? What would Toby do then? It bothers me.

'It's all right.' Momma laughs. 'You've got a while yet.'

'Will you still be able to ride Knight?' I say, quickly changing the subject. Knight is her Dutch Warmblood. The name makes him sound black but he's the colour of conkers.

'Ride Knight? Are you kidding?' Momma sits up straighter, winces. 'If I sit in this chair for much longer I'll go crazy. I can't *wait* to ride Knight. I'll damn well hop to Cornwall to ride him if I have to.'

Knowing Momma, this isn't as unlikely as it sounds.

'In fact, this evening I plan to talk to your father about leaving for Black Rabbit Hall sooner than normal.'

'When sooner?'

She shuffles on the cushions, unable to get comfortable. 'Next week – sooner, if Peggy can get the house ready by then.'

'Next *week*?' My head springs off her lap. 'But the Easter holidays don't start for another two weeks.'

'You can bring schoolwork if you want.'

'But, Momma –'

'Honey, you spend far too much time with your head in

17

a book anyway. Missing a bit of school is not going to hurt anyone. Too much school isn't good for any child.'

'I'll fall behind.'

'Nonsense. Miss Rope says you're racing ahead of the rest of the class. I'm not in the least worried. Besides, you'll learn far more at Black Rabbit Hall than in a stuffy old classroom in Regent's Park.'

'What sort of things?' I ask doubtfully.

'Life!'

I roll my eyes. 'I think I know enough about life at Black Rabbit Hall by now, Momma.'

She looks amused. 'Do you indeed?'

'And I'm getting too old for sandcastles.'

'Don't be silly. One is never too old for sandcastles.'

My life has been full of sandcastles. My first memory is of Toby, bent over on the beach, frantically digging, sand flicking over his shoulder in a golden arc. (He is left-handed, I am right, which means we can stand close together and not knock spades.) When it's done he sticks two razor-clam shells – 'Us,' he says and grins – on the very top: we are three years old.

'Apart from anything else, the air in London is just terrible,' Momma continues. 'And the relentless drizzle! My goodness, will it ever stop?'

'We spend most of our time in Cornwall wearing mackintoshes.'

'Yes, but it's a different kind of rain in Cornwall. It is! A different kind of sky too. A clear sky with stars. Shooting stars, Amber! Not that smoggy old thing.' She points at the grey ceiling of clouds outside the window. 'Hey, don't look like that. It's something else, isn't it? What is it?'

'It's Matilda's birthday party in nine days,' I say quietly, imagining all my classmates giggling into Kensington Palace's orangery in pastel party dresses; Matilda's older brother, Fred, down from Eton, the way one side of his mouth curls up when he smiles; Matilda herself, my closest friend, who is kind and funny and never pretends to be less smart than she is, unlike all the other girls. 'I absolutely cannot not go.'

'It's a shame it's Matilda's, I know. But it's still one party, honey.'

I don't say that I'm not the type of girl who gets invited to lots of parties. But I think Momma knows this because her voice goes soft: 'It may not feel like this now, Amber, but you have many parties to come, I promise.' She nods over to the window. 'Take a look out there. At the street. What do you see?'

I gaze out of the window at the crescent, the rivers of wet pavement, the black iron railings, the planet of grass in the centre of the square where we sometimes eat Bovril toast on sunny Saturday mornings. 'People shaking and closing their umbrellas?' I turn to her, wondering if this is the right answer. 'A nanny pushing a pram?'

'You know what I see? I see a whole world waiting for you, Amber. Look, there's a young woman in a neat little skirt suit walking to work.' Note: Momma doesn't work but she wears a navy skirt suit from Paris for church on Sundays. I guess that's work too. 'I see a couple on a bench kissing . . .' she raises one eyebrow '. . . rather passionately, I must say.'

I look away from the embracing couple quickly – obviously I wouldn't if Momma wasn't sitting next to me – and wonder how it would feel to kiss someone like that on a public bench, so lost in the kiss I didn't care who saw.

'I guess what I'm *trying* to say is that you're going to have lots of fun before you get married.'

School. Finishing school. A job at Christie's, maybe. It's hard to see that there's much room left for the fun bit before it stops.

'So you're not going to worry about missing one party?' Momma fixes the dress flat over her thighs where my head has rumpled it.

'Suppose.'

'Not a very convincing answer.'

I try to hide my smile beneath grumpiness, enjoying the pretence that Momma needs my approval, the pretence that I might not give it, that it matters at all. I know I am lucky like this. My school friends all get bossed about by their mothers, polite, faintly irritated Englishwomen in stiff dresses who never seem to throw back their heads and laugh so that you can see the wiggly bit in their throat. My mother can ride bareback. She wears denim jeans when we're in the country. And she's by far the prettiest mother at the school gate.

'Never forget how privileged we are still to have Black Rabbit Hall. So many of Daddy's friends have had to demolish their country houses and sell off the land, or open their homes to the public, awful things like that. We must never take it for granted.'

'It takes ages to get there.'

'We'll all drive down together. It'll be fun.' She nudges me. 'Hey, maybe one day they'll open an airport on the Roseland.'

'That's never going to happen.'

'Well . . . *good*.' She tucks a strand of hair behind my ear. 'We don't want to make it too easy, do we?'

'Then it wouldn't be our special place.' I say this shamelessly to please her. And it does.

'Exactly!' She grins and her eyes glint from green to yellow, a leaf and its underside. Filled with light again, distance gone. 'I always say to Daddy that Black Rabbit Hall is the one still sane point in this mad, changing world. It's our safe, happy place, isn't it, Amber?'

I hesitate. For some reason it feels as though everything rests on my answer.

Three

The storm will barrel up the creek around six o'clock, Daddy says, standing on the terrace in his crumpled cream suit, tilting back his fedora with one finger and sniffing the air, like a hunting hound. It's actually pretty obvious a storm is about to hit – the air is sticky, dark clouds are jamming the sky above a mirror-black sea – but it's not our place to point it out. We all know how much Daddy loves standing on the terrace, one hand gripping the balustrade, chest puffed, muttering about the weather and the fallow deer, complaining about the rabbits and the leaking roof. Not that anyone does anything about it.

Our house in London doesn't leak. Or drip. Or rattle in the night. Your hair doesn't get blown about as you cross the bedroom landing. Bits of the roof don't fly off in a high wind, like laundry from a line. And if it did my parents would get someone in to fix it. But at Black Rabbit Hall, none of that stuff bothers them. In fact, I'm beginning to think that, secretly, they may quite like it.

At the moment there's a bowl in the corner of my bedroom that Toby calls a potty. ('Oh, you've filled the potty again, Amber!' he hoots, and I whack him around the head with *Jane Eyre*.) There's at least six buckets in the old ballroom, which is so leaky only the little ones use it, whizzing up and down on their trikes.

Momma likes to keep things 'simple' at Black Rabbit

Hall: we don't have proper staff, just Peggy, who lives in, cooks when we're at the house, Annie, a distracted girl from the village who pretends to do the cleaning – Peggy dismissed her for laziness two summers ago, but she carried on turning up for work anyway – a loyal troupe of aged carpenters, one with a glass eye he'll tap with his screwdriver if you ask nicely, and even older gardeners, who have worked here on and off all their lives, stink of horse manure and look as if each gasping plunge of the spade might be their last. No nanny. Not when we're in Cornwall. None of my friends can believe it. But Momma didn't want us to be brought up by staff, like Daddy was, like Grandpa was, and all the other dead people hanging off the gallows of the family tree, hidden third drawer down in Daddy's desk.

You never know what you'll find stuffed in the drawers here: ration books, gas masks, a loaded pistol, a sheaf of golden curls from a dead baby, who, Daddy says, would have been our great aunt had she lived. Oh, yes, and Princess Margaret's glove. That's about as exciting as it gets.

We can only dream of a television set. Even the ancient wireless sparks when you plug it into the wall. It barely catches a signal, just a ragged stream of crackles, or broken messages picked up from local fishing boats about wind speeds and mackerel hauls. The pipes clank and groan all night, and if someone fills one of the big iron baths, it sounds like the earth itself is heaving open. There are constant power cuts – a brilliant flash, then mothy darkness – and we must make do with oil lamps from the storeroom until someone can fix it, which can take days, so the ceilings are all smudged with lamp smoke.

'It's like the twentieth century never started!' Momma laughs, as if this is the best thing ever, rather than the thing that puts me off inviting any of my friends to stay. Or maybe I just use that as an excuse. The truth is, I like it when it's just us down here. We don't really need anyone else.

I drag the Bottom Biter, the world's most uncomfortable cane chair that Great-Grandpa brought back from Bombay and can therefore never be replaced – when I'm married I'm going to buy new furniture from a department store – across the terrace. Not too far from Toby. Despite all the acres, Toby and I always seem to end up within five feet of each other here.

I'm now in prime position to watch the lightning tinselling the top of the woods. But the storm is indecisive. As if it can't quite summon the energy to break.

Toby sits on the stone balustrade in the stormy lemon sunshine, idly kicking his legs. The cat dozes beside him, tabby tail twitching against the tiny blue flowers that have seeded in the mortar. Daddy strides off to investigate the pterodactyl – according to Barney – nesting in the chimney. Momma is trying to brush Kitty's hair. Kitty squirms and protests as she always does, clings tight to the grubby scrap of cloth that is her beloved one-eyed Raggedy Doll. Barney puts his murky jam-jar of tadpoles on the ground and starts to kick a ball against the wall, his strawberry curls bouncing. The whack of rubber on dry stone sounds like every sunny spring day we've ever spent here.

That's the thing. I know this exact scene – me on the cane chair, Toby kicking his legs on the wall, looking at me, looking away, Momma brushing Kitty's hair, the smell of laundry and seaweed, me yearning for something, possibly a ginger biscuit – will repeat itself another day, as this day is a repeat of those that have come before it in other holidays. Nothing changes that much. Time goes syrupy slow. The family joke is that a Black Rabbit hour lasts twice as long as a London one, but you don't get a quarter of the things done. The other thing about Black Rabbit Hall is that when you're here it feels like you've been here for centuries but when you leave it feels like the entire holiday happened in one afternoon. Maybe that's why nobody cares that the clocks are all set wrong.

Not much ever happens.

Books help the time pass. But I have left my novel beside my bed and can't be bothered to climb all the stairs to the turret. Instead I press my toes against the armrest and steer my mind into the exquisite torture that is thinking about the birthday party I missed: Fred mostly. Thinking of him fills my body with a curious sweet heat. It comes out in a long sigh that sounds like something from the cinema, not mine at all.

Toby looks up instantly, eyeing me sharply through the spikes of his fiery lashes as if he knows exactly what I'm thinking about. Annoyingly, I blush, confirming his suspicions.

Toby and I were born fifteen minutes apart. I came first. Toby had the cord around his neck and Daddy almost lost his male heir that day. We're from two separate eggs, not connected beyond being siblings and sharing Momma's womb, yet sometimes weird things happen: things that aren't meant to happen to non-identical twins. Like when he smashed his nose crashing off the tree rope swing last year, I got a nose bleed for no reason. If I wake up unexpectedly in the night, I'll often get up and discover he's just woken too. Sometimes we even dream the same dream, which brings with it the mortifying possibility that he will dream about kissing Fred. We laugh at the same things, 'Dumb-rabbit stupid things,' as Toby always says – this is in itself a joke but I don't know why it's funny. He doesn't have to say much to make me laugh. It's the way he can hitch just the tiniest muscle in his face, or fill a silent pause with an unspoken rude word. He takes things too far. Always. It's my job to pull him back. But if I wasn't here I don't think he'd do it in the first place. He falls, knowing I'll catch him. Sometimes literally. He's usually covered with bruises. We both hate liquorice.

For most of our lives Toby and I have been at the same height, same stage, so that we've met each other eye to eye, our feet the same distance from the wooden end of the bed when he flumps next to me in the morning, chatting away while I'm trying to read. But I'm now one inch taller. I have two breasts with sore nipples hard as boiled sweets (still hopelessly minuscule, compared to Matilda's, but showing promise). On 22 January – identified at 3.05 p.m. in the girls' toilet – a sticky brown smear had appeared on my underwear, something that Momma later confirmed was the quietly triumphant arrival of the Curse. But Toby at fourteen is still the Toby that was: wiry, fiery-haired, 'weirdly beautiful for a boy', Matilda once said, denying it afterwards. His voice has gone crackly, a bit like the radio signal, and his shoulders wider, but we no longer look the same age. We no longer look much like twins either, apart from the hair. I don't think he likes that very much.

Toby starts to pick the moss from between the grey stones of the balustrade, roll it into hairy green balls and flick it off the ledge with his forefinger and thumb, seeing how far the balls will jump. We can kill hours like this at Black Rabbit Hall. We have to.

'Here, hold this for me, would you, darling?' Momma calls to me, brown elastic hairband dangling between her teeth. She waves some yellow ribbon above her head. Her hand – 'cured by Cornwall!' – is free of its splint now. 'Seawater just makes the most terrible tangles. Have you seen the state of your little sister's hair?'

I walk over to Momma, pendulum the ribbon while she brushes. 'She's been rolling around in the breakers, Momma.' Unlike the rest of us – who have Momma's scribble of a figure – Kitty is soft and plump and doesn't feel the coldness of the ocean. Like Barney, she doesn't have any fear of it either – wading out into the waves until Momma sprints in and yanks her back – which I personally think is pretty spunky for a four-year-old girl. She's quite something, our Kitty.

'Ow.' Kitty backs away from the brush. 'You're tugging Kitty's head off, Momma.'

'You should try not to get sand in your hair. Then Momma wouldn't have to brush it all the time,' I point out.

Kitty sticks out her bottom lip. 'If I was a crab I wouldn't have to brush my hair.'

'You tell me when you develop that hard shell then, Kittycat.' Momma gives up on the brush and uses her fingers to pull apart the knots in my little sister's fine blonde hair. Momma hums beneath her breath – the hum hasn't changed since I was Kitty's age: I could sing it in my sleep but I have no idea what it is – and squats down behind her, so that Kitty is tightly wedged between her knees and unable to fidget.

'Momma, will you take me to the den in the woods?' Barney heads the ball over the balustrade, wraps his twig arms around Momma's neck. 'I want to show you the den.'

'The den?' she says, like mothers do when they're not really listening.

'The new one.'

'Sounds very exciting.' Another thing mothers say when not really listening. 'You can show me later. After the storm. Easy, easy, Barney.' She picks off his fingers one by one. 'I can't breathe.'

My little brother is like one of those mini-monkeys in the Harrods pet shop, all eyelashes, mischief and bendy limbs. He'll hang upside down until his eyes pop pink. And he's at his happiest in the company of animals: a line of ants marching over his foot, a slowworm cupped in his hands, rabbits. Barney adores rabbits. He found a baby bunny on the lawn last year with sealed-shut eyes and fur like a dandelion clock and fed it warm milk through a pipette. When it died a few hours later, he cried for a whole day. He's been looking for a replacement ever since. But Barney's not a cry-baby, not normally, not like those whimpery little boys you see pulling on their nanny's hands in London parks. Barney's too busy, too curious to be miserable for long. Same as Toby like that: more alive than anyone else. The difference is that Barney is happy rushing about on his own – Peggy says he should be on a lead – while Toby always wants me around, close as possible. Until recently we'd curl up together, like two question marks, on the sofa. The tips of our fingers would touch beneath the table at supper. Now, we don't so much. We're a bit too old. Someone might see.

'Now, Momma. Please. There might be a badger in the trap,' Barney whines.

The 'trap' – a cage of twigs Toby made for him – is no more likely to catch a badger than a baby rhino. But Barney is convinced he's going to catch a badger cub and hand-rear it, even though this has never happened before and you wouldn't want to rear it even if you did catch one. They've got a terrible bite. We've been warned about the dangers of badgers. And riptides, adders and foxgloves.

'Please, Momma.'

'If you've got so much energy, how about you practise those neat little cartwheels Kitty taught you earlier?'

'I'm better at cartwheels,' says Kitty imperiously.

'So. Cartwheels are for girls. I'm better at rockets. You're completely useless at rockets, Kitty.'

'Mom-*ma*, Barney says I'm useless at rockets . . .'

'Don't you two start squabbling. Here, Toby,' Momma calls, over Kitty's head. 'How about taking your little brother for a kick-around?'

'Do I have to?'

'Yup.'

'Pssst!' Toby beckons him over. 'Better idea.' He lines up a moss ball on the balustrade and, using finger and thumb, flicks it across the terrace. Barney scrabbles up on the wall beside him. 'A bit of target practice?' Toby is looking at me, even though he's whispering into Barney's ear.

I shake my head like I'm above it all.

'Now, choose your moment carefully, Barney.' Toby

rolls a moss ball on his flattened palm. 'If you waste one you're in trouble.'

'I won't, Toby. Promise.'

'What do you think? Inanimate object, or . . .' Toby hushes his voice, glances over at me again and grins '. . . *Homo sapiens*?'

'Don't even think about it,' I hiss.

Toby glances across the terrace. 'Okay, let's do Peggy. But the deal is you won't blame me if you get told off.'

'Deal,' says Barney.

They sit and wait for a couple of minutes, two pairs of honey-brown eyes – flecked with gold, exactly like Momma's tiger-eye earrings – fixed intently on the small wooden gate that leads from the terrace to the area at the back of the kitchen garden, where the hens peck the ground and washing billows on the line. I settle back on my ringside seat, feigning disinterest.

'The target is in sight.' Toby flicks his red curls out of his eyes. His hair can't sit still either. He's got three natural partings, so it grows at different angles from his multiple crowns, and a cow's lick, so he always looks faintly electrified.

I sit forward, hugging my knees.

Peggy is out of the door. She is moving across the terrace, the wicker basket on her hip filled with white washing, wooden clothes pegs dangling in the cloth bag.

'At the ready, Barney.'

Peggy is two feet away. Toby stills Barney's eager thumb. 'Wait for it . . . wait for it . . .' Peggy is one foot away. 'And . . . fire!'

Barney's first moss ball falls short. Peggy doesn't even notice it. The afternoon already feels anti-climactic.

'Again,' says Toby, stacking up more balls on the wall. 'Fire!'

Again it falls short. Hopeless.

'Fire!'

The third lands in the basket of washing.

'Yes!' Toby and Barney raise their fists into the air.

Peggy takes a moment to realize what's gone on, first staring down at the green ball on her whites, gaze slowly moving to my brothers snorting on the wall. She sniffs – Peggy has all kinds of sniffs, this one is brisk, like she's smelling sour milk – picks the ball out and tosses it to the ground. 'Honestly.'

Peggy says 'honestly' like an older person, a teacher, a church-warden. But she is thirty-five, which is pretty old but not quite as old as Ambrose, Matilda's tortoise. It's hard to imagine Peggy any younger – or older – existing anywhere but here.

Toby says a fisherman jilted her at the altar and that is why she ended up at Black Rabbit Hall, cook, housekeeper and everything else. I have no idea if that is true, or how he knows it. But it feels true. Sometimes I catch her staring a bit too long at Daddy.

'Boys,' Momma calls. 'No monkey business. Peggy's trying to get on with things.'

Getting on with things is what Peggy does best, unlike the rest of us. She's always in a flap the first few days we arrive from London, walking too fast, like one of Barney's clockwork toys – I swear she ticks – swooping feathery dusters about like wands, wiping floury hands over and over on her apron even when there's no flour left on them, trying to remind my parents of her efficiency (and her famous pasties with gravy sizzling in their half-moon seams) even though we all know that Black Rabbit Hall would soon collapse into a pile of smoking rubble without her. And we'd have to survive on marmalade toast.

She has one of those faces you want to look at a little longer than is necessary – Matilda and I have decided this is the definition of prettiness – with round red cheeks that Peggy blames on the heat from our range ('Hotter than Hades!') and rain-grey eyes that always smile before her mouth. As my mother infuriates her by insisting she can wear whatever she wants, Peggy has imposed a strict uniform upon herself: an almost-black navy skirt that steams like a pudding if she stands in front of the fire on a damp day; a white shirt with a small frilly collar; a blue and white stripy apron tied around her waist, her name embroidered in cobalt cotton on its left-hand corner by Mad Mary in the village. I think there may be more than one apron, but they are all identical so I don't know. Whenever I think of Peggy, I think of that apron, the way it makes you notice her small, unlikely waist, then balloons over her tummy and wide hips, like the festive roof of a circus tent. Barney likes to hide in it.

It's no secret that Peggy loves Barney best, treating him to the forbidden jelly babies that she squirrels high up on a shelf in a battered tea tin. He reminds her of Little Lionel, she says, the youngest of her brothers. (Peggy is the eldest of eight, brought up in the teeniest, wonkiest cottage, like a gingerbread house made by Kitty at Christmas, five miles down the coast.) But it's also because Barney sticks daisies into her springy mat of frizzy brown hair – it's so dense the flowers never move – and slouches against her calves while he walks ladybirds from one finger to another. Peggy's calves are huge. But her feet are tiny so her legs suddenly swoop in at the ankles, like one of her nozzled icing bags. You'd think she'd fall over, but she doesn't.

'Barney!' Peggy says, pretending to be cross with him. 'Was that you?'

Toby slings a protective arm around Barney's shoulders. 'Oh, come on, Peggy. There's no mark on the laundry.'

'Not this time.'

Daddy is walking towards them now, shadow long and leggy, the sun a tinned peach half behind him. I wonder how it's going to play out. He lifts his chin, scratches his throat. 'What's going on here?'

Peggy's little silver crucifix swings on its chain in the dip of her neck. Barney holds his breath. Toby kicks his legs.

'Everything's just fine, Mr Alton,' Peggy calls over her shoulder, giving Toby a sharp look as she walks back into the house.

Not much ever happens.

'Well, that's just perfect timing, isn't it?' Momma stands up, gazes approvingly at Kitty. The wind fills her white blouse, like a sail. 'There. Sand brushed out. Plaits. Ribbons. Pretty as a picture.' She turns to Daddy. 'Isn't our Kittycat a beauty, Hugo?'

Daddy circles his arms around Momma's waist, dips his

nose to her neck and smells her like a flower. 'Just like her mother.'

Momma rests her chin on his shoulder and they stand like that on the terrace for a moment, swinging slightly, like they're being rocked by the wind. I look away. When they're like this, it's like nothing exists but them, and I glimpse the people they must have been in that unbelievable pre-history before I was born. Probably, Toby and I came out of an intimate moment like this. We all did. Barney, I know, was 'a happy accident' – I overheard Momma and Daddy talking late at night once – and Kitty born to be company for him, as there's such a big age difference between the top and bottom of the family. 'The bookends,' Daddy says. Last year Matilda offered a more detailed explanation – courtesy of her big sister, Annabel, the one who got expelled from Bedales – about what causes such 'happy accidents'. It makes me feel strange to see my parents like this now, knowing all the things I know.

'Did you find our little squatters then, Hugo?' asks Momma. Boris flumps down at her feet, panting.

'Gulls.'

'Oh, I was hoping for a nest of pterodactyls.'

'It's a bother, Nancy. We're going to have to get someone up there.'

'But who can blame them wanting to nest at Black Rabbit Hall?'

Daddy laughs, a low, rich laugh that could only come from a tall man.

'Now, Mr Alton . . .' Momma takes off Daddy's hat, leans forwards until the tip of her neat nose touches his.

No one else would dare do that. It feels like the rest of us have to knock to enter. Just like we must do at the library door when he's working. He works a lot. This is because the family fortunes never recovered from the crash of 1929, Grandpa's death duties or his fondness for the casinos of Monte Carlo. (Before we were born, Daddy had a brother who liked to gamble too, but he fell off a yacht in the Mediterranean, his body scooped up in a fishing net a week later. Disappointingly, Toby and I have been unable to extract any more gruesome details. His name was Sebastian, but he's never mentioned.)

'Mrs Alton.' He pulls her closer. Their shadow stretches like a cat on the lawn.

'I'm going to take Knight out for a quick ride.'

'Not with that gammy leg.'

'Don't be such a fusspot. I'll be quite all right.'

'Nancy, it's reckless.' Daddy's brow furrows. He has a short, square brow that furrows easily, thick dark hair and no bald shiny bit. Matilda says her mother keeps saying Daddy is the spit of Omar Sharif. 'Look at the sky. This sunshine won't last. And you know how Knight rides in a storm. He's a nutty creature at the best of times.'

'The storm won't hit until later. You just said so yourself.' She flicks Daddy's hat lightly against her thigh. We all know Momma will get her own way in the end. It's like watching butter melt in a pan.

'The doctor said your leg needs a good rest. And your wrist.'

'I'll ride Knight like a fat donkey on the beach, I promise, darling.' She puts his hat back on his head, kisses him on the mouth. 'See you soon.'

'You're impossible,' Daddy says, looking at Momma as if he wouldn't have her any other way.

When Momma leaves, our family huddle disperses, like when you take the magnet away from iron filings.

Toby and I joke that Peggy has shooed off the storm – 'It'll be back when it's hungry.' Toby tuts and I laugh at his Peggy imitation, far better than mine – and we drift lazily towards the kitchen, where our tea is running years late on account of the range dying after lunch. Barney and Kitty – who has manhandled Raggedy Doll into Great-Grandma's wooden toy pram and wrapped a red balloon around its handle – follow us, as they always do, until Barney suddenly shouts, 'Woo! Rabbits!'

He streaks off across the green lawn to the dashing brown dots, followed by Boris. The warrens are around the hydrangea bushes just before the woods. They always vanish into them before Barney gets anywhere near.

I roll my eyes. 'It's like he's spotting a herd of unicorn every time. He's five. He's seen millions of rabbits.'

'I reckon Barney will always be excited by rabbits,' Toby says. 'Just one day he'll pretend he's not.'

The dining room is at the bottom of the east turret, round and red and slightly damp, like the inside of a fruit pie. But it's miles from the kitchen, which makes Peggy complain about her feet. So when it's not Christmas or Sunday lunch or a meal involving Grandma Esme, who claims to be 'constitutionally unsuited to eating anywhere but a dining room', we eat in the kitchen, my favourite room at Black Rabbit Hall with its cornflower-blue walls – blue is meant to keep the flies away – and a larder with a happily broken lock. Unlike the rest of the house it's always warm.

Curious things go on in the kitchen: bread dough rises in china bowls, like a row of pregnant bellies; pig guts soak in salted water before being stuffed and turned into hog's pudding; tin buckets writhe with conger eels, awaiting dismemberment. There are often buckets of crabs, too, which Barney refuses to eat because crabs have character. I can't throw the poor creatures into the boiling water – a living thing must feel pain – but once they're cooked, I'll help Peggy pull out the dead man's fingers and suck the sweet white flesh from the claws. If they're dead, I don't see how they can mind. I wouldn't.

But there are no creatures in buckets today, just a greasy-looking soup bubbling on the stove that we fear is the dreaded kiddly broth, one of those recipes Peggy says we will 'learn to like' and never do. And the smell of the long-awaited scones: gusts of Heaven every time she opens the range door. Impatient now, we fidget around the old servants' table. When the scones finally appear, their tops are cracked a perfect gold. Toby bags the biggest, then has a moment of repentance and offers it to me. I let Kitty have it. Barney will be left with the smallest, of course, if he's lucky enough to get any at all. Rule is, if you're not here you don't count.

The clip-slip clip-slip of Momma's riding boots in the corridor. We sit up straighter, brighter, anticipating her walking through the door.

'Momma.' Toby wipes jam off his mouth with the back of his hand. He grins like he hasn't seen her for weeks.

'I declare myself officially alive again.' Momma tosses

the liquid copper of her hair. There is a splatter of mud up the back of her white blouse that makes me think she's not been riding Knight like a fat donkey on the beach at all. 'One. Two. Three.' She crowns our foreheads with wind-cool kisses, looks around the room and peers under the table. 'Where's Barney?'

We shrug, mouths full of clotted cream and seedy jam made from last summer's strawberries.

'Peggy, we're one down. Any idea where Barney is?'

Peggy slides another plate of scones on to the table. 'I thought he was with you, Mrs Alton.' She starts to hand around the second batch, deliberately slowly in order to test Toby's urge to grab.

'Well, he's not. The scamp.'

'He went off chasing rabbits half an hour ago, Momma,' Toby says, talking with his mouth full. 'With Boris.'

'Those two,' sighs Momma, with a smile. 'May I?' She takes a scone and dips it into the cream. 'Criminally good, Peggy.'

'I'm sorry about Barney, Mrs Alton. I should have checked.'

'It's not your fault, Peggy.'

'I do my best, Mrs Alton.' Peggy always says this, leaving a pause for confirmation afterwards.

'Of course you do, Peggy. I'll go fetch Barney. It's no problem.' Momma bends down to Kitty, flinching a little as she does so, as if her bad leg is bothering her again. 'Where will I find your imp of a brother now, Kittycat?'

'Is an imp like a limp?' asks Kitty. We ignore her. You have to or you'd be answering questions all day.

'He'll be at the new den with Boris,' I say.

'Should have guessed.' Momma bends down, adjusting her riding boot. 'Oh, wait a minute, *there*'s Boris!'

Boris skulks out from behind the kitchen door, tail flat, eyes doleful. He looks guilty, as if he might have eaten a tub of lard or chewed a favourite slipper.

Momma rubs his ears, frowning now, unsettled by Boris coming back to the house alone. 'Where's your partner in crime, mister?'

Boris presses himself against her riding boot. She looks up at me. 'Where's the den, honey?'

'Past the stream. On the banks of the creek.' I drop clotted cream on to my scone, squidge it down with the back of my spoon. 'Where we had the bonfire the other night – you know, just before the ground gets all marshy, near the big tree.' It's our favourite tree, an ancient oak on the muddy gum of the river, a long length of old rope tied from its upper branches. You wrap your legs around the bristly knot at the bottom, kick off from the bank and fly out over the river, filled with air, thrills and friction burns in funny places.

There's a rumble outside. It feels suddenly chilly, as if someone's whipped a blanket off the day. Momma walks to the window, presses her hands on either side of the dark wooden panelling, a knee on the window-seat, looking to the wild sky gathering above the woods. 'I fear Barney's about to get a proper soaking.'

Peggy joins Momma at the window, fingering the silver crucifix at her neck. 'I don't like the look of that, Mrs Alton. Looks like it's been blown in by the devil himself!'

Toby and I try not to laugh. This line will feed nicely

into a joke later. Neither of us feels in the least sorry for Barney, who could probably do with a good soaking.

'I'll get my boots and mackintosh and fetch him for tea. He can't be out in that.'

'No, Peggy, you get on with the tea.'

Toby stands up. 'Do you want me to go, Momma?'

'That's gallant of you, Toby, but no, you eat your tea. Knight's saddled up. I'll be back in a flash.' Momma walks to the door, calling over her shoulder. 'At least Barney will have worked up an appetite.'

Only Peggy doesn't smile, crossing her arms tight across her chest.

Not long after Momma leaves, the room flashes like a cellar bulb before it pops. Rain starts to clatter against the window, like hundreds of dropped beads. Through the open door I see that Kitty's red balloon has come loose from the pram and is caught in a whistling draught, bouncing along the black and white tiled hall.

Peggy stares out at the storm, scrunching her striped apron with her hands and muttering something about those 'poor fishermen out on the boiling waters' that makes Toby and me explode with smothered laughter. No one else talks like Peggy Popple, that mix of bossiness and biblical doom. We've missed her.

'Still not back?' Daddy appears, sticking a pen into his jacket pocket. He looks worried. Or maybe when you get old – Daddy is forty-six – you just end up looking worried more easily.

'They're not back, Mr Alton.' Peggy stands up straighter, sucks in her tummy. 'Neither Mrs Alton nor Barney.'

'When did Nancy leave?'

There's another crack of lightning. It highlights a long fine hair on Peggy's chin that I've never noticed before. 'Hard to say. Half an hour ago?'

'That boy has got it coming.'

The air tightens. Toby and I exchange looks. Momma and Daddy rarely fight but we all know that they disagree about 'strictness'. Unlike Daddy, Momma believes that children shouldn't be hit, however naughty, that our schools shouldn't have canes. She believes children should be listened to and understood. Daddy thinks this is 'new-fangled progressive nonsense, upon which empires rot and children spoil and great estates fall to rack and ruin'. Luckily, Momma's in charge, even if we have to pretend otherwise.

'I can't leave them out there in this weather. Peggy, my coat and a big umbrella, please.' Peggy scurries off to the boot room, a cold, stone-walled space that smells of leather, damp and, faintly, dog muck, all smells that should be horrible but somehow put together aren't as bad as you'd think. Daddy looks at Toby, then me. 'Amber, get your coat on.'

I don't know why he chooses me. I'm pleased he does but feel sorry for Toby, who looks a bit crushed, and I'm wondering how I can get him to come too when Peggy starts to grapple me into last year's coat. She pushes open the front door and the wind slams it wide open, showering the hall with rain. Outside it looks like night, not late afternoon, as if a giant mouth is sucking the light from the sky, like liquid through a straw.

As I take the last step, Momma's Stetson worn by one of our stone falcons blows off in a gust of wind. I reach forward to catch it. Daddy stops me, puts a hand on my arm. 'Leave the darn hat. We need to go, Amber.' He yanks Boris by the collar. 'And you're coming with us too.'

Boris pulls back from the door, whining, frightened.

'Oh, for God's sake, Boris!' shouts Daddy, above the howl of wind. 'What's wrong with you? Are you a dog or a mouse?'

Ears flat, probably deciding he'd rather be a mouse, Boris is pulled down the steps, sticking close to my ankles. 'It's only a storm, Boris,' I reassure him, ruffling his fluffy yellow fur. 'There's nothing to be scared of. Come on, lead us to Barney, good boy.'

It's a fight to walk into the wind, down the sloping lawns to the arched Gothic iron gate, glistening with rain. Daddy shoves it hard with his shoulder and we topple into the world of the woods. It is immediately quieter, the roar of the storm muffled by the mossy padding of the floor, the ferns and leaves.

'Where's this den, then?' Something about his tone makes me nervous. That and the way he's pulling on the lobes of his ears.

'Easiest to follow the stream.'

A thin trickle in summer, it has swollen to double its size, frothing and spitting over the small rocks, like the furious gush of a hose. We push our way through the umbrella leaves of giant rhubarb plants.

I can hear something, the brush and break of branches. Deer? I reach for Daddy's hand. Those antlered bucks are terrifying, even if they're not in rut. His hand is hotter than I expect, slippery with rain or sweat. I remind myself that we'll all soon be huddling in front of a fire, drinking cocoa, the irrepressible Barney chastened, for an hour or two at least. 'Deer, Daddy,' I whisper, pulling on his hand. 'Can you hear them?'

'Deer?' He stops still, listening, holding my hand a little tighter.

Something is definitely coming.

Twigs cracking, the muffled rhythm of feet. The something is heavy, big, fast, too fast. Boris's fur spikes along his spine. 'Daddy . . .'

Knight bolts out of the undergrowth, eyes rolling white, nostrils flared, bucking up with a terrible snort.

'Down!' Daddy throws me to the ground, out of the way of the demented wheeling hoofs. I only dare look up when the sound of them dulls. Just in time to see something white snapping from the empty stirrup. Then, darkness.

Four

Lorna

'Remember these guys?' Jon eyes Lorna curiously.

'You know, I think I do,' Lorna tells herself, partly because she wants to believe it. Memory can always be pushed into shape. 'Yes, I definitely do.'

More than five feet high, with beaks like swords, the pair of falcons on either side of Pencraw Hall's entrance steps look like they might stretch open their wings at any moment and lift into the sky, quite possibly having pecked your eyes out first. The evening sun – it has burnt through the rain clouds now, split open a blue sky – makes the wet stone sparkle.

'Your face is a picture.' He can't take his eyes off her.

Lorna laughs, trying to control her emotions and her long dark hair, which is whipping about like streamers. It isn't that Pencraw Hall is the grandest of houses – if anything, it's rather smaller than she remembers, more human in scale, its roof frilled with small, square battlements, two fat chess-piece turrets, a dinky castle sketched by a child. Years of neglect have left the house embedded in its grounds: wild flowers riot in the borders; ivy bristles up its walls, its leaves the size of plates, vines and mortar fused, like tissue and bone. But the house is . . . monumental.

Any wedding here would feel ancient, primal, part of the natural order of things. It would feel right. It does feel right. Like the way Jon felt right the first time she'd kissed him (on Waterloo Bridge in a blizzard of snow). And, as she did on that winter's night, two and a half years ago, she can't wait to call her sister, Louise, and tell her.

'Are you sure we can afford all this?' Jon pulls her towards him, circling her waist with the spades of his hands. Her yellow dress flips up in the breeze. 'You've not got jiggy with the figures?'

Lorna laughs again. 'No!'

A dazzle of sunlight swings across the steps, like a ship's boom. Jon shades his eyes, scans the roof with a cool, professional gaze. 'Although, I have to say, it's not far off being a hard-hat area.'

Lorna is not blind to the splintered upper windows, the chipped battlements or the tiles that have clearly flown off the roof and shattered on the drive, mixing with the honey-coloured gravel. But, in a funny way, the house's dilapidated state makes it more seductive, not less. She loves that it hasn't been turned into some soulless corporate away-day venue or a Farrow & Ball-painted tourist tearoom. It is a house literally crumbling under the weight of its past. Perfect, she thinks, with a sigh.

He rests his chin lightly on the top of her head. 'Hard to believe that anyone actually lives here, isn't it?'

'I guess.' Lorna decides not to mention that she's sensed someone watching them as they came up the drive, that someone is watching them now. There is life here all right, she is sure of it. She glances over at the cars rusting in the far reaches of the drive: a knackered green three-wheeler and a muddy blue sports car, wing mirrors secured with tape, a long gash running the length of its hooded roof.

Jon swivels Lorna to face him, bending down to kiss her.

'I feel we should burst into song or dance up the steps or something,' she whispers. 'It's that sort of place.'

He kisses her again.

'Come on, we're late.' She grabs his hand, tugs him impatiently up the remaining steps – all seventeen of them. She can't help counting, or imagining a white lace train sweeping behind her, although she's long decided that she is not a flowing-train type of girl. But what she wants – or wanted – is already shifting, new possibilities rising, like steam from the wet stone steps in the sun.

Facing the door – black, ridiculously big, lion's-paw brass knocker – she straightens her yellow sundress and clamps a little bit of fabric between her knees so that the wind won't blow up the skirt at the wrong moment. She wants to make a good impression. 'You do it, Jon,' she says, suddenly nervous, hit by the odd sensation – and the accompanying mental drum roll – that she is on the threshold of far more than a house.

Jon decides on the doorbell – actually a bell! It chimes deep in the belly of the building. Slow footsteps. A dog yapping. Lorna prepares to meet a shrill, blonde, horsey type in glossy riding boots, or an older lady, like the Duchess of Devonshire, trailing plush chickens and vaguely resembling the Queen. There's a stronger gust of wind. She clamps her knees together harder.

The door opens. Lorna can't hide her surprise.

A tiny woman, with startled grey eyes, an orb of brown

46

hair frizzing around her delicate face, like a giant seed head, is dwarfed by the door. She wears not a scrap of make-up, her skin rouged and crisped by the elements, and could be in her early forties or a decade younger. Smelling strongly of woodsmoke, she's as hard to date as her clothes: Land Girl baggy mustard jumbo cords, heavy brown boots and an enormous Fair Isle jumper, with a hole unravelling on its cuff.

'Hi, there! I'm Lorna.' She smiles brightly, pushes her straw bag back up her shoulder. The woman looks at them blankly. 'Lorna and Jon.'

'Lorna and Jon?' The voice is girlish with a West Country burr. She cocks her head on one side, stares at Lorna quizzically, fingernail travelling to her crowded teeth. 'Wait a minute . . .'

'We spoke on the phone last week? About our wedding?' Has the woman forgotten the arrangement? Is there something a little wrong with her? 'I'm so sorry we're late. I hope we've not put you to any trouble.'

'We got lost. Lorna was map-reading,' says Jon, trying to slide in a joke.

The woman doesn't laugh. But she glances at him for the first time, visibly starting at the six-foot symphony of broad shoulders, sandy hair and hazel eyes, speckled like hen's eggs. Her cheeks flare and she drops her gaze.

'It's true, no sense of direction,' chatters Lorna, trying to keep the conversation moving, deciding against petting the small moth-eaten terrier that has appeared, snarling, dribbling, between the woman's mud-caked boots. Not the stately Labrador she imagined might live in a house like this. 'It's En-Endellion, isn't it?'

'Dill.' At last there's a smile, a pretty, tentative smile with an honesty about it that makes Lorna warm to her immediately. Dill's clearly just very shy. In need of a bit of a groom. They do things differently in the country.

'And this is Petal.' She scoops the dog up, its claws catching in the wool of her sweater. 'A boy. But we didn't realize for a while. A bit of a biter, I'm afraid. Meant to catch the rats. He prefers fingers, don't you, Petal?'

Lorna and Jon laugh a little too loudly.

Dill rolls the dog on to his back and carries him like a baby. 'Well, um, I suppose I should say, welcome to Pencraw Hall.'

There is a cheekiness to Lorna's smile now. 'Black Rabbit Hall?'

Dill's eyes widen in surprise. 'Who told you that?'

'I think he was a farmer, wasn't he, Jon?'

'A tractor was involved.'

'We met him on the road, just before the drive,' adds Lorna, wishing Dill would hurry up and invite them inside. 'He said all the locals call it Black Rabbit Hall. Is that right?'

'They used to call it that,' Dill replies quietly.

'Why Black Rabbit?' Lorna glimpses a hollowed elephant's foot stuffed with broken old umbrellas behind Dill's trouser leg. 'It's such an unusual name.'

'Well, if you look down there . . .' Lorna turns, her gaze following Dill's pointing finger to the sweep of lawn that drops steeply away from the house, becoming a horizon for the bowl of countryside beneath it, the white studs of sheep and the silver glint of the creek through the trees as it coils towards the sea. 'Rabbits. At dusk. We get so many rabbits on this lawn. The warrens are at the edge of the woods there, you see. Behind the hydrangeas.'

'Aw,' sighs Lorna, because she's a city girl and she thinks rabbits are cute.

'When the sun sets – we're facing west – it silhouettes them. The rabbits look . . .' she pauses, tickling Petal's matted belly '. . . like shadow puppets, I always think.'

Lorna flashes a joyous smile at Jon, picturing the wedding invitation, the big B, the sweep of the R. The talking point of the name. 'Oh, I'm going to call this place Black Rabbit Hall from now on.'

'Mrs Alton prefers Pencraw Hall,' Dill says quickly.

They sense conflict. A moment passes.

'I'm sure I came here as a kid with my mum,' blurts Lorna, who's been waiting for a gap in the conversation and can't contain herself any longer. 'Did it use to be open to the public, Dill?'

'No.' Dill rests a finger on her freckled lips. 'No, I don't think so.'

Lorna's heart sinks. Has she got the wrong house after all?

'But we've always had people wandering up the drive, knocking on the door, offering the housekeeper a bit of money for a quick nose, you know. That sort of thing. We still get the odd one, actually. Tourists see the sign near the turn-off, get curious . . .'

Sounds like her mother. Lorna remembers how she'd shamelessly dip beneath a stately house's red rope to peep at a private bathroom. Her mother adored being horrified by toff toilets: 'Imagine, all that class and a wooden seat!'

'Oh dear, you're being dripped on,' says Dill, looking up at the flaking wet stone above their heads. 'You'd better come in.'

At last, Lorna thinks, stepping past Dill on to the warp of black and white tiles. The smell of beeswax, charcoal and damp. 'Wow.'

The entrance hall is the size of their flat in Bethnal Green, jaw-dropping in its battered glamour.

'Enough staircase for you, sweetheart?' Jon whispers in her ear. His eyes dance.

'Oh, my God, yes.' She'd never expected anything so beautiful. Twisting gracefully down from the floors above, sinuous, balletic, it is the sweeping staircase of old Hollywood movies. Long oyster-satin dresses. A hand-dyed silk slipper's soundless descent.

Her delighted eye flits around. So much to look at. An enormous chandelier, furred with dust, dangles above them like a planet. The wood panelling is dark, coffee-bean glossed. Stag heads strain from the walls, as if trying to break free. There's a petrified palm in a brass pot that looks like it might have died a century before. Above the central cave of a fireplace, a towering gilt-framed portrait of a startling blonde in an ice-blue dress that perfectly matches her eyes, head slightly thrown back, staring directly into the hall, like a ship's figurehead might the sea. But most intriguing of all is the tall black grandfather clock opposite: an exquisite face, moon dial embedded, intricately painted in cerulean and gold. Lorna reaches out, touches it lightly. The wood is as warm as human skin. 'I love this.'

Jon peers closer, absorbed in its craftsmanship. 'Beautiful.'

'Oh, that's Big Bertie,' says Dill, with a shy, proud smile. 'Just don't ask him to tell the time.' She drops Petal on the floor. The dog scuttles off, claws skittering. 'Um, I did mention on the phone that this is a new venture for Mrs Alton?'

'You did.' Details don't matter a jot now. Lorna is gazing at the staircase again, imagining how it must feel to walk up its ragged red runner, hand on the banister, head held high. 'No problem at all.'

'Oh, that's a relief. It's better you know.'

Lorna turns to smile at Dill, wonders if she's played a part in pricing Black Rabbit Hall. If so, they should be grateful to her. No doubt as soon as the bookings start flowing in the prices will rocket. 'We'll be very pleased to be the first, won't we, Jon?'

Jon flashes her a secret look that says, '*Really?*'

'So you want to get married in . . . ?' Dill frowns, even though Lorna had told her twice on the phone. She tugs at a loose thread on her sweater cuff. 'Next April, was it?'

'October.' Lorna loves Cornwall in autumn when the mists roll in from the sea and the earth smells damp and mushroomy. Also, it's cheaper out of season, which will help. She reaches for Jon's hand. 'I know it's a push.'

'*This* October? That is soon.'

Lorna winces. 'Well, it does need to be during a school holiday – I'm a teacher – but October half-term isn't to-tally set in stone, is it, Jon?'

'I suppose not.' Jon rubs his jaw vaguely. He always tends to drift off when they start making complicated arrangements that involve a degree of uncertainty. Lorna, for once, is thankful for this trait. She doesn't want Dill undermining his confidence in the house.

'Well, if you could be flexible . . . You see, this is all rather new for me too.' Dill's hands flutter. They are childishly small hands, Lorna notices, hands that look like they've done more than their share of hard work, the skin roughened, the nail beds black. 'Weddings. Dealing with the public. We haven't had people, lots of people, on the estate for years. Normally I just look after Mrs Alton, help manage the house.'

Well, at least she's not hitting them with a hard sell, like so many other wedding people do, Lorna decides, hoping Jon might come to the same conclusion.

'But Mrs Alton is quite determined to find a way to secure the house's future. Yes, an income stream.' Dill's mouth begins to work, chewing the inside of her cheek. 'We've tried various things over the years. It's been tricky for Mrs Alton to keep it all going, you see, since Mr Alton died.'

Lorna starts a little at death joining the conversation. 'Oh, I'm sorry.'

'This place eats money, even if you only live in a bit of it,' Dill continues.

'The central heating must cost a fortune,' says Jon.

'Oh, we don't use central heating!' Dill exclaims, as if Jon had suggested they might bathe in champagne.

Jon squeezes Lorna's hand. She knows he's trying not to laugh. That she must not catch it.

'It's a Victorian system, prone to the most terrible moods and blockages, so we burn logs from the woods. Much easier. But there's some electric heaters in the bridal suite,' she adds quickly, glancing down at Jon and Lorna's entwined hands, as if she'd noticed the squeeze. 'Not yet in the ballroom . . . Yes, that needs a bit of work too. But by next April . . .'

'October,' smiles Jon, letting go of Lorna's hand and buttoning up his light cotton navy jacket. It's quite chilly, far colder than outside. Lorna hopes he's not going to take an annoyingly practical stance on the place later. 'Ideally.'

'Oops. Sorry.' Dill blushes again. 'You did say, Tom.'

'Jon.'

'So can we see the rooms?' Lorna pushes on gently.

'Sweetheart,' Jon lowers his voice, his lips skimming her cheek, 'it's getting late.'

'We won't be long.' She turns back to Dill, dark eyes shining. 'Where shall we start?'

'Start? Oh, yes. That's a good idea.' Dill starts to stomp across the hall in her muddy boots. One of the laces is undone and trails behind her foot, like a rat's tail. 'This hall is the oldest part of the house, dating back to Norman times or something. But the place is a right old mish-mash, bits built and knocked down by different generations. The main bit is Georgian, I think, but the towers were added by some rather showy Victorians. Or it might be the other way round.' She pauses, finger pressed to her mouth. 'No, it's gone. Sorry not to be more accurate. I've never been good with dates and things. This way, please.' She pushes on a heavy oak door, lets out a small mew of exertion. 'I must show you the enfilade.'

'The what?' mouths Jon to Lorna, stepping on to a rot-softened board and following Dill into a poorly lit corridor.

'A row of connected rooms or something,' whispers Lorna, who has recently been Googling stately homes in her lunch hours.

'That's right.' Dill clearly has excellent hearing. 'It links this wing of the house.' Her face lights up with a smile, knocking ten years off. 'And you know what? If you stand at the far end of the enfilade you can roll a ball from one end to the other, all the way back to the original hall!'

The comment makes Lorna think of children. She can almost see the ball rolling across the floorboards, flying into the priceless antiques, and it makes her smile.

'Excuse me, Dill, your shoelace . . .' Jon points out politely.

'Oh, thank you. Thank you very much.' Dill blushes, bends down and stuffs the lace into the boot rather than tying it, pushing open a door with her behind as she does so. 'The drawing room. The Alton family's favourite room, although it's not used much, these days.'

The drawing room is so dark it seems edgeless. Only when Dill pulls back the heavy draperies at the French windows, filling it with crystal Cornish light, does it make any sense. Its walls pulse inky blue – the colour of deep ocean, Lorna fancies, far beneath the waves – and the paintings on the walls pop. The fleshy-faced ancestor portraits are there, of course, but Lorna is drawn to the moody seascapes, billowing skies, terrifying high seas, shipwrecks and crag-faced smugglers carrying booty on their backs along rain-battered beaches. What a comfortable place to witness man and nature at their worst, she thinks. Overlapping threadbare Persian rugs muffle their footsteps.

Plump chairs in rich velvets – petal pinks, ox-blood reds – huddle in gossipy clusters in the corners. Most inviting of all is the huge fireplace with its long leather-padded brass fender – glowing from generations of warming bottoms – and barrel-sized log basket. Lorna imagines that she could sit at such a fireplace with Jon on a cool evening and never want to leave.

'Mrs Alton suggests that you offer a glass of something here. Some fizz? A cocktail?'

'Perfect.' Lorna notices a globe standing on brass feet in the corner of the room, the greens and blues of its lands and oceans faded, the colonies it delineated long gone. Forgetting herself, she reaches out and touches its parchment surface, making the globe spin and quiver slightly on its axis. 'Oops, sorry. I shouldn't touch.'

'Oh, don't worry.' Dill shrugs, as if it were merely bric-a-brac. 'Spin it if you like. It hums. It's got a really nice hum.'

Lorna hesitates.

Jon smiles. 'Go on.'

Oh, the hum. The drone of fat bumblebees in lavender beds. Lorna closes her eyes, letting the sound fill her, the house start to weave its spell. When she opens her eyes Jon is staring at her with a confused expression bordering faintly on alarm.

'Perhaps we should move along, if you're in a hurry. Mrs Alton's adamant you don't miss the bridal suite.' Dill tugs at a thread. The cuff hole is expanding rapidly.

'Oh, yes! I'm desperate to climb that grand staircase.'

'We'll enter through the top-floor landing, then.' Dill

points out of the window to one of the stone turrets, reaching up to the pinking sky. 'That's where we're going. That's it.'

Lorna turns to beam at Jon: she hasn't seen anything prettier, or more romantic. But Jon is frowning slightly. Something has unsettled him.

'Mrs Alton thought most brides would prefer the turret to one of the grander bedrooms on the chamber floor,' Dill explains apologetically. 'It gets terribly cold, even in the summer. I'm afraid the chimneys are blocked with dead gulls. We need to get someone in.'

'I'd much prefer a turret,' says Lorna. 'Wouldn't you, Jon?'

He hesitates.

Dill bites her lower lip, sensing Jon's reservations.

'The bride's prerogative.' Jon digs his hands into the front pockets of his jeans with a boyish shrug that is disarmingly at odds with his big frame. 'Lorna must love it, that's all. I can sleep anywhere.'

'We've done the turret up specially,' says Dill, with a relieved smile.

'Who used to be locked up in it, then?' Jon asks, only half joking.

This visibly throws Dill. 'I . . . I . . .'

Lorna comes to Dill's rescue. 'Stop teasing, Jon.' She glances up at the turret again. And it is then that she sees it. The flicker of a curtain. A face at the uppermost window. She blinks and it's gone. A trick of the light.

Lorna pushes a snowdrift of dust up the dark banister as she climbs, her other hand holding Jon's tightly. She says nothing but is experiencing the electric snap of a *déjà vu* so strong – like a frozen memory abruptly thawed – that she has to touch her temples to neutralize the crushing sensation. The higher they get – first floor, second, third – the stiller, darker and more decrepit the house becomes, the tighter her head. She takes a sip of water from the bottle in her bag and feels a little better. Maybe she's just dehydrated. Or in delayed shock from the near-accident. She needs tea and cake.

'You all right, sweetheart?' Jon asks quietly.

'Of course!' She doesn't want to distract him, or say anything negative. More than this, she doesn't want him worrying that the house is stirring something inside. He thinks she's too stirred up already, she knows that, her mood giddily elated one day, flat and morbid the next, as she feels her way into this strange new world without her mother, all its contradictions and consequences, the grief, also the release. They walk up one more flight of stairs. The tightness in Lorna's head subsides.

Jon peers through a powder-blue door, ajar on the third floor. 'Looks like a bunch of kids have just left this room, doesn't it?' he observes, standing aside to let Lorna see too.

'Oh, it really does.' There are so many children's things, seemingly left where they were thrown. In the corner of the room, partially covered by a blanket, is a dappled grey rocking horse the size of a small pony. Beneath its front hoofs, a dolly's cradle. Closer to the door, a mildewed pile of books: *The Secret Garden*, *Jane Eyre*, *Wuthering Heights*, *Milly Molly Mandy*, *Rupert Annual 1969* . . . A shiver tingles up her spine – she'd read and loved many of these books as a child: an instant bond with the departed children, one that transcends both time and class.

'This floor's not used any more,' Dill says, reaching over and closing the door, as if she cannot bear to see its contents. 'Mrs Alton has no need for so many rooms.'

'Does anyone?' Jon asks, the seriousness of the question lightened by his smile. Lorna knows all too well what he's thinking: so many people without homes at all – and it's true that too many of her pupils live in hostels or B-and-Bs, one family to a room – and this vast house is populated by just one old lady and her housekeeper. Rationally, politically, she agrees with him. Secretly she's rather pleased that houses like Black Rabbit Hall still exist.

'How many rooms are there, Dill?' she asks. The house really feels like it might go on forever, doors behind doors, worlds within worlds.

'You know, I don't think anyone's ever counted them.'

'Bedrooms?'

'Hmm. Nine, I think. Not including the old staff quarters on the top floor. The house is actually smaller than it looks. Oh. Oh, no. I'm going off!'

The noise is shrill and insistent. *Beep beep beep beeeeep.* Dill pats her jumper frantically until she locates some kind of paging device beneath the layers of matted wool and silences it. 'Such a racket. So sorry. Mrs Alton needs me. I've got to go. Now . . . what to do . . .' She clicks a fingernail against her teeth. 'Could you come back tomorrow?'

'Today really would be better. As we're here.' And nearly got mown down by a tractor on the way, Lorna is tempted to add. 'A whiz around the bridal suite? We can be really quick, I promise.'

Dill looks torn. Another impatient beep.

'Come on, Lorna. Dill's busy,' says Jon, pressing his warm hand on her lower back. 'I reckon we've got a real taste of the house already.'

Dill's eyes brighten. 'Hang on! How about you wait for me downstairs? Mrs Alton will be very upset if you don't see her bridal suite, I'm sure of it. I won't be long.'

'I'm afraid we must be —' begins Jon politely, the jiggle of his foot revealing his impatience.

'A few more minutes,' begs Lorna. She grabs his hands. 'Please.'

'We've got a booking for dinner, remember? And I've still got to study the map, sort out how to get back to the B-and-B.'

Lorna seizes on this. 'Okay, you do that. I'll wait. Ten minutes, then I'll join you.'

As Jon walks away, Lorna feels the pang of separation, as if part of her is walking away too. They've been so close these last few days. She almost runs after him. But something holds her. The pull of the house is just a little too strong.

Lorna doesn't understand it at first. The star-shattered hole in the middle of the forehead. The shape of the skull. Then the bones come together, the animal emerges. For it is surely a horse's skull with its snooker-ball eye sockets, the long nose bone curving to meet the long jaw, like an extended beak. She shivers. The skull is brutal, pagan, luminous in the black box. She treads silently along the worn rug and peers into more of the dusty cabinets: stuffed birds, squirrels, baby deer, rabbits, spirited natural creatures sewn into a second life as stiff mannequins. She remembers Jon's aside earlier – 'This lot would stuff their own ancestors given half a chance' – and feels their dull glass eyes track her as she walks to the window-seat, mobile tight in her hand.

Lorna's search for phone reception has led her into this long, dim library – two brass doorknobs off the enfilade. Acres of books. An old oak desk the size of a small boat. A peculiar cluster of museum-style cabinets. Maybe too peculiar.

She's glad to have a view from the window of Jon and the car. He is sipping a bottle of water, studying the map, singing along to music. She loves to watch him when he's unaware of it. He's the least self-conscious man she's ever met, so quietly at ease with himself, sure of who he is, what he wants. She wonders what would have become of her if they hadn't both been at that party in Camden, the one she nearly didn't go to. If she hadn't clocked the glorious blond bear of a man in the crowded, smoky kitchen, pouring guests' drinks to help a stressed hostess. He'd had a nasty cut on his hand, the one that was pouring the vodka. A slipped saw, he'd shrugged when she'd asked, no big deal, would she let him make her a drink? Sexiest thing ever.

She texts her sister, Louise: *Amazing. Will tell u all l8r.* And she just has time to call her father. She has to call her father.

'Dad, it's me!'

'Hi, Sunshine!' Doug's voice lights up as it always does when she phones, making her feel guilty for not phoning him more often. 'Sorry, one sec – let me put my cup down. It's burning my hand off. There. I'm all yours. Everything okay? Is the jet stream ruining your week too? Can't be worse than here. Been raining all sodding day. Not that they've lifted the hosepipe ban. Do those ponces at Westminster ever actually look out the window?'

'Doubt it.' Lorna sits down on the window-seat's tapestry cushions.

'Hope you're tucked away in a cosy little pub somewhere.'

'Oh, no, we're still at one of the venues, actually. Well, Jon's sorting out the car. I'm in the house's library, waiting to see the bridal suite.'

'This late?'

'Yeah, well, the house was hard to find.'

'Ha! I bet Jon didn't like that. Tell him he needs to stop relying on that bloody satnav.' A recently retired London taxi driver, her father prides himself on never getting lost anywhere, ever, and thoroughly enjoys it when other men do.

'But we found the perfect house eventually. Well, I think it's perfect.'

'And Jon doesn't?'

'Hmm.'

Doug's laugh is still the gravel-truck laugh of a twenty-a-day smoker, even though he gave up ten years ago and now only smokes when drunk at Christmas. 'Something tells me you'll talk him round.'

'It's a wonderful house, Dad, tucked away on the Roseland Peninsula.'

'Oh, the Roseland, that takes me back. There's a smashing little caravan site down there, just outside Portscatho. Tiny. A cut above. Your mother loved it.'

Lorna's thrilled to have confirmation that they stayed so close. Her memories of their family summer holidays are scuffed, like photographs carried around too long in a purse: the blue loo smell of the supposedly state-of-the-art caravan that was always breaking down; Louise's mattress pressing through the wire mesh inches above Lorna's face; Mum cattle-prodding her around endless National Trust properties while Dad and Louise got to build sandcastles on the beach. Funny what sticks.

'The best shower block in Cornwall,' her father continues. 'Hot water all day. Free soap, the lot. Weren't many caravan sites like that in those days.' He's more talkative than usual. Lorna fears that this is because he is spending hours alone. 'Sorry, give us a moment, Lors.'

There is a squeak and she immediately knows it's the wicker chair in the conservatory, where he sits every morning, shaking out his newspaper, gazing at the empty seat next to him where her mother used to sit, the cushions indelibly squashed into the double dip of her neat bottom. 'That's better. Tight hips, according to the doctor. New doctor. Looks about ten. Told him he didn't need to talk down to me, I know my ischial spine from my sacroiliac joint.'

Lorna feels a wave of sympathy for the doctor. Her father has always unquestioningly accepted the bigger picture – namely, being a devoted husband to her exacting mother – reserving all his voracious curiosity for the world outside it. Despite having left school at fourteen, Doug claims to be 'self-educated up to mad-prof level', having worked his way through the shelves of all the local libraries, gobbling up what her mum fondly called 'a galaxy of utterly useless knowledge'. His passengers would always step out of his cab altered in some way – if only utterly exhausted – having sat through an explanation of a pigeon's digestive system or the physics behind the traffic flow around Piccadilly Circus. For this reason, and a few others, Lorna and Jon are both nervous about the father-of-the-bride speech.

'And you'll never guess what the name of the house is, Dad.'

She hears him take a short sip of tea. He drinks it too hot – all cabbies rush their tea, he says, which, like a lot of things he says, may or may not be true.

'Black Rabbit Hall.' She pauses, hopes for a start of recognition.

'Rabbits can run up to fifty miles an hour, did you know that? Zigzagging to confuse predators. Not as dim as they look.'

'Dad, does the name ring any bells?'

'Nope.'

'I'm almost certain Mum brought me here. It feels so familiar.'

'Possible. Possible. I wouldn't know. Never got along with those stuffy old houses myself. That was your mother's thing, heritage and all that. She preferred your company to mine anyway – said I slowed her down and asked embarrassing irrelevant questions.'

'How come Louise got out of it?'

'Too little, Sheila said. The odd times she did take her,

Louise would start whining for ice-cream, moaning that she was bored and whatnot.' He clears his throat. 'Your mum said you got more out of it.'

Did she? It certainly hadn't felt like it at the time. But here she is, all these years later, poking around a big old house, quite bewitched. 'I wonder if there are any pictures. I'd love to see them.'

'Why don't you pop over, have a rifle through the boxes in the attic? There's so much stuff up there.'

The Dunaways' black boxes, Lorna likes to think, recording a family rather than an air flight, everything from her mother's improbable years as a platinum Teddy girl in the early sixties, the subsequent buttoning down into marriage, a henna perm and prim, easy-iron dresses, the late, longed-for motherhood. A modest life collected and collated by someone who is now just a surprisingly hefty urn of grainy ashes on a shelf in the lounge.

Lorna tries not to look at it. She'd much rather remember Mum on holiday – she was one of those people who only ever seemed truly happy, and truly themselves, on holiday – bundled up in her woolly coat, sharing delicious hot vinegary chips on a windy beach, smiling at Lorna when their salty, greasy fingers briefly touched, the crashing of the waves removing any need to talk, relaxing with one another in a way they somehow never managed on the settee at home.

'I'm afraid I haven't really been able to face going through those boxes yet,' Doug says, in a hushed voice. 'I'm not sure I ever will, to be honest.'

'I'll do it, don't worry.' Poor Dad. She's by the cabinets

again, her eye sucked towards the horse's skull, the unsettling absence at its centre.

'Lorna.' The teary choke in her father's voice takes her aback, reminding her of how raw his loss still is. 'I'm sorry that I can't answer all your questions about the past, not like your mum could . . .'

Doug's words tail into a long, loaded silence that wraps around Lorna, like a scarf, tighter and tighter so that her throat locks too. Outside, a chatter of starlings lifts off the lawn. Memories of missed opportunities fly by just as fast. Oh, how Lorna wishes she'd made more effort to talk properly to her mother over the years. They'd never really connected – not in the easy, comfortable way she did with Dad – and she wonders if they avoided situations that made it obvious. They were always far better at *doing* things together – a Saturday cinema matinee, a ballet at Christmas, baking a Victoria sponge, taking turns to stir the bowl, Radio 2 blaring – than chatting intimately. And bringing up certain subjects about the past – the No Gos, Lorna and Louise secretly called them – had always felt so charged, horribly awkward, her mother usually jumping up to dust a skirting board or wipe down a clean surface, dispersing questions with mushroom clouds of Pledge. Then in May the conversation had ended for good.

The unfairness of it still taunts her. It turned out the council were due to mend the broken paving outside the Co-op the following day. Mum shouldn't have tripped, surrounded by her marked-down fruit and vegetables – she never tripped – or banged her head in a freakishly bad place to bang it. She wasn't meant to die at sixty-five:

perfectly healthy, she was part of that lithe post-war generation brought up on sluggy allotment cabbage and modest portions of home-cooked food, who walked to the shops rather than drove. Most unfair of all, Lorna thinks, pressing her nails into the palm of her clenched hand, is that when her life support was switched off it stole away any loving deathbed reckoning, made so much of her own past irretrievable. She blinks back a rush of tears.

'Oh, you're here!'

Lorna turns to see Dill standing in the doorway, dog in her arms, licking her mouth.

'Ready to see the bridal suite?'

'Dad.' She smiles at Dill, tries to collect herself. 'I've got to go.'

She hears a telling rustle and a sniff as he rearranges his feelings too. 'Well, try not to get lost in that big house alone, okay?'

'Don't be a doughnut. Love you.'

But when Lorna starts ascending the steep shaft of the tower's stairwell – dark, tightly enclosed, its exits unclear – she realizes that her father might be on to something. It really would be quite easy to get lost in Black Rabbit Hall. To think you were going in one direction but were heading entirely in another.

Five

Amber

Boris leaps out of the undergrowth. He noses Momma's face and whines. Daddy pushes him off and wraps Momma in his coat to keep her warm. 'Find Barney,' he shouts over his shoulder and charges out of the woods, Boris following, Momma in his arms, head lolling at a strange angle.

I don't know how long I stand there numbly, heart hammering, the image of Momma's head – the swinging red hair, the angle of her neck – everywhere I look, like the imprint of a light-bulb after it's been switched off. What do I do? What do I do now?

Then I remember. Find Barney, Daddy said. Find Barney.

The storm clouds are parting. A bone-white moon jumps from behind one tree to another. Full moon. High tides. The lower part of the creek often bursts its banks in an early-evening high tide, especially after a storm. The water will wash through the wood beside the den. I haven't got long.

I start running, praying over and over that it's going to be all right. Safe, happy place. Safe, happy place. Black Rabbit Hall is our safe, happy place.

Barney is not in the den, or by the soggy char of the

bonfire. My feet start to squish beneath me. The water is coming.

'Barney!' I shout. 'Barney, it's me! Are you there? Barney, don't be an idiot! Where are you?'

I wait, listening, heart pounding in my ears. There is movement in the undergrowth. Two yellow eyes. A hare? A fox?

I scramble deeper into the woods, calling his name, and it occurs to me he could be running away from me deliberately, hiding, playing a game – he loves to be chased – unaware of what has happened to Momma. 'Barney!' I shout louder, more desperate. Nothing. I stop, overcome by hopelessness. Unable to be brave any longer, I start to cry, the sobs rising out of me in blocked-drain snorts. And that's when Boris appears, tail wagging. Never have I been so pleased to see him. I sink my face into his smelly fur, gripping the fat around his haunches. 'Barney. Help me find Barney. Please.'

Boris cocks his head slightly to one side, as if he understands, hesitates for a moment, then dashes off into the woods. I follow him until he brakes beneath a giant beech, his paws sending a mash of wet leaves flying.

And there he is. Curled high in a tree. Owl eyes. I hold out my arms for him. He doesn't move. I keep tugging on his foot – cold and bare – and tell him everything's fine, it's safe to let go, and very slowly he starts to skim down the trunk. He wraps his arms tightly around my neck and, trembling, buries his face in my shoulder. 'What happened, Barney?'

He says nothing, his body heaving soundlessly.

'What happened to Momma?' I ask more gently. 'Did you see?'

He starts to sob then. I take off my coat. He is passive – Barney is never passive – and lets me butler him into it. The sleeves dangle to the ground. But he won't walk. 'Piggyback,' I say, kneeling down on the springy wet floor.

I run with him on my back all the way to the house. Fear makes me strong.

'Momma is dead,' says Toby, deadpan, leaning against Big Bertie in the hall, hands dug deep into his pockets, face scallop-white, staring up at the portrait of Momma. The clock ticks. The moon dial's gold glows in the stormy light. It ticks another ten times. Then Toby repeats, 'Momma is dead, Amber.'

Clearly Toby's got this wrong. I shake my head, set Barney on the floor, peel his fingers off my neck. 'Let go, Barney, will you? Find Peggy. She'll warm you up.'

'Excuse me. Raggedy Doll is late for tea!' chimes Kitty, bustling past us, rattling her pram across the hall. 'She's properly starving for scones and bramble jelly!'

'Is the doctor here?' I whisper. Barney wraps a hand around my leg.

'Too late,' mutters Toby, blankly. Something has changed in his face. There's a furious pulse in the hollow of his throat.

'Raggedy Doll is most terribly busy today.' Kitty sighs, pulling the doll out of the pram and frog-marching her up the first stair. 'So much to do, so little time.'

The black and white floor tiles start to flicker and slide,

sweating the sharp smell of the vinegar that Annie uses to clean them. 'Where's Momma, then?'

'In bed.'

I push past Kitty, leap up the stairs, two at a time. The staircase feels higher than ever, stretching as I climb. I'll find Momma in bed. I'll bring her tea. I'll stroke her hair, like she does mine when I'm ill. I don't believe she's dead at all. And if I don't believe it she won't be.

I throw my shoulder against the door of the bedroom. And she is in bed, just as Toby says, tucked up like a sick child in a white sheet, her hair brushed over her shoulder. The curtains are shut, the lights low, the flowers carved into the bed's thick dark posts picked out by the flickering candlelight. Momma's clasped hands hold a posy too, the pale yellow daffodils that were in the blue teardrop vase on her bedside table this morning. I move closer, refusing to acknowledge the way her head is caved in above the ear, the strange dip where her hair has mashed with blood and fragments of bone.

'Momma.' Her hand is not freezing but it's not warm either, like milk left out. The daffodils fall across her chest. She does not twitch them off. 'Momma, please. Wake up, please.'

And that's when I hear the groans coming from the other side of the bed. I peer over, still holding Momma's hand in mine, shocked to see Daddy hunched, crouched on the floor, his face sunk into the sheet that falls off Momma. 'Daddy?' My voice comes out as high as Kitty's. I want him to reach for me and tell me it's going to be fine, that Momma will heal and mend, fill with warmth and blood again, thaw back to life, tuck the daffodils back into the vase. 'Daddy, it's me.'

He does not look up. The groans become quieter, more intense.

'Amber,' Toby whispers, suddenly behind me. 'Come away.'

I let him pull me towards him. Toby's skin smells of me and distinctly of itself, like the top of a knee. He is hot to touch. A boy on fire. I can feel his heart through the fabric of his rugby shirt. He holds me tight, tighter, so that we are pressed into one, fitting together perfectly again, two babies curled in the soft warm blackness of Momma's womb. 'We still have each other. I have you.'

'Amber, Toby . . .' Peggy is standing at the door, hand over her mouth. 'What are you doing? Come out of there, please.'

'Momma's dead,' I say, not sure Peggy has cottoned on.

Toby tightens his grip. 'She's dead, Peggy.'

'And your father needs to be with her in peace, my love.' She walks over to us, peels us off each other, glancing down anxiously at Daddy. 'Amber, Toby, please. Let go of each other. Come downstairs.'

'I want to stay with Momma,' I plead.

'You can't, duck. Not right now.'

It's then that Daddy looks up, removes his hands from his head. His face is swollen and monstrous with grief, his eyes red bulbs. He does not look like Daddy.

'Is there anything I can get you, Mr Alton?' She squats beside him, resting her roundness on her tiny feet. 'Mr Alton?'

He looks at Peggy as if he can't comprehend her.

'A stiff glass of . . .'

'*GO!*' he roars, making us leap from our skins. '*GO!*'

*

Balancing on the fender, we sit around the drawing-room fire, into which Momma tossed a fistful of kitchen salt yesterday to make the flames dance blue for Kitty. There are still a few grains on the hearth.

Despite the heat, our outstretched hands, we're not getting warmer. Toby and I sit next to each other, quivering, skinless, wedged together. Kitty is chatting nonsense to Raggedy Doll. Barney stares blankly into the flames, his lips still blue, wearing the stripy pyjamas that Aunt Bay sends over from Bloomingdales every Christmas. He has not spoken since we returned to the house. We have no idea what he saw, if he saw anything at all.

Boris lumbers in, sinks down beneath the globe, head on his paws, watching us. The globe is tilting Momma's America towards us. I can see Seattle, a bit of Idaho, Oregon. Places she has promised to take me.

I cannot touch my hot chocolate. To drink hot chocolate while Momma lies still upstairs is impossible. After a few moments, Toby sips his. There is something brave about this, the attempt to be normal. I try to smile at him but my face feels frozen and I can't make my mouth turn up.

Click, click, click, go Peggy's knitting needles. She sits very upright in the pink velvet chair near the window, fingers trying to make this evening like any other, long red scarf pooling around her feet.

Kitty breaks the clicks. 'My hair needs brushing.' She shakes it with her fingers, sending sand flying. 'Momma doesn't like sand in Kitty's hair. Kitty wants Momma to brush the sand out. Where is she? Where is Momma?'

Peggy's knitting needles still. She puts them down on her lap. 'Momma's in Heaven now, Kitty.'

'She's not,' says Kitty, firmly, snuggling Raggedy Doll into the cradle of her crossed legs. 'She's in bed, Peggy. And she needs to get up and plait Kittycat's hair.'

Toby and I exchange glances. There are shadows dark as river mud beneath his eyes.

'I'll plait your hair, Kits,' I say, reaching out to her. 'Come here.'

Kitty shakes her head. 'Want Momma to do it.'

Toby drains his chocolate, glancing at me down the shaft of the mug, checking I haven't gone anywhere since the last time he looked a second ago. Gravelly bits of cocoa leave a clown's smile on his upper lip. He clinks the mug down hard on the hearth. We all flinch, watch the brown milk dribbling down the white enamel rim. Waiting.

Click, click, click.

Any minute now normal has to restart. Momma's footstep on the stairs. A cough. Rush out to the hall and there she will be, hair curled over one shoulder, hand on the banister, ready for dinner in a green dress ('A redhead has little choice'), her white rabbit-fur tippet over her shoulders, diamanté clasp winking. And after Momma, not long after, will come Daddy, pinging Barney's curls, punching Toby playfully on the shoulder, asking where Momma is, always looking for Momma, his eyes hungry when he first sees her, making me and Toby look away. We'll hear the chink of glasses. Smell pine cones on their fire. Laughter.

Bang! A gunshot shakes the night.

'Bang.' Kitty smiles, raises Raggedy Doll to eye level. 'Bang, bang, bang.'

Peggy throws her knitting to the floor, rushes to the window. The red skein of wool catches on her heel, unspooling behind her. 'Christ almighty.'

Six

Peggy tried to scrub all traces of Knight away with the bristle brush. But there is still a dark red splatter on the stone, like an exploding poppy, a smell of horse sweat and blood. The bobble of Knight's brains and the brown tufts of his mane were all over the side of the stable, too, but Toby nimbly scrabbled up and scraped them off. He laid the bits of brain on the wall to dry, like little red and white jewels, so he could preserve them, add them to his collection of things dug up from the gardens and fields, fossils, rabbit skulls, crockery shards, cartridge cases, and the shrivelled lambs' tails that drop off in spring. I think he'd do the same with Momma if he could. And I think that would be preferable to this: Momma buried beneath the soil like a broken butter dish.

That's going to happen today. It's the day of the funeral. Time has gone funny. Almost a week has vanished since Momma died, sucked into the hole that has opened up, black and deep and dangerous as a disused tin mine. It's impossible to believe it's Easter, that bluebells are budding in the woods. The sky is wintry, heavy and low, like something that's going to keep falling until it crushes you flat. A brisk, eye-drying wind, smelling of rotting things, dementedly spins the weathercock on the steeple of St Mary's, the church beside the old harbour. Its damp stone walls are pocked with yellow lichen, the stained-glass windows crusted with salt. Like being stuck in the underside of an upturned boat, Momma always said, making us laugh during intolerable services that went on for centuries, far longer than any in London. Seagulls and pigeons line its gable roof, hungrily eyeing the tiny graveyard, Momma's stomach-churning destination. The hole is already dug, the exposed worms kinking in the daylight. I hate the thought of her here. The graveyard is known to be a pickle of bones – bodies layered with more bodies, like thin blankets on a bed in winter – full of old dead Altons and mariners and drowned children who wandered out too far in the wrong tide or walked the mud flats of the creek for a dare or a sherbet fountain.

We gather outside the church door, avoiding the eyes of the people we might normally see at weddings or christenings, flinching when they hug us, unable to be comforted. They all talk in those whispery voices that adults use in children's bedrooms when they think the children are asleep. The women touch Daddy's arm, cock their heads. The men, with their chubby baby faces, clap him on the shoulder. Daddy nods politely, not quite meeting their eyes. If he did they'd see that the light has gone out of them as surely as a snuffed candle. I feel their gaze skating over me too. I hear them muttering under their breath, 'She looks so uncannily like her mother.' I let my hair fall in front of my face and hide there until the smiles slide off their faces and, slightly embarrassed, they move on.

'It's time, my darling,' Daddy says, hand on my back. He tries to smile but can't. I think about him sobbing last night, every night since Momma died. I don't think there can be a worse sound in the world than your father crying. He takes a deep breath. 'Ready?'

I nod. I know what to expect. I've been to funerals here before. There is something about funerals that is all the same, like weddings in reverse. So I will pretend it's someone else's, not Momma's. This is how we've decided to survive it.

The heavy church door opens with a pig squeal. The vicar apologizes, mutters something about rust. As if it matters.

Toby squeezes my hand. Stick together, be brave, the squeeze says. I squeeze back and we steer Barney and Kitty into St Mary's, our feet falling into step, like soldiers.

The church smells of old flower water. It is all dank gloom, apart from Momma's coffin, which is covered with pale pink ribbons and so many spring flowers – hyacinth, anemone, iris – that it looks like a garden. I like this. Momma loved gardens. She loved our garden. But it still feels impossible that she is actually in that box – my warm, pretty momma, who would bundle us up on cold, clear nights and take us outside to spot the Bear and the Plough glittering in the sky – packed up like a fancy Easter egg. I tell myself it's impossible. It is not her.

Still, we must walk towards it, Kitty pulling back on my hand, intimidated less by Momma's coffin than all the pomp. The crowd follows behind us in solemn, coughing silence. There are not enough seats in the church. I'm glad. It would be much worse if there were empty spaces. People are standing, staring, jostling for a prized view of the coffin through the forest of hats. We walk to the front row, eyes hot on our back. The church doors squeal again, clump shut.

'Psst!' Only Aunt Bay's full film star lips are visible beneath the cartwheel rim of her hat. She's in the row behind us wearing a black mini-dress – a glimpse of thigh revealed above the pew – that reminds me of all the reasons Momma adored her, and all the reasons Daddy doesn't really approve. She grabs my hand, trailing the smell of cigarettes. 'How are you, baby?'

My mouth opens, but nothing comes out. Aunt Bay's American accent is too much, too close to Momma's. It's what I would hear if she walked through that church door, lifting her hair off her shoulders, laughing, telling everyone it's all been a silly misunderstanding and another case of English fuss.

I can't stop doing this, imagining Momma bursting back into life at random moments. Neither can I stop replaying that day, making things turn out differently, pulling time back and forth, alive and elastic as gum, snipping out the day of the storm entirely and making Big Bertie's chains and cogs jolt forward to the day after, eating sandy sandwiches on the beach.

'Honey?' She pushes up the rim of her hat, so that I can see her kind, red-rimmed eyes, spidery long lashes.

'I'm very well, thank you, Aunt Bay,' I say, because this is what Altons are expected to say.

'That's my girl,' says Bay. She has a small chunk of lipstick on her front tooth that looks like pale pink icing. 'Nancy would be so proud of you. She loved you so much, Amber.'

My throat locks. I know Momma loved me. For some

reason, I don't want to be told that she did, as if that might not have been the case.

'Will you come and see me in New York?'

I nod, thinking of Aunt Bay's hotel apartment, where there is a fat man called Hank on a desk and you have to knock past guests arriving with suitcases, guitars slung over their shoulders. How Aunt Bay would leave us playing dominoes with Hank while she and Momma went to shows on 42nd Street.

'Please stand,' says the vicar. There is a rustle. Bay's hat obliterates the view for the row behind. There's a tut or two.

'I'll take you to Coney Island, up the Empire State,' she whispers. 'If you ever need somewhere to escape you come to me, OK?'

I don't nod then. Why would I ever want to escape what remains of my family? Just the thought of not being with them makes me feel dizzy.

'Right, Amber?'

'Shush, please,' whispers Mildred, one of my father's tall, cross cousins.

Aunt Bay turns and smiles at Mildred and carries on talking, only louder, which is very Aunt Bay. 'You're a quiet girl with a big heart, Amber. You need to make it a strong heart too. You're the lady of the house now.'

Lady of the house? I don't like that idea at all.

'But you can cry all the same. You're allowed to cry, honey. Really.'

I try to cry for Aunt Bay but my tears are stuck.

Mouths open, sing, exposing jam-red throats. I turn to check Daddy is not going to mess up. He is staring directly ahead, face blank, back straight, chin raised but shoulders shaking, little judders, like the engine of the boat made when he and Momma used to putter up and down the creek, laughing, sharing a cigarette.

Speeches. Poems. An American. A duke. A colonel. They talk about how Daddy fell in love with Momma's spirit. Her 'thirst for life'. Her love of home and family and horses. How Daddy brought her here from America and she fell in love with Cornwall. How she'd introduced the locals to the delights of pumpkin pie. How she didn't even like killing the rabbits. Because that's what Nancy was, a nurturer, a mother, an animal-lover, a Joan Baez fan, someone who saw the good in everyone and everything and liked to sing around the fire.

Everyone is snuffling quietly. But Aunt Bay is howling and saying, 'Sweet Jesus,' not very quietly at all, over and over, even though she doesn't believe in Jesus but a bearded man in orange robes who lives in India. 'My baby sister. Oh, sweet Jesus!'

I pretend to wipe away a tear, and keep focused on the others, making sure no one else causes a scene.

They are all under orders to be brave. Kitty is fiddling with a stray thread on her button, flicking it back and forth with her fingers, Momma's death still too vast for her to grasp. Barney is staring down at his shoes, polished to mirrors, biting his bottom lip, breathing fast and hard. Toby stares ahead, rigid, chest inflated, his neck blazing red at the back, as if his skin is bursting with the effort of holding the feelings inside. We all want it over. Anything but this.

When Daddy steps out of his pew the church stills and

the snuffling stops. He looks older and smaller than he did only days before, the hair at his temples the colour of cutlery. When he looks up at the silent congregation his eyes are blank and bloodshot and make me think of the fish that get caught on the creek as the tide rolls out, flapping on the mud until they stop.

The hush is broken by the crinkle-crackle of foil.

'Kitty!' I hiss, realizing that she is unwrapping a small chocolate egg in her pocket.

She looks up, indignant, hot-cheeked. 'It's Easter! Aunt Bay gave it to me.'

'You can eat it afterwards.' Mildred's mouth purses disapprovingly in the tail of my eye.

Kitty drops the egg into her pinafore-dress pocket. I pull her close. Barney too. He feels limp and cool, all his usual fidgety energy gone. No longer more alive than everyone else. The opposite. He still hasn't told us what happened in the woods – what he saw – and when pressed, he just says he can't remember anything before sitting at the fireplace, drinking cocoa, the bang of the gun. I'm not sure I believe him.

I think about Momma in London before we left sitting on the turquoise chair, saying, 'Worrying is a mother's job,' and I feel as if I'm going to shatter into a million pieces. Who will worry about us now? Who will look after us now?

The answer hits with a heavy punch. It. Will. Be. Me.

Daddy's mouth opens. At first nothing comes out. Toby and I exchange looks. From nowhere comes the urge to laugh. I bite down on my lower lip, terrified that I might actually do it. Then the piece of paper Daddy is holding

81

begins to tremble, like the feathers on the sobbing wo-men's hats. And the giggle leaves me as suddenly as it came. Someone help Daddy. Someone help him. After a long stretch of awfulness, the vicar walks up to him and, grip-ping one of his arms at the elbow, tries to direct him back to his seat. But he refuses to go. The vicar, unsure what to do next, sheepishly retreats.

'Thank you all for coming,' Daddy says at last, raising his shot-red eyes again. 'I know many of you have trav-elled many miles to be here.'

Shoulders drop. Legs stretch. We breathe again. Toby scuffs his shoe on the church floor.

'Nancy would be enormously touched to see . . .' Daddy stops. He is staring over my left shoulder, his mouth drop-ping open, his notes starting to slip from his fingers. Everyone glances over to see what has startled him.

At the back of the church, in the latecomers' pew, there is a woman with an almost-smile and an upward tilt of her chin, relishing the curious stares. I suppose you wouldn't have hair like hers if you didn't want to be noticed: silvery blonde, scraped hard off her face and coiled luxuriantly on the crown of her head in fat rolls, it's the kind of hair-do you never see south of the Tamar. Her face is sharply featured, handsome rather than pretty, with a thin, slightly curved nose and polar blue eyes made bluer by sweeps of the black eye-liner pencils Momma used when she went to parties in London. Tossed over the shoulder of her pitch-black coat, like something freshly killed, is a red fox fur.

The hush sounds whispery now, full of saliva. It takes an eternity for Daddy to start talking again.

'She'd be enormously touched to see our tiny church so

'crowded,' Daddy says at last, sounding less sure of himself. 'But there are some women who cannot help but change the lives of all those they meet . . .'

Daddy pauses, stutters, gazing at the blonde woman. Toby and I frown at each other, thinking the same thing: weirdly, it sounds as if Daddy is talking about someone else, not Momma at all. And it feels like this until Daddy says quickly, 'Nancy Alton was such a woman.'

Seven

Lorna

A liver-spotted hand emerges from the frayed flap of tweed cape. 'Mrs Caroline Alton.' It's the poshest voice Lorna's ever heard, roughened only by a faint wheezy whistle. 'Delighted.'

'Hi,' Lorna stutters. The woman's arthritic knuckles are like golf balls. But the handshake is firm. Out of the corner of her eye Lorna sees Dill shrinking back into the hall. She wishes she'd warned her that Mrs Alton would be in the bridal suite. 'I'm Lorna. Lorna Dunaway,' she says, trying not to stare rudely.

'Bones don't age,' as her mother always said. Mrs Alton's haven't: she's clearly the handsome woman from the portrait in the hall. But her face is etched with knife-cut wrinkles now. These are not laughter lines, like Lorna's late nan had, the result of a good life, lived cheerfully. The lines on either side of Mrs Alton's mouth and the arrowhead V stamped between her eyes suggest she has spent her privileged life in a state of perpetual disapproval.

'So you'd like to get married at Pencraw?' Mrs Alton pins Lorna with unstable pale blue eyes, eyes that stare out hard, rather than let you in. 'I am pleased.'

This is the moment when Lorna should point out that she's just exploring the option. She doesn't.

'Do take a proper look around.' Mrs Alton leans on a brass-tipped wooden cane, keeping her back perfectly straight. The hand clasping the top is locked with rings, their diamonds glinting dully in the evening light. 'Tell me your thoughts. And please refrain from politeness.'

Lorna smiles hard – she hears her mother's voice in her head: 'If you don't know the rules, just smile!' – and looks properly around the room. The ceilings are lower in the tower than they are in the rest of the house, the walls covered with cottagey floral wallpaper. The relative lack of dusty grandness is a relief, although there is a nod to it with the giant mahogany-black bed, vines and flowers carved into its four posts, which will surely impress even Jon. 'It's lovely, Mrs Alton.'

'I'm glad you think so,' she replies, in a manner that warns against thinking otherwise. That Mrs Alton lives in this remote spot almost alone makes perfect sense now. She is clearly not the kind of old woman – late seventies? – who could be settled into a comfy armchair in a retirement home off a seaside promenade and placated with sponge puddings. 'I suspected you might like it from the moment I saw you getting out of the car.'

So someone had been watching them, Lorna thinks, gratified that she hadn't imagined it.

'So, Lorna . . .' She fingers the row of skin-buffed pearls in the crêpe of her neck. 'Enlighten me. A little bit about yourself.'

'I'm a primary-school teacher from Bethnal Green, east London.'

'A teacher? Oh. My sympathies.'

Lorna is stunned. She wishes Jon was with her so they

could discuss it all to death later. Also, she just wishes Jon was with her.

'Your fiancé?'

'He works for his family's building firm,' she stutters, bracing herself for the reaction. 'Carpentry, that's his passion,' she adds, hating herself for trying to justify it, wishing she could convey quite how talented Jon is, the extraordinary deftness of his huge hands, the way his fingertips read the grain of wood, like braille.

'A carpenter?' Mrs Alton stamps her cane on the floor, turns to Dill. 'This could prove most useful, Endellion, most useful indeed. My goodness, we always need carpenters.'

Dill smiles apologetically at Lorna, stares down at her feet.

'Come closer, my dear.' Mrs Alton beckons Lorna forward with a long finger, crooked to the left, armed with jewels.

Lorna hesitates for a second, then steps forward. There is something about Mrs Alton that makes non-compliance an unappealing prospect.

Without warning, the cane slips, clatters to the ground. Lorna bends down and hands it back with a smile.

'Damn thing,' says Mrs Alton, pulling it to her side again. 'Bad hip, legacy from my time on the slopes. A terrible bore. Do you ski?'

'Oh, no. Not really,' says Lorna, not daring to cite the time she spent on an Austrian nursery slope two years ago, being overtaken by three-year-olds.

'Now, that dress . . .' Mrs Alton murmurs softly. Her head tilts to one side, trying to place it. Standing so close, Lorna catches an unpleasant sweet smell on her breath. 'It reminds me of something.'

'Well, it's vintage,' Lorna explains brightly, always happy to talk about clothes, crunching the yellow cotton between her fingers. Modern cotton doesn't crunch in the same way. Neither does it hang properly. To get this quality now you'd have to pay hundreds, which she'd never be able to afford. 'Late sixties, the woman in the shop said.'

Mrs Alton looks amused. 'Late sixties? Gracious. You like old clothes?'

'I'm prone to a rummage in a charity shop. I guess I just kind of like old things.'

'Well, that is probably just as well, isn't it?' says Mrs Alton, wryly.

'Oh, no.' Lorna hopes that Mrs Alton realizes she was referring to the house, not its owner. 'I meant that –'

'The funny thing is one *assumes* life is linear,' Mrs Alton interrupts, with a stagey sigh. She starts to walk to the window – very slight limp, otherwise perfect deportment – her cane tapping on the wooden floor. 'But then, as you get older, as ancient as me, Lorna, you realize life is not linear at all but circular, that dying is as hard as being born, that it all returns to the point you think you'd left long, long ago. Like the hands of a clock.'

'Really?' Lorna has absolutely no idea what she's talking about. Still, she thinks old people are hugely underestimated and that too often it's only children and old people who speak the truth. You just have to slow down and listen.

'Fashions come around again.' Her eyes sweep up and down Lorna's dress. 'Events. People. Yet we all imagine ourselves unique. You wear that dress without giving a thought to its previous life.'

Lorna is too polite to say that she frequently wonders about her vintage items, who wore them, if they're still alive. She's been known to make up biographies for them too, which Jon finds hilarious.

'As we never learn from those who go before us, we are all doomed to repeat mistakes afresh,' Mrs Alton adds wearily. 'Over and over. Like mice in a scientist's cage.' She gazes out of the window, as if she's quite forgotten anyone else is there.

Lorna glances at Dill for some kind of direction, some sign that it may be time to leave. But Dill offers only a nervous smile, gaze slipping away.

They really are the oddest couple. And this is the oddest day, Lorna decides. One of those extraordinary surreal days that pop up unexpectedly in an ordinary life, unrelated to anything that has gone before it or will come after.

'And when might we expect the first payment, my dear?' Mrs Alton whips around, smiling properly for the first time, revealing peculiarly small, antique-ivory teeth. 'In cash.'

'Oh.' Lorna is flustered. She'd thought posh people didn't discuss finances.

'I do hope I haven't embarrassed you by mentioning money.'

'No, no, not at all. The thing is, I . . . I love this house, Mrs Alton, I really do. It's wonderful, quite unlike anywhere else I've ever been. But my fiancé is not yet convinced . . . I need to talk to him first,' she blathers, feeling a tide of heat sweep her face.

'*Talk* to him?' repeats Mrs Alton, looking puzzled. 'And you, a modern girl.'

'It's really about the little details.' Lorna takes a deep breath, tells herself sternly not to be intimidated. 'We need a bit more information, that's all.'

'In-for-*ma*-tion?' Mrs Alton enunciates slowly, as if the very idea is preposterously bourgeois. Her lip catches on a dry tooth, staying hitched for a moment before falling. 'What sort of information might you require?'

'Um, where we'd actually have the reception, the dancing, the catering arrangements.' She reaches for her hair and twists it, feeling a wave of self-consciousness under the pin of Mrs Alton's gaze. 'That sort of thing.'

'But there are so many rooms! You could have four weddings going on and you'd never bump into each other.' She glares at Dill. 'Is there one job on earth that you could not mess up?'

'Oh, don't get me wrong! Dill has given us a fantastic tour,' says Lorna, quickly, hoping she hasn't got Dill into trouble. The meeting is unravelling fast. 'But we arrived rather late and we've run out of time.'

On cue, the car horn hoots jauntily from the drive below.

Mrs Alton frowns at Dill. 'Surely we haven't another visitor. Are the masses at the gate?'

'Oh, no. That's Jon.' Lorna wrings her hands, not quite sure how to make her exit gracefully, fearing he might hoot again if she doesn't hurry up. 'Thank you so much for taking the time to show me the bridal suite.'

Mrs Alton, sensing she might be about to lose her first customer, sharply changes tack. 'Endellion tells me you'd love to know more about the house.'

Dill nods enthusiastically in the corner.

'I'm just nosy, really,' Lorna says, a little wary now.

'Excellent. I like an enquiring mind. I don't get many around here, as you can see.' She tilts her head, considers something. A seagull shrieks, wheels past the window. 'The answer is obvious. You must come and stay. Then you can gather all this . . . information that you seem to need before you pay the deposit.' She sets her jaw. 'I must have that deposit.'

'I don't know what to say. That's . . . that's extremely generous of you, Mrs Alton. But –'

'Not at all generous,' says Mrs Alton, with a dismissive flap of her hand, the diamonds trailing a shimmer of light. 'Quite the opposite. It is imperative that I get this wedding business off the ground if the house is to remain in private hands, if it has any future at all. And that is all I care about. The house. Oh, and the dog too, of course.'

Lorna laughs nervously.

Mrs Alton smiles. 'Lorna, you are to be my guinea pig.'

'I am?' She's feeling more confused by the moment. Has she really just been invited to stay here?

'I'm no fool, Lorna.' Mrs Alton raises one smudged pencilled eyebrow. 'I'm perfectly well aware that the fees for such a house, even given its decorative state, are rather modest.'

Lorna blushes: she had assumed Mrs Alton and Dill knew nothing of the marketplace.

'But as I'm sure you are *also* aware, it is hard to get bookings until there is some evidence of past success. Such is the tiresome trepidation of modern couples. However, I can see that you are a young lady of imagination, style and . . .' there is mischief in her eyes now '. . . pluck.'

Even though she knows it's shameless flattery, Lorna

cannot help thrilling to the idea of being a young lady of pluck. It's such a wonderful old-fashioned word. She makes a note to share it with her class, come September.

Mrs Alton's smile hardens. 'I no longer have the constitution for suspense. Tell me, are you to be my guest?'

The urge to say yes is almost overwhelming.

'Sorry, sweetheart, there's just no way I can stay at Toad Hall this month.' Jon accelerates up the drive, gravel popping beneath the wheels. It is a clear evening now, smelling of rain and grass and blowy big sky. 'I can't take any more time off work, not with this big new project in Bow . . .'

'Don't worry about it.' Lorna sighs, digging through the detritus of the glove compartment for the mints. She's ravenous. All those stairs. 'I'll ask my sister.'

The atmosphere in the car tightens slightly. They drive for a few moments in silence. When they get to the end of the drive, Lorna gazes at the house's battered white enamel sign – stuck in the bushes, like a lost handkerchief that needs to be returned to its owner – and feels a wash of longing and frustration. She is certain that now she's seen Black Rabbit Hall nothing else will do.

They crunch off the pot-holed drive into the country lane. Behind the foam of cow parsley, farmed fields start to rush past. Electricity pylons, zingy road markings, stone cottages in the valley, all return the sense of normality, the shift from one world to another. Jon relaxes back in his seat. 'Am I allowed to point out now that Black Rabbit Hall is completely loony? Sort of like being trapped in a Kate Bush song.'

'It's a tad eccentric,' Lorna acknowledges, unwrapping a sticky mint. 'But I love it.'

The corners of his mouth twitch with a smile. 'Like you love flea markets and dusty little shops that smell of wee?'

She flicks the mint wrapper at him, laughs. 'Vintage shops don't smell of wee!'

'At least in a shop you can only waste a few pounds on something that's coming apart at the seams.' He changes gear a little too firmly. She can always tell his mood shifts by the way he changes gear. Something is bugging him. 'And there is also the minor matter of rats, my beauty, that manky mongrel having been bought to catch them.'

'Oh, rats are everywhere in the country,' she says authoritatively, even though she hasn't a clue if this is true or not.

'Just what I wanted at my wedding. A bit of bubonic plague.'

Lorna unwraps another mint, feeds it between his lips, skimming the grain of his evening stubble, pushing the sweet in a little too hard. He bites down on her finger, trapping it in his mouth. She feels the serrated ridge of his teeth, almost hurting but not, the wet heat of his tongue curling around her fingertip and something starts to clench inside. Their eyes catch and spark in the mirror, and it is this abrasion, this tension, that has always made things so exciting. They are such different people – Jon steady, considered, able to simplify any situation, she impulsive, instinctive, prone to over-complication – that most of the time they balance each other perfectly. But other times, the rare occasions when they don't agree on something – something big – it feels like those oppositions might pull them apart.

Not breaking her gaze, he releases her finger. She turns to look out the window, annoyed by her own arousal.

'Lorna, I know you love that house.' Their eyes meet in the mirror. 'I want to love it too.'

'You've decided you don't.'

He turns the radio on, swivelling the silver knob, trying to change the mood. But the dance anthem jars. Lorna turns the volume down in silent riposte.

'All I'll say is that we'd be better off putting your nephew in charge of the wedding than Dill.'

'Not fair. I like Dill.'

'So do I. But she's clearly been changing Mrs Alton's bedpans for the last thousand years and seems to have met barely another living soul, let alone supervised a wedding.' He winds down his window, lets the warm, damp evening flood in. 'If you ask me, it's only because they're posh that Social Services aren't knocking on the door.'

The rush of air makes Lorna's enthusiasm flame up again. 'Oh, forget Dill and Mrs Alton and everything else for a moment!' She closes her eyes, feels her hair swish about her neck. 'Imagine the house full of people dancing! The garden lit up! Kids –'

'– smashing the antiques. Getting lost in the woods,' he says drily.

'The house needs some life, some love, that's all, Jon.'

'And at least five hundred grand's worth of repairs. The buckets weren't decorative.'

'Oh, no one will care about the odd leak.' Well, only Jon's mother, Lorraine, a glamorous juggernaut of a matriarch – Botox, BMW convertible, big heart – who is never shy of complaining to café managers if there is toilet paper on the floor of the Ladies or a smudge on a wine glass. She'd grown up 'outside-toilet' poor and, now that she is not in the least poor, dismisses anything short of luxurious and absolutely spotless as a point of principle. 'They'll enjoy something different.'

He smiles. 'It will certainly be different.'

'Jon, it's *the* house. The one Mum and I visited. Even Dad thinks it is,' she adds, embellishing only a little.

'Your old man, bless him, being a wholly credible source of accurate information.' He winds the window down further, trucker elbow hanging out of the car.

'Black Rabbit Hall has got soul. That is all that matters,' says Lorna, with finality.

'It's also got dry rot,' he teases, overtaking a rattling Cortina, fog lights on, snorting black exhaust. 'And I don't fancy paying for the privilege of feeling like a toff for the day, thanks all the same.'

Lorna feels ridiculously tearful, aware of how silly and immature it is to cry about a wedding venue of all things, but unable to help herself. Also, she's not aspirational, not like that. Her mother's misplaced snobbery, her habit of telling Lorna's friends' mothers that Dad managed an 'executive car service' rather than drove a black cab had always been excruciating to her and her sister.

'Sorry.' Jon reaches across, hitches up the hem of her yellow dress to lay a hand on her bare knee, his eyes on the road. 'I know Cornwall is . . .' he glances at her, hesitates, choosing his words carefully '. . . special to you.'

'Don't try to read things into it, Jon,' she says quickly, warning him off. She knows what he's trying to imply, doesn't want to go there. 'I just think that house is amazing, the perfect place for a wedding, for us.'

They drive on for a bit in silence, the green fields smudging to graphite squares in the dusk, their normal easy intimacy a little jagged. After a while, Jon pulls up at a junction, turns to face her, his gaze warm and impossible to break. 'Lorna, I just want us to be married, that's all.' He switches on a Cockney accent, the one that always makes her smile. 'For yous to be me missus.'

'I will!'

'And the wedding to be about you and me.'

'That's all it's ever been about.'

He rakes his blond hair off his face. The air thickens between them. 'Then why can't I shift the feeling that the moment we stepped into that house it became about something else?'

'I don't know what you're –' She stops. There *is* something else, irrational, inescapable, a pull she doesn't understand. She doesn't know how to explain it.

'It's all right,' Jon says, as if reading her thoughts. 'Let's just get back, shall we?' He slams his foot on the accelerator.

Lorna twists in her seat belt, hoping to catch a final glimpse of the house in the distance. But it's gone. The miles tick past. The sky darkens. A thick eggy fog rolls over the hedges, whirling in the cones of the headlights. But as vivid dreams can fray the neat edge of waking hours, so Black Rabbit Hall stays with Lorna that night, during the days that follow: the smell of beeswax; the hum of the globe; the taste of the past, salty, moreish, on the tip of her tongue.

Eight

'This house needs a woman's touch again,' Peggy is saying, voice hushing as voices do when crossing into awkward dead-mother territory. 'That's what it needs. Gosh, let's get some air and light in here, shall we? It's been four months – God rest her soul – and Mr Alton's still keeping Nancy's dressing room like a mausoleum. It gives me the willies.'

Curtains rattle along a rail. A thin line of light spills through the edges of the doors. I huddle into the cloud of a fur-lined coat, press myself against the back of the wardrobe. I've always loved Momma's wardrobe, the giant mahogany paw feet that look like they might start lumbering across the room at any moment, its bloated belly full of silky dresses, furs (sable, mink, fox), the teetering column of circular hat boxes, mothy cashmere. It's the last place on the estate that still smells intensely of Momma: the waxy scent of her red lipstick in its bullet-gold case, old saddle leather, the bread-dough tang of her skin in the morning before she showered. I remember Momma by her smell. She'd understand: she used to sniff us all the time. But I suspect Peggy and Annie will think it's weird – and Daddy doesn't want any of us here messing up his memories – so I sit very still and try not to make a sound.

'The house just feels so dark these days,' continues

Peggy, sucking a sigh through her teeth. 'Dark and stagnant, however many windows I open.'

I've begun to realize this too. Without Momma's light, airy presence, Black Rabbit Hall feels heavy and still, too old and tired to move.

'Well, the children aren't helping matters,' says Annie, thinking Peggy is having a dig at her cleaning. 'I could make a sand dune just with what's in the stair carpet. And they never stop tramping river mud through the place. It's like a bog in their bathrooms. I'm not paid enough, Pegs, I'm really not.'

'Come, Annie . . .' Peggy sounds irritated now. 'Hardly the time.'

'I've never seen kids go feral so quick. They look wild. And they *are* wild, Peggy, wilder than any God-fearing kids should be, let alone a grand family such as the Altons. Everyone in the village is nattering about it.'

'Well, let them.' I hear a complaint of springs that can only mean Peggy's flumped down on Momma's baby-blue *chaise longue* by the window. 'If they've got nothing better to do than gossip about wretched children who've lost their ma.'

'I'm just saying they're not the same smart city kids who stepped off that London train at the beginning of the summer, that's all,' mutters Annie, under her breath. A swoosh of a polishing cloth on wood.

'No.' Peggy sighs. 'That they're not.'

I can only remember that early-July day vaguely: leaving Paddington in the morning, the grimy swing of the train door in the evening, Toby throwing his bag on to the sun-scrubbed platform. A lifetime ago already.

After Momma's funeral, Daddy decided that the best thing for all of us was to continue precisely as if nothing had happened. The next day Toby left for boarding school as normal; Kitty, Barney and I returned to Fitzroy Square and day school in London. The alternate reality of that summer term quickly took over, our broken lives held up by tight white elastic socks and the industrious routines of our earnest new nanny, Meg, who has a streak of grey hair like a badger, and says, 'Now, now, it'll all work out fine,' a lot, when it clearly won't.

Looking back on that school term now, I'm not sure it was actually me sitting at the pen-pocked desk, shooting my hand up to answer questions on Prospero and osmosis to prove that I was the same star student and nothing had changed, debating the merits of the school tuck shop's various boiled sweets with Matilda, as if I still lived in a universe where boiled sweets might actually matter. It was someone acting me, I think: I was huddled in a tight ball somewhere else, hands over my head, trying to protect myself from the unendurable sadness that would swoop down without warning, bloodied claws outstretched.

At least the days snipped past, vanished as soon as they'd happened, leaving nothing behind: everything felt inconsequential, pointless, and I missed Toby dreadfully. In a blink it was the end-of-term school fête: Union Jack bunting, fat strawberries and dollops of cool sweet cream, a shrill starting whistle and a fierce charge of mothers in fluttery pastel dresses, with thudding bare feet – but no longer my mother, who always won the mothers' race, light and graceful as a doe – and the summer term finished. It was time to return to Black Rabbit Hall for the summer holidays. Because that is what Altons do at the beginning of July. And nothing must change.

I even allowed myself to believe it wouldn't: that Black Rabbit Hall had such power of inertia that we would all just return to the days before the storm and Momma would still be there, the beads of her string bikini bouncing at the back of her neck as, whooping, she ran into the sea.

Counting down the days until we left for Cornwall, I'd lie in my bed in Fitzroy Square trying to conjure it all up: the pipes clanking, the bigness, the safeness. But when we got back here it wasn't the same. There was no safe feeling left, just an unhinged, manic freedom.

'Their mother wouldn't stand for it, all this a-roaming about the countryside from dawn to dusk,' says Annie, shaking me out of my thoughts. 'Not even an American, Pegs.'

I want to shout that Momma wouldn't mind at all. She was the one who'd wake us up to watch the red sunrise and make us sit, yawning, bleary-eyed, complaining but happy, wrapped in doggy blankets in the car, drinking hot chocolate from a Thermos.

Then I doubt myself: it gets harder and harder to know what she'd think. Or remember her face, her real face, not just the face from a photograph. I remember random things more vividly, a tiny biscuit crumb stuck to her lipstick as she smiled, the patterns of freckles across her nose. Other times, when I'm asleep, I hear her voice so clearly – 'Honey, lend me a hand in the stables this morning?'; 'Pancakes or crumpets? Peggy is demanding an answer' – that it wakes me up with a jolt, certain she's in the room. But she isn't. She never is.

One hundred and twenty-three days ago she was alive. And getting older. Now she won't get any older. In April it would have been her forty-first birthday. (I imagined her in the bronze dress, the one she'd wear with her tiger-eye earrings, that turned her hair a blaze of red and her eyes green as lettuce.) We planted a plane tree in Fitzroy Square and lit a candle on a pink cake adorned with a tiny American flag on a cocktail stick. As we walked away, mouths full of icing and sponge, I wondered how many of her birthdays we'd celebrate: dead people's birthdays go on forever. Do we stop when she gets to the right age to die? Like eighty. Or seventy-five. Daddy didn't answer.

Toby and I were fifteen in May. We couldn't face a party so Daddy took us to the cinema in Leicester Square. We stumbled out of the dark, smoky theatre unable to remember what we'd just seen. I didn't tell any of my friends that it was my birthday, apart from Matilda, because it's embarrassing enough being the Girl Whose Mum Died – the head threw a special assembly, crucifying – and I don't want to attract any more attention.

I am attracting attention outside school, though. When I walk down the street men stare much more than they ever did. Secretly, I quite like it. But Toby tried to hit one last week, a stringy boy with bulgy eyes, smoking, leaning against the red telephone box in the village.

I shift, trying to get comfortable, realizing how long my legs have grown, flamingo legs folding right up to my chin. I'm half an inch taller too – Toby double that. I'm finally wearing a proper bra. (I have never missed Momma more than when I was struggling out of my shirt in the stuffy Rigby & Peller changing room, watched by new nanny

Meg.) It's a relief to have a proper woman's body at last because I no longer feel like a girl inside. You can't feel like a girl if you haven't got a mother, I told Matilda. The generations jump about like months in a leap year. You have to grow up.

Barney and Kitty don't have a mother either, just a gap where she used to be. And as big sister, I have to try to fill it.

I'm pretty bad at all the Momma things – bedtime stories, kissing cut knees, untangling knots in fine baby hair – but I try to copy what she did and hope it's better than nothing. I remembered to put a coin beneath the pillow when Barney lost a tooth. I covered the dappled grey rocking horse with a blanket because it reminded him of Knight and made him cry. I poke the stuffing back inside Raggedy Doll's neck when it sprouts from the stitches, go along with the ritual of putting her to bed in the cradle, tucking the doll beneath her lacy sheets. I worry about Kitty being too cheerful – 'Worrying is a mother's job' – and not understanding the finality of death: yesterday I found her pushing Raggedy Doll around the stables, searching for Momma. I worry when Barney wets the bed or pours hot water down the ant hole on the terrace. I talk to Daddy about why he might have dropped to the bottom of the class at school and all the other bedwetty things, and Daddy mutters that he doesn't know what he'd do without me. And that makes me feel proud but panicky. It makes me want to push my siblings away as well as hold them close. And sometimes it makes me cry a bit. Those times, the times it feels like someone's hollowed out my heart with an ice-cream scoop, I slink into this wardrobe and pretend the dangling silk scarves are Momma's long hair.

I came in here after Boris appeared at breakfast with Momma's wooden Mason Pearson hairbrush between his teeth. It still had her copper hair in it. I always pay a quick visit after those nights when I wake up and forget Momma is dead for a few blissful moments, then remember. Or when I push open the drawing-room door, expecting to see her stockinged feet up on the footstool, but they're not there and my brain flings back to dark places. What do her feet look like now? Are they just a marble-bag of bones, knuckly white joints, like the ones in Toby's collection?

The longest I've had to sit here this summer holiday was in the first week: one morning Peggy started frantically removing all the stuff in the pantry 'left over' from when we were last here – Easter – which meant throwing away the things we ate when Momma was alive. Toby was mad about that too. But Peggy insisted it would upset our stomachs, even though she's not one even to scrape the mould off the top of the jam and hates wasting anything. It was about something else.

Luckily, Toby rescued a small half-empty jar of Bovril from the bin for me. I now have it safely hidden in my knicker drawer. I unscrew the lid to smell the sandwiches Momma and I used to eat on lazy, happy Saturday mornings. The girl I was – quietly confident, trusting, full of certainties – is somewhere in that gloopy, inky pot.

Toby is different too. He gets angry a lot now and he didn't before: angry with Momma for dying; with me for not being Momma; with Peggy for not being Momma; with Barney for chasing rabbits that day; with Barney for no longer chasing rabbits; with Daddy for shutting down – it's like Daddy's had a power cut and we're still waiting for someone to fix him. I don't like being around Toby's anger too much or it seeps into me too.

But I can still see the old Toby sometimes: I can see the old Toby more easily than I can see the old me. I think that's true for him too, in reverse. And we still laugh at stupid things. It feels disloyal to laugh with Momma dead. But it feels worse if we don't. We get these fleeting unexpected bursts of silly happiness that come from nowhere, glowing embers shooting on to damp ground. So anything is possible: that's what Momma always said. Well, most things. I'm not about to go looking for her in the stables like Kitty.

My leg cramps and I stretch it out, knocking a shoe to the floor of the wardrobe.

'What was that?' says Peggy. 'Did you just hear something, Annie?'

I freeze, heart in my mouth, wondering how on earth I will explain myself.

'I'm not sure.'

'Those bloody mice again.'

I muffle a sigh of relief in cupped hands.

'What was I saying? Oh, yes. I politely said to Mr Alton that the kids need to be brought in hand. Especially Toby. He slept on a bed of sticks in the woods last week. Did you know that?'

'Rather him than me. What did Mr Alton say?'

'That Toby's been a right pain in the neck – all sorts of problems at school – and if he's happy and out of trouble for once then let him be. And, oh, yes, had I starched Mr Alton's white shirts for his trip to Paris?'

'Sounds like he just wants them out of his hair, Pegs.'

My stomach goes watery. Is that true? It can't be.

'Little troupers, those kids.'

'But Barney's gone flat as a pancake. Toby, well . . .' Something in Annie's voice cracks.

'Toby will calm down,' says Peggy, firmly. 'Amber will make sure of it.'

'She's too young for all this, Pegs.'

'Time is a great healer. We must remember that.'

Everyone says this. Or, worse, 'In time, you will feel better . . .' That's like promising to someone who has lost their leg, 'In time, you will grow another.' Anyway, I don't want to feel better. I don't want ever to forget Momma.

'Well, let's hope the man has the good sense to remarry,' says Annie. 'And quickly.'

'Remarry?' Peggy's voice squeaks.

'It's all anyone can talk about at the Anchor, Pegs. How will he cope with four growing kids without a wife? The man desperately needs a wife.'

I scrunch a bit of fur into my fist, struggling not to shout, 'Daddy will never remarry because he will never find another woman like Momma!' Grandma Esme has told me many times – now the stuff of family legend – that she'd introduced Daddy to all sorts of suitable English-women, 'dressed up irresistibly for a good Season of husband hunting'. He wouldn't commit to any of them. 'Your daddy frustrated many a determined young lady, the rogue.' Grandma's eyes always light up when she gets to our favourite part of the tale, Daddy meeting a 'land-owner's daughter from America with poppy-red hair and a thoroughly improper laugh' at a party. That was it. 'He was like a lovesick puppy,' she'll say, shaking her head so that her chins wobble. 'Neither Grandpa nor I could talk any sense into him. We told him no American girl could cope with the harshness of Cornish country life.' She'll kiss my forehead at this point in the story, and end, 'How wrong we were! I'm so very glad he took not the blindest bit of notice of us. Very glad indeed.' Thinking of Grandma makes me miss her horribly. She's too old to come to Black Rabbit Hall as frequently as she once did.

'Well,' says Peggy, sounding flustered, 'it's going to be one brave lady to take on this old pile.'

'You've got a pretty enough face, Pegs.'

'*Annie!*'

'Well, he needs a fancy version of you, doesn't he? Someone practical. Motherly. Oooh, Pegs, you're blushing!'

I smile into the sable. Ridiculous. They're both completely ridiculous.

'Honestly, Annie. If anyone could hear you.'

'Well, I bet he wouldn't step on his partner's toes at the village-hall dance! Or stink of pilchards.'

'Stop it, Annie.'

'Not the kind of brute to jilt a young woman at the altar either.'

'Annie, for the love of God . . .' I hear the hurt and anger in her voice, then realize Toby's story about her past is true. Oh, poor Peggy.

'Sorry, Pegs. Sorry. All I'm trying to say is that our Mr Alton is not going to be on the widowers' shelf for long, mark my words. Oh . . . crikey.' Her voice flashes with embarrassment. 'Toby! We were just . . . just freshening your ma's dressing room . . .'

'I'm looking for Amber.' I know from the low growl in his voice that he has heard the tail end of their conversation too. 'Have you seen my sister?'

'I was searching for ages.' Toby is standing at my bedroom window. He scratches the back of his sinewy calf with his toenail. The sole of his foot is hard and dirty. None of us has worn shoes for weeks. There are still splatters of grey river mud behind his knees. 'Where were you?'

'About.' I lie back on the bed, tugging Momma's cheese-cloth mini-dress down over my legs, and pretend to read Aunt Bay's letter. (I know it almost line by line, having read it five times already.)

I need one place that is my own.

Fidgety and fierce today, bare-chested in ripped Scout shorts, he presses his hands on the window frame and leans into the view, as if he's squaring up for a fight, shoulder-blades rising on his nut-brown back like fins. All the swimming and climbing have made him strong and lean, knotted his once skinny shoulders and arms with muscle. His hair is matted and curled, sun-bleached bright as a bonfire. His fingertips are stained with blackberry blood. Annie's right: he does look wild. 'What does Aunt Bay's letter say, then?'

'Sold a painting. Lost an inch from her hips on some diet. Oh, and she's got homes for all the kittens in the Chelsea Hotel. That's good, isn't it? They can all stay near each other. I hate the idea of them being separated . . .'

Toby rolls his eyes, pretending not to care. But we both love Aunt Bay's letters. They arrive deliciously randomly, sometimes three or four in the same month – fast, fizzy, in looping writing that somehow reads like she talks – then she goes silent for weeks, which is also reassuringly in character.

'She's coming to visit soon anyway.'

'Please, God, don't let her go swimming naked in the creek again.' Toby is funny about nudity. We both are. The bathroom door is now locked when we bathe. 'Where are the others?'

'Messing about in the ballroom.'

Toby holds the windowsill and lifts his feet from the floor, soles on the wall below, like a swimmer launching from the end of a pool. 'There's something I want us to try, Amber.'

I don't like it when he says 'us'. 'You're breaking the windowsill.'

He springs down, barely making a noise. 'Put that letter away, will you? I know you've read it a hundred times.'

I stuff it between bed and wall to savour later.

'Shove up.' Toby wedges next to me. His skin feels hot and dry along my arm and he smells of sweat and sea. He throws one of his legs over mine. It's surprisingly heavy and I'm reminded again of how time has pulled our once-similar bodies apart. No one could call Toby pretty now. He's changing so quickly.

'Amber,' he says, resting his face on his hand and staring at me intensely through the blaze of his lashes.

'What?'

'Limpets. Eating them raw. Off the rocks.' He grins his crazy-man grin. 'What do you think?'

'Ugh. No, thank you.'

'You really can eat them raw. People do.'

'Mad people.'

He sits up on the side of my bed, rumpling my eiderdown. I kick one of my bare feet on to his lap, my toes wiggling in the breeze from the window. He holds my foot, fingers curling lightly around my heel. 'We need to learn how to survive, Amber.'

Not this again. Just as I imagine people dying all the time now, Toby imagines the world ending in different ways. He reads books on warfare and tales of survival against the odds in bleak, wild places and wakes up each morning prepared to meet impending catastrophe head on.

'We don't have to survive and certainly not on raw limpets. Or those nettles you boiled up to a disgusting soup on the fire. If you're hungry why can't you just pinch some ginger biscuits from the pantry? Or make one of your crushed-Twiglet sandwiches or something?'

He looks at me as if I'm stupid. 'You're just not getting it.'

I remove my foot from his lap, dangle my hand to the floor, searching blindly for *Wuthering Heights*. 'Getting *what*?'

'We've got to know how to look after ourselves, Kitty and Barney.'

'Right. What about Daddy?'

'He could die.'

'He's not going to die.' I pick up the book, hold it above my head and fold back the turned page corner.

'Everyone dies. We've got to be prepared for the worst. Bad stuff happens.'

'The bad stuff *has* happened.'

He shakes his head. 'I'm talking about worse stuff.'

I quickly turn the page, even though I haven't read it. 'How on earth could anything be *worse*?'

'I don't know but . . . I sense that it can. I dream about it all the time. It's like . . .' I see something pass over his eyes like a cloud, and I know that whatever he's thinking of is as real to him as the book in my hands. 'A black dot getting bigger. A hole. Maybe a meteorite hitting us or something.'

'A meteorite!' I lick my finger, ready to flick another page. 'How exciting.'

'You're not taking it seriously.' He lies back on the bed, arms crossed behind his head, revealing a damp red puff of hair in each armpit. 'Amber?'

'What?'

'Will you promise me something?'

I put my book down, stare upwards, inverting the room in my head so that the white ceiling becomes the floor and the green lampshade a solitary tree in a snowy field.

'We stick together, whatever happens?'

'That's always been the deal.'

'Promise?'

'I already have. Ugh, Boris.'

Boris shuffles through the door, bedraggled, wet, a crea- ture of the mud. 'Sit,' I say, before he gets any ideas about joining us on the bed.

'There's one more thing,' Toby says, ruffling Boris's filthy ears with his toes.

'What?'

A slow grin curls the sides of his mouth. 'You'll try a limpet?'

'Just absolutely no. Never.'

*

The limpets are not as disgusting as they sound, just chewier, sandier and more alive. I say, 'Sorry,' to it as I swallow. Next time I'm definitely raiding the pantry.

'Don't pull a face,' grins Toby. Secretly he's impressed. Eating raw limpets is not something I'd have done when Momma was alive. But after Momma dying, the small things don't matter so much. You don't feel a scratch on your foot if you've gashed open your head. Anyway, I'll eat raw limpets for Toby.

'Your turn.' I throw him the sharp, flat bit of stone and he whacks it hard at the base of a limpet, prising its muscular foot away from the rock before it has a chance to lock down. It occurs to me that we're all a bit like these limpets, sticking hard to our rock, what remains of our family, as the tide tries to suck us out.

'Got it.' He leaps up, so springy on his feet it's as if he's weightless. No wonder he's constantly in trouble at school. He can't sit still for more than thirty seconds.

'Amber.' Kitty wanders over, rattling a bucket of shells and crispy mermaid's purses scoured from the strand line. She looks at Toby, puzzled. 'What you doing, Toby?'

'Foraging for my lunch.' He gouges out the stringy meat of the limpet, holds it up on the tip of his finger, enjoying the gore, then casually drops it into his mouth. 'Delicious.'

Kitty is horrified. 'That's Kitty's limpet friend.'

'Not any more. Want to try one?'

She holds Raggedy Doll in front of her face. 'No!'

He chips off another. 'Hungry, Barney?'

Barney pretends not to hear and stabs his stick into the

rock pool's seaweedy edges, trying to flush out fish. He is at his least miserable on the beach, far away from the spot in the woods where Momma died. It's the only place where you can feel his old spirit stirring.

'Or are you a girl too?' teases Toby.

Eyes watering, Barney makes himself eat the raw limpet. He wants Toby's approval, correctly suspecting that part of Toby blames him for initiating the line of dots that led to Momma's death: chasing the rabbits, Momma heading out with her weak leg and wrist, and whatever else happened that Barney refuses to talk about.

Toby ruffles his hair. 'Good man, Barns.'

'Yuck. That's so yuck. Raggedy Doll wants to go back to London and eat Nette's cinnamon toast.' Kitty holds up the doll – gnawed, ferociously over-loved. 'Don't you, Raggedy Doll?'

'I'm never going back to London,' says Barney, quickly retreating to the rock pool in case he's offered another limpet.

'School starts next week,' I say, reminding myself. Toby and Barney may want to keep free-falling at Black Rabbit Hall but secretly I'm looking forward to being back with my friends and studies, the petty comfort of enforced bedtimes, rules involving indoor and outdoor shoes and brushing hair before bed. A bit of distance from Toby too, although it feels mean to admit that.

'I will hide here in the cove and no one will find me,' says Barney.

'You must never hide here on your own. It's dangerous, Barney,' I explain, for the hundredth time. We caught him just in time last week, blithely wading out into a rough sea with a net. 'The water comes right up to the cliff at high tide. You can get caught out.'

'I can swim!'

'Yeah, but it sucks you under. There are weird currents.'

Barney picks up a small crab by a claw, watching it scuttle helplessly in the air. 'Well, I refuse to go back to London. It's too . . .' he pauses, thinks about it '. . . small.'

I smile because I know exactly what he means. This last summer at Black Rabbit Hall has been vast, boundless.

We sit in easy silence for a bit, throw a stick into the sea for Boris. A black cormorant flexes itself on a rock, wings outstretched. A cloud slips over the sun. The temperature drops and the sea changes from clear blue to murky dark green, like a glass of Kitty's paintbrush water.

'Amber?' Kitty presses up against my legs, sand-gritted and chilled.

'Yeah?'

'Is London still there?'

'Yes, of course it is.'

'And Nette?'

'Nette and Nanny Meg and Grandma Esme. And your little bedroom with the Flower Fairy painting on the wall. It's all as it was, Kitty,' I say, stretching it a bit.

'I can't imagine two places at once,' she says, looking worried. 'I can't imagine London any more.'

It does feel impossible sometimes that both this place and London can co-exist. Our lives are so different. 'Busyness is a tonic,' Daddy says, which means school, prep, museum visits; tea at Matilda's and Grandma's; trips to

London Zoo, the Natural History Museum, fittings for shoes and coats, our lives ordered, arranged, the days backed up with things to do so that we have as little time to think about Momma as possible. But here, of course, it's a different story. It's always a different story at Black Rabbit Hall. It unspools everything.

Ghosts are everywhere, not just the ghost of Momma in the woods, but ghosts of us too, what we used to be like in those long summers when she was alive and not much ever happened: burying her long legs on the beach, Toby and I watching Daddy kiss Momma behind a veil of meaty barbecue smoke. When it rains, if I stare long enough, I can actually see those miniature moments caught in the fat drops that roll down the kitchen windows, just before they flatten on the sill. Momma pops up in odd places.

'It'll all be there, the moment we step off the train. Hey, you're shivering, Kits. Come here.'

I flick the worst of the sand off her skin, wrap her in my cardigan and sink my chin on to the cushion of her curls. I love the squidge of Kitty in my arms – she's plumper than ever on account of all the sympathy sweets. If I can't sleep I go into her bed, where she still sleeps like a baby, balled up with her bottom in the air. More often than not, I'll wake up to find Toby in the tatty tartan armchair opposite, as if he's been watching us and dropped off too.

'London is still there,' Kitty repeats, just when I thought I'd settled the issue. 'Our house is there. Momma's not there.'

'That's right, Kitty,' I say, pleased that she finally seems to get it.

She looks up at me, asks sternly, 'So where's Daddy?'

'Daddy's in Paris.'

Her eyes are blue and round in her face. She blinks, and it's like butterflies opening and shutting their wings. 'Why is he in Paris? What's Paris?'

'Paris is the capital of Germany, dumbo,' pipes up Barney.

'Paris is the capital of France, Barns.' Toby whacks him across the legs with a rope of seaweed.

Kitty is still looking up at me, blinking.

'Daddy is in Paris for business,' I explain more slowly. 'But he'll be back at Black Rabbit Hall at the weekend, okay?'

'But the weekend will take years to come.'

'Two days.'

Toby sits down next to me on the rock, pale beneath his tan, holding his tummy with one hand, where the muscles carve horizontally. Boris drips out of the waves and shakes stinky dog water all over us.

Toby pushes him away. 'Ugh, all I need.'

I smile, realize what's going on. 'Another limpet, Toby?'

'Don't.'

I wriggle my toes into the warm, powdery top layer of sand and stare out at the darkening sea, keeping half an eye on Barney, just like Momma used to do in the days when I was free to be a kid. Kitty hums beneath her breath. I recognize it as the tune Momma used to hum when she brushed Kitty's hair.

'Amber,' Toby says, after a while, knocking his knee against mine to grab my attention. He lowers his voice: 'Do you think it really is business?'

I turn to look at him, suddenly uneasy, unsure why. 'What?'

He frowns, his eyes flecking a dangerous gold. 'Daddy being in Paris.'

'Well, what else would it be?'

Nine

Christmas Eve, 1968

'Breathe in!' Peggy puffs, as she knits the hooks and eyes up my spine.

'This dress is far too small.'

'You'll fit. Lucky thing. I'd kill for a figure like yours.' She swivels me around to face her. Her cheeks are still a lively pink from the village dance the night before, hair prettily curled, traces of lipstick on the outer edge of her mouth, all suggesting the improbable idea that she actually has a life outside this one. 'Lovely.'

'I hate yellow, Peggy. I look like a daffodil.' I immediately think of the daffodil posy in Momma's dead white hands as she lay on her bed.

'Well, nothing wrong with a daff. The colour sets off your hair. There. Pretty as a picture. What a difference a nice dress makes. Don't look at me like that. If you think I'm going to let you all run around half naked like you did in the summer, you're very much mistaken. Oh, someone's moulting.' She brushes fine red hairs off my arm. I visited Momma's wardrobe this morning, wrapped myself up in her fox-trimmed coat. 'That's better.'

'My plait is too tight.' I pull at the French plait stitched to my scalp, trying to loosen it. Boris looks up at me sympathetically.

'Too tight! Too loose!' mutters Peggy, beneath her breath. She was at the 'end of my tether' two hours ago, so I don't know where she is now.

'You seem to have forgotten I'm fifteen years old. Not five. I don't even wear my hair in plaits to go to school now, Peggy.'

'Amber . . .' She suddenly looks very tired and baggy-faced. 'Your dad will want to show you all off to his smart London friends, you know that.'

I scowl, freshly enraged that he's invited another two families to share Christmas with us, especially other children, a boy of about Toby's and my age apparently. We want Daddy to ourselves. We want ourselves to ourselves.

'I'm not going to ruin it by presenting him with a huddle of ragamuffins, am I? The plait stays.'

Eight months since Momma walked out of the kitchen in her riding boots to her death. Things she's missed already: her favourite baby-pink clematis blooming on the garden wall; small sweet strawberries from the kitchen garden; the leaves in the woods crisping gold; her wedding anniversary surprise, a week in Venice; Bonfire Night in Regent's Park, the air scorched with gunpowder and smoke and wet, singed wool; Thanksgiving with American friends in her Kensington club, coming home smelling of cigarettes and other ladies' scent; the Oxford Street lights; Harrods; dancing; Christmas Eve.

Except it doesn't feel like Christmas Eve. When we woke up this morning there were none of the trails of ivy that Momma loved to thread between the banister posts, no freshly cut holly in bell jars, no slings of paper chains we'd all made together on the dining table. In fact, this year Peggy has barely used the old family decorations at all – 'Dusty and musty,' she groaned, sniffing the boxes from the cellars – and has bought new ones 'to cheer everyone up' from St Austell, shiny red and green baubles, snakes of thin tinsel in gold and purple, and new lights, which flicker on and off, then pop dead.

There is a giant stack of presents under the swaying, enormous tree in the hall – a gift from the villagers because everyone feels sorry for us. And the smells are almost the same – pine needles, woodsmoke, pastry – but not quite because Momma's candles aren't burning. Peggy prefers the electric lights. So it doesn't smell right. It doesn't smell right at all.

For the sake of Barney and Kitty (and, secretly, Toby, even though he says he couldn't care less), I tried to make some Christmassy things this morning, like Momma used to do. I found some old white tissue paper – the stuff Daddy uses to pack his suits – and got the younger ones to screw it into balls, coat the balls in glue, roll them in glitter and hang them up above the fireplace in the hall. They look silly – like balls of screwed-up paper dunked in glitter – but Kitty loves them. Next to these, Toby has hung some of his prized bones – horse's teeth, a sheep's skull, buffed white with his sock – on bits of string, like wind chimes. Obviously Peggy hates all of these things, especially the dangling teeth, but knows Barney and Kitty will scream blue murder if she dares to take any of them down. And Daddy's about to arrive so she cannot risk it.

'Just the bow now, Amber.' She gives the sash a yank.

'Too tight.'

She yanks again, harder than necessary. 'To think you used to be the obedient one. Whatever happened to —'

She stops. We all know what happened.

'There,' she says more softly, adjusting the sash at the waist, so the tortoiseshell buckle sits centrally among the folds of the full skirt, and nods approvingly. 'You'll do.'

I scowl at her then. I don't want to be in the yellow dress. I don't want to be at Black Rabbit Hall. The day we returned — three days ago — was a shock, like the coldness of the seawater is always a shock, even when you're expecting it: it creeps into every crevice of you just the same. I'd only just got used to London after the drift of the summer. We're expected to flip between our different lives, like acrobats twisting in mid-air.

I haven't dared tell Toby that I'm missing London — he'd see it as unforgivable disloyalty. He loves it here. Us together. The woods. The wildness. In a funny way, he only makes sense at Black Rabbit Hall. But I can't help yearning for those easy afternoons after school in London, chewing Black Jacks in Matilda's bedroom, painting each other's toenails with her sister's scarlet varnish, discussing the Christmas parties, boys we'd die to kiss. In London I can pretend I'm just a normal fifteen-year-old. Like the accident never happened.

I cannot pretend here. Not even the rabid winter storms can wash off the dull brown stain on the stone by the stable. Knight's skull is now in a velvet-lined black box in the library — Daddy's way of saying sorry for shooting Momma's beloved horse, I think — alongside all the animals in boxes. Whenever I see it I hear *bang bang bang*. Picture entrails of red wool trailing across the floor. Memories press up against the present, like bodies in a crowded street.

But London at Christmas helps me forget it all, for a few moments at least. Carols gust out of shop fronts. Singers call at the door. Bags of roast nuts, heavy and hot in the hands. Hundreds, thousands, millions of jostling elbows and clicking heels and shopping bags. A tug of life that forces you to keep your head above water whether you like it or not. But if we venture out to the village here, people stare and clutch their children tight, as if our bad fortune might be catching. Maybe it is.

London's lights glow gold as far as the eye can see. Look out of a window at Black Rabbit Hall and it's just sky, a bottomless black that goes on forever, with star after star, like dozens of glinting nail studs on the stable wall, mocking the idea that there is even room for a Heaven. Not that I believe in Heaven, or God. I only pretend to believe for Barney and Kitty's sake. I know He won't return Momma any more than He returns the gull-pecked eyes to the dolphin dying on the beach.

'The car's coming up the drive!' Peggy furiously pats her hair, tidies herself. 'Now, remember. Stand straight. Manners. Don't go frightening anyone with talk of the accident, for goodness' sake. There will be other children. Show them the ballroom or something, Toby. No, not your collection of bones. Just try to be – be normal, please. Make your father proud of you. Go on, then. Into the hall. What are you waiting for? Don't just stand there like frozen lollies. *Move.*'

He is not what I was expecting.

This 'boy' is at least a foot taller than his mother. He

stares at the floor, black hair flopping over one eye, like a pirate's patch, hands dug deep in his pockets, so that we cannot see his face. When he does look up it is straight at me, a jet gaze so defiantly charged it makes my breath hitch and my dress tighten around my ribs. I hear Daddy saying, 'Caroline, this is my eldest, Amber,' as if I'm under water. 'Amber?' Daddy repeats.

I quickly look from the boy to his mother. She is picking off white kid-leather gloves, one finger then the next, eyeing the portrait of Momma on the wall above the fireplace with a stitch of a frown. I remember her gas-ring blue eyes from the funeral, the sharp features, the confrontational tilt of her chin. I remember it all as if it happened five minutes ago: Daddy staring at her during his speech, the funeral lurching to its side, like a boat in a storm, before it righted itself. Of course it would be her.

Then I notice the differences, and these seem more important. The way her hair is no longer scraped up into a tight topknot but a soft puff of blonde on her shoulders, curling up beneath her small, high-set ears, mingling with the white fur at her neck. The heavy eye-liner has gone too. She looks older somehow – seeing her close up, it's obvious she's quite a bit older than Momma was – and altogether less racy, more sensible, more like one of the mothers at my school. It occurs to me that she's done this on purpose.

'This is Caroline Shawcross, Amber,' says Daddy, with fake cheeriness. I can tell he's nervous and about to start tweaking his earlobes. He takes off his trilby and passes it to Peggy, who is waiting to receive it as keenly as Boris waits for a ball on the beach.

'Good evening, Mrs Shawcross,' I say politely, keeping my expression blank, feeling the heat of her son's eyes on me. I suddenly know that I will always remember this moment, standing in the black and white hall in my too-tight lemon yellow dress. That it feels like the beginning of something that hasn't happened yet.

'It's lovely to meet you, Amber. I've heard so much about you from your father.' Even though she's smiling, her voice is metallic and her gaze flits, wary, fast, reminding me of a bird on the lawn. It darts from Momma's portrait straight to me, as if spotting the likeness that everyone says is so startling. 'Not Mrs Shawcross, please. You simply must call me Caroline.'

I nod, fighting the urge to look at her son.

Daddy introduces Toby, Kitty and Barney in brisk succession and takes the heat off me. Peggy propels them all forward with a nudge in the back.

'What a beautiful collection of children, Hugo.' Boris rudely sniffs her skirt. Daddy has to pull him back. She laughs nervously. 'Let me introduce my son, Lucian.' She shoots a sharp glance in his direction, as if she's already expecting him to do the wrong thing. 'Lucian Shawcross.' He does not move. 'Lucian,' she repeats, through a gritted smile. Reluctantly he steps forward into the space his mother has cleared.

I get to stare properly then.

Lucian is a different species of boy from anything I've ever seen, tall and slim but incredibly dense, wide at certain points, his shoulders straining in his heavy woollen navy blazer, sullen stoop failing to hide his height. His eyes are lamp black, unlike his mother's, his face all rough angles and juts, reminding me of the young men in bashed-up leather jackets who sit around on motorbikes, cigarettes dangling from their lips, near Grandma's house in Chelsea. Men, Grandma warns, whose eyes I must never catch: 'Very much the wrong sort.' Thrilling.

'Lucian,' murmurs Caroline, fingers twisting the pearls at her neck. 'Say hello, darling.'

'A pleasure to meet you,' he says, in a way that suggests it is no pleasure at all. The silence stretches.

Peggy smiles too hard into the awkwardness, freshly pressed apron a triangle on her hips. 'What time might the Moncrieffs be arriving, Mr Alton?'

The Moncrieffs! My spirits lift. I remember the Moncrieffs: their white house in Holland Park, endless stairs, sprawling palms in pots, children and dogs. There's a girl of about my age called Emily, who is transparently blonde and has an easy laugh.

'The Moncrieffs?' repeats Daddy, blankly. 'Oh, gosh, sorry, Peggy. I haven't told you, have I?'

'Lady Charlotte's youngest has terrible croup again,' says Caroline. 'Such a pity. She was determined to come, being Lady Charlotte, but I strongly advised her to stay in London near the hospitals. She can't risk being marooned in Cornwall. You can never be too careful with croup.'

Peggy nods politely, even though I know she'll be thinking that the best cure for croup is sea air. Peggy thinks it cures everything: coughs, rashes, broken hearts.

'Sensible advice,' murmurs Daddy, pulling at his left earlobe.

I glance at Toby, confused by what it all means. But Toby is glaring at Lucian, radiating his own peculiar kind of storm static. I fear it's only a matter of time before he blows.

'Well, the poor Moncrieffs are missing out horribly, aren't they?' Her smile reveals intriguingly small white teeth, each one like the tip of a blackboard chalk. 'The house is delightful. Oh, just look at that staircase. Do look at it, Lucian.' Her heels peck across the hall. She wraps her fingers around the banister. 'To find a house this grand so far west . . .' she says, as if it's a wonder we don't all live in beach huts.

Daddy rises on his heels, looking pleased. 'Well, admittedly a bit rough around the edges. But we like it, don't we, Barney?'

'So did Momma. That's Momma.' Barney points proudly at the portrait above the fireplace, his skinny wrist gaping from the sleeve of his too-small blue sailor suit. 'She's called Nancy. Nancy Kitty Alton. She's American. But she's gone to Heaven because I chased rabbits and there was a storm and she had a bad leg and Knight bucked like a devil and Momma got a hole in her head and we didn't have a big enough plaster.' He glances nervously at Toby, checking he's got it right. 'The doctor put a sheet over her face.'

Caroline's fingers seek her pearls again. 'I am sorry, Barney.'

'Daddy shot the horse. Toby has the brains in his special collection.'

Caroline adjusts to this news with a rapid succession of blinks.

'They've gone crispy,' says Kitty, matter-of-factly. 'Like seaweed purses.'

'Goodness.' A flush steals up her neck.

'Daddy put the skull in a box.'

Caroline's eyes widen. Peggy wrings her apron helplessly.

Barney looks up at her from beneath his mop of strawberry curls. 'Do you want to see it?'

'Don't be a clot. Of course she doesn't,' says Peggy, with a small, shrill laugh, clipping Barney affectionately around the head.

'That's enough, little man,' says Daddy, resting a hand on Barney's shoulder. 'Now, let's get on with enjoying Christmas, shall we?'

'We never have guests at Black Rabbit Hall,' spits Toby, suddenly. He is glaring at Lucian as he talks, puffing up like the kitchen cat to scare a rival off its territory. 'You always say the Altons stick to family at Christmas, Daddy.'

'Well, this Christmas is different, Toby,' says Daddy, wearily, raking his hair off his face, exposing the licks of baldness at either side of his forehead that appeared the week Momma died and seem to spread further every week. 'I wanted to jolly things along with a bit of company for you. I'm afraid Grandma can't be here this year.'

'But Kitty wants Grandma!' squeaks Kitty, her bottom lip trembling. 'Grandma brings rhubarb-and-custards in a glass jar!'

'Why isn't she coming?' demands Barney.

'She's not terribly well, I'm afraid. And she's getting a bit old now for such a long journey.'

I swallow hard, thinking of my beloved Grandma Esme on her giant rose-covered sofa in Chelsea. She's one of the few people who actually talks to me about what's happened. 'Your father does not find it easy to discuss feelings, my darling. I think, like most men, he'd much rather no one mentioned them at all,' she'd said, before I left, squeezing me against the brooch on her bosom so that I was left with an imprint on my cheek in the shape of a peacock.

'But she packed me off with so many presents,' Daddy continues, 'that I'm surprised the Rolls could move.'

'I want Grandma Esme,' says Kitty, with renewed vigour. 'I want Grandma.'

Caroline puts her hand to her throat and says, 'Aw.' I want to tell her that she doesn't know Grandma or Kitty and has no right to say, 'Aw,' in that stagey way, looking at Daddy as she does so because it's clearly entirely for his benefit.

'Where's Aunt Bay?' Kitty says. 'Does she need the doctor too?'

'Aunt Bay's not sick, Kitty.' Daddy bends down to Kitty's height, eyes warm and kind. 'But the storms over the Atlantic make the passage unsafe.'

My heart sinks. 'In her last letter she said she was definitely coming.'

He turns to me, not quite meeting my gaze. 'I know, I know. But it wasn't fair to ask her to come – Caroline is quite right. Not in this weather. I had to insist she didn't risk it.'

Why has Caroline had *any* say in this? I feel a creep of unease. Toby frowns at me, thinking the same thing.

'But what about the peanut butter?' perseveres Kitty. Caroline must think we're all obsessed with food, which we are. 'Aunt Bay always brings a big tub of peanut butter and doesn't mind if we stick our fingers in.'

'I might be able to find some up in Truro, love,' says Peggy.

Kitty scowls. It's not about peanut butter.

'Brrr.' Daddy claps his hands together, tries to change the subject. 'We certainly haven't had a Christmas this cold for a long while, have we?'

'The fires are blazing, sir,' says Peggy. Daddy has always made her a little nervous. Never more so than now – I feel for her, she's desperate to make a good impression. 'I hope Mrs . . .' She stumbles, unsure how to address her.

'Mrs Shawcross.' She smiles tightly.

I wonder where Mr Shawcross is.

'I've lit a fire in your room, Mrs Shawcross.'

'A fire?' Clearly she wasn't expecting her bedroom to be heated with logs. 'That sounds rather nice, thank you.'

'May I take your bag upstairs, Mrs Shawcross?'

It is made from toffee-coloured leather and stamped with gold letters, far smarter than any of ours. We have to sit on our trunks to shut them, or use the ancient steamer luggage chests stamped with peeling Indian labels and smelling of tea.

Peggy strains to pick it up. 'And may I be so bold as to recommend my famous mince pies, Mrs Shawcross?' I wish she'd stop repeating Mrs Shawcross's name. Maybe she's trying not to forget it.

Caroline glances at her son. 'You love mince pies, don't you, Lucian?'

Lucian looks at her as if he doesn't love anything, neither a mince pie nor her.

'I always say taking Lucian out of boarding school at the end of term is like taking milk from an ice box.' Caroline laughs, a shrill sound that lasts a beat too long. 'He needs time to warm up.'

'I can light a fire in Lucian's room?' suggests Peggy, nerves making her silly.

'Daddy . . .' Kitty's bottom lip starts to wobble.

'Yes, darling?' He doesn't see it coming at all.

'Kitty doesn't want this lady in the house.'

Caroline looks embarrassed rather than hurt.

'I'm so sorry, Caroline,' says Daddy, picking Kitty up. She pushes her face into his neck, peering out at Caroline between her fingers. 'The children are still a little unsettled, I'm afraid.'

'Don't you dare apologize, Hugo. I quite understand. Listen, Kitty.' She speaks more softly, leans in too close. Kitty backs away. 'I know I must look like a stranger. But your father and I have known one another for many years. And now I hope to get to know you too, don't I, Hugo?' The look she shoots him is not one I understand. 'I want us all to be best friends. You. Me. Your little doll.'

Toby makes a quiet snort of cynicism in the back of his throat that everyone pretends they haven't heard.

Daddy nods, pulls at his collar, hot all of a sudden. As if he'd rather be anywhere else. 'Indeed. We must all get to know each other.'

My mind flings back to the conversation I overheard huddled in Momma's wardrobe in the summer, the hushed voices seeping through the brass hinges: 'Let's hope the man has the good sense to remarry. And quickly.' I think of the stream of pies and cakes arriving at the door of Fitzroy Square, the women with their craning necks and made-up puffy lips, whispering, 'How *is* Daddy, darling?' to Kitty as she weighs up the donated cake tins in her hands, trying to guess the flavour of the contents. And I'm struck by a sickening sense of everything moving too fast, mechanisms pumping hard where we can't see them, like the pistons beneath our seats on the train that carried us away from London a few days before.

Caroline touches Kitty's arm. 'Maybe you can show me around Pencraw Hall later.'

'We don't call it Pencraw Hall,' growls Toby. '*Momma* calls it Black Rabbit Hall.'

Lucian shoots Toby a look of grudging respect.

'Black Rabbit Hall? Goodness. How . . . how charming.' Caroline smiles. It does not reach the frozen blue of those eyes. 'I'll be sure to remember that, Toby.'

Later that evening I overhear Caroline call our house Pencraw Hall many times. Not once does Daddy correct her.

'She must think we're dumb-rabbit stupid.' Toby plunges his penknife into the flesh of the big old oak. He never goes anywhere without it just in case the world ends and he needs to cut himself out. 'All this fake niceness. All the "Oh, Hugo, what beautiful children!" It makes me want to pick her eyelashes off one by one. Like legs off a spider.'

'Except you wouldn't do that to a spider,' I say, buttoning my coat with numb, clumsy fingers. We are hunkered in the marshier bit of woods. The sky is marble-white. The tide is out and the mud flats look both dreary and deadly, pocked with eel and crayfish holes, fog lapping at the far reaches: winter in the raw, not Christmassy at all.

'No. I respect a spider. A spider has a right to be here,' he says, pale face straining as he gouges the blade into the bark. Like Momma's, Toby's colouring changes with the seasons: freckles fading, glowing red thatch of summer hair dimmed like a lamp.

'Her lashes aren't real.'

He looks up, curious. 'How do you know?'

'If you look carefully you can see a sticky white glue line,' I explain, having familiarized myself with Matilda's older sister's secret make-up box.

'Right.' He looks impressed by my powers of observation. 'And have you noticed the way she's always trying to touch Daddy?'

'Horrible.'

'And she refused every mince pie.'

'Weird. What can it mean?'

A heron stalks its way along the bank, stabbing its long beak into the cold mud to pluck out creatures left squirming by the tide's retreat. Toby tracks it, blade at rest, thoughtful for a moment or two. 'Control.'

'Maybe we should offer her a raw limpet instead. That might loosen things up.'

'Did you see her face at lunch when Peggy brought out the stargazy pie?'

Remembering the look of appalled horror on Caroline's face, I start to giggle uncontrollably, seized by a mad, mirthless mirth that makes my front teeth cold. Stargazy pie – one of Peggy's favourite recipes passed down from her mam – involves six shrivelled pilchard heads poking out of slits in the pastry lid. 'I'm going to request conger eel next.' I snort, regaining my breath.

But Toby's face is sombre, which kills my laughter. He is carving the 'B' of his name. 'I reckon she's scared of us, you and me.' He leans back, squints at his handiwork. 'She's scared we can see through her.'

'Well, we can.' This isn't totally true. I can't quite work out if Caroline's a fairly nice woman who is nervous and has somehow, through social accident, landed in the wrong place at Christmas or a calculated troublemaker pretending to be fairly nice. Not that it matters. She shouldn't be here. Neither should she have suggested Aunt Bay did not fly out to see us because of bad weather. Aunt Bay is not scared of flying. She says she has pills for that.

'It's laughably obvious what Caroline wants.' He picks out more of the tree's flesh with a brutality that makes me wince, and looks up at me, checking my reaction as he speaks. 'To get into Momma's shoes, Amber. That's what.'

I close my eyes, picturing an ugly foot shoving its way into Momma's riding boots, the soft leather moulded to the shape of her high arches, her second toe slightly longer than the first. Ballerina's feet, Daddy used to say. 'She won't. They won't fit.'

'Just let her try.' He presses his hands to his neck, squeezes so that his face goes red, the blade in one hand sticking upright, threatening to shave off his left ear. 'Die! Die!'

'Don't be an idiot.' His intensity scares me sometimes. He acts out as if he means it. 'You shouldn't joke about things like that.'

He releases his neck, annoyed. 'Who's going to hear?'

I glance uneasily at the spot where Knight bucked, a few yards into the woods, beside the beech covered with yellow fungus ears. The feeling of being watched returns.

There's a presence in the woods today, and it can only be hers. 'Momma might hear.'

'Hope so,' he says more cheerily, bending down to the bark again. 'She'd hate Caroline.'

'Momma didn't hate anyone, Toby.' I think of the gap in Momma's smile, the way it invited you right inside her, like a door ajar. It was her natural resting expression, as Matilda's mum's is a frown. When people commented on her cheerfulness she'd say, 'I have a lot to smile about,' in a way that wasn't smug, but genuinely thankful.

'Well, she'd laugh at her too,' Toby decides. 'She'd definitely laugh at Caroline Shawcross.'

Probably. Momma used to find English pomposity very funny, and Caroline is full of it. I lift my chin, prepare to impersonate: 'Peggy, the water gushing out of my bath taps is *rusty*! It is brown! Quite brown! Is it safe? You're sure? Goodness. Well, if you're absolutely sure it's safe to bathe in such water I . . . I suppose one must just brace oneself.' It's not a very good imitation but it works. I'm pleased. It's not easy to make Toby laugh today. After that everything softens a bit.

I reach idly for the rope Toby tied from the upper branches one long hot summer a year or two ago, hold it in my clenched palm, remembering how it felt to fly free across the river, careless with ordinary joy. Toby stares at my hand, the rope, his mind turning over the same thing. The evening light ripens, then blanks back to white again.

Toby, still staring at my hand, says, 'You don't like him, do you?'

'Who?' I hold the rope tighter.

'Lucian. The spawn.'

'Don't be insane!'

Toby looks back to his blade, stroking his thumb along its edge, testing its sharpness. I can tell that he's not satisfied by my answer. He chips away another large flake of bark, jaw tense. 'Don't trust him. Lucian and his mother are cut from the same cloth, Amber.'

I think of Lucian's height, the surprising muscular heft of his shoulders, the cliff jut of his jaw. Yes, I can see Caroline in him. But there is something else, something that makes you want to stare at him for another reason. I don't understand it. It's not that Lucian is handsome, not like Fred Hollywell, with his movie-star blond hair, easy charm and ribbon-blue eyes. Lucian is rude, silent and dark. The air around him is not still.

Toby stares at me coldly. 'You're thinking about him right now.'

'You don't know what I'm thinking,' I say, feeling the betrayal of a blush heat my cheeks.

'I do.'

'Not any more.' He flinches at that and I immediately wish I could take it back. It's like denying we're twins. 'Sorry, I didn't mean . . .'

'Get lost, Amber.'

I leap off the low branch, twigs snapping beneath my leather boots. 'Fine. I'll go back to the house. You're in one of your funny moods.'

'Do what you like.'

I hesitate. For some reason I don't fancy walking back on my own. And I don't want to leave Toby like this either. 'Come with me.'

He shakes his head, lips pressed tight. I know he's angry

133

with me for thinking about Lucian. For cutting him out by not admitting it.

'Shall I bring you back a coat?'

'Who are you? My mother?' he scoffs.

It's my turn to flinch. 'It's cold out here. Your lips are sort of purple.'

'Did you know that you can freeze a scorpion in a block of ice for hours, then crack it open and the scorpion will walk out alive?'

I shake my head, stuffing my hands deep into my pockets to warm them. I hate Toby's funny moods now, their simmering violence.

'I'm like a scorpion, Amber.'

'Suit yourself. Freeze, then.' I walk away through the snatch of scrub and branches. After a couple of minutes, I turn to see if Toby's following me. Normally he'll catch me up, sometimes put an arm around my shoulders to say sorry. This time he doesn't. He's still in the tree, stabbing at it repeatedly. Then I can no longer see him at all. I feel a wave of unease.

The squawk and rise of dozens of tiny brown birds from the bushes make me jump. Something has disturbed them. I pause, heart thumping inside my chest, listening hard. Deer? Badger? Fox?

A cough.

Lucian is standing very still beneath the shadow of a tree, no more than a few yards away, one foot raised on a root, leaning against the trunk, watching me. He is taller than I remember, more menacing. Something of the wood.

'What are you doing here?' I fight the urge to step away but refuse to reveal my nerves.

'Same as you.' I wonder whether Toby will hear me if I scream. I wonder if I can outrun Lucian. 'No need to look quite so petrified.'

'Why would I be petrified of you?'

He shrugs. There is an odd, unquiet moment when neither of us speaks.

He digs into his pocket, pulls out a packet of Embassy cigarettes. 'Want one?'

'Not before dinner,' I say, hoping that this makes sense to someone who smokes. I'll be damned if I'll tell him I've never smoked a cigarette.

He fights a smile, as if he knows I'm bluffing. I realize at that moment that I haven't seen him smile, not properly, and that part of me – the bit that refuses to be scared of such an arrogant oaf – wants to make it happen, to wipe the infuriating smug coolness off those crag features. The other part of me just wants to get back to the house, extremely quickly. Kick him in the balls, that's what Matilda's sister says. If a bad man comes at you, kick him where it hurts.

'How old are you?'

'Fifteen.' My heart feels like it's going to beat right out of me.

'You look younger.'

I curse my slight frame, freckled baby face and stupid Cornish wardrobe that is kept down here in a mothy trunk, always a size too small. 'How old are *you*?'

He lights a match. The contours of his face flicker gold. 'How old do you think I am?'

'Too young to smoke.'

I get it then, the smile, a dazzling split of white that

transforms his face from something scowling and off balance into something . . . well, something completely else. 'Seventeen. I'm bloody well seventeen.' He squats down to the swollen tree roots, puffs white smoke rings into the gloom. 'Ding dong merrily on high, eh? Is it always this goddamn miserable down here?'

'Our mother died at Easter,' I say, unable to resist.

'This Easter?' He does not exhibit any of the expected embarrassment or shock, but sucks thoughtfully at his cigarette, gaze sharper, not leaving my face, as if this new fact changes the way he sees me slightly. 'Mother did tell me she was dead. But I didn't know it was so recent.'

'She came off her horse,' I add, trying to rouse more of a reaction. 'A few feet from where you're standing.'

A moment passes. 'That's rotten luck.'

I say nothing but am secretly grateful that he's not trying to dress up the accident as anything other than it is. I hate it when people pretend there was a grand master plan behind it. That she was taken for a reason.

'And now you've got me and Ma for Christmas. No wonder you all look suicidal.' He throws down the stub of cigarette, half smoked, where it releases one dying flicker before succumbing to the wet cold. 'Well, I suppose we only have to tolerate each other for another couple of days before we're released back to London.'

'If we survive that long,' I retort, riled by his bad manners, irritated that he isn't more impressed with Black Rabbit Hall. I feel protective of it in all its gusty dampness. In so many ways it is all we've got. 'But while you're a guest at our house you could at least make some effort to be polite.'

He flicks a lock of hair from his face. 'Am I breaking the

136

etiquette? Used to people bowing before you down here, are you?'

'You've got no idea. We're not like that.' My heart is in my ears now, my voice high. 'We're not rich.'

He shakes his head at me, as if he's marvelling at my stupidity. 'I wasn't talking about money.'

'I'm half American,' I say, because I know he's implying I'm some snobby upper-class English girl, like so many of the girls at school, and I'm not. I'm different from them. I don't care if someone says 'lav' or 'toilet', 'writing paper' or 'notepaper' or anything like that. Momma taught us that some things don't matter half as much as anyone thinks.

'Well, aren't you exotic?' The corners of his mouth curl, exposing a glint of shiny pink gum.

'And you're an idiot.' Not wanting to lose the last word, I start to walk backwards, slowly, keeping my eyes trained on him – like you walk away from a dangerous animal – only turning and breaking into a run the moment I'm hidden by trees. Shaky and breathless, I skid up the icy steps, shove my shoulder hard against the front door and barrel into the hall, slap-bang into Caroline.

'Goodness!' Her hand leaps to her throat. 'I'm looking for Lucian. Have you seen him?'

I cannot speak. I cannot believe my eyes. The hall suddenly seems very, very dark, the cape's diamanté clasp blinking at me, an enraged cat's eye.

'Amber, what's wrong? What in Heaven's name is the matter?'

Ten

Lorna

Lorna swings the torchlight over the plywood floor of the attic, starts at the sight of a lone clumpy-heeled court shoe of her mother's lying forlornly on its side. She shivers. What is it about shoes? More than a dress, a coat or anything else, a shoe somehow moulds itself to its wearer: the swell of a bunion, the ballet arch of an instep, a sole thinned on unknown pavements in runs for the bus, walks with a lover. It's for this reason that she doesn't buy vintage shoes: they are never truly yours. She reaches out and gently rights her mother's shoe, the patent leather hard and crackly against her fingers. Then she quickly throws the torchlight to the other side of the eaves.

More boxes. Shadows. A thin cut of sunlight at the edges of the roof tiles. No wonder she had nightmares about this attic as a child, imagining all sorts of ghouls crouched up here, waiting, ready to prowl her dreams at night. While the rest of the house – bar the chaos of the garage – was ruled by their mother, this was the one place only her dad ever went, carrying up bulging storage boxes, teetering unnervingly on his creaking metal ladder until his head, body, tartan slippers were swallowed into the chasm. She would wait anxiously for him from the safety of the carpeted landing, breath held until he returned to her, grinning, jumping the last few rungs, feathered in the tiny yellow insulation fibres that her mother said caused cancer.

The ghouls have long gone now. But the attic still feels as if it might hide other things, family secrets buried in the damp, mildewed boxes – labelled and taped shut by her mother's busy, determined fingers – waiting to be brought into the light.

Since returning from Black Rabbit Hall ten days ago, she's been desperate to have a rummage. And here is the box she's after, labelled 'Pix' in her mother's neat, hard-slanted handwriting, thankfully not too far from the hatch. She carries it down, rests it on the landing carpet, noticing the caterpillars of dust on the skirting board, which her mother would never have tolerated. Just one more sign that she has gone and they are living in a different era, messier, less tightly controlled.

Cocooned in the fussy florals and tasselled swagging of the lounge – her mother's take on stately home furnishings – Lorna lies on the rug, chatting to Louise on speakerphone while riffling through holiday snaps that are both horrifying and hilarious in equal measure. Why did no one tell her that her teenage 'highlights' were green? Who knew that her mother had once looked so hot in a bikini?

'If you came with me this weekend you could make up for all those hours I endured in historic lavender gardens while you licked 99s on the beach,' she shouts at the phone, slipping a sheaf of photos from one pile to another.

Louise laughs. She has one of those short, snorty laughs, the sound of something bubbling over. 'I could never make that up to you.'

'But you need a break, Lou.' She starts to flick through a stack of black-and-whites of her as a toddler, before Louise was born. She was actually quite a cute toddler, she decides, cherub-cheeked, raven-curled, always straining in her mother's arms, trying to dart out of the frame to something more interesting.

'Lorna, I've got no childcare and Chloë's got rampant impetigo so if you want a lifetime ban from ever visiting Black Rabbit Hall again, let alone getting married there, I'm your woman.'

It's true that Louise has got her hands full: Mia, aged nine, Chloë, aged eight, and her youngest, Alf, a six-year-old with Down's. Lorna has no idea how she copes, let alone with such good humour. 'Couldn't Will take them this weekend?'

'It's not his weekend.'

'Can't he be a *bit* flexible?'

'I'm not sure we're at the flexible stage yet,' Louise says, with a heaviness that pulls at Lorna's heart. Will and Louise divorced last year. It's not been one of those functional divorces you read about. A twenty-nine-year-old secretary called Bethany is involved. 'But we're getting there.'

'Hang on, can't Dad take them?'

'It would kill him off too.'

'Sacrifice for a good cause? I reckon you'll love Black Rabbit Hall, Lou.'

'Are there spa facilities?'

Lorna snorts.

'Why's that so funny?'

'When you see it you'll understand. We can swim in the sea, though.'

'I don't swim in the sea north of Brittany. Point of principle.'

'Where's your sense of adventure?'

'Left somewhere in the labour ward. Why can't Jon go again?'

'I've lost him to another project. Some tower of super-deluxe flats in Bow that each cost trillions, interior-decorated to death. The usual.' Lorna doesn't mention that Jon wouldn't have wanted to go, his reservations about the place growing since they got back. She starts flicking through a different stack of photos. 'I wish you could see these pics, Louise. Mum and Dad look so young.'

A child's screech. 'I've got to go. Listen, Lorna, I'm pleased you found somewhere to get married at last. It sounds *très* posh. And I'm sure Mum would have loved it, especially if it's got wooden toilet seats.'

'Wooden toilet seats a go-go.'

'Good. I was beginning to think you'd never find any-where you liked.'

'I was looking for Black Rabbit Hall,' says Lorna, the words forming as she thinks them.

'Alf, we're about to have our tea. Put the rice cakes down. Sorry, you were saying?'

'Black Rabbit Hall was the blueprint in my head. Nothing matched up to it. I only realize that now. That's why I couldn't settle on anything else.'

'Really? Weird.' The sound of a scuffle in the background. 'Well, it's been a funny old year to plan a wedding, I suppose. Mia, no more telly I said. Alf, leave the rice cakes.' A child's indignant sob. 'Sorry, Lor. It's witching hour. What was I trying to say? I can't hold a thought in my head for more than thirty seconds. Oh, yeah, that I got married young and you, free spirit that you are –'

'Had commitment issues? Always went for the wrong men?' Lorna jokes, a little too close to the bone. She's kissed a lot of frogs.

'*No*, that's not what I meant. I meant you travelled, lived a bit . . .'

'I didn't know what I wanted after dropping out of uni, Lou.' She remembers the spiking highs and lows of that time, working on the vintage-clothes stall in Portobello market, freezing hands in fingerless gloves, selling old furs and cowboy boots to fashion stylists, the waitressing jobs, bar work, teaching English as a foreign language in Barcelona. 'Permanent state of existential crisis, I think.'

'Until you met Jon.'

'Well . . .' She smiles but is reluctant to admit it. 'It wasn't just that.'

'True. You got yourself to teacher-training college and now have a proper career, unlike me, which you just happen to be completely brilliant at. Lest we forget, you also have a pension! My cool big sister with a *pension*.'

'Cool? Oh, the cool's long gone, Louise.' Lorna flips up the lip of a brown envelope with a fingernail.

'Baby next, Lor.'

'Stop it.' She laughs.

'Jon clearly wants a huge brood, like now.'

She loves that about him. It also scares her slightly. What sort of mother will she make? Will she be a natural like Louise? Pushing those questions away, she shakes out a photograph: black-and-white, one corner torn, her mother pulling her awkward photo smile, clutching her beloved boxy Margaret Thatcher handbag. Next to her, a willowy girl in patchwork dungarees. Behind them, trees. A white enamelled sign.

Doug shakes the biscuit barrel next to his large red ear. 'My biscuits appear to have mastered the art of cupboard travel, or I've got a poltergeist. Sorry, love. I'm out.'

'Dad, I don't care about biscuits. Will you just look? Black Rabbit Hall!'

'One sec.' Doug's belt buckle clinks against the counter as he leans forward, pushing the biscuit tin back on to the shelf.

'Not one photo, but three! More or less the same spot. Same sign, only I'm different ages in the pictures. I start off looking about four. End up about seven or eight. Gosh, I wonder if there are more in a box somewhere.'

'Right. Where are my bloody glasses?' Maddeningly, they spend the next five minutes searching for them. Eventually she finds them in the cutlery drawer, getting scratched by a potato peeler. 'The sign . . .' he mutters, sounding thrown. 'Pencraw Hall?'

'Yes, stupid of me, I should have said. That's the house's official name.'

He is silent for a few moments, stroking an invisible beard with his fingers. 'Blimey.'

'So you've heard of it?' Lorna's words trip with excitement.

'I'm not sure. No, no, I don't think so,' he says, correcting himself. Looking a bit taken aback, he carries the steaming teapot to the table and sits down, spreading his hairy dad hands on the delicacy of the lacy tablecloth.

Lorna is touched that it is the white one that her mother always kept spotless 'for special occasions' (this did not include her daughters' visits) but is now a rather dirty shade of grey, on account of her father's struggles with the concept of a white wash.

She spreads the photos, like a deck of playing cards. 'Why did we keep going back?'

Doug pours, not taking his eyes off the rope of dark stewed tea. His glasses start to slide down a thin skim of sweat on his nose. 'Your mother always did have her favourite spots.'

'But why are we standing at the bottom of the drive like a right pair of lemons?'

He pushes his glasses up his nose with his thumb. 'Lorna, love, let me explain something to you.'

Lorna groans inwardly, fearing exactly what starts to come.

'Men think with the brain's grey matter, which is full of active neurons.' He taps the side of his head. 'Women ponder the world with their brain's white matter, which consists of connections *between* the neurons.'

Normally at this point her mother would step in and say, 'Oh, for goodness' sake, do be quiet, Doug.' Lorna wishes she could do the same.

'I suppose what I'm trying to explain is that I had no idea what was going through your mother's pretty skull half the time,' he says, scratching his neck.

But Lorna is not satisfied. A neck scratch is normally a sign that her dad is slightly nervous. It occurs to her that he's not telling her everything. And if not, why not?

Also, the photographs are wonky, tilted at an angle. The smudge of a photographer's finger on one. In another, their heads sliced off at the top. Not the sort of photographs you'd keep for posterity. 'Who took the pictures, do you reckon?'

'Oh, your mother was never shy of asking a stranger to wield the Pentax.'

'This one.' She slides a photo to the top of the pile, watching him carefully. 'Can you date it?'

He leans in closer, nudging his glasses back up his nose. 'Summer, judging by all the leaves on the trees. You look about eight, I'd say. Late seventies.'

'Could those awful dungarees have come from any other decade?'

'Oh, you *loved* them.' His eyes grow distant behind his steam-milked specs and Lorna gets the feeling he is no longer seeing her – aged thirty-two, white T-shirt, denim skirt, silver Converse – but the little girl she was, wriggly in hot dungarees and T-bar leather sandals. 'Had very strong opinions about clothes from the year dot you did. It was like dressing Marie Antoinette every morning.'

A rush of memories starts to flow over the table then, swirling in powerful eddies around the photographs, like water around a rock. Doug stares at his hands, laced, thumbs circling each other. Resignedly, Lorna slides the photos back into the envelope. She's clearly not going to get any answers here.

Only then does Doug relax, leaning back in his chair, hands interlaced on his stomach. 'What were you two girls nattering about, then?'

'Oh, I was trying to persuade Lou to come with me to Black Rabbit Hall this weekend.' She almost asks him directly if he'll look after Louise's kids, but it occurs to her that he'll say yes and that Lou might feel uneasy about leaving them – Alf is a handful – imposing on Dad, so she just says, 'But she's got the kids.'

He doesn't take the bait, stirs sugar cubes into his tea with a grubby spoon. Back up to three. No one to nag him about it now. 'Sure Jon can't get this weekend off and go with you? I'd feel better about it if you went with Jon.'

'Big job on.'

He looks up at her, eyebrows exploding above his glasses, one of those looks that precede a probing, slightly personal question. 'Things okay between you two?'

'Of course.' She folds her arms across her chest. 'Why?'

'I sensed some discombobulation at our pub lunch on Sunday. Not like you two lovebirds.'

'Oh, that,' she says, trying to make light of it to herself as much as to her father. She couples the salt and pepper together in the centre of the table with the palms of her hands. 'He's not sure I should stay at Black Rabbit Hall. Thinks it's a hard sell.'

'Well, isn't it?'

'Maybe. Okay, it is. But we don't have to sign up for anything in blood. I mean if Jon really doesn't want to . . .'

'You'll just roll over and agree?' He laughs, belly rising and falling, pressing against the table. 'Come on, Lorna. We all know you better than that. You set your mind on something and that's it.'

'But it's such a beautiful house!'

He studies her over the rim of his cup, more serious. 'I

have to say I'm with Jon. Not sure I like this invitation from the duchess . . .'

'She's not a duchess. Mrs Alton is just a bit of a character holed up in a big old house and fancies some company.' This isn't entirely true – there is something a little more damaged about Caroline Alton, a little odder about the set-up with the nervous Dill, the invitation to stay – but she knows better than to expand on it right now. The main thing is that the school summer holidays are whizzing past at an alarming rate. In September she'll go back to catching lice, panicking about Ofsted inspections and freaking out about not having sorted the wedding.

'Another brew?'

'Thanks. But I should go.' This keeps happening: she looks forward to visiting Dad, then, once she's in the family home, she feels so sorry for him and so unsettled by the absence of her mother – and the person she was in her mother's company – that she yearns to step back into her own grown-up life. 'Otherwise I'm hitting rush-hour,' she over-explains, picking up her bag.

He looks disappointed, as he always does when she leaves, then rallies himself, pushing back the chair, standing up. 'Thanks for the fancy deli titbits. I'll enjoy that salami.'

'Call me if you need anything.' She kisses his cheek – smells aftershave, toast, a shirt collar not wholly fresh – glances down at the brown envelope on the table. 'Dad, do you mind if I take the photos?'

He hesitates, brow furrowed, then nods. 'You know, I think they belong to you.'

It is only as Lorna turns the key in the ignition that his

last comment strikes her as odd — why do the photos belong to her? — and something her father wouldn't normally say. But a Volvo is waiting impatiently for her parking space, another car stacked behind it, which has tooted once already, and it seems silly to go back and ask him now.

Eleven

The taxi vanishes into the trees, leaving Lorna alone on the shingle beach of Pencraw Hall's drive, weekend bag at her feet. It is quiet, unnervingly so, but for the wind and the laughter of seagulls she can hear but not see. The twin stone falcons at the entrance look alarmingly sentient, but the house itself seems sleepy and empty in the late-summer heat, a building patiently sitting out its own process of decay. For the first time, Lorna feels a twinge of apprehension. It's not just the remoteness of the house, the fact that she hasn't got a car – not keen to tackle those twisting narrow lanes on her own, she got the train from Paddington – or any means of getting away easily. It's also because she left London on such a discordant note, one that has jangled between her and Jon ever since they got back from Black Rabbit Hall almost three weeks ago, pitch intensifying the closer they got to the weekend she was to return.

Jon's seemed so quiet and preoccupied in the last few days, as if he's struggling with something about the house that he's not yet disclosed, or is unable to articulate. She's felt misunderstood, judged too harshly for missing his 'little' sister's twenty-seventh birthday party this weekend. She can't help but wonder if Jon is simply irritated that she has come here without him. He's always liked to keep her close. She loves him for this – the territorial male thing – but it also, contrarily, makes her want to push him away. To love someone so much – to be loved back – scares her. It makes her feel exposed. So she kicks against it, vowing to stay as independent as possible, married or not. Never to be a woman who lives through her relationship.

Anyway, it's no bad thing she's here alone, she tells herself firmly. It will be easier to explore the house, dig around a bit, see if she can discover an explanation for those strange photos of her and her mother on the drive, photos she's slid carefully between the pages of her book. On her own, she can immerse herself in Black Rabbit Hall. Conscious of doing exactly this, she closes her eyes for a moment, enjoying the warm breeze fluttering her dress, carrying delicious scents – seaweed, honeysuckle, lanolin – that are a tripwire back to her own childhood summers, country walks when she'd pick scuzzy bits of sheep's wool off the barbed-wire fences and hide them from her mother in her anorak pocket.

The high-pitched scream of a gull startles her. She hurries up the steps and rings the bell. Nobody. She rings again. Thumps the lion's-paw knocker. Nothing. Puzzling. She called a couple of days before, spoke to Dill and confirmed her time of arrival. Has Dill forgotten already? She checks her watch. Two o'clock. Could Dill and Mrs Alton still be having lunch somewhere? Yes, that makes sense. They'll be poking smoked salmon around a bit of priceless family china probably, deaf behind thick stone walls. Lorna decides that the best thing to do is leave her bag here and take a walk around the grounds, call back in twenty minutes, when they will surely have finished.

*

The ornate wrought-iron gate at the edge of the woods leaves a dried-blood rust on her fingers, as if it wants to stamp its mark on whoever passes through it. It isn't locked, but neither will it open easily, brambles snagging its hinges. This only makes Lorna more determined to get through it. She picks off the worst of the brambles without nicking her fingers too badly, then kicks the rest away, cursing the silliness of wearing thin-soled ballet flats. Pushing her shoulder hard against the metal, with a vaguely alarming crunch – she's not sure if it's the gate or her bones – it opens. She is through.

The narrow path through the woods kinks and twists away from the house so that when Lorna looks over her shoulder a few minutes later she sees that her route back is no longer visible. The trees become denser as she walks, the endless verticals of the trunks puzzling perspective so that she has no idea quite how far one tree is from another. Close up, the trees are enormous, gnarled, peculiarly human. They are the kind of trees Lorna dreamed about climbing as a child while she picked her way around her mother's immaculate 'no ball games' chrysanthemum borders.

Water? Lorna stops. That is surely the whisper of water. She remembers Dill saying you accessed the river through the woods. But she's lost all sense of direction, never having had much in the first place. Her pupils dilate, adjusting to the shadows. As she follows the sound, nettles lash at her legs. Carcasses of dead trees lie across the path, scorched by lightning. Oh dear. She is lost-*ish*. She now risks being the guest who arrived, wandered off into the woods and required a search party to retrieve her in time for dinner. The moment she decides to retrace her steps – a vague backwards direction seems sensible – she glimpses a metallic shiver through the branches, like the flick of a carnival streamer. The river! It must be. She gambols towards it, jumping branches, newly energized, and arrives, breathless and tangle-haired, on its soft, marshy bank.

Lorna stands there, grinning like a loon at the dimpled water, lifting her hair off her neck, mouth open, sucking it all in, the boggy salty smell, the luminous water plaited by the tide, the thrill of being alone, soon to be married, a guest at Black Rabbit Hall no less. It all hits her with a drug-like rush. And she is filled with certainty that she is absolutely meant to be on this riverbank on this particular August afternoon, that whatever ructions it has caused, it is worth it. Feeling really quite buzzed, she leans back against the nearest tree, the bark rough and warm through the thin cotton of her dress. Her gaze travels its thick trunk to the canopy – a sunlit lattice of leaves – and down again. Marks on the wood catch her eye. Ridges. Scars. Letters.

The graffiti has clearly been gouged into the flesh of the tree with a sharp instrument, she decides, peering closer. Some are hard to decipher, their edges blurred by the tree's growth, filled in by flaky lichen. They are old markings certainly, but how old she has no idea. Lorna reaches up, traces her fingertips over them. It's silly, of course, but she cannot help feeling that this tree has waited a long time for her visit.

Strange symbols, crosses, triangles, wiggles . . . the doodling of the tip of a blade on bark? Yes, definitely a blade, a small knife of some kind. Oh, a rabbit! A cartoon rabbit with long ears and two protruding comedy teeth. She smiles. And what is this? T-O-B-Y. Toby? Yes, quite clearly Toby. Who is Toby? She recognizes the hand behind the graffiti, not a young child, she decides, thinking of her primary-school pupils' scrawls, but someone older, an early teen maybe, nicely schooled. Something about the letters – the obvious energy and determination of the hand that carved them – makes her heart pound. It's like discovering the remains of an extinct tribe.

Lorna soon deciphers another group of letters. A-M . . . No, she can make out no more than that, the rest of the word rotted. But, oh, look. Here is another. Right down at the base of a branch. K-I-T. Kit? So there was *more* than one child living here at some point. An heir and a spare. She's heard that expression before. There's a brutal logic to it.

Lorna pulls a hairclip out of her pocket, twists up her hair into its jaws, away from the heat of her cheeks. And it's then that the letters start to leap, jostling, jumping, rushing up to her like small children. 'Little brother Barney,' she reads out, fingertip dipping into the deepest gouge. 'R.I.P. 1963–1969.' Toby's name is scrawled beneath this in the same hand. As the dates sink in, she clamps her hand over her mouth. Oh, no. The poor little mite was only *six*. The same age as her class, 1B. The same age as her little nephew, Alf. Feelings flip in rapid succession: sadness because she knows six-year-old boys so well, their kicky feet, gummy milk-tooth gaps, boundless energy; an aching sympathy for poor Mrs Alton, for this must surely be her child; and then, unexpectedly, a sense of responsibility to this poor forgotten boy, a similar tug that she gets on learning that any child in her class is vulnerable or needs rescuing in some way. She isn't one of those teachers who pretend not to notice, or who can switch off once she's left work. She'll lie awake at night thinking about those children. And she will about these.

She swallows hard. This graffiti – so close to being lost, swallowed by time and moss – is an epitaph to such a pitifully short life, the 'little brother' making it more heartfelt, more poignant, than anything on a grand marble headstone.

She feels a pulse of connection then. A quickening. She didn't need to find this tree – there must be thousands, what are the chances? – but she did. Something has drawn her to this little boy – and the older brother who carved his name so sweetly – inviting her to find out more about his brief existence. She's sure of it. Can she blithely get married at Black Rabbit Hall now *not* knowing what happened to him? No, she cannot. She needs to satisfy herself, make some sense of it, as she must the old photographs of her and her mother on the drive. The two things are unconnected, but as Lorna stands there – fingers on the crisp bark, sunlight dappling through the leaves – they start to stir in the same dark space in her head and chase one another like playful ghosts.

Twelve

Amber, Christmas Eve, 1968

'It wasn't, Barney, I promise. There's no such thing as ghosts.' Barney's a trembling fawn in my arms, all skinny limbs and long wet lashes. 'It was Caroline in Momma's white fur tippet, that's all,' I add, trying to sound like this was nothing. 'It gave me a bit of a shock.'

'Is my favourite monkey in there?' Peggy's at the nursery door. 'Look. I've brought you a blanket. We don't want you to catch your death, do we now?' She shrugs it over Barney's shoulders, tucks a fold under his chin like a bib. 'Look what else I've brought you.' She places a tray on my bedroom rug. 'Crackers,' she says. 'Cheese. And a nice glass of warm milk with a dash of condensed from the tin. Your favourite.'

Barney's arms loosen around my neck. He edges off my knees towards the plate.

'If you hadn't yelled blue murder at poor Mrs Shaw-cross, Amber, you wouldn't have scared the living daylights out of him,' Peggy hisses, in a furious whisper over Barney's head as he nibbles on the cracker. 'He's just turned six, for goodness' sake. It's no wonder he's upset.'

'So it's my fault?'

'Well, yes. This time it is. Oh, Amber, don't look at me like that. I know you still miss your ma, and you're hurting but you can't show it by flying off the handle like a fury, not in front of a sensitive boy like our Barney.' She puts her tiny hand on my shoulder. 'We all have our crosses to bear in this life.'

'You've got no idea.' I shrug her off.

'Well, maybe not.' She sniffs. 'But I do know it's Christmas Eve.' Her fingers walk to her crucifix. 'And I do know that Mr Alton's doing his best. And after a hard week in London he doesn't need it. He wants his good little Amber back, not some kind of . . . doo-lally demon.'

'*She*'s the demon!'

'What's a demon?' asks Barney, cheeks fat with cheese.

'Nothing you need to worry about, Barney. You just eat those crackers. Build up your strength,' says Peggy, quickly, whispering to me over his head, 'That Shawcross woman is trying very hard to be kind, if you and Toby would only let her. And spending a small fortune. Have you seen how many presents she's piled up under that tree? It's almost indecent. I've never seen so many. Or a woman trying to be liked more.'

'Caroline gave us pear drops,' Barney says matter-of-factly.

I flick away his sticky milk moustache with my finger. 'She gave you sweets?'

'Pear drops in a twist of paper.'

Peggy swivels her apron around her bottle-top waist, levers herself up with a sigh. 'Well, your tea isn't going to make itself.'

'Wait! Peggy, where did Caroline find the tippet?' The possibility that Caroline went anywhere near Momma's wardrobe – the place I can go and inhale the last atoms of her – makes me feel sick.

Peggy frowns, works her mouth. 'It'd have been hanging in the cloakroom, I believe.'

I shake my head. 'No. I've seen it in Momma's wardrobe, hanging next to the red fox fur stole.'

'Oh, don't get caught up on details, Amber. You can blame me if you like.'

'Why?' I say crossly, knowing she's going to try to take the blame to keep the peace.

'Well, I bumped into Mrs Shawcross coming in from the terrace earlier, shivering she was. You'd think she'd have more sense, wearing a dress like that in December, shoulders bare like a butcher's ham, but anyway. I suggested she might want to cover up, a fur or something, didn't want to come down with a cold, not when you can't find a sober doctor for love nor money during Yuletide. And the next thing I know . . .' Peggy's cheeks glow pink: she's enjoying the drama '. . . there's *only* Mrs Shawcross standing at the top of the stairs with your mother's tippet wrapped around her, like something you'd see on screen at the Truro Coronet!'

A shudder passes through me. I see the clasp again, winking, a cat's eye.

'And she did look Christmassy, all that white fur. I thought, There's a sight that might cheer up Mr Alton at least,' Peggy says, looking a little irritated by this idea.

'But it's our first Christmas without Momma!'

'Yes, Amber. And that's *why* Mrs Shawcross is here, isn't it? To jolly things along. Keep your pa's spirits up.'

I sink my chin into Barney's hair, all the fight sucked out of me, wondering if I've got it wrong after all and am being beastly selfish.

'Don't look so sad. Your ma would want you to be happy at Christmas, wouldn't she? She hated a long face.'

My eyes fill with tears. I try to blink them away so as not to upset Barney.

'Hey,' says Peggy. She pulls me into a hug. The smell of sweat and cake and talc puffs out of the frilled collar of her shirt. 'None of that, missy.'

'But I – I feel like we're all pretending things are normal, Peggy.' I pull away from her, wipe the tears on the back of my hand. 'Like Daddy's asking us to forget Momma.'

She shakes her head. 'No one's asking you to forget her, duck.'

'It feels like they are.'

'Mr Alton believes the best way forward is to put one foot in front of the other, stiff upper lip and all that. There's sense in it, Amber. If you live in the past . . .' Peggy's voice cracks a little '. . . you're only living half a life.'

Barney coughs on a repressed sob. We both turn, terrified we've upset him again. He gets upset so easily.

'Hey, mister, there, there. Don't you be starting your racket up again, or you'll send Mrs Shawcross running for the London train and we'll all get it in the neck.' She glances up at me, whispers, 'I suspect Mrs Caroline Shawcross is not a lady who likes screaming children.'

'I don't think she likes children at all. I can see it in the way she looks at us. Even at Lucian.'

'Well, Lucian doesn't strike me as the easiest lad to get along with.'

An odd sensation crawls over my skin as I remember my encounter with Lucian in the woods, the way he appeared from the shadows. I push the image away, trying not to think about him. But the more determined I am not to think about Lucian the more indistinguishable it becomes from thinking about him. Like how wishing yourself asleep only makes you more awake.

'You forget that not everyone's as soppy as your mother when it comes to children, Amber. Seen but not heard. That's the way it was for generations of Alton children. Maud Bean in the village, who knew your daddy's Nanny Toots, says your father only met his parents between the hours of five and six. It was your mother – bless her – who shook things up here, what with her American ways. No one had ever seen anything like it.'

She squats down. 'There's a good boy, Barney. Finish up all that milk. Boys need milk to get strong. You want to get tall and strong like Daddy, don't you?'

Barney nods, eyes wide, small pale fingers curled around the glass.

'My nanna used to tell me, drink a glass of milk every day and you'll live to a hundred.'

'Did she?' asks Barney.

'Ninety-two. But that's a long enough life for anyone.' She winks at Barney, ruffles his hair. 'We don't want to out-stay our welcome, do we?'

The seed heads nod like frosted skulls, caught in the bright shaft of light falling from the kitchen window. Silvery brambles steal across the ground in the borders. The ivy is denser than ever, as if it's been creeping over the house by stealth while we sleep, suckering to the windows like sticky frog's feet. Nothing in the garden has been cut back or pruned this year. Momma and her team of gardeners did it every autumn – I used to help, holding the sack open for the tossed clippings, bringing out plates of warm shortbread to keep everyone going. No one came this year. I press my hands against the cold glass, trying to see out into the dark.

Still no sign of Toby.

Grateful not to be summoned to a grown-ups' dinner, I attempt to eat the nursery food – a steaming slump of shepherd's pie, cabbage, carrots from the kitchen garden, the promise of apple dicky for pudding, another mince pie – but since I met Lucian in the woods I've lost my appetite, belly full of other things.

Fifteen minutes later, Toby sidles into his seat, covering his face with his hand as he sits, blanking me. Is he still angry? I notice a rip on the collar of his shirt, mud stiffening his hair.

'What's happened to your eye, Toby?' asks Kitty, cheerfully, as she feeds a carrot into Raggedy Doll's black stitch of a mouth.

'Nothing,' he huffs.

I crane forward to see what he's hiding. 'Crikey. What happened to your eye?'

Toby stabs his fork into the potato. 'It doesn't hurt.'

Fear clenches my stomach: three knuckle marks on his eyebrow. 'Did Lucian do it?'

'I don't want to talk about it.'

'Toby . . .'

'Get lost.'

*

It's pitch black now, the long velvet curtains pulled against the spiking cold. I stop outside the door to the drawing room, listening to the carols crackling on the record player, Daddy's cigar cough and the sounds of an unfamiliar woman.

Daddy's face is lit by the flare of his cigar. The record has stuck: '*Silent night, ho-oo--oo . . .*' He leans over, picks up the needle, places it back on a groove. The song jumps, the choir continues.

'*Holy night . . .*'

I steal a glance at Caroline. She is not wearing the tippet now. But she is sitting on Momma's chair by the fire – the plum-pink one opposite Daddy that none of us dares use – like it's always been hers, legs neatly crossed at the knee, sitting very upright, cocktail glass in hand, smiling in that tight way of hers, as if invisible strings are pulling her lips up. She's wearing a blood-red gown that shows off the flawless cream of her shoulders. Her eyes are the colour of a clear winter sky in the bleak cold hours just after dawn. 'Good evening, Amber,' she says, in a way that suggests she never wore Momma's tippet earlier, that I never shouted in her face. 'Excited about Christmas?'

I remind myself of Peggy's words, how Daddy wants the old Amber back, so I try, for his sake. 'Yes, thank you, Caroline,' I manage, my voice coming out high and strange.

Daddy smiles at me. A relieved, grateful smile. I wonder if he knows what happened earlier. I haven't had a chance to tell him because I've not been able to get him on his own. Maybe he's had Caroline's version.

'Oh, look, the poppets.' Caroline peers over my shoulder, hand at her throat. 'How adorable they look, Hugo!'

Barney and Kitty stand in the doorway in their night-wear, shuffling shyly from one bare foot to the other, their just-brushed hair haloed with static, their faces scrubbed. Peggy passes behind them, like a shadow. Boris thwacks his tail.

'Did you bring any more pear drops?' Barney pipes up, making Daddy and Caroline laugh as if this is the funniest thing they've ever heard.

'I'm sure I could find you another little something. Would you like that? Something rather sweet and naughty?'

Barney and Kitty nod enthusiastically. I want to point out to Caroline that they have brushed their teeth but Kitty will be furious if I do.

'Oh, Master Toby too.' She stiffens on the chair. 'Good evening, young man.'

'What's happened to your eye?' asks Daddy, quietly, as if he's not sure he wants to know the answer. Sometimes with Toby it's best not to ask.

'Fell off a tree. Branch snapped,' mumbles Toby, barely audible.

Daddy says, 'Mmm', pretends to believe him.

'Oh dear, quite a shiner,' Caroline remarks, and is about to say something else but stops, as if it's just occurred to her where he might have got it. After that no one mentions the eye or Lucian's obvious absence from the room.

After a snap of awkwardness, Daddy opens his arms. 'Come on, give me a hug, then.' Barney runs up to him and leaps on to one knee. Kitty takes the other alongside Raggedy Doll. Boris lies down on his feet, dribbling over his shoelaces.

Toby stands firm, punishing Daddy for inviting the Shawcrosses to Black Rabbit Hall.

I hold out for a second or two but am unable to resist and press my face against Daddy's chest – he feels safe and solid, smells right – and run my fingers through the back of his hair, not something I'd normally do but Caroline is watching. I stake my territory.

'I've missed you all these last few weeks,' Daddy says, dropping his chin into Kitty's curls, watching Toby from the corner of his eye. 'It's just been impossibly busy at work.'

'Raggedy Doll still loves you,' whispers Kitty. 'She's made you a pink stocking.'

'Has she indeed?' Daddy's eyes go soft with love. We laugh. And for a moment I almost forget about Caroline. 'I'm very proud of you all. I hope you know that.' He glances over at Toby as he speaks and I think this is because he wants Toby to know he means him too. But Toby looks away, spinning the globe in the corner of the room with his finger.

Caroline coughs, shifts on the chair, uncomfortable, as if she doesn't quite know where to put herself.

'You've all been so brave.' This is the closest Daddy has come to mentioning Momma since he returned home for Christmas.

'Next year will be better,' says Caroline, a little shrilly, watching us over the rim of her glass with darting eyes.

'It certainly will.' Daddy smiles at her over Kitty's head. I don't like the smile. I don't like the way it is full of conversations we've not heard.

'Do you swear on your life, Daddy?' Kitty's gaze is fixed on Caroline's sapphire earrings, glinting from her tiny, high-set ears. 'That it will get better, and then better again?'

'On my life, Kittycat.' He kisses her forehead, eyes closed.

Caroline stands up abruptly as if the tenderness is too much. Her glass hits the marble fireplace with a sharp clink. 'Who's looked outside in the last few minutes?'

Barney and Kitty shake their heads. Toby spins the globe faster. The way he's spinning it makes me think it will go faster and faster, then break away and fly across the room. A bit like Toby.

'I've got something magical to show you.' Caroline offers her hand. It hovers in mid-air, the jewelled rings glinting in the firelight. 'Come, children.'

Kitty and Barney stare at the hand, then back at Toby, unsure of their loyalties. A muscle twitches in Caroline's jaw. Kitty can't resist the rings, of course. Caroline looks relieved and smiles over her shoulder at Daddy. Look at me, the smile says. Look how Kitty loves me and is holding my hand. They walk to the window.

'Amber. Toby. The window.' There is an edge to Daddy's voice as he refills his whisky glass from the crystal decanter. 'You'll regret it if you don't.'

Curiosity gets the better of us. We yank back the heavy velvet curtain and gasp. Huge, furry white snowflakes are tumbling down in the golden light of the window, spiralling, swimming, in the wind.

'Wow!' Barney starfishes his hands on the glass. 'Is the snow real?'

Caroline cups his tiny shoulder. 'As real as you or me, Barney.'

'But it never snows at Black Rabbit Hall,' says Toby, frowning. Something about it really bothers him, doesn't add up. 'It never snows by the sea.'

'Well, it does now, Toby.' Caroline lifts her chin, staring out of the window with a look of unmistakable triumph. 'Isn't this all just too perfect for words?'

I buck awake, hands protecting my face from falling, and lie there panting in the darkness. How dare Lucian? How dare he hurt Toby, then hide away? I won't let him hide any longer.

I tug the lamp switch, squint through the shade's peachy fringing, adjusting to the light. Out of my warm bed, a slap of cold. Avoiding the floorboard directly outside my door that squeaks like a kitten, I close my bedroom door carefully, leaving the comforting glow of lamplight, and pad along the corridor to Toby's room. I hover outside, listening hard – nothing stirring, good, he'd go mad if he knew where I'm going – then check on Barney and Kitty, as I always do when I wake in the night, just to be sure they're not dead.

They are both in Barney's bed, a sticky tangle of curls and limbs, crushed against the patch of wall where Barney sticks his flapping collection of bloodied plasters, trophies of cut knees and thorned fingers. There's a faint smell of wee. Kitty's bottom is in the air. Barney's elbow is jutting into Kitty's nostril. The book I read them before bed – *Milly Molly Mandy* – is crumpled beneath the pillow. Raggedy Doll dangles over it, head first, arms outstretched. I tuck her next to Kitty, slide the book out and watch them breathe sweetly for a moment. Then I kiss them both on the forehead and tiptoe out. My anger feels wrong in here.

I hesitate at the landing window outside their room – the floorboards drenched with mercury moonlight – and breathe out a mask on the glass. Outside the whiteness is as still and flat as milk. I think about how much Momma would have loved to see Black Rabbit Hall like this, the fields, the woods all iced. And I think of how fierce she would have been if someone had hurt Toby.

She's not here. But I am.

Anticipating the twist at the top of the stairs, my finger-tips brush something solid in the liquorice dark. I jump, fisting my hands. But it's only the grandfather clock – the noisy little brother of the one in the hall, Momma called it. I try to read its pearly face: two a.m., which means it's probably nearer three. Late, far too late, but Toby made confronting Lucian impossible before bed and I couldn't risk getting Toby involved. I will just have to wake Lucian.

But there's already a thin stripe of light beneath Lucian's door. I creep towards it and stand outside, lining up insults on my tongue, ready to be spat out like hard peas.

'Who's there?' The door springs open. I'm not sure who is more shocked to see the other. My insults aren't ready.

His eyes round with surprise. Then he lets out a low, relieved whistle. 'I thought you were Toby.'

I scramble myself together from the unlikely sight of him in blue striped pyjamas. 'I know what you did.'

'Better come in, then.' He opens the door wider for me like the gentleman he isn't.

Over his shoulder I see embers glowing invitingly in the

166

grate. But something stops me stepping into his room, as if there's an invisible line I must not cross. This is already not how I imagined it.

'Freeze in the corridor, if you prefer.'

I put my chin up and stride in, as if I was about to anyway.

There is a distinct smell in the room. Smoke. Cigarettes. Something else. A bit like Toby but different. I don't quite know where to stand, or where to look.

'Just thrown the last log on, sorry.' He sits down on his bed, tugs up a blanket. 'Want this?'

'No, thank you.' I'd rather get frostbite than accept a blanket from Lucian. Still, I curse myself for not putting on my dressing-gown. For wearing a nightie covered with rainbows and looking like Wendy from *Peter Pan*. Worse than his pyjamas. Much worse.

'You're shivering.'

'I'm used to winters at Black Rabbit Hall.' My voice is clipped, furious, gritted against the chill. 'But I'm not used to idiots like *you*.'

He looks at me as if I've suddenly become more interesting. 'Black Rabbit Hall,' he repeats, a slow smile curling his mouth. 'I want to see the silhouettes on the lawn. Failing the timely appearance of a bunny, will you stand against the setting sun tomorrow so I can test the theory?'

'Don't be soft.' I sneak a quick glance around the room, the stack of novels – some French! – the neck of a guitar resting against his bed. It looks so much more grown-up than Toby's room, which is littered with stray socks and ancient copies of the *Boy's Own Paper*. I haven't seen a guitar close up since visiting Aunt Bay in New York. We only have classical instruments at school. Guitars – not a respectable instrument for a girl – are forbidden. My eye is sucked towards it.

Seeing my interest, he reaches across the bed for it, settles it like a baby in his lap and fingers the strings, silently mimicking a chord. I notice the pink bruising on his knuckles. That hand smashed Toby's face.

'What sort of music do you like?' His eyes flicker across my chest, linger there for one tiny moment before he pulls them away.

I cross my arms, fighting a wave of self-consciousness. I don't have a clue how to answer his question. It occurs to me that he looks right holding a guitar, as I might holding a book, like they belong together somehow.

'Is it that embarrassing?' There's mischief in his eyes now. Clearly he's enjoying me standing here in my nightie, caught in the glare of what suddenly seems an extremely bright bedside light.

'Sod off.'

He plucks a string on his guitar. It shivers sweetly in the silence. 'You know, I always spend Christmas in Hampstead with my grandmother, which is pretty bloody dull but preferable to this.'

'We don't want you here, Lucian. You or your mother.'

'The feeling is mutual,' he says mildly, plucking the string again. 'Ma normally celebrates on a black run at Gstaad. God knows why she's dragged me here.'

'You mean she doesn't spend Christmas with you?' I ask, forgetting I'm not in the least interested.

'You obviously don't know my mother.'

'And nor do I want to.'

He doesn't look up from the guitar.

'You punched Toby in the woods, idiot,' I hiss. My arm-pits are wet, despite the chill spiking the hairs along my arms. 'Worse, you hid afterwards. You are . . . pathetic.'

'And you are some wildcat,' he says, a confusing note of admiration in his voice.

'Is that all you have to say?' My voice shakes. 'No apology? No – no explanation?'

'That's right.'

'You're lucky Toby didn't report it to Daddy. But I want you to know that *I* will, Lucian.' I reach for the brass door handle, use it to steady myself. 'I will tell Daddy every detail of this conversation in the morning! And he will demand that you and your mother leave immediately.'

'Something to look forward to, then.'

I stomp out of the door, then stop. Something doesn't make sense. 'Tell me why you did it,' I say, back still turned.

'I don't have to tell you anything.'

I whip round. 'Toby's my twin brother.'

He rolls his eyes. 'Yeah, I rather got that.'

'Just tell me.'

Lucian stares down at the guitar, rubs its neck with his thumb. For the first time I see vulnerability in him, a hesitation in his long, slim fingers. 'Amber, it's no big thing. There was a skirmish in the woods, that's all.'

'A skirmish?' I lean on the door, close it behind me, its ridged wooden panels pressing into my spine.

'After I saw you this afternoon, I went down to the river and there was Toby, sitting on a tree, this massive old tree with a rope dangling down. He was carving it up. We got . . . talking.'

'What about?' My scalp starts to creep.

'Well, he kind of accused me of . . .' he clears his throat, falters '. . . er, staring at you at lunch.'

'Staring at *me*?'

'Those weren't his exact words. But if you want the gist, that was it, yes.'

'Well, how . . . how insane.' I twist a snake of my hair around my finger, no longer sure where to take the conversation. My face is on fire. Was Lucian staring at me at lunch? I was so determined not to look in his direction, twisting away from him, that I wouldn't have seen. 'How perfectly stupid.'

'I'm genuinely sorry about your brother's eye.' His are so dark they're almost entirely black, embers flickering in each.

'You don't look very sorry.' I sniff, trying to hide my embarrassment.

'I don't say things I don't mean.' He shoves the guitar to one side and sits up on the bed, bending at an awkward angle, feet on the rug.

My eye is drawn to a dark crease on his red pyjama top. 'What's that?'

Lucian looks down, pulls the fabric away from his stomach.

'It looks like . . . blood.'

'Knocked an old rugby scratch.'

More blood spilt at Black Rabbit Hall! I clamp my hand to my mouth, wondering what I'll tell Caroline if he dies.

'Don't look spooked.' He yanks up his pyjama top. 'Nothing, see?'

It's about three inches long, a thin, straight gash, like a scissor slit in a pillow. 'You need the village doctor.'

'No, I don't.' He laughs.

'Your mother. I'll get her.'

'No! Not Ma. Jesus. Don't even think about it. Just find me some tissue or something, will you?'

I try to remember the St John Ambulance first-aid lesson at school as I run into the bathroom, yank a towel off the hook and fold it up to make a pad with trembling fingers. When I get back into the bedroom Lucian is naked from the waist up. My breath catches in my throat. I squat down, wishing I'd never visited his room or asked any questions and, not knowing what else to do – he doesn't take the towel – start to wipe the blood off his smooth, firm skin, refusing to look at the wiry V of sooty hair that arrows down from his belly button to an unknowable place beneath his waistband. The wound is superficial, but surgical. 'It doesn't look like a rugby scratch,' I say primly.

His stomach muscles clench. And I know then. I close my eyes, prepare myself, like you do on a fairground ride, rising up, up, up, ready for the horror-swoop down. 'Toby?' I whisper, barely able to breathe the word out.

'Stupid penknife.' His voice is so low and restrained that I know he doesn't want to tell me, any more than I want to hear it. But we're holed up in this room in the dead of the night, the snow swirling outside the window, and it suddenly seems impossible that either of us could say anything that wasn't true.

'I don't think he meant to, Amber,' Lucian says, with an unexpected gentleness that makes me want to cry. 'He just wanted to frighten me. Things went too far.'

'Toby's not a bad person.' I can't stop my voice breaking, imagining Daddy's fury when he finds out. 'He – he just gets angry sometimes.'

'I know. It's all right.'

Struggling not to cry, I drop the towel to the floor. The wound is dry now. 'Why didn't you tell?'

'I understand, that's all.'

Everything I thought I knew about Lucian Shawcross starts to slip and slide beneath me, like melting snow. But I'm still not sure whether to believe him.

We sit in silence for a few moments. The embers in the fire flare up one last time, then fade to black, making the room feel dreamy, under water. 'My dad died.'

'Oh.' Now I believe him.

'It was snowing then too.'

'I'm sorry.'

He shrugs. 'It's not like it happened at Easter or anything.'

There's not much to say after that: it cuts through the soft stuff straight to the bone. We both know things that most people our age don't. We've both had to stick ourselves back together again. Rotten luck. That's it, really.

'I'd better go.' I stand up quickly, a sweet heat puffing out from my nightie. Not looking back over my shoulder, though I long to do so, I climb up the stairs in the moonlight, trying to take it all in. But there's too much to fit: a night tucked within the night. I feel more awake than I have ever been. As if I will never sleep again. The grandfather clock says it is three. Can an hour really have passed? Where did it go?

As I creep along the landing towards my bedroom, I

notice that the door is ajar and my lamp is off, even though I left it on. Something moves in the darkness, shifts on the springs of my bed. 'Toby?' I push open the door slowly, safe only for a few more seconds, fear a moth in my stomach. 'Toby, is that you?'

Thirteen

Lorna

'Yes, Lorna, there was a – a Toby who lived here once, a long time ago,' stutters Dill, the back of her wrist pressed to her forehead, as if the name hurts her head. She heaves Lorna's weekend bag to the leather luggage rack, making it wobble. 'Oh dear, towels. I forgot your towels.' She tuts, although Lorna senses she's grateful for the distraction. 'I knew I'd forget something.'

'Toby is Mrs Alton's son?' Lorna perseveres. She can still feel the ridges in the rough bark beneath her finger-tips, the names of those children, and she cannot stop thinking about them. It's hard to believe she kissed Jon goodbye and caught the train from London only this morning. Black Rabbit Hall has already reeled her in, pushed her other life back.

'Oh, no, not her son,' says Dill, looking startled by the idea. 'No, no. Her stepson. Let's get some air in here.' She pulls back the floral curtains, flings the sash window up, as if trying to disperse Lorna's questions with a bracing breeze. 'That's better.'

Lorna joins her at the window. The view is different from how she remembers it, simultaneously bigger and more intimate. The sweep of lawn makes her think of an outdoor summer stage, the players long departed. But *not* forgotten. No child should ever be forgotten. 'So, Dill, this tree in the woods . . .'

'We're all running rather late. Mrs Alton will be waiting for her tea in the sunroom,' Dill says, backing out of the door. 'She doesn't much like a late tea.'

If Mrs Alton is impatient for her tea she has the manners not to show it. Dressed in slacks and a cloud-blue bouclé collarless jacket that has matted with age – there is an air vent of moth holes in a perfect circle on the left shoulder – but looks suspiciously like the Chanel ones that go for small fortunes in the better vintage shops, she is sitting very still in a snug, goldfinch-yellow room. She steeples her fingertips together, presses them lightly against her lips. 'You got lost in the woods, I gather.'

'I did,' Lorna admits. 'I'm very sorry if I've made you wait.'

'Oh, those paths were purposely designed to make a visitor lose their bearings. Some sort of Alton mischief at the turn of the nineteenth century, I believe. Do sit. You look quite flushed by your little adventure.'

Mrs Alton's cool detachment is the kind to bring out a fluster in anyone, Lorna thinks, careful not to put her elbows on the linen-covered table. She feels grateful for her mother's insistence on good table manners.

'Tea.' Dill slides an Oriental black tray, the lacquer peeling off in long, curled shards, in front of them. 'A slice of ginger cake, Lorna?'

The cake is a gleaming bronze ingot. 'Oh, yes, please. It looks delicious.'

'I simply cannot function without Dill's ginger cake,' says Mrs Alton, slicing into hers with the side of a dull silver cake fork.

'My mother's recipe,' Dill explains, looking surprised and pleased, as if such a compliment is rare.

'One of the more digestible,' adds Mrs Alton, briskly.

The cake pirouettes on Lorna's tongue. It's the best she's ever tasted, and she's tasted a lot. Before she can say so, Dill vanishes from the room, soundless as a kitchen cat.

'So the grounds are romantic, are they not, Lorna?' Mrs Alton dabs at the corners of her mouth with a thread-bare linen napkin that looks like it's been boil-washed every day since the fifteenth century. 'A perfect backdrop for a wedding?'

'They are the most beautiful grounds I've ever seen.'

Mrs Alton picks up her teacup between finger and thumb, brings it to her pursing lips and sips. 'Excellent.'

'Mrs Alton, I found this tree beside the river . . .' Lorna begins gently, not wanting to disturb any buried grief, but curiosity getting the better of her. The room may be still – all old rooms feel still, undisturbed by WiFi clouds and hidden wiring or whatever it is that makes the air in modern houses jiggle – but her mind is racing at a million miles an hour. Even as she sits there, she feels like she's in motion. '. . . covered with sort of carvings, names.'

'I am aware of such a tree.' Mrs Alton sighs, as if Lorna has disappointed her by mentioning it. The arrowhead deepens between her eyebrows and her gaze hardens over the rim of her cup, daring Lorna to probe any further. 'It is diseased and must come down.'

176

'Oh, no, you must leave it! It's part of the house's history.'

'It's *one* history, Lorna.' She clinks her cup to the saucer sharply. 'In a family such as mine there are many, many histories, most of which contradict each other. We cannot be sentimental about them all. Now, would you be so kind as to cut me another sliver of cake? I find it is quite pointless to deny oneself a second slice at my stage of life.'

'I quite agree.' Using a heavy blunt silver knife, she cuts a fat piece, probably too fat because it makes Mrs Alton's left eyebrow arch. And although she'd happily eat another herself, a genius idea freezes the knife mid-air. 'Mrs Alton, I've an idea about how you might establish a successful wedding business here on the estate.'

'Really?' She brings a dainty morsel of cake to her mouth. 'Do go on.'

Lorna leans forwards over the table, forgetting all about her elbows. 'Can I be frank?'

'I have no time to waste on those who are not.'

'Well, the website isn't very . . . enticing.' She is being diplomatic: the 'website' consists of a grainy photo, an elusive address – 'Pencraw Hall, Roseland, Cornwall' – and a grab of text, 'Site under construction.'

'I see,' Mrs Alton says curtly, laying her fork on her plate. The thunderous expression on her face suggests that frankness might be a relative concept. 'Believe me, Lorna, it is little short of a miracle that we have one at all.'

'I . . . I just mean that the website doesn't quite do the house justice.'

'Endellion will be taking some more photographs. What

she lacks in skill she makes up for in quantity. That should do it.'

'What about the house's history? Everyone will want to know that.'

'They will?'

'Mrs Alton, this is a venue for people who, like me, love old stuff, couples looking for somewhere far removed from the modern and everyday.' She recalls the other bland, anonymous wedding venues that left her cold and tries to work out what was missing. 'For authenticity too. A peep inside your world.'

'A peep inside my world? None of their darned business.' A crumb of ginger cake dislodges from her front tooth, torpedoes across the table and lands on Lorna's wrist.

'I'm talking purely from a commercial point of view, Mrs Alton.' She's not, of course, but she lets the words hang there, wonders when she's going to have an opportunity to discreetly wipe away the cake crumb.

'You are certain it would bring in more business?'

'I would think so. It doesn't need to be much information, nothing intrusive, just a little bit of background.' She takes a deep breath, goes for it. 'I'd be very happy to help you.'

Mrs Alton's eyes narrow. 'It won't get you a discount, you know.'

'Of course not! I'd just love to do it as a thank-you for my stay. I'm a quick writer. It wouldn't take long and it would be a pleasure, really. I find that sort of thing fascinating. History is my favourite subject to teach at school,' she adds, fearing she might be overdoing it.

'I see.' Mrs Alton doesn't withhold the scepticism from her voice.

In the awkward hush, Lorna hears the house creak and sigh, as if the stone and wood and crumbling lime mortar are also trying to make up their minds about the urban imposter.

'More cake, ladies?' asks Dill, pushing open the door, eyeing them curiously. 'Everything all right?'

Lorna holds her breath, doesn't dare look up. She's about to get asked to leave. Well, that was fun. All four hours of it.

The old lady clears her throat with a bullet crack. 'Lorna has had the audacity to suggest we flip the family's bed sheets for public inspection, Endellion.'

Christ! 'Mrs Alton, I really didn't mean –'

'And I think it's about time, don't you?' Mrs Alton stands slowly, levering herself up with bunched knuckles on the table. 'But I'll need a stiff drink in the drawing room first. Sherry, please, Endellion. Not the finest.'

When they pass the moon-dial clock in the hall it says midnight. But Lorna's watch says five. Neither time feels right. The drawing-room walls are a dark foggy blue and the spitting fire in the grate that Dill has hurriedly lit makes the room airlessly sleepy, as if caught in the late unreal hours of a cold winter's night. Thick grey woodsmoke curls up the huge chimney before changing its mind and rolling slowly back into the room like a sea fog, making Lorna's eyes water and the back of her throat burn. The sherry doesn't help either. Feeling disoriented, she licks a finger – it tastes inexplicably of the milky sap of a dandelion stalk, a bitter grassiness recalled from childhood – and flips the page of her notebook.

An hour later it is scribbled with random facts about the house, bouncing back and forth in time like a confused student's notes: Pencraw, in the Alton family for five generations, bought with trade money – sugar, originally – from a duke 'with far too many houses, a thoroughly spoilt wife, running out of cash'; used as a convalescent hospital for injured troops during the First World War, taking in at least twenty evacuee children in the Second; farmland, once extensive, now largely sold off; ditto, most of the estate cottages; the house itself coming near to destruction, demolition being cheaper than its upkeep, in the early 1950s, as did its infamous rabbits, hit by myxomatosis; a glorious Reynolds in the drawing room, where a smuggler's landscape now hangs, scandalously auctioned off by her husband Hugo's grandfather; a rogue alcoholic heir, Sebastian, who, hallucinating on absinthe, simply stepped off a yacht in the Med, naked but for his Panama hat, and drowned, much to everyone's relief; a yew tree in the garden, 'older than America'; Princess Margaret, who once came to a party, danced all night, and left behind a long white silk glove, now stored in a drawer but no one can remember exactly which. There are many.

The more recent family history is harder to tease out. Sketchy, elliptical, it escapes from Mrs Alton inadvertently in small salty drops, each one leaving Lorna thirstier than the last: Hugo's 'horribly beautiful' first wife, who 'couldn't survive her horse', four stepchildren including 'disturbed, difficult twins', her own son, Lucian – whose name Mrs Alton voices in a low, husky whisper – and an admission that the role of stepmother 'was not one in which I particularly excelled', spoken with notably little, if any, regret.

As they talk, the carriage clock ticks and the flames start to crackle salt-blue. Smoke hangs in the corners of the room, just out of reach, like the stories Lorna is after. Lorna realizes she's been circling Barney, not daring to ask directly about his death: she fears Mrs Alton's reaction, an explosion of grief, and knows that she won't be able to shake the details from her head once she's let them in. No one can forget the death of a child. It goes against the natural order of things. And order – age, gender, status – in a grand family, she is beginning to grasp, is everything. Defying it is dangerous. Defying it leaves elderly women living alone in vast damp houses, throttled by their precious, worthless strings of pearls.

'I have made mistakes, Lorna,' Mrs Alton says abruptly.

'Everyone makes mistakes with houses, Mrs Alton.' Lorna warms her sherry glass in the cup of her hand. The first two sips were challenging, but she's grown to rather like it. 'You should hear some of Jon's building site stories.'

Mrs Alton shakes her head, mouth pursed tight. 'Not *those* kind of mistakes.'

'Oh.' The candid turn in the conversation catches in Lorna's throat, making her splutter on the smoke.

'I was like some of our hens, Lorna, no maternal instinct at all. I was supposed to have one, all women were back then, but I didn't. I found that rather difficult. And those stepchildren – Amber, Toby, Barney, Kitty – I . . . I found . . .' She searches for the right word, shaking her head. '. . . unfathomable.'

181

'I'm sure you did your best, Mrs Alton.' She reaches out and touches Mrs Alton's arm lightly.

Mrs Alton jolts, stares at Lorna's hand, startled by the human touch. 'Obviously, I'd rather you didn't include any mention of such in *l'histoire*,' she says coolly.

'Of course not.' Lorna removes her hand, retreats to her sherry glass. 'It's your story, not mine. You only share what you're comfortable with.'

But Mrs Alton doesn't look comfortable now, not at all. She is agitating her pearls with crooked fingers, frown lines deepening on her forehead. 'I fear I am talking rather too much.'

'Not at all!'

'You are frighteningly easy to talk to.' She leans forward in her chair, eyes narrowing suspiciously beneath the drooped skin of the lids. 'Have you done this sort of thing before?'

'Never.' Lorna can't help but smile at the idea that she makes a habit of interviewing grand old dames in country-house drawing rooms.

'Well, you're a natural. We certainly didn't have teachers like you in my day. My school days might have been rather more tolerable if we had.' Mrs Alton smiles, but distantly. Her energy seems to be waning. 'I trust you have enough information now.'

'Um, not quite.' If she doesn't ask now . . . She steels herself, takes a deep breath, speaks as gently as she can. 'What happened to Barney, Mrs Alton?'

'Barney?' Mrs Alton reaches for the decanter, refills her glass, a visible tremor in her grip. 'Barney paid the price.'

'The price?' Lorna repeats, shocked. 'The price for what?'

A soft knock at the door steals the answer. 'Sorry to disturb you. It's time for your pills, Mrs Alton.' Dill walks over, carrying a tumbler of water. The scrappy terrier follows, claws tapping on the wood, trailing the smell of wet dog.

'Petal!' Mrs Alton's face softens. She dips her finger in her sherry, and, not seeming to care if she loses it, lets the dog lick it off. 'Good boy, Petal. Aren't you my beautiful boy?'

'You've missed your snooze today, Mrs Alton,' says Dill, pulling a fistful of pills out of a grubby plastic freezer bag. She shoots Lorna a sweet smile. 'That's a first.'

'Funnily enough, I didn't notice. Time has quite flown.' Mrs Alton knocks the pills back with efficiency, dismissing the tumbler of water with a flick of the hand and using the sherry to gulp them down. 'But I suppose I should rest now, or that dreadful doctor will start pestering again.' She reaches for her cane. 'Yes, that is quite enough for now. Quite enough.'

Lorna's heart sinks. Just when she felt she was getting somewhere. Still, to be fair, Mrs Alton looks quite drained beneath the powdery blooms of blush on her cheeks, giving her the eerie appearance of an aged china doll.

Seeing Mrs Alton rise, Lorna leaps up and helps her to her feet, supporting her gently beneath her forearms, just as she used to do with Nan. Only Nan's arms had felt soft and plump, like socks filled with warm sand. Mrs Alton's are sinewy, stringy, the tendons crunching beneath the wool of her jacket. Thankfully, Dill takes over.

'I may be a while,' Dill apologizes to Lorna, as she walks Mrs Alton to the door, the cane reaching out in front of them like an insect's proboscis. 'Will you be okay just knocking about on your own until dinner?'

'Perfectly,' Lorna says. She could do with a chance to recover from the intoxication of sherry and smoke. 'Please don't worry about me. I'm quite happy moseying.'

'You could have a look in the library. There are lots of photos, house records, that sort of thing in there.' Dill coughs, waving her hand in front of her to clear the air. 'If you're happy with that, Mrs Alton?'

'Happiness has nothing to do with it, Endellion.' Mrs Alton raises her cane and steps forward. 'It is about survival now.'

Lorna decides to take that as a yes.

Lorna swoops the phone around the bay of the library's window-seat, like someone trying to catch a butterfly in a net. Yes! One signal bar. Connection to the outside world. 'Jon, can you hear me?'

There is distant chatter at the end of the line, the sound of someone who has left their mobile switched on in their pocket and is walking down a busy London street.

'Jon, it's me.'

A crackle, a hiss, silence. She tries again. The same happens. Lorna cannot help but wonder if the disconnection is symbolic of something else, something about the state of their relationship, the bickering before she left for Cornwall. Downhearted, she drops the phone back into her handbag. She'll phone him later. He won't be able to talk properly if he's on site anyway. At least her number will have come up: he'll know that she's tried.

She looks around the library, eyes hooking on the horse's

skull in the box. Does it have something to do with the first wife's riding accident? No, of course not. That would be far too gruesome.

She looks away, turning her back on its unsettling lunar stare. If she wants to have a good poke around before Dill reappears, she needs to get a move on. She peers up at the floor-to-ceiling bookshelves – endless gilded spines – and trails a finger along a shelf, thrilling at the sheer abundance of books.

There were books in her house when she was growing up but they were always borrowed from public libraries, their jackets encased in floppy plastic sleeves, with strangers' sticky thumbprints at the bottom of the pages. And there were only ever six at a time. Occasionally she'd glimpse libraries like this in a National Trust property – rarely stopping. Mum wasn't interested in books unless they were bodice-ripper romances, which she'd read in a scalding hot bath, foamed up with a squirt of Radox – and the young Lorna would marvel at the fantastical idea of having a library of her very own, dozens of books just sitting there, waiting, books you could stick your 'This book belongs to . . .' label into, books that didn't attract pocket-money-gobbling fines if you didn't return them in time.

She steps back, catching her heel in a hole in the rug as she tries to make out the tomes on the upper shelves: a row of fat burgundy leather spines that could easily be photo albums, each labelled with a different decade in pale gold letters. She decides to risk the library stepladder, a leggy contraption that protests noisily when she rests her weight upon it.

Lorna climbs until she's on a level with the lowest tear-drop crystal of the chandelier. The dust is even thicker on the shelves up here, mixed with dead bluebottles and mummified bees. It feels notably cooler too – confusing: isn't warm air supposed to rise? – and as she reaches up and pulls down a leather-bound book that reads '1960s' her scalp prickles. Judging by the dates carved into the tree, this should be the decade that Barney and his siblings lived here.

She flumps to the threadbare rug and slaps open the heavy covers, revealing a starry swirl of green marble end-papers. Yes, it's a photo album: eight small pictures to the double page, their corners tucked into lacy creamy card, each page covered with a thin sheet of waxed paper.

Lorna parts the paper like curtains, smiles. 'Hello.'

Four children. All startlingly pretty, popping off the page. The eldest two – Toby? Amber? – must be the twins, although they don't look in the least disturbed. The youngest – Kitty? – is cherubic, like a girl from an old Pears ad, hugging a funny cloth doll. And there he is, the little boy who called out to her from the woods. For it must be him, cheeky grin, hands stuffed deep into the pockets of his shorts, shoulders raised, as if he's struggling not to explode into giggles. Barney is so animated, so full of life, it's almost impossible to believe he died so young. She strokes his image gently then, lump in her throat, quickly turns the page.

The most noticeable thing about the Altons as a troupe – and they do look like a troupe, bundled together, arms thrown casually over each other's shoulders, mischievous rabbit-ear fingers above each other's heads – is their spirit, which shines through the fade of the years, written in a beautiful Italianate hand – 'Summer '65'; 'Easter '66' – at the bottom of each page. You can't disguise happiness in children, Lorna knows from experience. Those who have it own it. They gleam and glow. And it hangs around this group of children like a golden aura in every photo: yelping into the sea, hanging upside down from branches by their knees, eating sandwiches on a windy beach, huddled grinning and frozen beneath tents of towels.

Oh. Who's this? The first wife? No. She can't imagine the current Mrs Alton feeling overshadowed by this lady. Curvy girl-next-door-pretty, she stands at the back of some of the photographs, wearing a boldly striped apron.

Flipping another page, Lorna sees her mistake. No, no, that must have been a nanny or a housekeeper. *This* is the wife and mother. Blimey. What a beautiful smile. No wonder Mrs Alton struggled. In one photograph the first wife is laughing on a beach, lithe and model-like in a white bikini, her long hair wet, arms crossed, shoulders braced, as if emerging from a freezing sea. In every other shot there is a child attached to her: wrapped around her leg, sitting on her shoulders, little hands around her neck, lying on the ground playing with her toes. And Mr Alton presumably – pretty hot himself in a posh old-school James Bond kind of way – is gazing devotedly at her in almost every photo. It's obvious this woman is the humming heart of the family. How on earth had it coped without her?

The answer perhaps lies in the following few pages, after a gap in the dates. Rejoining the family in late '68, the mood is sombre, the pictures no longer labelled by that lovely handwriting. And the mother is, of course, nowhere to be seen. While the earlier pages of the children – the family as it was – seemed to pour light into the room on opening, these puff out a fine flour of dust, suggesting no one has turned to them for years. Or maybe it's just that the times have so obviously changed.

Mr Alton, where he appears at all, is grim-faced, hollow-cheeked, his once lustrous hair thin, salted with silver. The golden glow has leached from the children too, taller now, lanky, mistrustful of the camera. Still, Lorna's relieved that they're huddled together, like young animals bunching for protection and warmth. They've got each other at least.

Ah, here she is: Caroline, the new Mrs Alton, towering at the back of the photograph, a striking glacial blonde in her forties, hand resting stiffly on Kitty's shoulder. Mr Alton is not looking at this wife but out of the frame, his eyes distant, posture slumped. Next to him stands a sullen, handsome teenage boy, awkward in his height and jacket. Lucian? It must be. Yes, he has Mrs Alton's sharp good looks. Something else too. A handsome boy indeed.

The twins are shadows of their former selves, their gaze often bewildered, as if they've been picked from one life and buried in another. In one Christmas photograph – there is an enormous tree, like something from a town square, buried in presents – Toby looks ready to explode. Amber has her hand on his arm, as if trying to restrain him from doing or saying something. The scowling carries on into the wedding pictures – oh dear, that's a second marriage portrait and a half – and into a blazing summer that . . . suddenly vanishes. Lorna skips ahead, searching for the rest. But no: for some reason, the photographs abruptly stop in August 1969, the decade closing prematurely in a flutter of blank waxed pages. She slams shut the photo album, feeling drained, as if she's lived ten years in as many minutes. No more photographs. Not today. She has a wedding to plan, she reminds herself. She must get on.

Black Rabbit Hall is not a house that lends itself to 'getting on', any more than it does phone calls, Lorna soon discovers. It unfolds at its own pace, its corridors, anterooms and the repeated pauses of its views fostering a dreamy kind of lingering, an openness to getting lost. Is this because it was built for the leisured classes, she wonders, or is it something else?

Just when she thinks she's done with a room at Black Rabbit Hall and is about to leave it, Lorna notices something she hasn't before and it holds her there a little longer, not only in space but also in feeling, as if the house somehow forces the external and internal to synchronize.

The drawing room is proving particularly sticky. She blames the globe. There's a technique to the globe: it hums better if you push it, lightly, from the left. The longer you let it hum, the deeper and louder the hum becomes, as if you're walking towards a hidden beehive. And she's noticed another funny thing too: a small circle – wonkily drawn in green biro – around New York. Why?

Her mother never really got it, Lorna decides. She assumed that grand, gilded rooms and old masters told a stately home's story, the historical details filled in by an obsequious tour guide. But the real story is hidden, scribbled somewhere by a human hand that was probably doing

189

something it shouldn't. Like this inked circle. Or the carved tree in the woods.

Then she stops short. What if she is underestimating her mother? What if her mother always knew of another story bubbling beneath Black Rabbit Hall, like an underground stream? The idea makes her skin contract, the hairs rise. After all, the house sign must have had some significance. Why else would she make them both pose against it for photographs? It doesn't make sense. But it will. The answer has to lie here in the house somewhere. Where next?

Annoyingly, the ballroom is locked. She stands outside it in a vast, grand corridor that has all the warmth of a walk-in fridge. Maybe she can get a view of it from outside. She follows the kitchen garden's crumbly red-brick wall, until she sees a long line of windows. The glass is so dirty it's hard to see anything through the bottom panes. But in a nearby blanket of buttercups she spots a cane chair splitting apart, like a huge old basket. With some effort, she drags it over and clambers up, fearing she might plunge through its seat at any moment.

The ballroom ceiling is a field of pale green with corn-rows of gilt moulding, the floor a huge expanse of wonky dislodged parquet. Two teetering columns of stacked white chairs and the carcass of an old grand piano, its lid smashed. And . . . yes! A hydrangea! There really is a hydrangea growing through the floor, pressing its blue petals against the glass, like a hothouse flower. The tractor driver hadn't made it up. She can't wait to tell Jon.

Or should she?

There is a possibility he'll use it as evidence of the

house's unsuitability. Feeling a prickle of irritation – mostly at the idea of Jon, the one who's defensively taking form in his absence – she jumps off the chair, refusing to dwell on what the state of the ballroom might mean in terms of wedding practicalities, how the guests might eat and dance on such a floor in such a room. She's barely thinking about their wedding at all. No, other things have taken over.

There is still no sign of either Dill or Mrs Alton as she crosses the hall's chessboard tiles and creeps up the staircase, heart drumming at her own audacity, speeding up when she gets to the point on the first landing where she felt so peculiar on the first visit. There is one room in particular she's dying to revisit. She finds it easily enough on the third floor, the powder-blue door, the one Jon peered through and thought looked as if the children had just left. She nudges it open, immediately trips over a shoe.

She picks up a dirty white plimsoll, flexing it back and forth, light and rubbery in her hands, wondering to whom it might once have belonged. Desiccated sand falls from its heel and scatters across the floor, each grain a beach in miniature, a sandcastle, a summer long gone, she fancies. She respectfully places the plimsoll back where she found it, steps into the room, sure she can hear the chatter of children in the wind that blows through the gaps in the window frame, the repressed giggle of a child hiding behind the long yellow curtain, making the fabric shake.

There is the dappled grey rocking horse: it makes her think of the skull in the library now, so she quickly looks away. The well-thumbed books, some of their corners bookmark-turned. She crouches to the grubby floor, picks through bent boxes of Monopoly, broken toy tea sets, Matchbox cars, blunted colouring pencils, discovering a rickety wooden toy pram that looks like something that has endured centuries of bossy little girls. These must have belonged to the Alton children. She cannot help but tidy them, wiping away the dust, putting lids back on boxes, settling an old, balding teddy in the pram.

She remembers that her own mother kept many of her and Louise's favourite toys, wrapping them in old tea-towels and tucking them into boxes in the attic. Louise's have since been brought down, given to her own children. Lorna's remain, waiting. She always assumed, a little harshly, that her mother was a careful hoarder rather than a sentimentalist, but seeing this room, where toys really have been left to decompose in the damp, she's no longer so sure. Clearly things she took for granted are not taken for granted by all children. The idea makes her sad.

No, Mrs Alton is just not the type to treasure a child's beloved toy. But she is the type to treasure old clothes, Lorna thinks more cheerfully, standing up, brushing sand from her knees. After all, Mrs Alton still wears Chanel, albeit ragged. There could be a wardrobe of priceless dresses – Hardy Amies, Yves Saint Laurent, Courrèges – waiting to be discovered. Lorna steps back down the darkening stairway, almost tripping in her haste to get to the chamber floor, fingertips tingling at the thought of all the liquid satins and butterfly-wing silks waiting to be stroked.

The main bedroom on the first floor is enormous, cold and dusty, with an abandoned air. It does not smell of sleep but of time itself, a sort of dead mustiness. Lorna parts the heavy velvet curtains so that sunlight spills into the room, revealing Tiffany blue walls bloomed with damp. She explores the three doors leading off the bedroom. One opens into a bathroom, a free-standing copper bath stained green. Next to this is a small, pale blue dressing room. There is a silver hairbrush on the kidney-shaped dressing table. A powder puff the size of a side plate. A small portrait of what is unmistakably Mrs Alton in her blonde younger years posed, poised, perfect. Crushingly, nothing is in the wardrobe – tall, white, intricately carved – except a stack of blankets and a lethal-looking hair dryer sprouting wires. Perhaps Mrs Alton has taken all of her prize possessions to her living quarters in the east turret. Yes, that would make sense.

Still one more door off the bedroom. It's stiff and finally opens with a sigh of dust. Lorna coughs, covers her mouth, looks around, eyes widening as the air clears. Weirdly, this, too, seems to be a dressing room. Painted a pearly clam pink, prettier and bigger, it has its own door leading directly to the landing. Against one wall is a giant Narnia wardrobe, dark wood, carved paws for feet. There is also a wing-mirrored dressing-table, the mercury glass mottled and milky, and a *chaise longue* beneath the window. But it's the small photograph on the wall that pulls her towards it: a black-and-white photograph of a family – shiny quiffs, lampshade prom dresses, very 1950s – standing on the stoop of a house in front of the stars and stripes of an American flag. The first wife? Oh, God. Did Mr Alton preserve his first wife's dressing room, while letting his new wife use the smaller one opposite? Oh, poor Mrs Alton.

'Lorna?' Dill's voice sails towards her.

Lorna turns to see Dill standing in the dressing-room doorway, puzzled, beneath a filigree of backlit hair.

'I . . . I . . .' It occurs to Lorna how it must look – sneaking around the house, poking through a dead woman's things – and her cheeks burn.

'It's your fiancé, Tom. Jon, sorry.'

'Jon?' His name sounds strange. As if he belongs in another life entirely.

'On the office phone. He says it's urgent.'

Fourteen

Amber, Fitzroy Square, April 1969

'Go on, say, "Cheese!"' Barney steps backwards on to the pavement, squinting, camera skew-whiff in his hands. 'And stop blinking, will you?'

Matilda and I crush ourselves together, arm in arm, heads cocked, her straight brown hair mixing with mine, red and unruly.

'Done.' Barney unloops Matilda's camera from his neck and runs back up the steps into the house, pleased to have helped Matilda at least.

Barney likes Matilda. Everyone who matters likes Matilda. The show-pony girls at school tease her for being too big and too tall and wearing glasses. Matilda says she's not looking for any more friends. From anyone else this would sound like a cover-up but from Matilda it isn't. Matilda doesn't suffer like the rest of us. She's not bombarded by feelings all the time. Neither does she doubt herself. I've never seen Matilda blush, hide her body in the showers or apologize when something's not her fault. Matilda just is. She doesn't change for anyone. I cannot bear to say goodbye.

'You should be coming with me, Amber,' she says, picking up her overnight bag from the stone step and swinging it over her shoulder so that the messages we scribbled each other last night on the inside of the strap are hidden. She starts to walk down the steps, stops. 'Last chance to change your mind? I'm sure Mummy could still get you on the flight.'

I bite my bottom lip to stop myself saying, 'Let's go!' and bolting down the steps with her into the sparkling spring sunshine, away from the anniversary of Momma's death.

Greece for the Easter holidays. Matilda says we'll turn as brown as our school brogues and eat salty black olives and swim in a sea that doesn't scald you scarlet with cold. Fred and Annabel will be there too, which is particularly exciting as Annabel has dropped out of Swiss finishing school to work in a Kensington boutique and have sex: she says that sex is like smoking, horrible the first time, but if you persevere it can start to feel quite nice, and then you cannot imagine life without it.

'Amber? Come. Please.'

'I can't – really.' It's not that Daddy would stop me: he's become so vague recently he can be persuaded into most things. But I haven't seen Toby for a whole term now. I miss him so much, even the things about him that frustrate me, especially those: the way he makes every moment so intense. It's hard to explain any of this to Matilda, who simply thinks her brother Fred is irritating and to be avoided, so I don't even try.

A few days after I'd found Toby sitting on my bed in the dark, incandescent with fury that I'd 'sneaked into Lucian's room to be Nursey', he was expelled, and shunted to a new school in the depths of Hertfordshire. To be fair, he'd hit a notorious bully, who just happened to be a cabinet minister's son, taking out a tooth. Daddy was furious about this – the boy's father is a founding member of his London club – and even more furious, I think, that Toby has grown so unlike him: Toby with his brilliant, quicksilver brain – 'like a ferret in a sack', one tutor wrote – his disrespect for school and loathing of rugby, the sheer bloody-minded impossibility of him. Momma, of course, thought all these traits (admittedly less marked then) charming – 'The world doesn't need another dull old-school tie,' she'd say – and would advise Toby to be true to himself and find 'that little precious thing that makes you happy', as if you could sort through life as you would the beach, slipping the shiniest bits into your pocket. She never wanted Toby to be anything but who he was.

'Last chance?' asks Matilda, shaking me out of my thoughts.

I feel the dead weight of Black Rabbit Hall on my shoulders. 'It's not that I don't want to.'

The Hollywells' driver arrives. Matilda blows me kisses from behind the car window, then she's gone, taking all the carefree fun of being fifteen with her.

The train judders west, slowly at first, through the sooty bricks of Paddington, then speeding up as the houses get smaller and lower and cleaner and the gardens lengthen before disappearing entirely into a rush of fields, green, yellow, green, the view somehow synchronizing with the flavours of the boiled sweets – lime, lemon, lime – that I shake out into my palm. Other things too. The push and pull of Black Rabbit Hall.

Toby – who has been there a week already as his new

school finished earlier than ours – is sucking me towards the place, like a magnet. But there's the opposite charge too, the knowledge that this new Easter holiday – one year on, how have I survived it? – will push Momma even further back into the past, widen the gap between now and the last moment I heard the click of her riding boot on the kitchen floor. Someone will take a photograph of us all and she won't be in it. Worse, the house and gardens will be stirring with life – wallflowers, bluebells, dew steaming off the lawns in the morning – and she loved that. She'd hate to miss it. Momma's pleasure in spring was one of the pleasures *of* spring. I wonder then if all children just love the things that make their mothers happy. If that's what it comes down to, really.

Momma liked trains too, especially sleepers. But the open road made more sense to her. Before we were all born, she and Daddy drove from America's east coast to its west in a green Cadillac so she loved the drive to Cornwall. This time last year we were driving down in the Rolls, oblivious to what was going to happen, Daddy at the wheel, Momma singing at the top of her voice, seats down in the back, Barney and Kitty rolling about in sleeping-bags, my head on Toby's lap, book swaying over my head, windows wide open waiting for the first smell of the sea.

A year on, that's all gone, all the insignificant bits you don't think you'll miss but do. Daddy says I'm old enough to manage the others on the train without Toby – 'I dare say it will be far easier without your twin brother, as most things are these days' – and that we can no longer afford to waste money on luxuries like chauffeured cars because the investments aren't working as they should.

It doesn't feel that easy.

Every time my head drops against the window, Kitty pulls at my sleeve, demanding I cut the crusts off Nette's cheese and pickle sandwiches or read to her (*The Tale of Peter Rabbit*, over and over), or else Barney needs the loo. As I don't want to leave Kitty on her own in case something terrible happens – Nanny Meg leaves her newspaper open in the nursery and it's full of terrible things happening to children at the hands of strangers who look just like the passengers in the corridor outside our compartment – we all have to tunnel into the narrow aisle, Kitty moaning, Barney holding his crotch, Boris beating his tail. We clear our own compartment pretty quickly.

By the time we get to the station, Barney, Kitty and Boris are all asleep. I have not slept. Olive groves, Greek boys and hot white alleyways, heavy with the scent of jasmine, have kept me restless on the itchy carpeting of the seat. They distract me from an irrational terror that Toby might die just before we arrive.

'Wake up! We're here!' I shake their shoulders.

Barney sits up, rubbing his eyes, but I can't rouse Kitty. We struggle out of the train on to the empty platform, Kitty slumped in my arms, her sweaty cheek stuck to my neck, Barney dropping bits of luggage, Boris barking. The train rumbles down the track, leaving us alone on the platform, separated from Toby only by a taxi ride and the river Fal.

'Amber?' Barney squints up at me.

'Not now, Barns.' I'm sweating under the dead weight of Kitty, unable to see the taxi, hoping that Peggy has not forgotten to arrange one.

'It's just that Kitty's wetting herself.' He points to the back of Kitty's skirt, drops splashing to the platform.

The taxi driver is called Tel and fat, car-tilting-to-the-right fat, but nice. Most Cornish taxi drivers are pretty nice, I've discovered, and always seem to have a cousin once removed who worked at Black Rabbit Hall or know Peggy's sprawling family down the coast. 'This Easter is going to be a scorcher.' He smiles at me in the mirror, dangling his elbow out of the car window, like a cut of meat. 'Hope you've packed your cossies.'

'We have, thank you,' I reply politely and stare out of the window, hoping he's not going to talk all the way to Black Rabbit Hall, or complain about the wee smell, which is quite strong, even though I managed to shove Kitty into fresh knickers and stuff the soiled ones into an empty sandwich box.

But Tel doesn't say anything, either because he knows about Momma and feels sorry for us or because the smell is masked by other smells, like Boris. But he does wind down his window. It jams halfway. Sea air rushes through the gap and blows our heads from London to Black Rabbit Hall. We slowly feel more like ourselves. Familiar landmarks blink by: tea shops, old people's homes, undertakers, the King Harry Ferry grinding across the glassy green river on clanking chains. More twisting lanes. Then, at last, the sign at the bottom of the drive. My heart starts to beat faster. Boris's ears arrow.

Black Rabbit Hall rises on the hill, daring us to doubt its existence ever again. Toby sits on the steps, waiting.

'Toby!' I jump out of the cab, flying across the gravel.

We hug tightly and it feels like all the bits that are

scattered – the parts of me that never settle without him around – root back to their rightful place. But I quickly spot the difference in him. It is not just that Toby is taller, skinnier, his body hardened and sharpened, as if he's spent the last few months bare-fist fighting in a pit, there's something else too: a wariness in his manner, as if he has forgotten how to be with someone he trusts. There are things going on behind his gold-flecked eyes that I can't quite read. I'm about to ask him what the matter is, what he's been up to these last few days down here without us, when the last of our bags hits the gravel, puffing up golden dust.

'That's yer lot,' shouts Tel, turning the car back down the drive. He winks at Toby. 'Nice motor.'

I follow the blaze of Toby's eyes to the gleam of dragon-fly blue beneath the bushes, its silver snout more bullet than motor-car.

'Wow, whose is that, Toby?'

The twisted scowl on his face is my thrilling answer.

Lucian smokes at the edge of the woods, like a dead person come brilliantly back to life. My stomach lurches. I hadn't expected to see him again, which is why it's been safe to think about him in the stuffy dark of my bedroom all these months, pillow clamped hot between my thighs, reliving the hard smoothness of his stomach beneath my fingertips, the sticky warmth of his blood, the way that snowy winter's night in his bedroom pulsed with heat and stars.

And here he is! His sports car in the drive! Smoking in our garden! It is so improbable, so unexpected, that I can do nothing but stare dumbly. The cigarette travels with compelling speed back to his mouth the moment he exhales. He flicks his fringe – longer than I remember it, winging across one eye – off his face, grinds the cigarette out with his shoe, lights *another*.

'Smoking himself silly.' Peggy appears at my shoulder, making me start. 'Will you go and tell him it's time for tea?'

I nod, but am unable to move from the kitchen window. The idea of approaching Lucian – talking to him! – fills me with terror. What if he takes one look at me and *knows?*

'He must be hungry. Came down from London this morning to meet his mother, who wasn't here, of course.' Peggy shakes her head, tuts beneath her breath. 'I don't believe he even had lunch.'

'When is she coming?' I can already hear the chilling tack-tap of Caroline's heels across our hall.

'This evening. With your father, I believe. Manners, Kitty. Use your cake fork, not your fingers. You're not a skipper.' She sniffs, looking rather put out. 'I was only told yesterday. Been rushing around madly ever since, getting things ready. Of course, sod's law, there's something nasty brewing in the first-floor bathroom pipes.' She suppresses a small smile. 'Now sit yourself down, Amber,' she says, mercifully forgetting about me going to get Lucian.

I lock myself between Barney and Kitty, heat of the range against my back.

'You're all of a fidget today.' Peggy eyes me curiously. 'A slice of fruit cake?' The door slams. She looks up. 'Oh, Toby, there you are. I was wondering where you'd got to.

Oh, just look at you. All skin and bones! Is the new school canteen that bad? Don't worry, I'll cut you a good fat slice. No, not you, Kitty. Not unless you want to turn into Billy Bunter.'

Toby wedges in, foot scuffing anxiously on the floor, muttering about how we must spend tomorrow morning on the beach, first swim of the year. Peggy topples cake on to our plates, chattering to anyone who will listen. 'A *birthday* present that car was!' She lowers her voice, a raindrop gleam in her grey eyes. 'Can you imagine? Don't you be getting any funny ideas, Toby.'

'Unlikely,' he says, and for the first time since we got back, we laugh.

We know that we're lucky to get a bicycle for our birthday. Most of the time we're given things we don't particularly want, a gold brooch handed down from a great-aunt we don't remember, Grandpa's chipped glass marbles in an ivory box. Only Aunt Bay is known for her brilliant presents, deliciously plasticky things, smelling of America, often edible.

'Can we have a ride in the car? Lucian's car?' asks Barney, standing on tiptoe, trying to catch sight of it through the window.

'Certainly not. Sit down.' Peggy bends over Kitty from behind, firmly wrapping her fingers correctly around the fork. 'It looks like a right death trap. I wouldn't set foot in it if you paid me.' She wipes her brow with the back of her hand and looks up at me, irritated, remembering what she'd asked a few minutes ago. 'Amber, will you *please* go and get Lucian in for tea? No, really. Now.'

*

'Tea,' I say matter-of-factly, scared to meet his eyes. But I can see he is looking at me, through the strands of his fringe, shyly. The shyness is surprising.

'Sorry about turning up again like this.' He digs into his black blazer pocket – he's dressed all in black, like a highwayman – pulls out another cigarette and lights it with the kind of chunky silver army lighter that Toby would kill for. 'It's my girlfriend's party in Devon in a couple of days. Ma insisted on me visiting her at Pencraw first.' He pulls on the cigarette. 'But she's not here.'

'Devon?' The word 'girlfriend' echoes mockingly in my head. It is at this awful moment that I realize I haven't changed out of the clothes I wore on the train and probably smell of Kitty's wee.

'Bigbury Grange.' His voice trails off and he looks at the ground, as if wishing he hadn't mentioned it.

'Oh.' Bigbury Grange is one of the finest houses in the West Country, a huge estate, sugar-paste white, and much gossiped about a few years ago when the Brace-wells – 'Newly minted frozen-food millionaires,' sniffed Daddy – had bought it from old friends of my parents, the impoverished Lord and Lady Fraser, who could only afford to heat the gatekeeper's cottage and eat pheasants and raw honey from the hives. 'Well, tea if you want it,' I say, trying to hide my crashing spirits, turning back to the house.

He throws down his cigarette, unsmoked, and stamps on it. 'I'll come with you.'

We walk up the slope of lawn, his hand swinging about six inches from mine. I sneak a sidelong glance at him and blush furiously when it meets his.

When we reach the terrace, he says in a fast, garbled way, words pushed up together: '*Doyouwanttogoforadriveto-morrowmorning?*'

'I . . .' I glance back at the house, see Toby watching us from the kitchen window, a fleshy pale dot where his forehead is pressed against the glass.

'It's a Lotus Elan.' His jet eyes glitter. 'The roof rolls down and stuff.'

'I said I'd go to the beach with Toby,' I say, forcing the words out against my will, like when Matilda asked me to Greece.

'Of course,' he says quickly, as if it didn't matter anyway, and we walk into the house in embarrassed silence.

Tomorrow arrives, flat as a cancelled party. From my bedroom window, I spot Caroline, who arrived late last night but is already up, inspecting the flower borders, lilac headscarf knotted under her chin, enormous white-framed sunglasses. Worse, after breakfast she announces an 'Easter family luncheon', chin raised, eyes showing too much white, like a declaration of war. 'One o'clock sharp in the dining room,' she adds, shooting an expectant smile across the room to Daddy, as if anticipating praise for taking control of a household where nothing has happened 'sharp' in living memory. 'Latecomers will pay the price in lost Easter eggs.' She laughs shrilly.

Unwilling to take the risk that she might not be joking – not after last year's chocolate wash-out – Barney and Kitty scamper between Big Bertie and Black Rabbit Hall's other clocks, trying to work out the right time. Then, sensibly deciding that none are to be trusted, they hover beside the sundial on the terrace, impatiently waiting for the shadow to creep across its bronze face like a frown, leaving me and Toby to go to the beach alone.

'Well, I'm not going to the lunch if you're not,' I say, as we trudge back from the beach along the cliff path, bags heavy with sandy towels and wet swimming costumes, watching out for the adders that nest in the long grasses, stirred by the unexpected spring heat.

As I walk I start to feel my fingers and toes again. The sea – a shimmering iceberg blue today – was bearable for only a few seconds. Toby stayed in far longer than I did, his skin boiled red, gasping at the cold, as if he was enjoying the pain of it. I insisted he get out in the end, worried that he'd stiffen and float out into the ocean, like a driftwood log.

'A *family* lunch!' snorts Toby. 'Since when were that ridiculous woman and her spoilt son family?'

I swing the heavy straw beach bag over my shoulder, thinking that Lucian should be spoilt but isn't somehow. His joy in the sports car seemed genuine. 'It's all a bit odd, isn't it?' I say mildly, hoping to calm him down.

'No, it's not odd! Or random or coincidental, Amber. That's the flipping point! The Shawcross invasion is going *exactly* to plan. It's been executed by Caroline, sure as a military exercise. Why else would they be here again?'

'You know why. What Daddy said.' The Shawcrosses were to join friends in Gloucestershire for Easter but the friends had cancelled at the last minute, leaving their guests at a loose end. So Daddy had done 'the decent thing' and invited them here, 'as everyone got on so terribly well at Christmas'.

'That's rot and you know it.' Toby kicks a stone over the cliff, spinning it into nothingness. He shoots me a sidelong glance. 'I've been working on a contingency plan, these last few days. Since I heard they were coming.'

'A what?' I ask, not liking the sound of it.

'It's a surprise. In the woods.'

I like the sound of it even less.

'It's not quite ready, though.'

'Oh, Toby. Just go along with lunch today,' I say, trying again, fearing yet another row between Daddy and him. I realize now that Momma was the bridge between their two clashing personalities. The long school terms don't help: Daddy looks at Toby as if he doesn't recognize him sometimes. 'Please?'

'Stop trying to be peacemaker. Incredibly tiresome.'

I look away, furious that Toby is beyond manipulation, even when it's in his best interest. It's almost as if he sees things too clearly, in unforgiving sharp focus, like someone looking at skin through a magnifying glass and seeing only its ugly bumps and hairs. 'Daddy will be awfully upset if you don't come.'

'Well, *I'm* awfully upset he's invited the Antichrist to stay on the anniversary of Momma's death. Aren't you?' With no warning, he lurches towards the cliff edge and, to my horror, poles off it on one arm, so that in a blink only his shock of red hair is visible, two fists gripping the snake-nest cliff grass. I lunge forward, reaching for his hands. 'Tob –'

He releases his fingers. There is a sickening scuffle of stones, the sound of something heavy falling. Wild laughter.

I peer tentatively over the edge. He is on a ledge a few feet below, a narrow band of flat rock, like a camp bed sticking out from the cliff. It's a ledge I've seen hundreds of times from the beach but never considered attempting to land on. But the parts of the estate that seemed dangerous when Momma was alive seem less so now. After all, if you can die just falling from a horse, you may as well climb to the top of a tree.

'Swing your feet over, sis! Don't look down!'

I hesitate, wondering if I can play it to my advantage. 'Only if you come to the Easter lunch.'

'Boring,' he says, which means yes.

I have to do it then, crawling backwards on my hands and knees, one foot dangling in mid-air.

'Foot hole to the left. No, no, left, not right, you twit! I've got you. Really, I've got you. Let *go*. Amber, you actually have to let go of the grass. The dangling is the dangerous bit. Believe me, I've been practising. You can't hang there. Trust me. Leap of faith.'

'Argh.' I grab him as I land – the drop only a few feet but feeling much more – making us both wobble precariously. I squat, root myself on the rock floor: it feels safer than standing. 'You scare me sometimes, Toby.'

'Why? I'll always catch you,' he says simply. And I know he will.

'This must be how gulls feel.' The view is dizzying, almost too beautiful. It makes my eyes water. 'Like we're sitting in the sky.'

'We are.' He grins — one of his charming, crazy grins — and peels off his shirt, exposing a startling winter-white chest, spinning it above his head before tossing it over the edge with a whoop. He leans over fearlessly, watches it flutter to the rocks below.

'You've gone quite nuts alone here,' I say, rolling my eyes, wondering what Daddy and Caroline will think when he struts into the house half naked.

He lurches back, stretching out his legs, head rolling heavy on my crossed knees, as if he doesn't need to ask because I belong to him again. The distance I felt earlier is closing. But I still feel uneasy.

We stay like this in silence for a while. A grey-winged kittiwake eyes us warily from its seaweed nest in a crevice nearby. The wind picks up. My legs go dead. Toby closes his eyes, lids flickering madly. I peer down at him breathing, quick, intense breaths, like inside he's still running, and wonder about the yellowing bruises on his biceps, the surprise waiting for me in the woods and how the splatter of fiery freckles stirring on his cheekbones somehow look like warnings about the days to come.

Fifteen

Toby makes it impossible for me to behave normally around Lucian. The most mundane moments – passing the water jug, or each other on the stairs – have become oddly charged and clumsy. When I have to speak to Lucian in Toby's presence my voice always sounds too high, my laugh too shrill. Even when Toby's nowhere near, the self-consciousness follows me like an awkward friend, made worse by the fear that Toby will pop up at any minute, eyes narrowed, territorial as a tom cat.

This morning, thank goodness, I don't have to worry. It's D Day: Toby is finishing the project in the woods. After wolfing his breakfast, he'd stalked off, swinging a mallet from one hand, a tent of rusty chicken wire over a shoulder.

As soon as Toby's out of view, Caroline presses the napkin to the corners of her mouth and suggests that I show Lucian the cove: he and I glance at each other for a blaze of a second, look away in embarrassment. But Caroline's suggestion remains, shimmering above the bowl of cold stewed apple, just within my grasp.

'Well? Gracious, you're both very silent this morning, I must say.' She sips her tea delicately. 'But I do think you should get some colour into those pale cheeks before you leave for the shooting party at Bigbury Grange tomorrow, Lucian. The Bracewells are terribly outdoorsy. You don't want Belinda to think you're just a city boy, do you?'

I try to hide my crush of disappointment at him leaving by playing with the edge of a fork.

'What the beach lacks in amenities, it makes up for in seclusion,' Caroline continues, placing her cup carefully on the saucer, sunlight catching on its gold rim. 'It's rather like being marooned at the end of the world. You won't see another soul.'

'Crabs have souls,' Barney points out shyly, throwing a crust to Boris beneath the table. 'But Momma says the soul has probably gone by the time you actually eat the crab sandwich, so it's fine to eat the sandwich.'

Caroline's smile vanishes at the mention of my mother. 'What a curious idea,' she manages, the words sliding between her tiny teeth. She gets up abruptly, cup of tea not finished, and leaves the room. Which is something.

I discover that I'm far less likely to be a twit around Lucian when I'm in motion. Walking, I can hide an unexpected blush with my hand (and there is only one hot cheek to hide). I don't have to look into his eyes either, reveal things I don't want to. And knowing that Toby is nowhere nearby stops the words knotting quite so thickly on my tongue. This is not so bad.

We climb the cliff path like stairs, up and down the headland, cutting over the dry-stone walls, the scrambles of windblown pine. The spring sun feels hotter – closer – on the cliffs. Wind gusts beneath my skirt, trying to flip it inside out like an umbrella in a storm. I push it down and secretly check to see if Lucian's looking at my legs. He is.

But Kitty is trying to make him look at her, swinging from his hand, chattering and giggling. If Lucian finds her as trying as I do, he doesn't show it. Neither does he dismiss Barney's endless patter of questions – 'Would someone with fifteen fingers play the guitar better than someone with ten?' – but patiently answers each one, so that we have very little time to talk about anything that might matter. He smiles at me sometimes, looking up through his dark fringe while he's talking to them, when I least expect it, and it's a funny, shy half-smile that makes me forget about Toby and nesting adders and the fact he has a stinking-rich girlfriend called Belinda who lives in a house in Devon with central heating and no blood splatters outside the stables.

When we get to the edge of the cliff – just above the ledge where Toby and I lay the day before – Barney pulls on his arm and points proudly. 'That's our beach.'

Lucian glances across at me, a smile playing on his lips. 'You made it sound huge.'

'Did I?' I don't know how to explain that it felt huge when I was a little kid and somehow still does.

Barney starts to gambol down the narrow rumble of stones to the sand. He gets there before anyone else, happily wading where the underground stream skirts out as a bubbling petticoat of water. Back in his element.

In the distance, the sea is jelly green, the tide so far out you can see the stumpy brown ribs of the little rowing boat poking out of hard rills of sand. I tell Lucian the locals say it's the remains of an old smugglers' boat and he listens intently, staring at my mouth as I talk.

We sit down on some rocks, smooth and grey as seals' backs, almost a yard apart. He takes off his shoes. I can't help but notice that his feet are very pale and soft-looking, as if they have been wrapped in socks far too long and never run free. Something about them makes me feel rather sorry for him.

We chat about nothing much – the weather, how a high tide can cut this beach right off – and Kitty wanders away with her bucket, scouring the foamy strandline for shells and smooth green glass. Barney rolls up his trousers, paddling along the shore. I watch Barney closely – you can never take your eyes off him by the water – but still manage to sneak the odd glance at Lucian, while pretending not to.

'You're lucky having all this,' he says, pulling one leg towards him, letting the other dangle long. I notice how the black hairs on his legs stop in a perfect bracelet around his ankle, his very own strandline.

'I know.' I squeeze my skirt between my knees so that it doesn't fly up again, even though a part of me rather wishes it would. 'We don't need a bigger beach.'

'I don't mean the beach.'

I turn to him, puzzled, pulling a lock of hair out of my mouth. 'What then?'

He gazes at Kitty, rattling her bucket of shells. 'Brothers, sisters, you know.' He shrugs.

I try to imagine a silent world without responsibilities and divided loyalties and squabbles over the biggest slice of cake. 'It must be nice to have peace and quiet too.'

'Not really,' he says, digging his toes into the sand. 'That's why I started to play the guitar.'

'Well, if you had noisy brothers and sisters you'd probably never have learned to play it like you do.' Realizing I've revealed that I've been listening (ear pressed to the floorboards), my face explodes. I cover my cheek with my hand, feel the heat of my blood pulsing through my fingers.

'You know what?' He drags his heel across the sand, leaving a trench that quickly fills with water.

'What?'

'I wanted a twin.'

'That's funny.' I laugh.

'A brother twin. Someone to do boy things with.'

'I do boy things,' I say indignantly.

'Yeah, I know.' Is that a funny sort of respect in his eyes or is he mocking me? I can't tell.

The uncertainty makes me say the wrong thing: 'I cannot imagine you being a twin.'

'Why not?' He looks put out.

'You're too . . .' I'm not sure how to explain that he has solid edges and Toby and I have blurred ones. That Toby is left-handed and I am right-handed, that sometimes it's like there's a mirror line between us. '. . . complete as you are, I think.'

His laughter erupts across the beach. I've never heard Lucian laugh like that before. Like something smashing out of him. I see then what I suspected in his bedroom at Christmas: he is impossible not to like. Beneath all his deadpan sullenness there is warmth and laughter: it's like finding shiny gold coins in mud.

'So you feel incomplete without Toby?' he says, when the laughter subsides and his face closes once more.

'It's not quite like that,' I say quickly, even though in many ways it is.

He frowns up at the cliff. 'Where is he? I haven't seen him all morning.'

'Woods.' I shrug, even though the question makes my heart patter. It's as if in asking he's creating the possibility that Toby isn't in the woods but scrambling furiously along the cliff path towards us. 'Making something. He won't tell me what.'

'Intriguing.'

I feel a bit embarrassed on Toby's behalf. It strikes me how much more grown-up Lucian is than Toby, far more than the extra two years. I cannot imagine Lucian making things in the woods at fifteen, or whooping across the river on a swing. Did part of Toby stop developing when Momma died? Did part of all of us? Our bodies changed but inside we stayed the age we were then.

I suddenly want to grow up, and quickly.

'When do you reckon he'll finish?' he asks hesitantly.

'Oh, he'll probably be out there all day. Won't leave anything alone until it's done.'

'Right.' Lucian pushes his foot into the sand, back and forth, as if trying to decide whether to ask me something. Then he does.

'Faster!' I shout over the engine, sounding thrillingly unlike myself.

'Sure?' He laughs.

'Yes!' The car roof is pushed back like a pram hood. The air rushes into my mouth. 'Yes, yes, yes!'

'Hold tight!'

The engine growls – and it's like we're riding a living thing, not a car at all. It splices the cliff road in half, scattering gulls and butterflies, throwing me against the side on bends. I twist, steadying myself with a hand on the glossy wooden dashboard. Black Rabbit Hall is a doll's house in the distance.

'My hair!' I shriek, because it's candy-flossing above my head, catching in my mouth.

'I love your hair.'

I love your hair. Could that really be what he said? It's so hard to hear over the roar of the engine. But it makes me grin stupidly anyway. I never want to get out of this amazing little car that can take you away so quickly from somewhere so big and inescapable that, within seconds, it's like it never existed at all.

'Fun?' he asks, his hair streaming too, flat black feathers. 'Damn.'

A huddle of sheep is pouring out of a farm gate into the lane. We're going to crash into them but we don't – the brakes screech and I'm thrown forward in my seat, laughing – and I love this, the cheating of the bad thing, the writing over the disaster. The sheep stagger up the bank, push up against the fence. Lucian reverses back down the lane, while the farmer shakes his fist.

We park, then sit on the white bench at the edge of the cliff, gazing out at the slowly shifting purple and green patches on the ocean, like a pod of whales deep below the surface. My legs feel wobbly, disoriented, just as they do on solid ground after I've been on a boat in choppy water. The back of my cotton dress is sodden with sweat. Lucian is sitting so close to me that if I moved my leg just two inches to the right it would touch his. And I can feel him staring, as if his eyes are all over me, soft and warm as hands. I'm not sure I can remember a nicer feeling. I try to store it up, so I can tell Matilda about it in detail when I'm back in London.

'Sorry for nearly killing you.'

'That was the best bit actually.' I dare to meet his gaze. His pupils have eclipsed the chocolaty iris and he has an odd expression of awe on his face, as if he's not seeing me but someone wondrous.

Then, because I'm overexcited and scared that I'm going to say the wrong thing, I say, 'I have dead flies in my hair,' and ruin the moment completely.

He reaches over and, with agonizing slowness, picks out a midge, running it down the hair shaft, flicking it off at the end. He does it again. Everything sucks tight inside. This is already the most perfect moment of my life so far.

'Done.'

'Thanks.' I sound almost normal. Inside, everything is liquid.

'Toby's going to go mad, isn't he?'

'I won't tell him,' I say, panicking less about Toby finding out and stabbing Lucian repeatedly with the penknife than the drive coming to an end. My eyes fall to his lips and I wonder what it would be like to kiss him, if a boy's mouth has a particular taste. 'I love the motor-car. Let's go out again.'

'Amber . . .' he says, then stops. For a wild, magical moment, I think he's going to kiss me. That everything – the night in his room at Christmas, sitting on the rock in the cove watching Kitty fill her bucket with shells – has been leading to this point. I brace myself, trying to remember how people kiss in books, terrified about doing it wrong, clashing teeth and noses.

But he doesn't kiss me. He stands up. 'Let's go.'

My spirits crash, then fly again when he pulls me up by my hands. His are hot, quite damp and feel wonderfully big. My skirt flutters in the wind and I'm sure that if he lets go I'll fly off the cliff like a kite.

'I'll get you home.' He grins, that wonderful surprising grin. 'And this time I promise to drive like a vicar.'

'Thank you,' I say, desperately wishing he would do neither.

Sixteen

I should have known Toby would lead us all the way up here. Not in our usual place by the swing but further upstream where the trees get confusing, the creek narrows, seeming to flow in two directions at once, and the bank drops so steeply that if you slip in it's really hard to get out.

Barney holds my hand a little tighter. We stop, tense in the restless solitude of the deep wood. Where is he? And that's when we hear a hoot.

'That's him.' Toby does owl hoots better than anybody.

And there he is, a dart of red, nimble as a deer. When we finally catch up with him, he is leaning, barely out of breath, against an old apple ladder that reaches into the swollen belly of a huge tree. At the top of the ladder – about ten feet up – there is a platform made from old planks, willow and stolen bits of kitchen-garden fencing, leading into the tree's lightning-charred hollow.

'You built this tree house?' I say, beginning to grasp the level of feverish activity that must have taken place in the days while he waited for us to return to Black Rabbit Hall.

'Caroline has her plans. I have mine.' Toby nods, eyes sparkling, hair in tight sweat-damp curls. 'I am one step ahead, Amber.'

'Kitty doesn't like it,' my little sister says, tugging on my hand. 'Nor does Raggedy Doll. It's too high.'

'Think of it like a Wendy house.' Toby squats down to Kitty's eye level, trying to reassure her. 'You've always wanted a Wendy house, haven't you? Come on, let's go up.'

Kitty shakes her head. 'I will fall.'

'You won't. Not if you tell yourself you won't.' Toby taps his head. 'Falling is all in the mind.'

'He's right, Kitty. That's why I don't sink in the sea,' says Barney, matter-of-factly. 'I tell myself I won't and I don't.'

Toby ruffles his hair. 'Good man, Barns.' He leaps up the first two steps, making the whole structure sway.

'Are you absolutely sure it's safe?' I ask, anxious about Kitty, not known for her climbing skills, going so high.

'Safest place on the estate,' says Toby, sounding slightly weird again, making me wish I hadn't asked.

I'm the last to go up, pushing through a hatch of chicken wire. I cannot help but imagine Toby jamming it behind us and being stuck in here forever, no one knowing where to find us. As I crawl in, knees sore against roughly nailed planks, I sense that I've crawled into Toby's head. And, for once, I'm not sure I like it.

The interior seems airless, as if we were underground, even though we're high enough to break our backs if we fall. There is a narrow bed – an old camp mat on top of a bed of pine needles – a neatly stacked pyramid of tinned foods and beers, dusty bottles of wine stolen from the cellars, a tin cup and a hand-drawn map of the estate on the wall, with odd red arrows labelled 'escape', which make the hairs on my arms prickle. Worse, I spot the small pistol from the drawer in the library lying beside the bed and a huge knife hanging perilously from a nail, a knife that Great-Grandpa used for skinning stags.

Toby switches on a torch, bringing to life strange bits of his face: tunnel of nostrils, the angry shelf of his eyebrows. 'I can tell you don't like it.'

I try to smile. 'I do, it's just . . . that knife.' I point to it, dangling perilously over Barney's head. 'I don't like that.'

'Out of the way, Barney.' Toby pulls it down off its hook, shoves it under the pillow. 'Happy?'

'The gun. We're not allowed to touch the guns.'

He shrugs. 'We're not allowed to do lots of things.'

'Is it loaded?'

'Stop the old-lady fussing, will you?' He crouches forward to the edge of the platform and pushes back a bit of garden netting that he's camouflaged with leaves. 'Barns, come here.'

Obediently, Barney crawls forward. I stare at the gun, a chill running up and down my spine like cold fingers, wondering how I will remove it, if I should warn Lucian.

'If you sit still at dusk, you can see badgers, deer . . .'

Barney's eyes grow wide. He flicks them back at me for reassurance. 'Ghosts?'

'No ghosts, not yet,' says Toby. 'But there are rabbits. Many, many rabbits, and hares.'

'I don't like rabbits.' Barney crawls back from the edge, pushes up against me.

Toby and I exchange glances and I know we're thinking the same thing: nothing will ever be right until Barney loves rabbits again. This is just another of those things that we don't want to be true but is.

'Anyone for a jelly baby?' asks Toby, because it's depressing to linger on rabbits and the way each of us is no longer who we were in the process of becoming when Momma was alive. 'I've stolen Peggy's secret supply.'

Kitty starts pushing the sweets into her mouth faster and faster. For a while there is just the noise of the trees and birds and us chewing, until she says, 'Why isn't Lucian here?'

Everything silences, even the birds. Kitty freezes, the jelly baby a small lump in her cheek. Only her big blue eyes move from side to side, from me to Toby and back again.

I stay silent, fearing that whatever I say will be misinterpreted by Toby or, far worse, will invite Kitty to make a direct reference to our beach trip. Although I'm not sure why it must be kept secret – Caroline suggested it, I haven't done anything wrong – I have decided it's easier to say nothing.

'I like Lucian,' says Barney, coming to Kitty's aid. 'And I like his car because it's really shiny, isn't it, Amber?'

I swallow hard. Did Barney see us drive off after lunch? How could he? I deliberately took them to the ballroom to play on tricycles, so they wouldn't see me get into the car or ask questions.

'But I *don't* like Lucian's mummy,' Kitty adds, starting to chew more cheerfully again. 'She's like a seagull that wants your chips.'

Toby laughs, a short, hard laugh that breaks the tension, a karate hand through glass. It's actually quite useful to have an enemy to laugh at, I realize. Everything will be okay as long as the enemy is someone else.

Seventeen

Daddy looks up from his papers with a frown. He takes off his glasses and rubs his eyes, leaving a crease on the bridge of his nose that gleams in the morning light filtering through the tall library windows. 'What can I do for you, darling?'

'I wondered if we could talk, Daddy.'

'Talk?' Daddy says, as if I've suggested something outlandish. 'Oh, I suppose I could do with a break from this lot anyway.' He pushes the stack of papers away from him. Sticks his silver fountain pen in his breast pocket.

I glance out of the window to see a slice of Lucian's car, already packed, the neck of the guitar sticking out of the open boot. Should I go and say goodbye? I have no idea when I'll see him again. Today – the day Lucian leaves and everything returns to normal – already seems greyer, full of the old problems, a world looking back not forward.

'Peggy's done a formidable job of managing the estate in the last few months, but I'm afraid some things have inevitably passed under the radar.' Daddy looks glumly down at the papers.

'What sort of things?'

'Bills, goddamn bills, Amber. I'd be better off tossing my cash into the Fal than throwing it at this house. But don't look so worried. The Altons always find a way.' He blows out, lifting his coarsened silver hair. 'We won't lose the house. I'll make damn sure of it.'

This fighting talk makes me feel more anxious.

'But I've had my head in the sand far too long.' He loosens his collar. 'About time I dealt with it, Caroline's quite right.' What's *she* doing advising him? Daddy impatiently gestures at the other side of the desk. 'Sit, darling.'

I pull up the stool, elbows on the spongy green leather top of the huge desk – Toby says Daddy makes us sit on the other side of it to shrink us to a more manageable size – trying to ignore Knight in his black velvet-lined box, everything that happened that night still whirling silently in the star-shattered hole of his skull.

'So?' says Daddy, his smile not quite as open as it was a few moments ago.

I shift on the stool. 'Well, it's Toby.'

'I feared it might be.' Daddy shuffles papers that don't need to be shuffled, thumping them into a straight pile. 'Nose put out of joint by Lucian, I gather. Devilishly unfriendly. I expected better of him.'

'Well, it's not really that,' I say, wondering who suggested this version of events. Caroline probably. 'Daddy, he's built this tree house.'

'A tree house? Really? Where?'

'At the far end of the woods. Upriver. He's got food in there, a knife, a bed . . . a gun. Daddy, he's taken the pistol. The one from the drawer.'

'Did I not lock it?' He rubs his face wearily, stifles a yawn. 'No, I suppose he shouldn't have the pistol, although I had a collection of guns at his age so I do understand the attraction.'

'But, Daddy . . .' sometimes my father seems to belong to another age entirely '. . . it's as if he's making preparations for the world ending,' I say, hoping that he'll grasp the nuttiness of it. 'He keeps talking about this bad thing that's going to happen at the end of the summer holidays. Some sort of disaster.'

'Like going back to school? I dare say it will be a shock to the system – September always is after a summer down here.' He smiles kindly, and I feel a moment of hope that he might be willing to listen properly. 'He's got a bit of time at least.'

'I think it's more serious than that.'

'Serious? Amber, darling, dealing with Toby since . . .' there is a hiccup of silence where Momma's death should be '. . . these last few months has been damn near intolerable.' He pushes a large box of dusty pink Turkish delight towards me. 'Rather good, I must say. Try one. Caroline brought them from London.'

I shake my head. 'It's just that there's something properly not right with Toby. He's less himself than ever. Than at Christmas, say.'

Daddy looks out of the window, grim-faced, the cheerful Turkish delight moment gone. 'Well, he's started a new school. I dare say that requires some getting used to, especially as he arrived with a bit of a reputation.'

'I don't think he likes the school much, but it's not that.'

Daddy pulls on his earlobe, uncomfortable. The papers on his desk start to shift and flap in the breeze coming through the open window.

'Daddy, he's worse now than he was straight after . . . it happened.'

He considers this for a moment – chin sunk into hands – then seems to sit straight, flick it off. 'Amber, darling, I hope you know how I appreciate your kindness to your siblings this past year. It hasn't gone unnoticed.'

For some reason the praise makes me feel even worse. Like I'd had a choice in any of it.

'I think we're all guilty of thinking you older than your years sometimes. But there are many things you still don't understand, my darling.'

I see then that while Daddy has thick skin – 'thicker than the rump of a Gloucester Old Spot', Grandma Esme says – Toby barely has skin at all. He feels everything far too much, Daddy too little. And this is part of the problem.

'But I understand Toby, Daddy. I understand him better than anybody else does.'

He coughs. 'Amber, you're not the first person to draw my attention to this.'

'Did Grandma say something?'

'Toby's last school suggested . . .' his face clouds '. . . some kind of doctor. Some charlatan from Harley Street. But I won't do that to Toby, turn him into some dead-eyed creature, however difficult he is.' He adds, more emphatically, 'Nancy would never forgive me.'

So rarely does Daddy mention Momma directly that her name sucks all the air out of the room. Even he looks shocked. This is how we miss her now, less with a sadness that we swim about in and more with sharp spikes of feelings that pop up unexpectedly, like foxgloves in the woods.

'I want him to be happy, Daddy. Well, not that so much,' I say, realizing the impossible reach of my ambition. 'Just more like he was, I suppose.'

Daddy smiles at me then, vague, full of love, like he used to smile when I was Kitty's age. And I feel a pang for that time, when I didn't yearn to know anything beyond what Daddy knew, trusted his judgement completely.

'Amber, remember that strength of character is forged through hardship, not fun. If we aspire to duty and hard work then, *if* we are lucky, and only if we are lucky, happiness may come.' He slams a paperweight on top of the papers, crushing them flat. 'Pleasure is a by-product, not a bloody right, as my brother Sebastian believed.'

My mouth drops open. I feel my drowned rogue uncle in the room. I can almost see him, slipping beneath the gentle Mediterranean waters.

'If Toby is to inherit this estate – learn how to be the custodian of this house – he needs to pull himself together, sooner rather than later.' A muscle is pulsing in his jaw, sweat forming on his brow. 'That's all there is to it.'

'But what if Toby *can't* pull himself together?' I stutter.

'"Can't" is not a word we use in this family.'

'No,' I say, looking down, biting my lip. 'Sorry.'

'So, what do you think we should do?' he asks a little more gently.

'I don't know.' I was hoping he would. 'I guess something has to change. But, um, I'm not sure what.'

He stares at me, mind turning behind his eyes, like the invisible chains pulling the King Harry Ferry across the smooth surface of the river. Then he stands up, fists punching down on the desk's leather top. 'Thank you, Amber. I do believe you've unwittingly answered a question, a rather enormous question, that I've been tussling with for a few days.' He sets his jaw, as if forcing himself to consider something unpalatable. 'Something has to change. You are quite right. It is my duty as a father to make that change.'

'What?' I ask, puzzled, hoping it's nothing too drastic.

'I dare say you'll all find out soon enough.' He retrieves his silver pen from his lapel pocket, pulls off its lid with his teeth. 'Now, if you'll excuse me, I've got bills to pay.'

Eighteen

Lucian stops at the end of the drive, the engine purring, and opens the passenger door for me. 'I'm glad you agreed to make me late.'

'Well, it beats feeding the chickens.' I hop out of the car, trying to hide my pleasure in delaying his departure to Devon. That he chose me over Belinda, even if only for twenty-odd minutes.

'Good. I'm glad.' He glances up the drive warily. 'I hope Toby won't be too cross.'

'Oh, he won't find out,' I say quickly, my heart starting to race at the thought of being caught. 'He's still in the woods. Tree-house business.'

'I wish he'd show it to me.'

Unlikely, I think. 'One day,' I say.

The afternoon light slips behind his dark eyes so that I can see their hidden toffee colour, like the coloured-ink twist in the centre of a marble.

'Well . . . until next time.'

'This summer?' I say unthinkingly, as if I'll be counting the days until the next school holidays. Embarrassed, I brush the flower heads and pollen off my poplin dress, the one I'd chosen so carefully this morning because it brings out the green of my eyes and makes my breasts look bigger.

'I hope so.'

'I thought you hated Black Rabbit Hall.'

'I did. I changed my mind.'

'Oh,' I say, failing not to grin stupidly. 'Well, bye then.'

I go to step past him, but the space between us seems to contract and we awkwardly bump against each other. Flustered, I move backwards, tangling my hair in the low branches of the tree. He slams the car door shut. And it should be a final sound, the promise of an ending. But it isn't. The noise cuts through the summer air, like a starting whistle. We stare at each other, see it in each other's eyes. Something is out, released.

I know it's going to happen the split second before it does. But the kiss is still a raw shock, nothing like I ever imagined. His hands grip my waist, yanking me towards him, his breath fraying in my ear, my hair pulling on a twig until it snaps, the taste of salt and saliva and honey. We kiss and kiss until my jaw and tongue ache and I can't breathe and he suddenly pulls away and pants, 'Sorry. God, I'm so very sorry.'

'I'm not.' The words just blurt out before I can stop them. Mortified, clamping my hands to my mouth, I stumble up the verge into the woods, hearing him call my name, once, twice. Then, when I'm hidden by foliage, I lean back against the tree, catching my breath, resting my hands on my knees, and listen to the rumble of Lucian's car fading. I know I need to move, that Toby will soon be returning from the tree house, wondering where I am, the distance between us closing.

I walk shakily back to the house, the air fluting through my fingers, the taste of him on my lips, the birdsong wild and ecstatic. When I get to the stream, where the water pools beneath the giant rhubarb, I peer in, checking my reflection, sure that guilt must be written all over me. But the water cuts my glowing face into shimmering ribbons, smudging my hair, my smile, making sunlight dance in my eyes. Will Toby know? Will it be obvious? I lick my fingers, frantically smooth my hair – picking out the snapped twig – and my creased dress, pulling at the sticky dampness where my bottom met the leather car seat.

If I can run upstairs before anyone sees me, have a hot bath, brush my hair, change my clothes, who will ever know? No one could possibly have seen us. And no one would guess in a million years. But as Black Rabbit Hall rises above the ridge of the lawn, this all seems less certain. The stone falcons glare down their sharp beaks as if they know exactly where I've been, and, as I climb the grey stone steps, a different girl from the one who ran down them half an hour ago, the thrill of the kiss mingles with a small sting of fear.

Nineteen

Lorna

Dill's office is a small brick-walled room, tucked above the steps to the wine cellars. Dill mutters something apologetic about it being only temporary and not ideal as it was the place where pheasants used to hang – there are metal hooks along the walls – so she's sorry if it pongs a bit, and if the phone starts to crackle it can be remedied by a vigorous shake of the handset. But Lorna isn't listening. Jon wants her urgently. She's worried. 'Jon?'

Dill shuts the door softly behind her. A bee the size of a mouse appears from nowhere and starts to throw itself at the small-paned window in hopeless bristly thumps.

'I was about to hang up.' Jon's voice sounds muffled, distant, as if he might be phoning in from a different planet. 'Come and rescue you.'

'Don't be silly.' She laughs warily.

'You could have called me.' He can't hide the hurt in his voice. In London they normally speak on the phone two or three times a day. 'I didn't know if you were all right.'

'I tried to phone. The signal is terrible, you know that. But I'm fine, honestly. Why wouldn't I be?'

A moment passes. She pictures his large hand running through his golden hair. 'I just worry about you.'

'I'm not a child,' she says, a little irritated, perching on the swivel chair, trying to find some space for her elbows among the clutter on the desk: bills – overdue, red – falling out of a wire rack; an ancient beige PC; a tea-stained copy of *Country Life*. 'Is that it? The urgent thing?'

'No, it's not. Lorna, listen, I did a bit of digging around about your Black Rabbit Hall.'

She doesn't like that idea. Almost as if he's checking up on her. 'Er, why?'

'Something didn't feel right. Didn't add up.'

'You've lost me.' Lorna tries to open the window to let the bee out but it's stuck tight. So she draws the curtain to contain the bee for the duration of the phone call, plunging the room further into gloom.

'I can't really let you down gently, I'm afraid. Lorna, there's no wedding licence.'

She feels it like a temperature drop. 'I . . . I don't understand.'

'We can't have a wedding at Black Rabbit Hall. The owner has no licence to hire the place out to a member of the public as a venue. No insurance. None. *Nada*.'

'But they can get one? It must just be a formality.' She curses Jon's attention to detail, his respect for the kind of rules that beg to be broken.

'I don't think so. Health and safety, fire regs, they're just . . . miles off, sweetheart. Given that, asking for a cash deposit up front sort of stinks.'

She's sure she can smell it then, a metallic smell like the trace of coins. A faint meatiness. She bites the edge of her finger, wondering what to do. Does her dream end here?

'I'm sorry. I know you'd set your heart on that house.'

She sits up straight, mind made up. No, it is not the end. 'We will still have the wedding here.'

'You're not serious?' He laughs in disbelief.

'Why not? Come on. What's the harm? Who's it hurting? The last time I saw a policeman was at Paddington station. There are no neighbours for miles to complain about noise or parking.'

'The whole thing would be closed down like some . . . illegal rave or something. Just forget it.'

'I won't. I can't, Jon. I just can't.'

'What's got into you?' Jon says quietly.

She hesitates, tells him the truth. 'This house has got into me. It's got under my skin.'

Lorna feels his judgement then. His confusion. The gap stretching between them, gathering speed, like a train pulling away from a station.

'Okay, listen. You need to leave. Today. That place is messing with your head, sweetheart.'

'Don't be silly. I've only just arrived.' She wraps the telephone cord tightly around her finger. 'And I'm having a wonderful time.' She doesn't intend it to sound so charged – as if the wonderfulness excludes him – but somehow it does. She shuts her eyes for a moment, trying to recalibrate, feel close to him, say the right thing. But it's as if they've been parted for years, not days. 'I'm not going anywhere.'

He is silent for a moment. 'Is there some bloke there, or something you're not telling me?' He's only half joking.

'A *bloke*? Here? Like a gardener? A handsome young butler? Jon, please.'

'I don't know what to think.' He's cooler now. 'You sound so . . . weird.'

'Thanks.' Hating being shut out of his warmth, she goes on the defensive. 'Is this about the fact I'm here at all? That I dared to go away for the weekend without you? Because if you think I'm going to turn into some 1950s housewife just because we're engaged, well, we – we need to talk, we really do.'

'I didn't want you to go because it was an odd invite, okay? And it's so far away. There's no one around for miles.' He hesitates, changes the timbre of his voice, something harder to ignore. 'You're vulnerable at the moment, Lorna. You're still grieving, all over the place.'

All over the place? She most certainly is not. And she doesn't feel vulnerable. She doesn't even feel as if she's grieving now. No, she feels alive, fully charged for the first time in months, in a different place altogether. She just doesn't know how to explain this to Jon without sounding even loopier than he evidently thinks she is.

'Ever since we visited that house things between us have been, I don't know . . . off. You get a fevered look in your eye when you talk about it.'

'Oh, for God's sake, just shut up, will you?' Shocked by the hardness of the words, she tries to make amends. 'Sorry. I didn't mean . . .' But part of her did mean it. And her words limp off into a punishing silence, broken only by the bee's futile battle to escape the curtain. For a moment it feels like her behind that curtain, pushing against something thick and strange, something she doesn't understand.

'You know what, Lorna? I'm not going to shut up. I

think it's time you were honest with me – and yourself – about why you can only think and talk about that half-derelict old house in Cornwall.'

'I love it.'

'It's more complicated than that, isn't it? It's about your mum.'

She flicks her finger against the rusty wire letter tray, tries to swallow the lump that has hardened in her throat. 'I want to find out why there are photographs of me and Mum on the drive. It's bugging me, okay?' She decides against telling him that she also desperately wants to know what happened to the Alton children at the end of the summer of '69, especially to a little boy called Barney. 'I know it sounds silly.'

'Not at all. It's natural to try to put the pieces of a puzzle together after . . .' He stops, searches for the right words. 'To make some sense of the senseless. Give me a bit of credit, I do understand.'

'You don't,' she mutters.

He ignores this. 'But it's not just that. It's not just about those photographs, is it?' The telephone feels hot and heavy in her hand, a loaded gun. 'You can't keep running, Lorna, circling your past rather than facing it head on, pretending you're searching for one thing when you're actually digging for something else.'

Jon is tugging her somewhere she doesn't want to go, pushing her into the bricked-up space in her own head. He's been trying to get her there for a while: she resists, he keeps trying. The urge to slam down the phone is almost overwhelming.

Jon takes a deep breath. 'Lorna, I always wondered if

you'd want to search for your birth mother after Sheila died.'

The trapped bee bursts out from a gap beneath the curtains and spirals dementedly into the air, like a pilotless plane. Lorna is rigid, her fingers cramping around the phone, fighting a rising nausea. 'That's not what this is about,' she manages, a tremor in her voice. 'I've got her name. I could find her, if I wanted to. But I decided not to trace her long ago, you know that.'

'No. Sheila decided. She made you feel guilty for even wondering about it, let alone asking any questions. She was terrified that one day you'd go off searching for another mother, rejecting her. That's why she couldn't talk about it. That's why she didn't even tell you that you were adopted until you were nine. She couldn't bear the idea, could she?'

'I'd better go, Jon.' Her voice is barely a whisper now. She feels unexpectedly protective of her mother while recognizing the painful truth in his words.

'Lorna, please. We can search for your birth mother together. We know she was Cornish, that you were adopted from Truro. I want to help. That's why I suggested we might visit there, that time in the car.'

'I remember,' she manages.

'Please, let's do it together. There will be leads. It may be easier than you think.'

'I'm not looking for that woman. I don't want to find her.' She doesn't tell him she could never risk rejection twice: she knows that uttering those words out loud will make her cry. So she says, more emphatically, 'I've never wanted to find her,' and feels her resolve harden.

'Not consciously.'

A sharp intake of breath. She can think of no smart response.

'Shit. I wish I was with you now. This is no conversation to have on the phone.'

She hears footsteps outside the office door, faint, getting fainter, someone walking away. It occurs to her that someone might have been listening.

'But I should tell you . . . since your mum's funeral you've mumbled your birth mother's name in your sleep a few times.'

She starts, a cold sensation in her stomach. 'Why . . . why didn't you tell me?'

'I was waiting for the right time. There wasn't one. I'm sorry.'

Her eyes fill. She blinks back the tears.

'You'll let me in everywhere else but there, won't you?' Jon's voice breaks, which makes her feel worse, that her past is affecting the people she loves, seeping out despite her attempts to contain it. 'I lay awake all last night thinking about it, missing you, wondering why I've allowed it to go on so long. You come with no-go areas, Lorna, you know that? You won't let me in. But I want a wife who tells me everything.' His voice chokes again. 'I want all of you or . . .'

'Nothing?' She gulps.

'That's not what I said.'

Lorna suddenly remembers an ex-boyfriend – the one before Jon – telling her that she tested relationships to destruction to prove they weren't worth saving. That she built walls around herself that made true intimacy impossible. The relationship imploded shortly afterwards. And here was Jon trying to say the same thing. But she cannot break down those barriers, even for Jon. She doesn't know how.

'Sweetheart, are you there?'

She will lose him over this. Deep down, she is certain that will happen: it's what she's always feared, that she will lose the one man who makes her feel anchored and safe and loved. And if you fear something you imagine it, and can recognize it when the process starts to happen. And it starts like this.

'Say something.'

The bee settles on her bare knee, almost weightless, a small tickle of life. She stares down at it, this beautiful frightened thing, and she knows the moment is pivotal. That it matters more than anything. That she might still have a chance to save her relationship. But something locks her throat. No words come out at all. And the bee flies off towards the window, trapping itself behind the curtain once more.

Submerged beneath the cloudy water – the bath is more like a wild pond – Lorna holds her breath until her lungs hurt. It helps to stop her thinking about the awful conversation with Jon, the lack of connection between them, as if someone has come along and snipped the wires. She'd tried to call him back once she'd composed herself and her hands had stopped shaking but she couldn't get through on the mobile. When she called on Dill's phone it went straight to voicemail. And, shamefully, she was enormously relieved. After the crab salad supper with Dill on the terrace – Mrs Alton wasn't hungry – she didn't try to call him again.

A little voice inside her head cannot help but wonder

whether it might even be easier to walk away now, call the whole thing off, than look deep inside, risk searching for answers to painful questions that Jon seems to be demanding she ask. If this is the beginning of the end, why not get it over with?

Lorna blasts up out of the water, gasping for air.

Alarmed by the escalating negativity of her thoughts, she stands in front of the bedroom window in her pyjamas, hair whipped up in a towel. The starless dark presses against the dimpled glass. There is no comfort of a moon tonight, no glowing dot of an aeroplane, nothing that might prove she isn't sealed off in Black Rabbit Hall's bridal suite as completely as a figure in one of the snow globes she used to collect as a child. She hears a faint fizz of rain against the glass. With a rattle of curtain rings, she shuts out the night with heavy brocade, herself in.

The bed's four posts loom like ebonized tree trunks. She clambers between them, tries to settle against the stack of pillows that smell of unfamiliar washing powder, old linen dried in the salty outside. She wonders who else has slept in this ancient bed, who was conceived on its lumpy mattress, who took their last breath on its sagging springs before a white linen sheet was lifted over their face. She can see it so vividly. The sheet. The face. God, she's so tired.

She must sleep. If she sleeps, all will be surmountable again, all the floating bits of the day will come together, like a slow-motion film of a cup smashing to the ground, played backwards. She parts the swishy silk fringing of the lamp, switches it off and waits for sleep to take her. It doesn't.

Instead, the day flies at her, like that frenzied bee in

Dill's office: the names scratched on the bark; the haunted children's faces in the photo album; the phone's spiralling cable, Jon's oddly unfamiliar voice; the wrongness of their conversation, the way it doesn't actually sound like them at all, the people they were before they came to Black Rabbit Hall.

She wonders then if Black Rabbit Hall, the planning of the wedding, is a secret test of her and Jon's compatibility, one that carries the possibility of failure. Like those couples who go together into counselling expecting it to fix their relationship, only for it to confirm that it is beyond saving.

What if Jon is too straightforward for her? Too nice? Too untroubled? When they first met she worried that his unquestioning, cheerful upbringing, his relaxed, large family, put him out of her league. That he'd soon grasp his mistake. That it was impossible to straighten an emotional kink bestowed on you by your past: anything else was unsustainable pretence. She'd confided her fears to Louise, who'd simply said, 'Don't be a plonker.' And she'd agreed with her. Jon and she loved each other. And yet. What if that initial worry was intuition, not paranoia? What if she'd been right the first time round?

Lorna tries to calm herself by taking yoga breaths. But they only seem to rush oxygen into the fire of her brain. She feels disoriented now, off balance. It is so dark in the room it's as if her eyes are closed. There are so many different shades of black, from oily kohl to something that is beyond colour, an abyss in the shadows beneath the drop of the curtain. The darkness is not still either. It moves, billowing, contracting, alive. As she stares into it, heart galloping in her ears, she can see flickering clips of her childhood: a felt-tip heart drawn on the back of Louise's delicate hand with her and Louise's names on it; the same hand, bigger, protectively holding newborn Alf, beautiful, sticky with birth wax, the shock of his Down's diagnosis still a doctor's round away; her adoption certificate in the torchlight under her Barbie duvet, the letters marching across it like ants, the sound of her mother violently re-arranging the linen cupboard in the corridor, waiting for Lorna to be 'done' with the bit of paper so she could shove it back in the box file in the attic and pretend once again that it didn't exist.

She bolts up on the pillow. Has she internalized her mother's anxieties about her adoption? It's never occurred to her before. Has she learned to see her own pre-Lorna Dunaway past – caught between the first beat of her tiny heart and the moment her adoptive parents bundled her into their arms – as a sheet of thin ice crackling over dangerously deep waters? Tread carefully, very carefully, preferably not at all. Her mind races in the dark, thoughts dashing about blindly, like creatures freed from a cage, until her eyes close and she sinks into the deepest black of all.

Some hours later, sickly yellow light waffles the floor beneath the folds in the curtains. Lorna's head roars. She's drenched in sweat, her engagement ring twisted around on her finger, diamond pushing into her palm. She stands up to use the bathroom, sinks back to the four-poster. What is the matter? Has she eaten something bad? Was it the crab at supper? That sticky ancient sherry?

She shivers beneath the sheets, hot, cold, hot. Someone

is banging against the inside of her skull, trying to get out. Or something. She imagines this is how a migraine might feel. Except she doesn't get migraines. She doesn't get headaches. She's as strong as an ox – good genes, ha – and is rarely, if ever, ill.

The only thing to do is close her eyes. Close her eyes and pray for sleep.

A knocking on the door. She squints across the room. The yellow dawn has gone now. The room is stifling and razor-sharp sunlight is pouring through the gaps in the curtains.

A voice swims across the room towards her: 'Everything okay?'

Lorna tries not to groan. A groan – and a self-pitying plea for tea and painkillers – is the noise she'd normally make on a morning like this, except she can't because she's a guest and her mother taught her that it's bad manners for guests to be ill. So she says weakly, 'Come in.' The sound of her own voice crashes sickeningly against her eardrums.

'Oh, what's the matter?'

Lorna can only focus enough to make out the giant frizzy orb of hair, a human allium.

'You look terrible.'

'It's my head . . .' Her hand goes to it. She is half expecting to find it changed in some way, elongated, squashed or pulped. It is damp and hot.

'You really do look pale. No, no, don't get up.'

Lorna couldn't even if she tried. 'Must be a bug. Something I picked up on the train.'

'Oh dear. Can I get you anything?'

'Paracetamol would be good.'

'I'll do what I can.'

Lorna lies back in the bed, feeling as if she may never get out, that it will eat her alive. The pounding intensifies. It has words. Jon's words. Questions she doesn't want answers to. It has a rhythm too, a nauseous swoosh, the sound of arterial blood, a river overflowing its banks.

Dill finally appears. 'I couldn't find any paracetamol.'

Lorna's eyes rush with tears.

'But Mrs Alton gave me these for you.' Dill holds up an innocuous white cardboard box. 'Painkillers. She gets migraines. Swears by them.'

Lorna will do anything to stop the sledgehammer in her head. She weakly shakes the box: two pills in a silver blister pack fall to the eiderdown. She tries to read the back of the packet – she can see a chemist's sticker, they're prescription – but the letters blur and smudge. She shouldn't take them. It's madness taking someone else's painkillers, the sort of thing it warns you against on the side of the box, if only she could read it.

'Shall I bring you a glass of water?' Dill asks kindly.

She nods. She doesn't ask about the dose.

What day is it? Where is she? Gripping a bedpost, Lorna pulls herself up. Her head is foggy, vision smoked at the edges, her stomach loose. It takes a few moments for the previous day and night to come back in a soft-focus mush, the moments falling apart as she reaches for them, the magical removal of pain, feeling, all sense of time. But . . . no . . . surely she wasn't stupid enough to take someone else's prescription pills. But the empty white box is on the floor. The bed is a mess, as if she's been trying to plait the sheets during the night. And the room stinks. She staggers from the sweaty tangle of linen, slams open the window and inhales, dewy ivy brushing her face. Seaweed. Wool. Bacon.

Bacon? Oh, no, she's late for breakfast. A day late for breakfast. She tries to text Jon – 'message unsent' – and after a brutal cold splashing from the bath's shower hose, dresses in a hurry, hopping across the rug, one foot stuck in a shoe, running her fingers through her hair. She trips down the narrow stairway until she gets to the door that leads directly to a floor she doesn't want to be on. One more flight down. Two. Another landing. Bewildering. Three tin buckets, plinking with drips. Finally, at the bottom of the staircase she looks around. A stuffed stag stares back at her, seeming faintly surprised.

Where's the dining room? It isn't making itself at all obvious. She turns into an unfamiliar long, dingy corridor, crashes into a room full of brooms and mops and upright floor polishers, another with furniture draped in white sheeting, lumps of pale ceiling plaster scattered across the floor like split bags of icing sugar. She retraces her steps, cloud-headed, cursing beneath her breath until she sees the words 'Dining Room' shimmer in faded gilt letters on a dark grey door. The relief is short-lived. She hears the clink of cutlery. Damn. They've started.

'I'm so sorry I'm late . . .' Her words trail off. She was not anticipating the dining room to be quite so grand or red or the table so enormously big. Mrs Alton still manages to dominate it, sitting upright at one end with perfect posture, a fork of scrambled egg poised mid-air. Petal, the ratty terrier, sits on her knee, one muddy paw on a lace-edged tablecloth, greedily eyeing the fork. Mrs Alton's lips twitch, but she says nothing.

'My alarm didn't go off,' Lorna mutters, as if she would have heard it if it had.

'Oh, it wouldn't. Not in this house.' Mrs Alton brings the fork to her mouth. 'I'm just glad you're feeling better and that the bridal suite has proved itself to be so suited to such deep slumber, Lorna,' she adds, making no mention of her little gift of the catatonic pills, horse tranquillizers, whatever they were. 'Do sit down.'

Lorna sits between some complicated cutlery. As she does so, she gets a sudden, vivid recollection of waking up and seeing someone standing in the doorway of the bedroom. Clearly, she was wired.

'I trust you're hungry.' Mrs Alton feeds the dog a triangle of buttered toast from her fingers but is watching Lorna intently, her gaze precise, as if something has sharpened her interest since yesterday.

'Oh, yes,' Lorna says, even though she's not sure she is. Her body still feels as if it might not belong to her. She wishes she couldn't smell the dog.

There is endless toast, different shades of burnt, in a silver toast rack. A fruit bowl full of strawberries and, if she's not actually hallucinating, tiny black ants scrabbling over them. Four jars of marmalade, some looking decades older than the others. Mushrooms swimming in butter. A horrifying limb of black pudding. Her hands stall on the table as she wonders when to declare her vegetarianism, whether etiquette dictates that she should just help herself or if she should wait to be invited. She half expects a maid in black and white to come up behind her with a pair of silver tongs.

Instead, Dill appears, wearing a battered navy overall and a look of delighted surprise. 'You're here!' she trills, as if she'd expected Lorna to do a runner in the night. 'How are you feeling?'

'Much better,' she says, embarrassed, hoping Dill hadn't witnessed her at her most spaced.

'Tea?' Dill pours it through a silver strainer into the prettiest gold-rimmed china teacups. 'Bacon and eggs? One of Betty's eggs. Most of our hens are menopausal, but our Betty Grable is hanging in there, isn't she, Mrs Alton?'

'Indeed. Dear old Betty.'

'Lovely.' Lorna is unsure she can face an egg but can't help feeling that it would be a personal slight to turn it down as the chicken has a name. 'But no bacon for me, thanks.'

'No bacon?' Dill looks baffled.

'I'm a vegetarian. Well, I eat fish.'

'Good heavens.' Mrs Alton presses her napkin to her mouth.

'I should have mentioned it earlier. Sorry.'

'No problem. Eggs coming up,' says Dill.

'I must warn you that it will be rather cold, especially the scrambled,' says Mrs Alton, recovering herself, gritting her breakfast with salt. 'Unless Endellion sprints from the kitchen, a form of exercise to which she is not naturally disposed.'

Dill smiles, not rising to the bait. 'The kitchen is not very convenient, Lorna, too far from the dining room,

247

which is why we usually keep ourselves to the east tower kitchen. But this is a special room and you a special guest. We thought you'd enjoy it.'

'It is an amazing room. I love the red walls.'

'In the early days, when I first came here, Lorna, I tried to use this dining room for every meal but it beat me in the end. All that lukewarm food.'

Lorna finds it hard to imagine Mrs Alton being beaten by anything.

'Pencraw is a wild horse, Lorna.' Mrs Alton sighs. 'Quite impossible to control. It took me many years to accept that. Such a determined new wife I was.'

A wild horse? An unfortunate turn of phrase, considering the manner of the first wife's death. It makes Lorna wonder if so much time has passed that Mrs Alton no longer makes the association or, more chillingly, if she does and says it anyway.

'I hope that the peeling wallpaper won't put you off your food.' Mrs Alton smiles. 'It is in a rather worse state than I remembered.'

'It feels like a palace to me.' Lorna reaches for some toast, self-conscious under Mrs Alton's tracking stare. 'We can't even fit a proper dining table in our flat.'

Mrs Alton coughs on a mushroom. 'I beg your pardon?'

'Too small,' explains Lorna, wishing she hadn't mentioned it. 'But we're hoping to move somewhere bigger soon.'

'I wouldn't recommend anywhere with more than six bedrooms for a couple starting out,' says Mrs Alton, thickly buttering another triangle of toast for the dog. 'Anything bigger can become a terrible chore unless you've got the staff. Endellion, Petal is still hungry.' Mrs Alton tickles the dog under the chin. A string of dribble ropes from Petal's mouth to the table. 'One of his doggy biscuits, please.'

'Coming up.' Dill's espadrilles make a squelching sound. The moment the door closes it feels like the last bit of normality has left. Lorna feels faintly claustrophobic, despite the room's generous proportions. It's not unlike the feeling she had in the turret after she'd closed the heavy brocade curtains. Mrs Alton's gaze is still boring into different parts of her: fingernails, nape of her neck. She's never felt so blatantly scrutinized and wishes she'd had time to brush her hair.

She peers over Mrs Alton's shoulder to the window. 'The lawn is extraordinarily lush and green this morning,' she says.

'That's what you get after a night of rain here. Not that you'll have rain on your wedding day, of course.' She grimaces. 'Not like I did.'

At the mention of the wedding, Lorna's heart immediately quickens: the phone conversation in Dill's office feels like something hard and indigestible in her stomach. Should she mention the wedding-licence issue now? Or is this the least of her worries?

'The weather is rather good down here in the autumn. The sun comes out on the weekend the tourists leave. Nature has a wicked sense of humour.' Mrs Alton eyes her coolly over the gold rim of her teacup. 'You are still set on an autumn date, I trust?'

Now she must mention it. For all she knows, Mrs Alton may not even realize that a licence is necessary. 'Well, there are a few things we need in place first. It's the wedding licence, you see. Jon couldn't find a record of one at the council.'

Thunderous silence. A flush of fury spreading up Mrs Alton's scraggy neck.

'Eggs!' Dill calls, oblivious, pushing the door back with her bottom, the two boiled eggs rocking in their cups. She puts the plate down, looks from Lorna to Mrs Alton and back again. 'Everything okay?'

'Lorna seems to think we are ill equipped for a wedding,' says Mrs Alton, tightly.

'I was just wondering about the – the wedding licence,' stutters Lorna, wishing she'd sent an email after she'd got back to London, rather than try to have it out here while she's feeling so delicate.

'Ah, yes.' Dill clears her throat, colours slightly. 'Soon. We'll have one soon.'

'Is this yet *another* ball you have managed to drop, Endellion?'

'Mrs Alton, I did explain that it was going to be very tricky getting the sign-off before we do the necessary repairs and alterations . . .' begins Dill, knotting her fingers around her overall's fabric belt.

'Endellion, do I really need to spell it out? We cannot afford repairs without income. Money must come first. You are approaching it, like most things, entirely the wrong way round.'

'But it doesn't work like that, Mrs Alton,' says Dill, in a manner that tells Lorna she's had this conversation many times before.

'*Make* it work like that, then.' Mrs Alton stands up to her full height, levered on the bulbs of her arthritic knuckles. 'Offer that troublesome little inspector man, I don't know, some firewood or something. A year's free mooring. That should buy a blind eye. It always used to.'

'Things have changed, Mrs Alton,' Dill protests.

Lorna stares down into the yellowest yolk she's ever seen, a sun within a shell.

'Well, do *think*, Endellion!' barks Mrs Alton. 'Because we are running out of time. *I* am running out of time. And patience.' She tosses down her napkin, reaches for her cane and starts tapping towards the door, the two-beat percussion of cane and footsteps receding down the corridor.

'God, I'm so sorry, Dill,' whispers Lorna. 'I didn't mean to cause trouble.'

'Don't be silly. It's nothing.' Dill strokes the dog, who eyes her dolefully.

'It's not nothing. I've made things difficult for you.'

'Mrs Alton is just overtired. Really, I'm used to it.'

'It's having me here, isn't it?'

There is just the slightest pause before Dill says, 'Of course not. She's rather excitable today, that's all.'

Lorna's eyes drop to the plate. She can't stay on. She's tangled things at home and now she's done the same at Black Rabbit Hall. She doesn't know which way to run, only that she cannot stand still. 'Dill, I'm going to catch the afternoon train today.'

'But you had to spend yesterday in bed, poor thing! You haven't even seen the cove. Surely you'll stay another night.'

'I'd love to,' she says honestly. 'But ... I just can't. Not now.'

'I wish you wouldn't leave.' Dill looks stricken. 'It's so

251

nice having a bit of company for once.' She puffs into the chair beside Lorna, refills Lorna's cup, pours some for herself. As they sip their tea, things normalize a little. It feels like Mrs Alton's outburst might have cleared the air. Or the pills are finally out of Lorna's system.

'Don't go because of Mrs Alton's outburst, please, Lorna. It's just her way. She's had a tough life. I know it doesn't look like it.'

'Well, I guess I wouldn't want to be rattling around such a big house at her age.' Or any age, Lorna thinks, wondering why on earth Dill sticks it out. She takes another sip of tea, enjoying the sensation of the warm liquid slipping down her parched throat. 'Could she not move somewhere . . . easier to heat, maybe?'

'Last time I suggested she move she threw a riding boot at me.' Dill points to a small pink crescent beneath her jaw. 'She will never leave Pencraw.'

Lorna sits up straighter, sensing that Dill is opening up. This is her chance to get some answers. 'But why? What keeps her here, Dill?'

'Well, it's a long story.'

'I love long stories.' Lorna smiles, cradling her cup in her hands. 'I bet you tell a good one.'

The flattery works. Dill, who is clearly starved of it, brightens. 'Mr and Mrs Alton were in love a long time ago when they were young, you see,' she says, in a hushed voice, glancing at the door. 'But after he left her for Nancy . . .'

'No! He dumped her for the first wife?'

Dill's eyes shine. 'Years ago. When they were young. Broke Mrs Alton's heart he did.'

'Okay, wait, wait . . . But Mrs Alton did marry someone else, didn't she?'

'Two weeks later. Mr Alfred Shawcross.'

'*Two* weeks?' She clinks her teacup to the saucer in surprise. 'Wow. That's quite some rebound.'

Dill glances at the door again, more nervous now, and lowers her voice further. 'Mr Shawcross was rich, very rich.'

'Aha, sweet revenge.' Just like one of the historical romances her mother used to read. Brilliant. She reaches for some cold toast, spreads it with marmalade and bites into it, wonders why marmalade toast always tastes better cold.

'So when Mr Shawcross died a few years later – he was old, much older than her – she was left a wealthy widow.' Dill pauses dramatically, letting Lorna fill in the blanks.

'Who, after Nancy was out of the picture too, could marry her first, true love.'

'Bringing with her a small fortune. It was *that* money that saved Pencraw from being sold off.'

'So he married her for her money? Oh. How depressing.'

'I don't think it was just that, actually.' Dill fiddles with the napkin, stalling. Lorna gets the impression she's desperate to talk, bursting at the seams in fact, but has been warned against it. 'The word is that Mr Alton wanted a mother figure for his children. They were going off the rails apparently, wild as you like, after his Nancy died, especially the eldest son, who took her death terribly hard. I think he thought a new wife would steady the ship.'

'Did she?' asks Lorna, doubtfully. The faces in the photographs she's seen suggest otherwise.

Dill shakes her head. 'I don't think the children ever accepted her. But she did bring financial security, which is not to be sneezed at, is it? They kept this house.'

Lorna looks around her, taking in the grand ceilings, the crumbling cornicing, the inky oils on the walls. Everything has a price.

'Nothing was managed on the estate after Nancy died, and the word was that Mr Alton had made some *very* bad investments in London.' She taps her temple lightly. 'Not sure he was quite himself by all accounts. Drank far too much. Mrs Alton was the one who kept everything going. But Mr Alton died over twenty-odd years ago now. That's a long time to live here alone – she was never interested in anyone else – and to shell out. Little wonder there's nothing left of her own fortune.' She checks the door once more, whispers, 'Although sometimes I do wonder if she had less of it in the first place than she let everyone imagine.'

Lorna bends forward, sensing the true story is about to spill out over the table. 'Surely it's time for the younger generation to take the reins.'

'Petal!' Dill jumps up, as if physically ejected from her chair. 'Petal, you horrid hound!'

Petal stares sheepishly at a yellow puddle on the floor.

'You and your bladder problems. Off with you.' She shoos the dog crossly away and its claws skitter across the floor. 'Go and find Mummy.'

'What about Nancy and Mr Alton's elder son?' Lorna tries again, cursing the dog for distracting Dill at such a critical moment. 'You know, the twin boy, the heir . . .'

'Toby?' Dill whispers, as if the name itself is so delicate

it might shatter on airing. 'Toby has not been seen for decades.'

'So he is alive? I assumed from the way Mrs Alton was talking . . .'

Dill looks away, biting the inside of her cheek. 'I shouldn't be nattering like this. I'm sorry. I don't know what's got into me. I'd really better get on. Clean up the dog's pee.'

'I'll help you.' Lorna stands and looks around. Anything to prolong the conversation. Why is Toby not here? Where is Lucian?

'I can't let you do that!'

'What shall I use to clean it?'

Dill dumbly hands her a napkin, as if she cannot quite believe the question has been asked because no one has ever before offered to help her do anything.

Lorna swiftly mops it up, trying not to breathe in.

'That's ever so kind of you.'

Lorna leaves the sodden napkin on the floor. She draws the line at handling it wet. 'It's a lot of work for you, Dill. Why do you stay?' she asks, touched by Dill's dedication and loyalty. There's something so sweetly old-fashioned about it.

'Me? Oh, I don't know, really. I can't imagine any different. Not many places to earn good money around here. Not with board and lodging thrown in.' She colours, gaze sliding away. 'I've never worked anywhere else, to be honest, Lorna.'

'No! Really? You must dream of –'

'Double glazing.' She looks up with a shy, endearing smile. 'I dream of double glazing.'

Lorna laughs. She's about to direct the conversation back to the Alton children when Dill's face grows suddenly solemn.

'Lorna, Mrs Alton is ill. It's a matter of weeks, I'm afraid.'

Lorna's laughter tails into a shocked silence. 'No . . .' She is so taken aback she doesn't know what else to say. She thinks of Mrs Alton's consumptive pallor, the sense of decay that hangs about her, like the scent of wilting cut flowers. It puts her headache into perspective. 'I'm so sorry.'

'She calls the tumour Nancy.'

Improbably, the world has caught up, the texts loading bullet-fast on the twelfth step of the grand staircase. Lorna stares at them with rising panic, the liberty of being non-contactable lost.

> Louise: *Jon freaked out! Wotz going on?*
>
> Dad: *Just checking all OK? *@$, how to put iron on non-steam setting?*
>
> Jon: *Can u call me bck?*
>
> Jon: *Worried now.*
>
> Jon: *Hs she locked u away? Call the cops?*

Lorna hurriedly thumbs a text to him, something about how she's only just picked up his messages and has been ill but not to worry and she's going to get the afternoon train. But for some reason it reads like an excuse, something one of her toxic exes might have sent in her pre-Jon life, offering the kind of insecurity that drew her, like a moth to a flame. She presses send. Just in time. The signal bars vanish, the window of communication closes.

Two hours left before she leaves, Lorna realizes with a pang. For all its oddness and tragedy, she knows she will miss Black Rabbit Hall, as you do miss places that make you rewrite your own map, if only slightly, places that take a bit of you away, give you something of their spirit in return. The feeling is made more poignant because a wedding at Black Rabbit Hall seems unlikely now. A wedding anywhere not entirely certain. It's as if the door to her future is blocked by the past.

She drops the phone back into her bag, hears a faint thudding coming from outside, the sound of a dusty rug being beaten with a broom. She wonders if it's Dill. She looked so crushed when Lorna had told her she was going to try for the five o' clock train, and ever since has kept a polite distance, turning off the rush of stories and candour like a tap. Mrs Alton also seems affronted, vanishing into the dark belly of the east turret, leaving Lorna to drink a cup of instant coffee in the sunroom alone while the dog pees against the skirting board. This time, she leaves the mess alone.

How to spend her last precious hours? The moment she steps off the train at Paddington, she's sure it will be impossible to conjure up Black Rabbit Hall again, to believe it exists at all. Everyday life takes over far too quickly.

The cove, of course. She mustn't miss it. Dill is quite right.

Lorna takes off her shoes – rather childishly, she wants to feel Black Rabbit Hall between her toes – and crosses the lawns to the woods, happy to be out in the warm summer air. She deliberately goes past the carved-up tree in the woods (she kisses her fingertips lightly, presses them against Barney's name), then walks through the seeding long grasses on the banks of the creek until she finds a nice spot in the dappled shade of a tree. She tosses in a stick, dreamily watching it bob on the luminous green water, remembering how, when she was a kid, Louise would deliberately get their Pooh sticks muddled at the finish line so Lorna could win. She'd forgotten that. She's forgotten so many precious things from childhood. The way long grasses catch and pull between bare toes. The way Louise would swing her hand and declare it 'fairy fate' that they were sisters. Even though Lorna couldn't explain 'fairy fate' in words then or now, it makes a funny sort of sense here. She throws in one more stick. Then, putting her shoes on, she cuts across the sun-buffed fields to the cliffs.

She finds a rickety white bench, a little too close to the crumbling cliff edge. Pressing her bare feet down on the fine blades of grass, she shields her eyes with her hand and admires the cove below. It is like an illustration from a 1950s children's book, lolly-shaped, nestled into jagged grey rocks, pristine and wild, its rubbly narrow beach path resisting easy access. She can imagine smugglers' boats sliding on to the sand. She can imagine all sorts of things. It has that air about it, a sense of things having happened here. Also, slightly unsettling, a sense that things might be *about* to happen. Partly for this reason, partly because she's worried that she'll miss the last London train of the day, Lorna doesn't hang around, slipping on her shoes and walking quickly away. But the imprint of her bare feet on the grass remains, a little bit of her left to await her return.

Twenty

Amber, June 1969

A bead of sweat slips down my nose. I wipe it away on a silk scarf, peering at Peggy through the crack in the wardrobe door, appreciating the tender way she feather-dusts Momma's things on the dressing-table, wishing she'd get a move on. Peggy's *so* slow today, wiping her brow with the back of her wrist, swaying a little, as if every movement is making her feel sick. I hope she's not sick in here. Like she was in the kitchen garden yesterday morning. A stomach bug, she says. I hope I don't catch it.

Peggy clicks the door behind her at last. I scramble out into the room, feet prickling with pins and needles – glad to be free of the hot furs and even hotter feelings – and sit down on the dressing-table's stool to breathe. The wardrobe is stuffy right now, but it is the only place I can think about Lucian without worrying that Toby will see the pictures in my head.

Toby suspects, I'm pretty sure of it, but he has no proof. If he did he would have confronted me. And the truth is that nothing *has* happened since the kiss at Easter. Daddy's announcement on the last day of the Easter holidays, crashing into us like a ball into a huddle of skittles, means it never can: 'You are to have a mother again, children. I hope you will warmly welcome Caroline as such, and Lucian as your new elder brother.'

A brother. How can he ever be a *brother*?

Matilda says it is possible, as long as I'm not wilfully romantic. She says I must train myself out of yearning for Lucian, much as you can train yourself to like the bitter taste of the olives she ate in Greece. I must fall for someone else. I am sixteen now, the perfect age for courting. How about her brother, Fred? Could I not fall in love with him instead? He's always been sweet on me and is a good dancer. I can't tell her that Fred now seems far too dull and far too innocent.

Matilda says if I'm to see Lucian strictly as a brother, I must remind myself that he farts, picks his nose and pees all over the loo seat. Do this, and how can the attraction not fade? But I've done exactly that. Nothing has faded. It's quite hopeless.

Worse, I can't resist replaying the kiss over and over, adding bits, making it go on longer, relocating it to different settings: beach, cliff ledge, the long grasses by the creek. Everything reminds me of him: I see someone with dark hair and a loping gait in the street and my heart flips; I sit on a bench in Fitzroy Square and think about the couple Momma and I spotted kissing from the window, so lost in the kiss that they didn't care who saw, and how – on that one miraculous spring afternoon – I kissed someone in just that way.

I cannot help but remember Lucian's sweetness to Barney and Kitty, his unshowy forgiveness of Toby, the quiet delight he takes in Black Rabbit Hall. Sometimes I swear

I can hear the faint strum of his guitar through the floor-boards, even though there is no guitar in this house now.

'Amber?' The door bursts open. Toby swaggers into the pink room with an angry, hard-bodied energy that can barely be contained within his vest and shorts. 'What are you doing in here?'

'I like to be near Momma's things.'

He stands behind me and our eyes clash in the mirror. 'I found a cake in the larder.'

'A cake?' I run my fingers over the boar bristles of Momma's hairbrush. All the wavy red hairs have gone from it now, plucked out and squirrelled in our secret places. It makes me think of something Matilda said: that if Momma had lived longer she'd have become irritating because all mothers become irritating eventually. Touching her hairbrush, I find this impossible to believe. 'What about the cake?'

'Five cakes. Different sizes.'

'So?'

'Don't be thick. A *wedding* cake, Amber. Peggy's rotten wedding cake.'

'Ugh.'

He lets out a wild hoot. 'I let Boris at them.'

'That is so – so dumb-rabbit stupid, Toby.' I shake my head, trying not to laugh. As terrible as it all is, he can still make me laugh like no one else. 'Peggy will feed *you* to the dog for that.'

He picks a long white hair off my bare arm and, puzzled, holds it between his fingers, glancing at me, then across to the wardrobe and away. I breathe again. I need one place he won't follow me.

'Peggy will only make another cake.'

'Well, if I were her I'd sprinkle the sponge with rat poison. It'll be far worse for her when they're married. It'll be worse for all of us.' He squats beside my stool, bouncing as if he's on springs. 'The moment the ring is on Caroline's finger she'll become even more monstrous, believe me.'

I turn my face to the side, try to see myself in the mirror as Lucian might have seen me, in profile, on the passenger seat. 'But she'll have what she wants then.'

'That's not how Caroline works.'

I roll my eyes.

'What?'

'Don't make it worse, Toby. It's bad enough.' I stare at myself in the mirror, mind turning. A moment passes. 'Caroline has yanked us all out of school early just so she can have a June wedding. She *must* be worried that Daddy will change his mind, Toby. Maybe . . .'

'No, Caroline will make sure this wedding happens.' Toby rips at his thumbnail with his teeth. 'And then she'll ruin Black Rabbit Hall. She'll destroy all our places.'

'Not the woods. The beach.' They still absorb Toby, the fortresses of old planks and chicken wire, the cold wet sand and the vault of sky. They are the places he is happiest. In his blood. It occurs to me then that, in a funny way, Toby is Black Rabbit Hall, more than anyone else is anyway. 'She can't destroy those.'

'The house, then. The bits with people in them.'

'Thanks.'

'You know I don't mean you.'

I get up from the stool, weighed down by the responsibility of being his more rational other half, and peer through the ivy pawing at the window. 'No more doom-mongering. Momma told us the world was a good place, remember?'

'That's because she didn't know what was going to happen to her.'

Outside, the garden is in full bloom, untended, spilling over itself. 'I'm glad of that.'

'Why? If she'd known, she wouldn't have gone out looking for Barney. She'd still be alive.'

I turn to face him, exasperated. 'But she *didn't* know. None of us knows anything. Ever. Not until it happens!'

'The problem is I do, Amber.' He covers his nose with his hands, breathing hard, as if trying to restrain panic. 'I don't want to. But I do. And I've got a chart showing exactly when.'

Twenty-One

The church is not nearly as full as it was for Momma's funeral. Daddy said he wanted 'a small affair'. But still. Faces are missing. Old London friends of my parents. Some cousins on Daddy's side, the ones who smell of horses and wet dog and adored Momma. Aunt Bay, whom I overheard rowing with Daddy on the phone last week, Daddy bellowing, 'And when is not too soon? I will never stop loving Nancy, so there will be no *right* time. Don't you understand, Bay? It can never, ever be right.' Not one American is here, in fact. I miss hearing voices that come from far-off places and motion pictures, proof that there are worlds outside mine.

Caroline's side of the aisle is fuller: a different crowd, louder, more excited, not in the least awkward at being back so soon in the church from which we buried Momma. The men guffaw and flip the tails of their morning suits so that they hang out of the gaps in the back of the pews like black tongues. Sweat bubbles on their thick red necks. Their slim wives arch over each other, like grasses, eyes tracking each other's outfits and shoes. They fold the order of service in half and fan fiercely in the church's still, unlikely heat. One woman actually takes her stockinged feet out of her shoes and lays them on the flags, leaving unthinkable sweaty marks on the ancient Norman stone.

'Gracious.' Grandma Esme raises an eyebrow, peering across at the feet in amused horror. 'I'm not sure I've ever seen so much Pan Stik in June, have you, darling?' She squeezes my hand. Her emerald rings dig into the flesh of my fingers. 'I fear that the bride's lady friends might actually melt to the wick if she leaves it much longer.'

Daddy is standing at the top of the church, back straight, fists clenched, less a groom than a soldier facing the firing squad. Toby's nail continues its *scratch scratch scratch* along the edge of the pew, his feelings conducted through it, picking at the hard brown polish like a scab. Barney's arm wraps around his leg. Unlike Kitty, Barney can still remember Momma's funeral clearly, enough for this to feel the same: the invasive hugs of strangers; the flowers; the pig squeal of the salt-rotted hinges as the church doors part.

At that squeal, everyone starts to swing around, straining to see the bride, smiling, fanning, whispering. The organist starts to thud out a tune. Daddy stiffens in his suit, pulls on the lobe of his left ear. The word 'Beautiful!' ripples from pew to pew behind cupped hands and beneath the brims of hats.

And he is. He is so beautiful I gasp.

Hair greased back, his mother's hand locked on his arm, Lucian walks slowly up the aisle, jet-cold eyes straight ahead, face stern, unreadable, taller and bigger than I remember him at Easter. With every step he takes closer towards me, my body tightens. I don't know how I will stand it when he actually passes, a mere twelve inches to my left. The urge to reach out to him is almost overwhelming. I want him to see *me* one last time, the girl he kissed, not a stepsister he will be forced to tolerate. But Lucian doesn't look at me, at anyone, hesitating only once to encourage Kitty, who is shuffling shyly behind them, a powder puff of pink and white tulle, hugging her brides-maid's posy close to her chest like a doll and looking for me in the crowd.

A small triumphant smile sets hard in the pale plaster of my new stepmother's face. Her sharp chin is raised and there is something studied and queenly in her walk, as if she's been rehearsing. Her dress – long, cream, seeded with tiny pearls – rocks back and forth as her legs scissor beneath it. She doesn't glance at any of us either. Maybe she doesn't dare: she surely knows Toby's likely to explode, if not when or in which direction. Better not to tempt it.

But, unbeknown to her, Toby has promised me not to make a scene, for Kitty's and Barney's sake. I feel so proud of him for his restraint, knowing how it goes against his nature. During the vows, he squeezes his eyes shut, hands fisted at his sides, only flicking them open in the tense hush that clamps the church when the ring doesn't fit the finger. We exchange a glance full of horror and hope – *please don't let it fit!* – and watch, transfixed, as Daddy bends down again, ears throbbing scarlet. He shoves. Nothing. Caroline's smile is frozen, her eyes darting, panicked, the wretched finger protruding into the sweating silence.

'Oh dear,' Grandma whispers, behind the order of ser-vice. 'Her finger must have swollen in this ghastly heat.'

But Daddy gives the ring one more hard, desperate shove. And it is on, sealing all our fates in a band of tight white gold.

I wave at Peggy through the car window as a column of vehicles pours up the drive from the church to Black Rab-bit Hall, the bells pealing faintly in the distance. But her expression doesn't change. I don't think she can see me behind the glass.

She is standing on the bottom step, next to Annie, lips pressed tightly into a fixed smile, wearing a new formal uniform: a black dress that makes her look really quite fat and a frilled white apron, cap pinned to a fuzzy bun of brown hair.

I roll the window down, suddenly desperate to connect to her, to everything that was good, warm, solid, smelling of bread. She sees me then. Her smile becomes genuine, full of teeth, and she flicks her eyes up, telling me to look at the sky.

Dark clouds are slugging towards Black Rabbit Hall, shadows over the woods, across the lawns, until, in no time at all, they are directly above us and releasing their load. Rain! Wild, wild rain that spits when it hits the gravel, flattens the flowers in their beds, makes the guests yelp and pick up their skirts, their feet spraying water as they run from the cars to the house.

Toby and I lose each other in the resulting pandemonium. The hall is a scrum of wet legs, dripping hats and women dabbing frantically at the sooty streams of make-up dribbling from their eyes. Boris – soggy, stinking – nudges his nose into their skirts. Big Bertie confuses everyone by chiming loudly and dementedly on the wrong hour, then chimes on and on, as if a cog has stuck, until a bloated man in a morning suit gives it a hard whack.

Peggy and her army of maids – pretty young fishermen's daughters, scrubbed up but still smelling faintly of mackerel, buttoned into ill-fitting black and white uniforms – flit about in the crowd, desperately trying not to spill their trays of champagne as they get knocked and shoved on the slippery floor and the hands of Caroline's male friends skim their bottoms and grin at them, with mouths full of crowded yellow teeth.

I'm only interested in one person.

Lucian is standing dutifully next to his mother, staring out at the crowds, through them, as if pretending he is anywhere else: something tells me he senses my gaze, but he doesn't meet it. A woman in pink is bending over Caroline's white silk shoe – brushing her bottom on his thigh – frantically trying to rub the muddy gravel splatter off it with a handkerchief, while Caroline hisses, 'Why the bloody hell is it raining? The weather forecast said it would be fine . . .' and glares out at the bruised Cornish sky, as if it's raining on purpose, which I think it might well be.

The rain continues to fall in sheets, creating, Grandma Esme notes with the tiniest glint of a smile, 'utter havoc with poor Caroline's carefully laid plans'. There can be no champagne reception on the lawn now, no dynastic wedding photograph framed by the rolling acres of the estate or the envied show of hydrangeas. Instead the guests are trapped behind the rattling windows of Black Rabbit Hall, watching slack-jawed as the wind tears at the pink and white gazebos, plucks pegs from the ground, the bunting from the trees, and blows a tower of white napkins high into the branches of the trees, where they flutter like surrendered flags.

'Wanton destruction!' Toby comes up behind me, eyes bright. 'Absolute carnage!'

'Maybe there is a God after all,' I whisper, and we both snort with mirthless laughter, less than miserable for the first time that day.

Peggy busies past – sweating, plum-faced, as if she might burst. Grandma pulls her to one side and whispers something in her ear that makes Peggy clamp her hand over her mouth and go even redder. Soon her army of local girls appears with tin buckets, which they shove beneath the ribbons of water pouring from the ceiling (the ceiling that Daddy promised to fix before the wedding but, of course, didn't). Caroline's friends watch, appalled and fascinated, muttering things about Caroline having her 'work cut out for her', as if she was the one holding a bucket, rather than ordering Peggy about, with a fixed smile, then disappearing upstairs to change into yet another dress.

The leaking is at its worst in the ballroom: Caroline was warned, but refused to accept that it might rain on her wedding day. And although the ballroom floor hasn't yet caved in under the weight of all the people, Peggy thinks this a real possibility, which has improved our mood a little. For the moment we have to make do with watching a drip bounce off the black lid of the grand piano and a bit of cornicing starting to crumble, carrying with it the hope of larger lumps of plaster falling down to knock the dull guests out cold.

At one point Grandma Esme looks so bored she might actually be asleep, eyes half closed over her untouched pink meat terrine. Kitty crawls on to her knee, overwhelmed and exhausted, sinking into her bosom, which is floral and pillowy, much like her sofa in Chelsea. If I could lie there I would.

Lucian still refuses to look in my direction, which makes me yearn for and hate him equally, but Toby's gaze is trained steadily on me – and only me – throughout most of the meal, as if this is the only thing that is stopping him from yanking off the tablecloth or storming along it, kicking salmon into people's faces.

If only he would. I now regret asking him to behave.

After an eternity, the meal is over and the guests, unsteady on their feet now, hooting, sloshing wine from their glasses, flow into the drawing room, where flickering candles singe swishing scarves and light the women's painted, exaggerated faces from beneath their chins. Voices rise, fighting the jazz band that seems to get noisier and less tuneful with every number.

Strangers finger the stone busts and paintings, leaving greasy marks all over Great-Great-Grandpa's face. They pull at the servant bells on the walls, blow the hunting horn, spin the globe too hard, loll on the furniture that has been pushed to the edges of the room, and rock with senseless laughter. The music changes, gets louder, faster, more confusing: it sounds as if we've been invaded by a charge of drunken fairground horses.

I stand on tiptoe in my silk pumps, craning above the bouncing curls, the sweating bald pates and sprouting ears, trying to spot my brothers and sister or Lucian, any familiar face. But I can't. Caroline's friends are starting to dance now, shimmying, doing funny things with their hands, making escape across the room to the door impossible. They grab me by my arms, try to get me to dance. Swollen bellies, hardened by champagne and gas, press up against me as I squeeze past.

In the end, I give up and flatten myself against a wall, waiting for the tune to end. A man with a moustache, foam-tipped with champagne, sidles up, stinking of drink, asking whether I like my new 'fabulously rich old stepmother' before snorting at his own wit. A woman in a white mini-dress pushes him off – 'Out of the cradle, you old beast, Bradley!'– introduces herself as Jibby and, with a startling lisp, starts telling me how my 'dishy new brother, Luthian' has broken her poor niece Belinda's heart by not contacting her: would I give him a nudge and get him to visit the poor girl?

The peacock brooch! The relief of finding Grandma Esme is so great – almost as great as hearing Lucian has broken Belinda's heart. I almost burst into tears. The Jibby woman excuses herself, staggering off into the crowd in silver knee-high boots.

'Oh, darling. You look quite exhausted,' Grandma says, grabbing my hands. She doesn't look so well herself, older than I think of her in my head.

'Where are the others, Grandma? I've lost them.'

'Kitty and Barney were happily demolishing a bowl of candied nuts in the hall when I last looked. I've no idea what Toby is up to. But I think, considering, he's behaved impeccably, don't you? Let's leave him be now, poor chap.'

I almost ask after Lucian, too, but think better of it in case something in my face gives me away.

'Why don't you sneak off, darling?' she whispers. 'This lot are far too pickled to notice.'

But at that moment Daddy walks back into the room. He is immediately cornered by Caroline and her tubby male friend, who vines his arm around Daddy's neck and shouts in his ear, making Daddy recoil. I wonder if Grandma can see well enough to notice how uncomfortable he looks for a man in his own house, the way he seems to be stepping back from both the man and Caroline, who responds by moving even closer, taut and anxious, repeatedly touching the studded jewels glinting in her hair. 'Won't Daddy mind? Aren't we all meant to wave them off on honeymoon?'

'You leave your papa to me.' Grandma squeezes my hands. 'I dare say if it weren't for you there would have been a somewhat more colourful scene at some point in today's rather lengthy proceedings. You've done enough.'

'I didn't do anything,' I say truthfully.

'You did everything. They take their lead from you, Amber. You were stoic, therefore so were they. You make them strong.' Grandma smiles tearfully. 'Nancy would be so proud of you.'

'Thank you, Grandma.' It's the first time anyone has mentioned Momma all day.

'Now just look at you . . .' She sniffs, centres the bow at my waist. 'You hold yourself with such dignity, unlike most of the women here. And you are quite, quite beautiful in that frock.'

I smile, unsure whether to believe it. Daddy's secretary bought the shell-pink dress from Harrods. It isn't something I'd have chosen. I'd wanted something shortish and sharp with black and white stripes, a big buckle and belt, something from Biba or Mary Quant, like the ones Matilda's sister wears, but this has a tight bodice and a full skirt pushed out by two layers of petticoats, reminding me of photographs of Momma in New York in the 1950s. 'The dress is a bit old-fashioned.'

'Ah, that's its charm. It's quite perfect on you. No wonder you're attracting such attention from all these bad-mannered brutes. You're quite the belle of the ball, darling.' She raises one eyebrow, glances over at Caroline. 'I'm surprised Caroline didn't make you wear sackcloth quite frankly.'

'She's barely acknowledged me. I don't think she's even noticed I'm here.'

'She's noticed you, my darling. Be assured of that.'

'I can't bear her, Grandma,' I say, feeling it fiercely. 'I just can't.'

At that moment Caroline looks at us, perhaps sensing we're discussing her, and her gaze hardens.

Grandma waves cheerfully, speaks to me from the side of her mouth. 'I suspect the new Mrs Alton is one of those women who needs to feel well liked before she becomes likeable, my dear Amber. It is down to us to ignite such a process, however testing.'

'Well, I can't. And I don't think Daddy loves her either.'

'In situations such as this, my darling, we must all find ways of getting on with one another, even if that means dampening our own judgement for the greater good.' She lifts her glass to her lips, mutters beneath its rim, 'Good gracious, I fear Caroline intends to honour us with her company. If you want to scoot, I suggest you do it right now and pretend you haven't noticed her intentions.'

I slide along the wall, dash out of the room, and find Barney and Kitty in the hall, fists full of sugared almonds. I have to push the exhausted pair up the stairs, hands on their bottoms. On the landing I look down at the boiling sea of people below and vow not to return until every last one of them has left.

In the nursery Kitty starts to sob because she's ripped her bridesmaid's dress and Peggy's cap makes her look not like Peggy. Barney confesses he drank half a glass of champagne and feels a bit peculiar and could I please carry him into bed? I make him drink three glasses of water and settle them both to sleep.

As I swish his curtains shut, the sound of fevered clapping rises from the drive, then the rattle of tins on gravel as a car zooms away. Well, she's gone at least. And tomorrow the guests will also be gone and the house will be ours again, I think, trying to lift my spirits. I must tell Toby the same thing. I must find him, check he's okay.

Toby is not in his bedroom. The window is gaping open and there is a black puddle in the middle of the floor – the moon gleaming in its centre like a glass eye – where the rain has been lashing in. I lean right out of the window to check he's not scrambling down the ivy. He's been known to do this to avoid company.

'Amber?'

I cannot move. My stomach flips.

'Everything okay?'

Slowly, I turn to face Lucian. The room suddenly feels impossibly small and charged, full of things we cannot say, our mutual embarrassment electric. I don't know where to look either.

'I'm . . . trying to find Toby,' I stutter. My mouth is dry, my heart beating so fast now that I'm sure he must be able to see it pumping beneath the silk of my dress. 'He's gone.'

'I can't blame him if he's bolted.' Lucian walks across the room, shuts the window. He has taken off his tails and I can see the blades of his shoulders beneath his shirt. 'My mother's set are boring when sober and beastly after a drink, I'm afraid.'

'I hadn't noticed.'

He laughs then, and some kind of understanding sparks between us. Music drifts up from downstairs, the rise and fall of voices. It feels another world away, the distance between it and us completely unbridgeable. His hand reaches to flip away his floppy fringe but it isn't there because it's all slicked back, making his handsome face seem more open and strangely vulnerable. 'May I help you look for Toby?'

For some reason it feels like he's asking something else, so I nod, feeling that he could ask me anything and I would only ever be able to say yes.

He holds open Toby's door. 'After you.'

The petticoats under the skirt of my dress rustle against his leg like sheets. I feel that tug deep inside. The same desperate tug I'd felt when he kissed me at the bottom of the drive. How can I feel this about a stepbrother? How is it right?

It may not be right. But it is. And this, I tell myself firmly, is how it will stay, a bud, never a full flower.

'Up?' he asks, stealing a glance at me.

I blush and nod, rather than suggesting we start outside, where Toby is most likely to be: I no longer care what Toby is doing.

On the topmost landing, I wipe away a circle of condensation from the window, then peer out into the night.

'See anything?' he asks.

'Not much.' The rain has stopped. The party is moving outside again, a flurry of hurricane lamps darting like fireflies on the lawns. But it is far too dark to see anything beyond the edge of the woods, black and dripping, where Toby, no doubt, is curled in his tree house – he has slept there twice this week already – to return at dawn to doze on the end of my bed like a dog, damp, muddy, with twigs in his hair and, when he wakes, strange lights in his eyes.

Lucian slides back the heavy lock and pushes the window up. There's a metallic smell of rain on leading. 'Can you hear something?' he asks.

'Voices in the garden, I think. Sound sort of bounces along the roof. Things get distorted up here.'

'Really? That's the roof?' He pushes his head eagerly through the open window into the night. 'Possible to get out there?'

'Kind of,' I say hesitantly. I've never much liked this bit of the roof. Daddy goes up there sometimes to try to fix things, check chimneys for nests, but Momma banned us from going anywhere near it. She was always terrified of Barney finding his way out there and falling off.

'Oh, come on. I've never been on the roof of any house before.' He offers a hand to pull me up after him, smiles. 'I promise not to jump if you won't.'

I take his hand, our palms sparking as they touch.

The dim landing light spills across the lead only a few feet, but far enough for us to see the short, chunky battlements. We step towards them gingerly. The wind sucks my dress to my legs. The sky is bright now, stitched with stars. And I feel alive, more alive than I've ever felt, like I'm going to burst out of my own skin.

Lucian's leg is about ten inches away from mine.

'I did my best to talk Ma out of the marriage,' he says quietly.

I steal a glance through my whirling, night-tangled hair. We are standing closer now, although I wasn't aware of either of us moving. The awkwardness between us in Toby's room has become something else.

'She's never been particularly interested in my opinion unfortunately.'

I feel a little sorry for him. Momma always made me feel that my opinions mattered.

'You don't get to choose your parents, do you?'

'No. No, you don't.' I'm struck with my own sheer luck in getting my mother out of all the millions of potential mothers in the world. I lost her. But I'd *had* her too. This has never occurred to me before.

'Ma wants me to rule the world, all that nonsense.'

'Daddy hoped Toby might rule the world once. I'm not sure he dares hope now.'

'Ah, Toby, Lord of Misrule,' says Lucian, not unkindly, making it sound like a compliment.

'What about your father?' I ask, emboldened by the furry lateness of the hour, the strangeness of being up on the roof on such a charged night. Up here, it seems, we can ask each other anything, anything we want, but the moment we descend back into the house, all the old rules will apply and we'll be back to talking about the weather and asking the other if they would be so kind as to pass the bramble jelly and pretending to be brother and sister. Also, I sense that Lucian quite likes blunt questioning.

'Father? He was a good man.' He is silent for a moment and when he speaks there is a crackle in his voice. 'I still miss him. It's been years. Stupid, isn't it?'

I shake my head, afraid that if I speak my voice will

crack, too, or, worse, I'll cry. And I absolutely hate it when people cry on my behalf, as if what happened to me happened to them when it didn't.

'He was seventy-three,' he says, as if trying to remind himself. 'So he had a fair innings.' He is silent for a moment. 'I'm aware that your mother didn't.'

'Forty is pretty old.'

'Just not old enough.'

'No. But she was happy, really happy. Whenever I think of my mother she's smiling. She had a gap between her teeth. You could stick a match end in it.' Talking about her doesn't feel stretchy or awkward as it normally does. Oddly, she comes alive again in the retelling to Lucian. 'I'm not sure if it's better to die happy, or worse because more is lost.'

He considers this. 'I think it makes it better.'

'She was beautiful too,' I say, unable to keep the pride from my voice.

'I know. I've seen her portrait in the hall.'

I start to grin at the craziness of the night. I can feel the ridge of his shoe against my pump.

'You look just like her,' he whispers, in a voice so soft I can't be quite certain he's said it.

We stand there, buffeted by wind and feelings, bats dancing figures of eight around the battlements.

The band starts a new song. The wind carries some notes up high, swallows others. Inside my body, things are happening too, a strange kind of music all its own.

'Look, I'm sorry about the kiss. If I'd known that they'd marry . . .' His words trail off in a fug of embarrassment. 'But we mustn't let it . . . ruin this . . . our friendship.'

A loud bang, like a gunshot, splitting the sky. I jump,

clench my teeth. Another. Louder. I hear it in every cell of my body. Feel it. See it. Blood splattered across the stable floor. Brains. A shattered skull in a black velvet box. I squeeze my eyes shut, feeling sick and faint, that terrible night rushing up.

'Amber, what's the matter?'

'Nothing,' I mutter, trying desperately hard not to make a scene, braced against the next shot, which comes loud, louder. I see the fingers bouncing from the jolt of the gun. Squeeze my eyes tighter shut.

'It's nothing to be frightened of. Fireworks. Really. Trust me. Look.'

So I do trust him and I do look.

Skipping ropes of fairy lights twist in the sky, over and over, before dissolving into a stream of silver. Bang. Bang. Bang. I flinch each time but Lucian's arm is around my shoulders and this makes it bearable. I press closer, my body remembering the fit of him, the smell of him, and all these sensations make the dreadful wrongness, the reasons, the rules for me not loving him completely irrelevant. There is no one I'd rather be with here on the roof. No one with whom I feel so myself. In hushed voices, our warm mouths close to each other's ears, we marvel at the bats, that a man might soon step on to that white pimpled moon, that we are on a roof high above the world. After a while the fireworks become quieter, less like gunfire than applause, clapping from high in the gods, and the space closes between us completely – that last inch – and we kiss and kiss as if we might get inside one another's skin and the sky shatters gold through the gaps between my eyelashes. His mouth drops to my neck. Whispering my name over and over.

Twenty-Two

'Amber! Amber!' Toby's eyes are glassy and pink. His hand wobbles my shoulder roughly. 'Wake up!'

I groan, pull my blanket up to my chin. 'What is it?'

'Has something happened with Lucian? Give me the word and I'll thump the living daylights out of him.'

'What? What are you talking about? Go away. I'm asleep.'

'You're not hurt? Nothing's happened?'

'For God's sake, Toby!'

He sinks down in my velvet bedroom chair, face in his hands, one knee juddering urgently, like he needs the loo.

I feel his eyes on me as I roll on to my side and face the wallpaper, heart scudding. I think, He knows, deep down, in the animal bit that doesn't need to be told stuff.

'Sorry. I . . . I couldn't sleep, you see. I got it into my head that something had happened. That you needed protecting.'

'Go back to sleep.'

Secrets are thrilling but deceit is horrible. It's been ten days since the wedding. I want more than anything to be able to be honest with Toby. But I can't think how this is possible. I can't really think at all. I feel less like a human being than an iridescent bubble flying across a summer sky. Less a sister. Less a child. Less of everything I was and yet somehow more myself than ever.

In Daddy's and Caroline's honeymoon absence, Black Rabbit Hall has become epic, ungoverned, ours. Peggy is too exhausted to object to anything much, leaving Annie to keep a lazy eye on Kitty and Barney, the rest of us to swim and amble, picnic on pasties, strawberries and broad beans eaten raw from the pod, while Lucian and I shoot secret smiles, wondering when we can next be alone. Usually we don't have to wait long: Toby has been hammering new 'cells' – higher floors – with sole-tingling drops, to his tree house, the ambition of his plans ever more fevered in the summer heat.

He was in the tree the night of the wedding, of course.

Toby's bedroom was empty at dawn. I'd left Lucian not long before but couldn't sleep a wink, so I'd walked into the woods to find Toby, cool dawn singing through my fingers, passing a pair of satin knickers stuck on a hydrangea bush and a fat man beached on the lawn, champagne bottle still in his hand. It seemed to take forever to get to the tree house, and I was glad of that, as if time, like water, could wash away any incriminating traces of the kisses. Finally, I spotted Toby's dirty bare foot through the trees, dangling in mid-air, his straggly red hair poking through the gap in the planks, like a giant bird in a nest. I was about to call out to him and bring him back to the house. But I lost my nerve – fearing he'd see my swollen lips and guess – and crept away soundlessly on the carpet of fallen beech nuts, leaving him to sleep peacefully among the knives and guns and stolen beer. As I retreated, I vowed that I would never kiss Lucian again. The risks were far too high.

A few hours later Lucian and I were kissing again, more urgently, knowing it to be wrong but quite unable to stop.

We kiss whenever we can now. On the cliff ledge. In the tall fluffy grasses at the back of the field, hidden by the stamping cows' hoofs. Beneath the surface of the river, slippy limbs entwined. And in the wardrobe, our favourite place, where we whisper furtively about everything that matters – music, books, why it's impossible not to giggle at funerals – and lick the salt off each other's swimmer's skin, peeling ourselves back, discovering each other inch by inch.

We did it there.

The first time the fierce burn of pain made me cry out. But now, after further fumbling and practice, I let out different cries, strange sounds that I have to stifle in the furs, the sounds of my body melting and opening, revelatory as a strange new planet. I know that it's against the rules – although no one but Annabel, Matilda's sister, has ever fully explained what 'it' is – but as far as I'm concerned, the rules broke the day Momma fell off her horse. Besides, I don't feel dirty or used, any of those things that girls are meant to feel. I feel . . . worshipped. Adored. Connected to the world again, no longer floating numbly in the cold black place beneath it. And, despite the danger of being caught, safe for the first time in months.

We are careful. Lucian always pulls out of me, just in time. And I've been bathing twice a day so that Toby won't smell it on me, the sweat, the sweetness, the betrayal. If Toby is in the room, I try not to look in Lucian's direction, and sit as far away from him as possible, or the urge for us to touch – a soft tap of the knee, a brush of the foot – is irresistible.

Yet I find myself thoughtlessly saying his name under

my breath. And it still feels as if Lucian is spread inside me like a colour. Which leads to the problem. The bigger problem, much harder to hide.

It is this: I am stupidly, shockingly happy. More than anything else, I worry that this will be the thing that gives me away. There is so much to be unhappy about – Daddy duped by Caroline, Momma's bones picked clean in the soil, the stupidity of loving *anyone* if you don't have to, when people die so easily – and yet . . . It's like watching the knife cut, seeing the blood and not feeling a thing.

Twenty-Three

A few days later, Caroline and Daddy return from Paris, smiling, not holding hands. Black Rabbit Hall isn't ours any more. And everything feels far more dangerous. Will Daddy notice something different? Will some grass stain or dishevelment give me away? It has all happened so fast I feel as if I must radiate a brilliant heat. But Daddy doesn't notice anything. He asks vaguely if we all had fun – lifting his chin, rubbing the back of his tanned neck – and, not long after, leaves for London on 'urgent business'. *Not* taking Caroline with him!

Disaster.

Caroline notices far more. She observes that Lucian 'is looking quite feral' and that, considering the state of the house, Peggy and Annie 'appear to have been struck down by some sedentary illness'. Worse, she promises to stay on until the end of the summer holidays 'to keep an eye on things' – my blood runs cold – and get the house 'in order, one that befits it'.

No one knows quite what this new 'order' might mean for Black Rabbit Hall – 'How can we when her whims change as often as her bed sheets?' mutters Peggy, who thinks daily fresh linen wasteful and unchristian – until Caroline mentions that the house must appear in *House & Garden* magazine one day. This makes all of us, especially

Peggy, shake with suppressed laughter, then subside into a kind of helpless gloom in the still heat.

Happily, Black Rabbit Hall puts up a good fight, rattling and leaking, spewing treacly brown water into Caroline's bath, as well as an extended family of mice – Caroline's petrified of mice – scuttling through her bedroom at night (greedy for the oats Toby scatters beneath the bed). Even when Daddy returns the following weekend, Black Rabbit Hall keeps it up. After one particularly eventful night – the cat coughing up hair balls on Caroline's silk slippers, the lights blowing, a dead crow rotting in their bedroom chimney – Daddy suggests that Caroline spend the rest of the summer holidays in the comfort of Fitzrovia while he 'makes things a little more to your liking here'. Clearly suspecting that this will not happen – it wouldn't – Caroline stands in the hall, jaw set, staring up the staircase, like a climber surveying a perilous mountain, determined to conquer it at any cost.

She wants to conquer us, too, of course, and has a variety of tactics up her silk sleeve to do this, all revolving around the abhorrent idea of 'Our New Family'. For some reason she wants to record the misery. There are endless forced photos: Caroline and Daddy standing stiffly side by side, me and Lucian shifty, Toby scowling, Barney and Kitty arranged like dolls, failing to smile for some fashionable photographer, who has stumbled sweaty and disoriented off the slow London train. Caroline also insists on 'family luncheons at the proper hour' in the dining room ('staff eat in the kitchen') while the constant threat of 'family activities' – walks, sailing, trips to St Ives – hangs over every summer day like an approaching storm, making me, Lucian and Toby shudder for different reasons.

We quickly learn that the easiest way to detonate such things, send the day spiralling off from the original plan, is by casually mentioning Momma. Within seconds a startling green vein starts to pop on Caroline's forehead and the whole charade shatters into a million sharp pieces, like a crystal tumbler dropped to the stone flag floor.

As it maddens Caroline when we are late, we also try to be late as much as possible, which is easy enough. Only Kitty – a survivor who prioritizes her food – arrives at the table before the meal is even colder than it is when it arrives after its Alpine trek from the kitchen. Barney usually has to be hastily dressed on account of his aversion to clothes in the heat and Caroline's insistence on 'a civility beyond that of apes', a comment that ensures Toby's underarm ape-style scratching behind her back while Lucian, loyal to his mother only to a point, tries not to laugh and almost breaks the uneasy truce that relies on them ignoring one another.

It's not that Lucian hasn't tried to be friendly, but all attempts are met with utter disdain and indifference: the last thing Toby wants is to have his prejudices contradicted. In a way this is a relief. If they were friendly, would it not make the dishonesty all the harder?

However, Toby does not ignore Caroline: he goads her, drawn to confrontation like a ship to a wrecker's lamp, knowing he has the enormous advantage of not giving a fig, while Caroline cares far too much. He refuses to join us in the dining room: 'I won't play any part or engage in the sort of forced conversation that makes me want to chop my tongue off and feed it to Boris. I will dine on Twiglets in the comfort of my tree house.' When Caroline, sherry glass trembling in her hand, tried to exert her authority – 'I don't give a damn what you think, young man. We will *all* sit down to eat like a normal happy family' – Toby crisply pointed out, 'We are not normal. We are not family. And, thanks to you, we are certainly not happy,' then casually wandered off, picking dirt out of his fingernails with the tip of his penknife and flicking it at the newly buffed wooden panelling.

The less Caroline can control us, the more she asserts her authority over the house. To general disbelief, she announced the appointment of a new live-out trained cook – this is akin to shoving the Queen off her throne and hiring a 'more professional' one – hurtling Peggy into a white-faced wordless fury, involving much crashing of copper pans and slamming of pantry doors.

Bartlett started yesterday.

It is all too peculiar for words. While Peggy is soft, round and getting rounder, Bartlett is skinny and stooped, rather like a bent soup spoon. Peggy and Annie are on high alert – 'Never trust a thin cook' – and suspicious of her spotless white apron, muttering beneath their breath about how Bartlett won't get her hands dirty dismembering eels, and doesn't know her stargazy pie from her hog's pudding. I haven't dared tell Peggy that I think this is the point: I'm not sure Caroline ever fully recovered from the sight of blackened pilchard heads poking through that pastry lid. We haven't had any Cornish family dishes since Bartlett started. I never thought I'd miss them but I do.

Lunch today was a whole salmon, dead-cold, fairy-pink, studded with medals of green cucumber, far more formal than anything we'd normally eat. The boiled potatoes were smooth and white as eggs, with not so much as one muddy eye. The silver has actually been polished – we pull faces into the convex mirrors of spoons – and now gleams on an unfamiliar tablecloth, something lacy and Victorian, dug out from the archaeological depths of the linen cupboard. And the napkins are confusing, forced into stiff fan-shapes that Barney flicks over with his fingers.

Daddy – shockingly – has also agreed to the garden having what Caroline calls 'rejuvenation' and Toby calls 'desecration'. After declaring that 'the beds have gone quite rampant!' – making Lucian and me pale at the table – Caroline fired Black Rabbit's loyal gardeners ('stuck in the past and older than the yew hedge') and hired a band of new ones, who arrived in a shiny black van with 'Ted Duckett and Son' picked out in gold lettering on the side, and started hacking at Momma's beloved rambling roses.

Caroline has also hired a fat man in half-moon spectacles – he has a meaty pink stump rather than a little finger – to fix the clocks. ('A hell of a job,' he huffed, sticking his doughy face into the weights and toothed cogs of Big Bertie, Barney peering over his shoulder, mesmerized by the glorious ghastliness of the finger stump.) Although the clocks are now supposedly accurate, it has made little difference to anyone's timekeeping. We are so used to adding a loose hour or so that it has merely confused us and we've gone back to judging the time by the rumble in our stomachs and the slip of the sun.

I'm sure if Caroline could hire a man to come and correct our settings – make us like her, forget Momma – she would. But she can't. And she hates that. She really hates that. She has tried being nice – presents! – and being vile. Neither makes a blind bit of difference. She walks into a room and makes the walls contract, so that even the biggest room here soon feels like a stuffy metal lift trapped between floors. If Daddy's not around, she doesn't bother pretending to like us and eyes us all, even Lucian, with undisguised irritation, as if her life would be so much more enjoyable if we didn't exist and she had Daddy to herself.

Daddy will not hear a word against her. He is loyal to her version of events, mostly, I think, because she has his ear first and can prepare the ground in her favour. When I told Daddy that she behaves very differently to us when he is away, he sighed. 'Caroline warned me that you'd say something like this, Amber.' And when I said I thought her 'vinegary', he became furious: 'How exceptionally ungenerous, when she is so very fond of you!'

Oddly, her presence sends him into a strange state of dumb passivity: he ambles about the estate now, absent-eyed, with a glass of whisky in his hand, while Caroline continually refills his glass and coos, in the soft voice she only uses with him, 'Don't you worry, everything's being taken care of, my darling,' as if he were a giant baby. Worse, Daddy doesn't seem to mind one bit.

Toby says Daddy's just relieved not to be in charge any more. That Momma dying made him suddenly old, and the old are like infants: 'They want to be led.'

If I thought Daddy actually loved her, maybe I wouldn't judge him so harshly. But it is always Caroline who reaches for his hand, not him for hers. Caroline who rests her hand on the thigh of his yellow cord trousers. Caroline who anxiously awaits his return, dressing up, ankling down the staircase in her heels, pausing on the lower step, frowning across at the portrait of Momma, like a woman checking her reflection in the mirror, not liking what she sees. Although Daddy compliments her regularly – 'Charming dress, darling' – he says it with little passion. There is none of the embarrassing smooching that there was with Momma, no long kisses or secret lights-off drawing-room dancing, no softening in his eyes whenever she walks into a room. I think Caroline's aware of this. When he's in London, she sometimes sits at the dining table, chin in her cold-creamed hands, just staring flatly at his chair, as if she'd never expected it to be so empty.

She's growing suspicious too. I'm sure of it. Lucian thinks I'm worrying unnecessarily – 'She'd never guess in a million years, Amber' – but in recent days I've noticed her razor gaze cutting to Lucian then back to me, as if something about us doesn't make sense. And she's endlessly probing Lucian: where has he been? With whom? Why has he got bits of hay sticking to his shirt?

I can't help but feel that things are taking shape, even though I can't see that shape yet, that a sequence of small irrecoverable moments is hooking fast together and pointing in one direction like the barbs of a feather.

Twenty-Four

Lorna

Leaning against one of the carved posts of the bridal suite's bed, Lorna slips the photographs into their brown envelope and sighs heavily. Will she ever know why her mother kept visiting Black Rabbit Hall? Maybe it doesn't matter. Maybe she's reading too much into those photographs. Trying to force a narrative shape on random events. After all, her mother was odd in many ways, an obsessive character drawn to old houses, the comfort of repetition. Maybe she just liked the drive. Yes, that could be reason enough.

She shouldn't dwell on it. She should get organized for the journey home. She stands up straight, scans the room – its prettiness a little tarnished by memories of her day spent doped – for things she's left behind. She always leaves something behind. This time it's her bronzer and the lid of her lip salve, rolling on the frayed edge of the rug by the door. She reaches for it and, as she does, spots strange dots in the dust immediately outside. About two centimetres in circumference, up the corridor, a wide footstep apart. The marks of Mrs Alton's cane, she suddenly thinks. Perhaps she had not merely imagined that someone was standing in the doorway watching her sleep. The idea is not a pleasant one.

Lorna retrieves the lid, then goes into the bathroom to refill her Evian bottle at the tap. It's so close today and she feels dehydrated so she's going to need it. The water spluttering out of the rusty tap is very brown, browner than it was yesterday. The heat probably. Not wanting to risk sickness on the long train ride home, Lorna pours it out. She'll find the kitchen. The water there will surely be cleaner. She has time. Just. And she can drop off her bag in the hall.

Surprisingly, Lorna finds her way easily, as if it wants to be found. Large, cheerful and square, its walls painted a peeling cerulean blue, sunlight pours through its paned window on to a homely wooden table that feels like the heart of the room. Opposite, there is an old range cooker, blackened with grease and age. Copper pans and oversized enamel kitchen implements hang above it. Cutlery – silver gone black – protrudes from grubby ceramic jars on the warped wooden work surfaces: Lorna sees each piece being pulled out by impatient children's fingers. Bowls, so many bowls. Someone must have been a keen cook. There is a larder too, circular air holes punched into its door in the shape of a heart. She can't resist.

Her mouth drops open. While the usual supermarket coffee, tea bags, sugar and pasta are on the most easily reached shelf, the ones above are crammed with things that look older than her – faded, ancient tins of marrowfat peas with vintage labels, a tin of Spam, like the ones Nan used to keep at the back of her cupboard. Hearing a faint rustling and fearing a mouse, Lorna quickly shuts the door and steps away.

Right. Water. No more poking around. No more

diversions. She needs to put her London head back on. After a tussle with the copper tap above a bath-sized butler's sink, the twisting cord of water finally runs into something that looks less of a health risk. She leans over, fills her bottle. And that's when it catches her eye, the blue and white apron hanging on the brass hook beside the sink. Something about it takes her aback. She's seen it before. Where?

Lorna's brain searches for the association, alighting on one possibility then another. Finally she's got it: the housekeeper in the background of the photographs. Yes, she thinks. The round pretty face. The striped apron, always in that apron. Yes, it's hers. She puts down her water bottle, picks the apron off the hook. Amazing it's still here, although perhaps not, given the state of the larder. She rubs it between her fingers because the fabric feels soft and old and she loves old fabric and . . . and her fingertips keep moving back and forth across the blue embroidered letters on the hem, catching on the drag of the years, back and forth, back and forth, until she is under her Barbie duvet with a flickering plastic torch, running her fingers across the ink of the Ps on the birth certificate, over and over, too many Ps ever to forget.

'You left these behind in your room.' Dill puts down her small wire basket of eggs and pulls from her overall pocket the brown envelope containing the photographs, offering it to Lorna. She doesn't make any mention of the fact that Lorna is sitting on the floor of the kitchen, face buried in an old apron. She's seen far stranger things at Black Rabbit Hall.

Lorna can barely move her arm to take them. She has stiffened on the linoleum floor, has no idea how long she's been there, only that the sunlight hitting the copper pans is gold and thick, and it wasn't this dark when she first walked into the kitchen.

'I couldn't find you, Lorna,' Dill says politely. 'We had to send the taxi away.'

'The taxi's gone?' She rubs her eyes, which are red and dry, but is far too shocked to cry. A black woodlouse lumbers across the floor, avoiding the puddle of water spilled from the water bottle that slipped from Lorna's hands.

'It's gone six.'

'My train . . .'

'There's nothing tomorrow. Bank holiday. But the morning after.' She smiles uncertainly. 'Mrs Alton will be pleased you're staying on another night or two.'

The floor is sticky against her thighs where her skirt has rucked up. She imagines herself stuck to it for ever, like an insect on a fly paper. How will she ever get from here to a train, the normality of London, to her life as it was? It feels unreachable.

Dill hovers uncertainly. 'Lorna, is, um, everything okay?'

Lorna stares down at the apron on her knee. Its waistband is shiny, once tightly tied. She imagines her mother loosening it as her belly got bigger. Did she use the apron to hide her pregnancy? Was she single or already married? Did her employer abuse her? Oh, no, please. Don't let her be a product of rape. That has always been one of her worst fears. To discover the genes of some beast helixing inside her.

'A cup of tea?' asks Dill, hand lost in her hair, not quite knowing what to do next.

'Yes, thank . . . thank you.' If only Dill would leave the room she could try to pick all the bits of herself up again, scrape herself off the walls, put herself back into some recognizable form.

Dill smiles shyly, nods at the envelope in Lorna's hands. 'I had a peep, hope you don't mind.'

'Oh.' She looks down at the envelope. No, none of this is possible. Why would her mother keep returning to the place where Lorna's biological mother lived and worked? It doesn't make any sense. Why risk Lorna accompanying her?

'I think I took those photos.'

'Sorry?' Lorna must have misheard.

'I'd sit at the front of the drive when I was a kid, while Mum was working up at the house. Did I mention she worked here?'

Lorna numbly shakes her head. She doesn't know. She wasn't listening hard enough. To herself, to any of this.

'Plonk myself high up in the tree and wait for local friends to pass. Mrs Alton didn't like the village kids on the estate, you see, so I'd wait for them at the end of the drive.'

Something somewhere is knitting together: a little girl's feet dangling from a tree; scuffed brown Mary-Janes – 'Say cheese!'

'She was pretty, I remember that, your mum, her mustard coat. For some reason I remember that coat.'

The mustard coat. She'd forgotten it until this moment but now remembers it exactly, the pill of the wool, the

296

glossy big brown buttons. Her mother had worn it all year round: she was permanently cold.

'She stood in that drive staring up at the house like it was . . . I don't know . . . Buckingham Palace or something. Always asked if I'd take a photograph for her. Gave me a bag of fudge as a thank-you.'

The hairs on Lorna's arms lift as she remembers the candy-striped paper bag of fudge in her hand. The envy and disappointment when her mother made her pass it to another girl. The girl with the shoes. The camera.

'My age you were, only you had better clothes and sounded so exotic, coming from London. Do you remember it? Me?' Dill glows with excitement.

'I – I think so. Yes, I do.'

Dill shakes her head in amazement. 'Well, isn't that something? You were right all along, Lorna. You definitely have been here before.'

Lorna bows her face to the apron.

'Is it something I said?'

'It's not you. Sorry. You see, it's the apron . . .' Lorna tries to explain, sniffing. 'The name on the apron.' She holds it up for Dill to see. 'Look.'

'Peggy, that's right,' Dill says, puzzled. 'Peggy Mary Popple. That apron belonged to my mum.'

Lorna hears Dill call. But she keeps running, faster now, into the dazzle of evening sun. She crashes through the washing on the line, fights the sheets with her hands, into the kitchen garden, flattens the tomato plants. A flip-flop flies off her foot. The kitchen-garden door swings shut behind her. The ground surface changes. The patio, hot as plates. Dry spiky grass. Sharp gravel biting into the sole of her foot. Another flip-flop lost. She keeps running. She must keep running. She must outrun Dill's stuttering explanation: her own Big Bang, every bit as catastrophic as she'd feared.

A tea dance. A tipsy tryst in the church hall. A single housekeeper wowed by a Scandinavian fisherman – 'father unknown' – who had left for a foreign port before she'd got his full name or the trawler's. Not a naïve young woman but an older woman, someone who should have known better, who went to church and dreamed of marriage to the local baker but got a bellyful of fatherless twins instead. And kept only one.

She'd kept only one. It was not her.

She was not chosen.

Lorna speeds up, trailing a plume of dust. But she can't outrun that rejection. And she is crying so hard that she cannot see. And all she wants is to go into the darkness of the woods. To disappear.

'Whoa! Stop!'

The voice is familiar. A voice from another life. But Lorna doesn't stop. She sees a blur of a car – squat, dirty silver – and hears the bristle of its engine as it reverses back down the drive. A screech of brakes. The slam of a car door.

'Lorna!'

She's grabbed. She's entangled in the smell of scent and shampoo. She sobs into Louise's neck, like a baby.

Louise explains that Jon is going out of his mind because she wasn't on the train and no one can get hold of her and he's stuck on site and – 'Bloody hell, Lorna, what on earth's happened? No wonder I got such a bad feeling about this. Shall I call the police? A doctor?'

No, no, no. Lorna tries to explain. She really tries. But it doesn't make sense. And she can tell Louise doesn't believe her at first. That Louise is making the soothing uh-huh noises she makes to Alf when he rambles nonsense. But then there is a moment: Louise is frowning down at Lorna's bleeding dirty feet, as if the feet reveal a truth, and something changes between them. She takes both Lorna's hands in her own. '*I'*m your sister,' she says softly. 'Lou and Lor, joined at the hip, remember? Lou and Lor. That's all that matters.' She squeezes Lorna's hand. 'Fairy fate.'

Fairy fate. Lorna wonders how she could ever explain to Louise that it was simple once – before she'd seen the apron – but that it would never be so simple again. Because she's coloured herself in, filled in the gaps. She's no longer a biological family tree of one, something ownerless to be claimed. There is a history. No great love affair. Just a small, shameful mistake. A rejection. A real twin sister with whom she feels little connection.

'Are you sad, Aunty Lorna?' Stubby fingers cup her knee. 'Have you lost the rabbit?'

There is something about the sight of Alf, his huge grin, his simple anticipation of it being returned, that makes Lorna's breathing come easier. She wipes her tears away, knowing how he hates people crying, unless there is an injury that explains things and requires him to stick on a plaster. 'I can't believe you're here, Alf.'

'Daddy said there were too many kids to look after me too.'

Louise rolls her eyes above his head.

'So Mummy put me in my car seat and gave me Wotsits. Grandpa didn't use the map because he said taxi drivers don't need maps. But Grandpa got lost.'

Lorna clamps a hand over her mouth. 'Dad's not here? Please tell me Dad's not here.'

'Insisted. He said he guessed what it might be about.' Louise winces, eyes flicking towards the car. 'I went with it, sorry.'

The car's passenger door flings open and Doug stumbles out into the dusty evening sunshine, wearing a loud Hawaiian shirt and rubbing sleepy eyes beneath his glasses. 'Wowzer.'

Lorna is so stunned by the unlikely sight of her father in his ridiculous shirt that at first she is speechless. Then she collects herself and is just furious. 'You knew, didn't you?'

'Dad, I think you and Lorna might have a bit of chatting to do.' Louise shoots him a hard stare. 'Come on, Alf. Let's go for a walk, a bit of adventure.'

Alf's round face grows serious. 'But I want to find the black rabbit.'

'That's just the name of the house, Alf. We can chat about it as we walk, eh?' Louise takes his hand and pulls him away from the car. But he breaks free of her grip and runs back to Lorna, hugging her legs tightly. 'Don't be sad, Aunty Lor,' he shouts, in his too-loud voice. 'I'm going to be the black-rabbit finder.'

Twenty-Five

Amber, August 1969

'You're not taking that filthy creature into the house!' Caroline's voice bounces off the brick walls of the kitchen garden, like a handful of tacks, carrying right across the terrace.

Toby and I stop arguing and crane our necks in the direction of the kitchen garden. And there is Caroline, wearing a red dress, sliced into four by the wooden slats of the gate like a magician's assistant. She has her hands on her hips and is towering over Barney, who is cradling something in his arms.

'What's the rotten old pike prattling on about now?' Toby's shoulders square for a fight.

'God knows,' I say, clipped, still annoyed with Toby. We've been arguing about who gets the last dry towel that doesn't stink of wet dog, but really we're arguing about the fact that he is coming swimming with me. I know he's checking that I'm not meeting Lucian behind his back – which I resent hugely, especially as this is precisely what I was hoping to do – and would much rather be alone in his tree house, shooting at squirrels with his pistol.

The tree house has three or four levels now, although it's hard to tell, and he has nailed a calendar to one of its rotten planks, counting down the days until a meteorite or something equally bad crashes into Cornwall, currently scheduled for the last week of August, our last day at Black Rabbit Hall. He has worked out the statistical probability of this event – not that probable, but possible – meticulously, with an enthusiasm that he never exercises at school, and is waiting with great relish for impending catastrophe.

I don't believe anything will happen – another of Toby's doomy prophecies – but it still somehow adds to the piquancy and melodrama of these last days of the holiday. Everything feels loaded, as if every hour counts.

The shortening sunny days are also overcast by the knowledge that Lucian will be going up to Oxford in September: the thought of being separated from him is almost unbearable. All we can do is cling to our sketchy plans for escape, which involve running away to New York together when 'the time is right', which it obviously never is, and descending on Aunt Bay. Much as I long to go – this morning I found myself dreamily doodling a circle around New York on the globe with a scratchy green pen – I can't bear the idea of leaving everyone else behind. Can I really break Toby's heart to save my own? Leave Kitty and Barney at the mercy of Caroline? What would Momma think about me deserting them? Would she forgive me?

As I cannot answer these questions, all I can do is wait to unite with Lucian back here at Christmas, and pray that, until then, we remain undiscovered. That in itself will be a small miracle. Even standing here on the terrace, goose-bumped in my swimming costume, I feel I might say or do something that will give me away at any moment.

'Here she comes.'

Caroline marches across the terrace, tossing the words 'Dinner at seven,' at our bare feet as she clips past.

'At least I know when to make myself scarce,' retorts Toby, in earshot, as we walk into the kitchen garden.

It is a strange sight: Barney is sitting on the raised strawberry bed, huddled over what looks a bit like a black cushion. He glances up at us with a smile I'd forgotten existed, pure, wide, revealing the twisted milk tooth that has been threatening to fall out for days.

'What's that?' asks Toby warily, although we can see what it is. We just don't believe it. I pull Boris back by his collar.

'A rabbit.' Barney beams. 'Look.'

'A rabbit?' We lean in closer to double check that the ball of fur is really alive, the nose peeping over Barney's arm twitching. 'A wild one?'

Barney shakes his head. 'Lucian gave it to me.'

Toby's lip curls in disgust. '*Lucian?*'

Barney drops his chin to nuzzle the bunny's head. 'Yeah, in a cardboard box. From the pet shop.'

'But I thought you didn't like rabbits any more,' I say, realizing where Lucian shot off to this morning so furtively, refusing to tell me why. He'd said it was going to be a surprise.

'I didn't want to touch him. But then Lucian made me . . . He held my fingers against his ears and it felt strange and I didn't like it and it made me breathe funny, but then he made me do it again and again until it felt nice.' He looks up at me, honey eyes shining. 'Feel how soft he is, Amber. Feel.'

I tickle the bunny behind his floppy-sock ears, awed by

Lucian, who in one sweet, insightful move has healed Barney of the irrational rabbit fear that set in after Momma's accident, succeeded where we have not. Even Toby has to grant him that.

'I wanted to call him Lucian . . .'

'Oh, God,' groans Toby, covering his face with his hands. I try not to laugh.

'But Lucian said that probably wasn't a good idea. So I'm calling him Old Harry. Like the ferry. Lucian says he'll grow into the name. Even rabbits get old.'

'Welcome to Black Rabbit Hall, Old Harry.' My fingers track a path in the gleaming fur.

'Bartlett will have you in a cooking pot in no time,' Toby says, lifting one of Old Harry's comical ears and peering into its soft pink pocket. 'Tasty.'

'Stop it,' I say curtly.

Barney's smile is already starting to doubt itself. 'Don't you like him?'

'I'm not sentimental about animals.' Toby shrugs. And it's true, he isn't. He loves them, but not like that. He'll eat anything that moves.

'I didn't want to love him, Toby,' Barney blurts apologetically. 'I thought something bad would happen if I did.'

'Bad things don't come out of love, Barney,' I say, hugging him towards me.

Toby looks up at me fiercely. 'What makes *you* so sure?'

I feel the helpless horror of a blush, made all the hotter for knowing what he'll read into it.

'Is there something you're trying to say?' The morning snaps then: the row over the towel, Lucian's rabbit, Toby's clenched fists. It breaks in two. 'Well, is there?'

'Don't be such a berk, Toby.' I steam away, my secret hanging by a bloody thread. Like Barney's milk tooth, one small tug and it's out.

I've discovered that life doesn't always turn on the obvious things – people dying, marriages, all the stuff that gets carved on the tombstones – but little unrecorded things too. Kisses. Rabbits.

In the last week or so, Old Harry has become less a bunny, more a little god with miraculous Barney-healing powers. As befits such a creature, he sleeps in the chicken coop on an old silk eiderdown at night. The enfilade has become his racetrack during the day. Kitty wheels him about the hall under blankets in the toy pram, calling him Baby Harriet when Barney isn't listening. Even Peggy, who says rabbits are pests and is still cranky with a horrid bug that makes her sick in the mornings, feeds him her sweetest carrots with her fingers.

Caroline, of course, has claimed the success as her own: Old Harry is living proof of Lucian's kind nature (as opposed to Toby's brutish one) and, by proxy, her own maternal prowess. She's turned Old Harry into something that pits Lucian against Toby and Toby against Daddy and the past against the future. (No wonder Toby loathes Old Harry, who scampers from the room in fear whenever he enters it.) A couple of days ago, I overheard Caroline murmur sweetly, 'Hugo, darling, Lucian reminds me so much of you, you know. Isn't it uncanny that you and he are so very alike, both in character and looks, and you and Toby so different?' She paused in a silence that I could only imagine was punctuated with Daddy's whisky sip or baffled smile. 'We must take comfort that there is now a like-minded young man in the family who could manage Pencraw . . . should anything happen.'

Worse, Daddy has been inviting Lucian into the library to listen to jazz. Toby's never been invited into the library to listen to jazz. It really makes me mad that Daddy is making an effort to get to know Lucian, but he never tries to get to know Toby. Maybe he's scared of what he'll find. Maybe he thinks he knows Toby already. Well, he doesn't. Daddy doesn't know Toby, any more than he knows me now. He has no idea that we are both different people from whom we were even at the start of the holidays, that everything has changed.

I think that adults must get sort of worn away over time, like rocks out at sea, but remain who they are, just slower and greyer with those funny vertical wrinkles in front of their ears. But the young are a different shape from one week to the next. To know us is to run alongside us, like someone trying to shout through the window of a moving train.

Caroline does not knock. 'Still not dressed, girls?'

I cover the back of my neck with my hand, where Lucian's mouth has left a pink mark. Kitty, who is lying across my pillow, looks up mildly, then carries on making her wigwam of Kirby grips.

Caroline glares at the piles of books and discarded shoes on the rug, the knickers hanging off the back of the velvet chair. 'This room is wanton. Tidy it, Amber. Tidy it at once. Peggy's attention should be on the public areas of the house now. I don't want her wasting her working day clucking after you lot, especially since her digestive problems are proving such a distraction.'

I start shoving the scatter of novels into a pile. Poor Peggy. It's not her fault she feels rotten.

'I've brought you some new dresses.' Caroline dumps a sheaf of clothes on to my bed, smelling of shop.

'I never get new things,' sighs Kitty, adding one more Kirby grip to the wigwam. They all collapse, scatter like matchsticks.

I tentatively hold up a calf-skimming, bulrush-brown pinafore, buttoned up to the collar, quite the ugliest dress I've ever seen.

'Ew,' says Kitty, sympathetically.

The next dress is even worse, sickly yellow and made from a fabric as rough as hop sack.

'A thank-you would be good manners, Amber,' says Caroline, sharply.

'Kitty shouldn't like to wear those either,' Kitty points out reasonably. 'Nor would Raggedy Doll.'

'Shut up, Kitty.' Caroline's mouth presses together. The morning light – filtered through the ivy – makes her look almost ill with irritation.

'It's . . . it's awfully generous of you, Caroline . . .'

'I want you dressed properly. Smartened up. I've booked a hairdresser to come tomorrow.'

'A hairdresser?' Lucian loves my hair just as it is. He's made me promise never to cut it.

Ignoring this comment, she flings open my wardrobe doors, flicking dismissively through my favourite dresses on the rail. 'I'll get rid of these old things.'

'Oh, no! Not those.' I can't tell her that I stuffed all my

favourite London clothes into a suitcase this summer – not risking the usual tatty Black Rabbit wardrobe – because I knew Lucian would be here. 'There's nothing wrong with any of them.'

'Nothing wrong with them?' She snorts, laying them over her arm. 'No one but your father could fail to notice that your dresses are far too tight and ridiculously short, Amber. They are no longer appropriate on a girl your age. You are too . . .' Her gaze guns to my breasts. Mortified, I cross my arms over my nightie. She stares for an eternity, fingering the pearls at her throat, almost as if she's forgotten herself, then turns on her heel and snaps, 'Get yourselves dressed, girls, and come down to breakfast before it becomes luncheon.'

I cannot bear the idea of Lucian seeing me in something so ugly so I throw the brown dress aside, slip on one that I bought shopping with Matilda in Chelsea – peach, skimming the knees with big white buttons the size of tea cakes – and wear it defiantly down to breakfast.

Caroline's eyes slice into the dress like scissors. But she says nothing. Instead she rests her knife calmly on the snow of the tablecloth and turns coolly to Lucian. 'Darling, I thought we might invite Belinda over this weekend. Before you go up to Oxford. We're running out of weekends now.'

A dry bit of toast catches in my throat. I cough and splutter and pick up my water glass too abruptly, making it splash across my front.

'It's not really Belinda's kind of place, Ma,' he says, straining to sound casual.

'Nonsense. Belinda will love Pencraw.' Caroline picks

up her knife again, scrapes a thin layer of butter on to her toast. 'Jibby Somerville-Rourke, Belinda's aunt – remember Jibby? At the wedding. Unfortunate lisp.'

Lucian nods, shoots an alarmed glance at me. I'm suddenly very glad that Toby hasn't bothered to come down to breakfast. He'd pick up on our unease right away.

'Well, the poor woman has written again, *hounding* me for an invitation to Belinda and herself, of course, as a chaperone. She says Belinda has been rather hopeful of one all summer but it has proved inexplicably elusive.' She leans towards Lucian, who backs away minutely. 'I do believe she's pining for you, my darling.'

I play with a button on my dress, cheeks burning, throat tight. Belinda. Rich, beautiful Belinda.

'I planned to help Toby this weekend.' There is a breathlessness to Lucian's voice now. 'He's set on some engineering project over the river, isn't he, Barns?'

'A rope bridge.' Barney sucks greengage jam off the back of a spoon. He grins. 'Scary. No sides.'

'The best kind,' Lucian says, trying to make things light but not managing it.

'But Toby won't want you to help, Lucian,' Kitty points out cheerfully. 'He doesn't like you joining in, remember?'

Caroline smiles to herself, glad to have more evidence of Toby's hostility. I know that she will repeat this to my father later.

'I so want to meet Belinda. I love the name Belinda,' Kitty continues maddeningly. Raggedy Doll lolls forward on her knee. 'There is a girl called Belinda at school. She has the longest plait in the class. Her nanny ties it with a pink ribbon on Fridays.'

'That grubby little doll is in the marmalade, Kitty. Please remove it.' Caroline turns back to Lucian, speaking more sternly now. 'You've not seen any of your set for weeks, Lucian. I think you could certainly do with a reminder of civilized society before returning to it. And you have every right to invite them to stay. This is *your* home now too.' She glances at Toby's empty seat. 'Don't let anyone make you feel differently.'

'Then I exercise my right not to invite them here,' Lucian flashes. 'Not Belinda. Not any of them.'

There is a terrible pause. The dining-room walls get redder.

'I see,' Caroline says tightly. The vein on her forehead pops. 'Well, let us leave this discussion for now. I cannot stomach such passion before nine o'clock. I really cannot.'

The next day, the hairdresser – a heavy, angry-looking woman, with a heavy, lid-like fringe – clomps up the steps, clasping a large brown leather bag and wearing a look of grim determination. Like a doctor arriving to perform an amputation, Toby jokes blackly, then belts into the woods to think about meteorite storms.

The hairdresser – Betty, she says tightly, as if she'd rather remain anonymous – sets up in the kitchen, out of the way of the workmen, who appeared at the door earlier this morning and are now thumping about upstairs doing who knows what. She arranges her tools – comb, scissors, blue glass pot of oily pomade – on the wooden table with fat butcher's fingers. Bartlett offers her tea and cake, which she works from one side of her jaw to the other as she snips.

I insist on being last to have my hair cut and sit on the stool, watching, worrying.

The hairdresser is not as brutal as she looks. Lucian is even more handsome with his new short back and sides. (I pick a glossy dark lock of his hair off the floor and slip it into my pocket.) Kitty's sweet curls aren't massacred. Barney no longer has to blink through his fringe. He scampers off, rabbit over his shoulder, waving at me from the bottom of his spine, fingers like a tail.

'Let's get on with it, then, dearie.' The hairdresser points at the kitchen chair, kicks the pile of hair out of the way.

I sit very straight, hands laced on my knee, firm that I want no more than an inch off. A smell of scalp trails from her moving fingers as she works the comb and cold metal scissors. It takes forever. 'Done,' the hairdresser says at last, shoving her things quickly into her bag.

My head is weightless, as if it might rise off my neck and float away, like a balloon. There are the long red tongues of hair on the stone floor. I reach behind me for where my hair should be swinging but isn't: it is skirting my neck.

I run, horrified, in search of a mirror. Lucian is the first person I see, hovering by the boot room, as if he's been waiting for me all this time.

'Don't look at me!' I hold my head with my hands, feeling the tears burning in my eyes. 'Don't look!'

He pulls me into the room, shuts the door and kisses me all the way up my neck, which he says he can now bite, like a vampire, and makes me smile despite everything. Then, hearing steps on the stairs, we leap apart.

I feel a little bit less as though the world has ended until I walk into Toby's bedroom. He is lying on the floor – bare feet up on the wall – peeling a hard, late-summer apple with his penknife above his head. 'Look,' I say, hoping he'll tell me it's fine. I still need his approval. 'Look what the hairdresser did!'

'Yeah, she's cut Momma right out of you, sis,' he says mildly, returning his attention to the apple. 'I knew she'd do that.'

'Well, you could have warned *me*,' I yell, walking off, slamming the door.

I hear him shout, 'I did.'

'Toby, something's happened,' I cry breathlessly, throwing his bedroom door open again a few minutes later. He is exactly where I left him, lying on the floor, the apple peel now one long unbroken spiral, the fruit's white-green flesh exposed.

'You've already shown me your hair.' One last expert twist of the knife and the peel drops to the floor. 'It'll grow back.'

'No, not my hair. Forget my hair. Something much, much worse.'

He looks at me then, puzzled. 'But nothing's meant to happen until the last day of the holiday.'

'Not one of your stupid planetary-event fantasies. Something properly awful. In the hall. Come. Come and look.'

The portrait that replaces Momma's is far bigger. Not just in size. Caroline's presence seems to bulge out of the vast ornate gilt frame, radiating its own particular chill into the hall. It captures not just Caroline's likeness – even if she does look years younger than she is – but somehow the scale of her ambition.

'*Bitch*,' hisses Toby, lips barely moving. 'Stupid bitch.' He drops the peeled apple to the tiles and pulls his penknife from his pocket. 'I'm going to gut it like a fish.'

I grab his arm, making the knife waggle in the air. 'No. When Daddy comes back later he'll take it down.'

'Daddy! Why do you still have faith in him?' He snaps free of my grip. 'Don't you understand what's happening here?'

'He loves that painting of Momma. He'd never let anyone remove it from the hall.'

'Wouldn't he? Don't you get it, Amber? It's not about love now, it's about power. Money.'

'What?'

'Caroline is rich. We're poor.'

'Don't be ridiculous.'

'Daddy's blown it, Amber. He's blown the lot since Momma died, and there wasn't that much to begin with, not enough to keep this house going anyway. Honestly, I've seen all the unpaid invoices, the ones he hides in his desk drawers.'

'Black Rabbit Hall's never been smart. Nobody minds.'

'*Caroline* minds. And she's going to keep spending on the house until she's made it hers.'

'It's still Daddy's. Ours. Yours.'

Toby's face closes, cold, impassive. 'The person you think of as Daddy, he's no longer Daddy. He's someone else.'

'No,' I say, refusing to believe it. 'Don't say that.'

'None of us is who we were, are we?' he says pointedly. 'And it's all because of Caroline and Lucian.'

'None of this has anything to do with Lucian,' I blurt before I think, the urge to defend him instinctive.

'It's nothing to do with Lucian,' he mimics in a girl's voice. 'Lucian the bunny lover. Lucian the perfect son. When will you bloody well *wake up*, Amber?'

I'm shaking. I can't trust myself not to say the wrong thing. I start to walk away, but Toby won't let me.

'Look.' He grabs my arm, gesticulates wildly with his knife in the direction of the portrait. 'This is nothing. This is not even the start. It's a warm-up. All traces of our family will soon be gone, scrubbed out of this place, just like that portrait. And because we are part of Momma, we will be rubbed out too, eventually. Especially you. Yes, you, Amber. In her eyes, you *are* Momma. You look more and more like Momma every day. That's why she cut your hair. That's why she's putting you in those foul dresses! Can't you see?' he shouts, as if somehow this is all my fault. 'The only way she'll get rid of the last trace of Momma is to get rid of *you*!'

I don't dare suggest that I think she might be making me as unattractive as possible because she suspects me and Lucian. I can't risk watering the same thought in Toby's head, the dark seed that is waiting for its moment to push into the light, like a spiked bramble through the floor.

'Black Rabbit Hall won't be anything to do with the Altons in a generation's time.' Toby stares up at the portrait, dwarfed by it. 'It won't even be here, most probably. She'll sell it. They'll turn it into flats, an old people's home or something.'

'Rubbish,' I say, voice shaking. 'You are the eldest son, the heir.'

Toby lets out an odd hollow laugh. 'Caroline is man-oeuvring Lucian into position and you know it.'

'Lucian would never accept –'

He whips around to me. 'How do you know? How do *you* damn well know what he would or wouldn't do?' His breath is sweet and sickening in my face.

'Because . . .' The words fail on my tongue.

'Because what, Amber?' His eyes narrow, a cold light glinting between the red barbs of his lashes.

'He's on our side.'

'Is that what he tells you? Are you that gullible?'

'None of this is his fault.' I know I should shut up. But I can't. If only I can make him understand.

'*Don't* . . . Just don't defend him.' He speaks very quietly, a low growl. His eyes are crazy, pupils dilated now. 'Not when I'm holding a knife.'

'What are you going to do? Stab me?' I hold out my bare arm, press it up against the blade, daring him to push it into my pale skin. Something in me – fury, frustration, love – comes loose inside. 'You'll have me forever then, won't you? It will just be us. You can put me in your room,' I shout back, 'sit me on the velvet chair and – and leave me there until I rot and then you can buff my bones with your special cloth and put me in your bone collection!'

Toby looks hurt. He moves the knife away from me. 'What? What on earth are you talking about?'

'You. Won't. Let. Me. Go,' I sob, all the tears rising up at once.

'I'd never hurt you. I'd never ever hurt you.' He throws the knife clattering to the tiles. He grips me by the shoulders, trying to shake something out of me. I carry on gabbling, Toby saying, 'Stop, stop, stop,' until I do.

'Remember our promise when Momma died?' I close my eyes to block him out. But he is inside me too, so I can't. 'Do you?'

I want to say yes. But guilt makes the word clot.

'Look at me.' He searches for something in my eyes. Not wanting him to find it, I look away but he tilts my jaw up roughly, forcing me to meet his gaze. 'You. Me. *Us.* Always us. That's what we promised. Do you remember? Tell me you remember. Say it. Say it out loud.'

'Us,' I whisper, the simple word making my eyes swell with tears.

Twenty-Six

Lorna

'You can't cherry-pick what you remember, Dad. Not any more.' Lorna turns away in fury. But she can still sense her father behind her, still see him slumped on the parched edge of the lawn, chest rising and falling inside his Hawaiian shirt, head in his hands. She hesitates only for a moment then starts to walk up the drive towards Black Rabbit Hall, which is shimmering in the haze of late-summer heat, something made of air not stone.

'Sheila might have mentioned a big house once,' he calls weakly.

Lorna whips around. '*What?*'

Doug rubs his face with his hand. He's spent most of his married life learning how to tread carefully around this subject: it is hard to unlearn these things, even now when it matters more than ever. Lorna's garbled tale – something about a name embroidered on an old apron, an unknown twin – has knocked him sideways. 'She . . . she said that the lady at the adoption agency in Truro had let something slip . . .'

Lorna runs back, kneels down on the grass, face millimetres from his so that she can read every twitch of truth in his soft brown eyes. 'Did Mum mention Pencraw Hall?'

'I'm not a hundred per cent. But I think that she might

have.' He stares down at his hands sheepishly. 'Or some-thing like it. They all sound the same these houses.'

'So that's why you didn't want us to have the wedding here?' She wishes that Louise hadn't felt the need to give them privacy and disappear into the woods with Alf. Her sister wouldn't let Dad wriggle out of any hard questions.

He nods, pulls the collar of his shirt away from his sweating neck. 'I knew it would stir up no good, if it was this place. And I was right, wasn't I?' He looks very tired, as if he's ageing in front of her eyes. 'Look at you. It just breaks my heart. It breaks my heart.' His eyes bulge with tears. He nudges them away with a knuckle. 'Your life's with Jon now, love. Not here.'

'But it *is* here, Dad. I think a part of me knew it – I felt it the moment I walked into the house. On the stairs. That moment on the stairs.'

'I'm sorry. I'm so sorry, love.'

She shakes her head, gasping back tears. 'And now I *know* that I'm screwed up, not that I might be,' she says fiercely. 'That I am.'

'Lorna, stop that. You're not screwed up, not at all.'

'The rejected twin! How can I *not* be?'

'You're made of much stronger stuff than that, Lorna, and you know it.'

'No, I *don't* know it, Dad. All I know is that Jon comes from a nice, normal family and will not want this in his life. Who would? A mother to his children, handing down her own weird issues to her kids, I don't think . . .' Tears tie her tongue.

'Why would Jon ever think that? Jon adores you. And you're amazing with kids. You always have been.'

'But what if I'm like my biological mother? The kind of woman who could choose one twin over another. What sort of woman could do *that*? That's what he'll be thinking. That's . . . what I'm thinking,' she says despairingly, covering her face with her hands.

'Oh, love. Come here.' He hugs her to his chest and she hears the ba-boom of his heart, smells tea, washing powder, sweat. 'You're getting carried away now.'

But she's not. Something has become horribly clear. She pulls away from him. 'I can't marry Jon. I'm going to call him and tell him.' She starts digging in her bag for her phone. 'I can't put him through all that.'

Doug holds her by the shoulders. 'Stop. Just stop. Remember what Nan said? Don't rush into big life decisions when you're upset or on an empty stomach.' He nods at the phone in her trembling hand. 'Put that back in your bag. Ask me what you like. I'll tell you anything I know.'

She wipes her eyes, puts the phone back. 'I need the whole story, Dad.' If you don't have the beginning of your story, she realizes – even a not very nice beginning, one you wouldn't write yourself – you can't understand the middle, let alone the end. 'Don't miss anything out.'

He blows out long and hard, stalling for time. 'Well, first, you've got to remember that the adoption agency didn't tell you a lot in those days. And your mum kept so much to herself.'

'Stop. Are you trying to say you know the weight of a sperm whale, and what was in the top ten in March 1952, all that complete and utter *rubbish*, but you don't know your own daughter's origins?'

He winces. 'Well, yes. Sort of.'

'For fuck's sake.'

'I never gave two hoots if you came from the primordial soup or Buckingham Palace – don't you see?' He tucks a lock of damp hair behind her ear. 'You were my beautiful Lorna. You still are. You always will be. It doesn't matter where you came from. It made no difference to me then and it doesn't now.'

Her eyes flash. 'It makes a difference to *me*.'

Doug looks genuinely baffled. 'But you always said it didn't. You told me and Sheila you didn't want to find your birth parents. If you had, we'd have helped you.'

'How was Mum going to help exactly, given that she could barely even say the word "adoption" without looking like she was sucking on a hornet? Why did no one ever *talk* about it?'

'It – it sounds so weak now. But the truth is, your mother suffered so many miscarriages – five in all – before we got you. She'd had so much loss, so much heartbreak, Lorna. She never thought she'd bear her own child. And I think the thought of you . . . not being fully hers, maybe wanting to look for another mother one day, it was just too painful.'

'I had feelings too. I had rights,' Lorna whispers. She'd known about the miscarriages, although she'd never known it was so many. Poor Mum. No wonder her childhood memories of her mother pregnant with Louise involve her lying in bed for endless anxious months, lest she lose the miracle baby.

'Seventies, eighties, it was a different era. No one talked to kids about anything, not like you're meant to these days.' Doug frowns. 'Some kids were never even told they were adopted at all. It was thought for the best. Not to muddle things up.'

'Why come to Cornwall, then? Why not stay away?'

Doug's face softens. 'She loved it, always had. Came here as a kid herself. And I think she always felt it was the land that had . . . given you to her in a way. It was the happiest day, Lorna, the day you were put into her arms, really. It happened so quickly. We only got the call a few days before. A Cornish baby, they said, were we interested? Sheila thought it was Fate.'

'But I still don't understand why she brought me to this house. It doesn't make sense, Dad. It just doesn't.'

'I'll agree with you there.' He shakes his head. 'But she did get fanciful about these things. Stuffed her head with those silly historical romances.'

'She didn't need to. She had her own secrets and melodrama, didn't she? Only it was all hidden away.'

He reaches for her hand. 'Lorna, I'm sure she would have told you everything one day.'

'One day? Dad, I'm thirty-two!'

'She didn't know she was going to trip, did she?' His reddening eyes plead for understanding. 'No one knows exactly when they're going to die, do they? If we did, we'd all unburden ourselves in time, Lorna.'

'Oh, my God.' She claps her hand across her mouth, heart skipping a beat. 'Dad, you're right.' There is no time to waste. She leaps from his arms, kicking up a milk of gravel dust. If she runs fast enough she might just run back through time, she thinks, push a pinhole of light into the dark.

*

In the drawing room, Dill's eyes widen beneath her plume of hair, dustpan brush slipping from her grip. Lorna pants, hands on her knees, looking up, searching for a connection, the recognition of blood. But she finds only a pulse of disbelief, faint embarrassment.

'Hi.' Dill smiles awkwardly.

What should long-lost sisters do? Hug? Kiss? Lorna isn't ready for that. So she stutters something improbable about her father, sister and nephew having just arrived at Black Rabbit Hall – the word 'sister' trailing an uncomfortable choke of smoke behind it – and needing to find Mrs Alton urgently, before it is too late.

Dill does not ask why – Lorna wonders if she guesses – and suggests she goes to the white bench above the cliff. Look out for the blue sports car. Dill glances down at Lorna's bare feet. Would she like to borrow some shoes? There are a lot of wasps on the ground. All the windfalls.

Yes, Lorna thinks, mind racing. Cidery autumn is pressing in. And after the harvest, death and decay. Mrs Alton could be dying right this moment, starting to rot, like a soft black apple. Why *not* die now? Or in five minutes? Or ten? That's what her mother had done, after all. Died, sucking down all the secrets with her. She won't let it happen again.

Lorna yomps away from the house in heavy borrowed wellies. She stills only at the edge of the woods, breathless, fingers on the flaking metal of the gate: it began here, she realizes, with a sharp intake of breath, the syrupy smell of pine. The woods – the tree – were the gateway to it all.

A child's whoop. Lorna flinches, unsure if she heard the sound in the roar of her own head, until it is followed by the joyful boomerang of Alf's laugh through the trees: Alf laughing at himself laughing. That's what Barney might have sounded like, she thinks, closing her eyes for a moment, sucking the laugh inside, letting it fill her with a funny kind of strength.

Lorna cuts across the field, no longer wary of the horned cows lumbering towards her. There are three twists in the cliff road before she hears flapping – like a tent loosening from its pegs – and glimpses the shredded car roof through the hedging. Beyond it, Mrs Alton is perched on the white bench, cane extended, staring out to a sea that fades from parrot blue to green. A breeze buffets up the cliff, playing with her grey cape and curls.

Lorna hesitates, on the edge of retreat. Does she really want to know the answers to her questions? Would it be possible for her and Jon never to refer to Black Rabbit Hall again? To pretend this summer never happened? For a moment she almost believes it would work, that she could just turn around and walk away, stuff the past into a box, like her mother had done. Then she pictures Peggy Popple sitting on this bench – over three decades ago but the sea, the sounds, the smells just the same – her tough housekeeper's hands loosening her apron, resting on the warm fleshy swell of her babies, swimming in their own dark waters. And she knows she cannot go back. That it is already too late. 'Mrs Alton,' she calls quietly.

Although a tremor of recognition passes through the old woman she doesn't turn around.

'May I?' Lorna walks over to her, sits. The wood feels damp and cool through the cotton of her dress, gumboots heavy on her feet.

'Of course.'

In the unforgiving sea light, Lorna can see that the tips of her lashes are frosted with fallen face powder. Her ermine features are pinched. The heavy make-up cannot hide the spongy lilac shadows beneath her eyes. She doesn't look well at all.

'Mrs Alton, I need to talk to you.'

'Indeed you do,' Mrs Alton replies, with the resigned air of someone who knows interrogation is inevitable. The wind flaps up her hair, exposing an unsettling patch of white scalp.

'It's about my . . .' the words stick in her mouth '. . . my mother.'

'Yes, Dill warned me. She was gabbling terribly. I didn't know what had got into her.'

'You . . . you knew my mother?' she stutters. There is a rushing in her head – fear, excitement, blood – that sounds like water.

'All too well.' Her face remains unreadable.

'What was my . . . she like?' A curlew dives down the cliff, feather-ruffling the air.

'What was your mother *like*?' repeats Mrs Alton, making the question sound even more pedestrian, unequal to the enormity of the subject. 'It depends, my dear, as everything does, on whom you ask.'

'I'm asking you,' Lorna says quickly. She's not going to take any of Mrs Alton's tricksiness today.

'I will be diplomatic.' Mrs Alton stares grimly ahead at the dip-dyed sea. 'Your smile is her smile.'

Oh. Lorna closes her eyes, hit by a wave of relief. She has a smile like someone else's smile. Just this tiny nugget of knowledge feels unexpectedly precious beyond words. How many times over the years has she looked in the mirror and wondered?

'When you sleep . . .' Mrs Alton coughs, spluttering into a handkerchief '. . . you sleep with abandon, arms above your head. She slept in exactly the same way.'

So Mrs Alton *had* been watching Lorna sleep. They were the marks of her cane at the bridal suite door. Had she checked on her when she was wiped out by those pills too? Had she even given her those pills for that purpose? Lorna shudders slightly, the light fingers of unease starting to tap down her spine.

'Lorna, my dear.' Mrs Alton moves closer, her face a bleak landscape of powdered pores. 'That night you interviewed me under the guise of writing the website pamphlet or some such, I knew there were other forces at work.'

'Forces?' The hairs on Lorna's arms lift. 'I – I don't understand.'

'Oh, you will,' Mrs Alton says coolly, returning her gaze to the sea. 'Over the years, I have learned not to underestimate Pencraw.'

A flock of gulls mews wildly, spiralling upwards as if disturbed by something on the rocks. Lorna suddenly wishes she could lift off, too. Stupid, but she feels vulnerable.

'Your mother hated me, of course. I won't pretend otherwise.'

'Sorry?' She hasn't heard it right.

'I was not Nancy. I was not the American airhead, perfect and dead. That was the problem that would never go away.' Her jaw tightens. 'I was set up to fail.'

Lorna recoils. Something about the cruel description of the first wife. Or maybe it's just that there is something repugnant about being old, so close to the end, and not at peace.

'It was a battle from day one.' The cane starts to tremble in its nest of crooked fingers. 'A battle to the death as it turns out.'

The wind picks up then, starts to rush up her nose, tug at her hair, as if Mrs Alton's words have unsettled the atmosphere itself. Lorna edges away.

'I keep going back to the beginning, trying to make sense of it. Oh dear.' She shakes her head. 'That terrible moment in the dressing room.'

'What happened in the dressing room?' Lorna asks, her voice high, hands gripping the edge of the bench.

'I became the monster everyone said I was. *I* became that woman, Lorna,' she says, swinging to face her with fierce intensity. 'Don't you see? You can see that, can't you?'

'Sorry, I don't really understand . . .' Something dark and chaotic is tugging at the corners of the conversation now. She presses her feet into the boots, readying herself to stand up.

'It was a lie, a silly, desperate lie, but it grew . . . it grew so big.' Mrs Alton squeezes her eyes tightly shut. The wind flaps her cape like wings. She looks so odd, swaying on the bench, Lorna is no longer sure if she is cogent, whether this is the looping of dementia, or something else. 'The most perfect August evening,' she mutters. 'Blue skies. It didn't look like a day anyone might die.'

Lorna becomes certain that Mrs Alton has done something unspeakably terrible. 'You don't need to tell me this.'

'Oh, I do.' She opens her eyes, smiles. 'Endellion has informed you that I am shortly due for dispatch?'

'I'm sorry.'

'Oh, don't be,' she says dismissively. 'I've lasted longer than anyone expected, or hoped. Stay out of hospitals and you stay alive. Remember that.'

Lorna stands up, desperate to run from this strange talk of terrible lies and deaths on perfect summer evenings. 'Perhaps I should find Dill. Would you like that, Mrs Alton? Some help getting back to the house?'

'It made keeping the baby utterly impossible, you see.'

Lorna runs the words through her head again, feels her way around each one, checking it for faults, misinterpretation. 'Mrs Alton, do you mean that my mother wanted to keep . . .' Something stops her finishing the question, too scared of the answer.

'Oh, yes, she wanted to keep you,' Mrs Alton replies matter-of-factly. 'Very much.' She raises her hand, holding it in mid-air until Lorna takes it, helps lift her slight frame off the bench. 'Come. I'd like to show you the room where you were born. If you would guide me to the car first. My sight is not quite what it was.'

'Blasted steering!' Mrs Alton whacks the leather wheel with her hand. 'Hasn't been right since 1975.'

'Wait. Don't. Move.' Lorna clutches her stomach, inches her nauseous gaze to the drop below: the nose of the blue car sticks cleanly, surreally, into the sky, like an aeroplane wing seen from a passenger's window. Out of the corner of her eye, she sees Mrs Alton's left foot lift.

'No!' Lorna lurches for the gear stick, yanking it into

327

reverse a second before Mrs Alton can hit the accelerator and propel them over the cliff. The car judders, with a spit and spin of dust and grass, then reverses at high speed into the gorse hedge where the engine stalls, sending a cloud of tits fluttering upwards.

Still Mrs Alton will not be persuaded to swap seats – 'Don't be ridiculous. I can drive this road with my eyes closed!' – and bends forward, pearls knocking against the steering-wheel, nose millimetres from the mud-splattered windscreen, speeding down the winding cliff road towards Black Rabbit Hall.

Lorna clings to the door handle, but it comes off in her hand. The roof flaps above her head, whipping rags of air into the cramped confines of the car. There is an alarming gash in the floor by her feet, where the road races past. The relief of not flying off a cliff to certain death is quickly superseded by fear of the car wrapping itself around a tree on the drive.

It bucks to a stop in front of the falcons. Mrs Alton pats her curls. 'Car always did play havoc with one's hair.'

Lorna shakily helps Mrs Alton out. It is disconcertingly quiet in the evening heat. She wonders where the others are, if they're looking for her inside the house.

'Tower,' Mrs Alton barks, shielding her eyes from the sun, nodding up at the gloomy ivy-strangled east tower – her living quarters – with an unreadable look on her face.

In the hall, Lorna hears Alf's faint chatter coming from somewhere in the direction of the enfilade. Mrs Alton catches her hesitation. 'This way. Let's not tarry.'

The east tower's door is off the grand hall, sunk into a

pointed arch of mottled stone. She must have passed it countless times in the last couple of days, never noticed it. Mrs Alton swivels its brass knob one way, then the other. 'After you,' she says, when Lorna doesn't move. 'Goodness. Don't look so terrified. I won't lock the door behind us.'

As Lorna hadn't considered this scenario, she lets out a high, nervous laugh, and has to force herself to step into what seems to be another hall, only on a much smaller scale. It is dark in here, stuffy. Its walls are a buffed boot-brown. The smell is distinctive, Lorna thinks, different from the rest of the house. Wet coats. Lavender. Dog. And something else. Something that smells of things hidden away for a long time. The smell you can never get out of clothes that have been stashed too long in an attic.

Mrs Alton unceremoniously pushes open another door with the tip of her cane. 'This, my dear, is what I call home.'

It's the suburban normality of Mrs Alton's sitting room that steals the words from Lorna's mouth: the twee china animals that look as if they've come from a market stall trotting along a modern pine fire surround; the hazardous five-bar electric heater; rose pink velveteen slippers, heels squashed flat with wear.

The oddest thing is that it is not unlike her nan's house. The difference is that Nan's place – a two up, two down in Hounslow – was so clean you could eat off the floor and this has a decidedly sticky patina. And while it was wallpapered in photographs of her nieces and nephews and grandchildren, the only family photo here – notable for its solitariness and prime position on the dresser – is a faded photograph of a handsome teenage boy with a floppy

1960s haircut, a little like one of the early Beatles. Mrs Alton's armchair and slippers are positioned directly opposite the photograph, not the telly, as if she might spend hours just staring at this alone.

'I find a smaller space much easier to manage,' says Mrs Alton, briskly, as if reading Lorna's mind. 'And unlike the rest of the house, it is not so cold that the blood freezes in the veins come October. But fear not, you did not enter the world down here.'

Lorna tries not to look relieved.

'Starward.' She points at a door beside some book-shelves.

Heart jacking, she slowly follows Mrs Alton up a narrow, bare wooden staircase, up, up, up, past numerous other doors that lead, Mrs Alton says, to the landings of the upper floors in the main house. On a couple that are open, Lorna notices bolts. She shudders. How must a pregnant woman have felt, toiling up this tube of stone, knowing she could be locked behind them?

The staircase narrows and darkens. Dead bare light-bulbs swing on frayed cables above their heads. The acoustics are peculiar, their footsteps echoing against the hard, bare wood, sounding like a crowd of feet, not just four, as if every past inhabitant of this house is hot on their heels.

Finally, one simple white door. A black doorknob. Nowhere else to go.

Lorna stares at it, knees weak. The door is like a stone blocking an entrance to a tomb. She's not sure she can go through it. She's not sure she can do any of this.

'It used to be the maids' dormitory, back in the days when the family could afford them.'

Lorna nods, swallows. Staff quarters: that makes a sort of sense.

'A perfect little hideaway with glorious views.' Mrs Alton rattles the doorknob. 'There was no reason for her to make such a ghastly fuss, no reason at all.'

Twenty-Seven

Amber, a week before the end of the summer holidays, August 1969

'It's over,' Toby whispers, ripping a fingernail with his teeth. 'It's started.'

Nothing's started. Nothing's over, I tell him. Things are admittedly pretty bad, but we've been in dark, fractured spots before, then good things suddenly happen and light shines through the cracks. I'm thinking of Lucian as I say this, so I quickly correct it to: life is strange and unpredictable and anything can happen and one day Toby will run Black Rabbit Hall exactly as he pleases, serve Twiglet sandwiches for supper and put Momma's portrait back up in the hall.

Toby stares at me uncomprehendingly, the haunted look in his eyes just like Daddy's cousin Rupert's whenever you asked him about the war.

It is not good. Ever since Momma's portrait was taken down, Toby's spirits have shelved sharply, unexpectedly, like a treacherous beach. Something in him – maybe the last bit of fight and hope – has gone. The look in his eyes makes me feel panicky, as if I may not be able to fix him this time.

In the end, it was Daddy who failed Toby, not Caroline. Even though Toby said he was expecting it – he'd warned me, after all – when Daddy's betrayal came it cut too deep.

As soon as Daddy returned from London, I rushed to the library, only to find that Caroline had got there first. Pressing my ear to the door, I heard the heat of their voices, Daddy shouting that it was goddamn insensitive, that she must take the blasted portrait down tomorrow. Then those sounds turned into other sounds, grunting, moaning, the telling thump of furniture against the wall, a long, high howl. Caroline's portrait stayed.

That night Toby slept in the tree house, and the next, returning to the house to lie lifelessly with his head on Peggy's lap, feet tangled in her knitting. Peggy picked out the twigs and earwigs from his hair, tried to feed him her ginger cake, breaking off small bits and dropping them into his mouth: it was an odd sight, the lithe teenager opening his mouth for Peggy's tiny fingers. I think that's all he's eaten. You can see the buttons of his spine through his shirt.

Caroline says Toby's 'performance' is 'weak and tedious'; she has warned him he must snap out of it, 'lest you achieve the remarkable feat of slipping even further in your father's affections'. I don't think she wants him to snap out of it, though. She's clearly enjoying his suffering immensely, her own mood improving as Toby's sinks. Daddy, on the other hand, did try to talk gently with Toby – 'man to man' – but the gentle talking quickly turned to shouting. Doors were slammed. Curses hurled. Daddy's London diary got a whole lot busier. He returned there this morning.

The rest of us are trying to help. Lucian – mortified by his mother's behaviour – has apologized on her behalf: Toby didn't seem to hear, looked right through him. I've been sitting with Toby on the cliff ledge or in the tree house, mostly in silence, as he doesn't want to talk much. Boris waits loyally on his bed for him to return from the woods, nosing him when he stares out of the window, tears running down his cheeks. Kitty steals him jelly babies and wraps Raggedy Doll's floppy arms around his neck. Barney even offers Old Harry for a cuddle – 'He has soft ears that make things better, Toby' – but is always fiercely rebuffed. Sometimes I think Toby blames that rabbit for everything.

Twenty-Eight

Two days before the end of the summer holidays

'Lucian, darling, an invitation to Bigbury Grange.' Caroline presses the stiff pale pink card to her flushed clavicles. 'Jibby has left me under no illusions that refusing it will ensure our quick and painful social death in the West Country. What do you say?'

Lucian and I privately agree that he must go, and with good grace. Caroline's questioning of him has intensified in recent days, her appraisal of me – eyes sweeping over my horrible dresses, my neck, my chest – more blatant. We're getting twitchy.

Now Lucian's been gone six hours. The 'light luncheon' has turned into high tea. Big Bertie's long, thin brass hands shudder from one minute to the next with agonizing slowness. Will Lucian even be back for the last day of the holidays tomorrow? It seems possible that he won't. All sorts of bad things seem possible.

I try to talk myself round. Apart from anything else, he wouldn't want to miss the high tide, would he? The locals say it's going to be a big one, the biggest of the summer, a tide that will smash against the bone-dry bottom of the cliff, suck up treasures from the deep. No, no. He won't want to miss that.

The next moment I'm racked with doubt. Of course

Lucian's not interested in full moons and high tides! What am I thinking? He's not Toby! He's being entertained at one of the finest houses in the country, plied with cold champagne and lobster and the beauteous Belinda Bracewell.

Or he's dead. Or about to be dead, the clock ticking down until the accident happens. I picture the car rolled upside down, like a beetle, wheels spinning in the air. I pray to God to keep him safe, pull him out of the tiny window before the flames leap. If He must take someone, please, please, take Caroline. Actually, take her anyway.

But God doesn't take Caroline. Later that afternoon, she's on the telephone, telling Peggy that the weather's turned – liar, the sky is blue as a plate! – so they'll be staying the night. Everyone is having a simply marvellous time.

By dusk there is no longer the slightest satisfaction to be found in sobbing. All I can do is stand on my packed suitcase, chin on the flaking windowsill, waiting for the little blue car that never comes up the drive.

A cough.

I turn and there is Toby, gaunt and wild-eyed, leaning against the wall. He has started talking more today, which, I hope, is a sign that the black gloom is lifting. 'Hi. How are you feeling?' I say, trying to sound cheery, hoping I don't look swollen-eyed.

He speaks out of the corner of his mouth, lips barely moving. 'You may as well get used to it.'

'What?'

'Lucian is an alley cat, Amber. He doesn't give a damn who feeds him, least of all Belinda Bracewell.'

'I wasn't thinking of Lucian,' I say quickly, taken aback. I thought Toby far too fogged and self-absorbed to notice where Lucian had gone. I was wrong. Today his eyes are glittering, hard and knowing again. This could be reassuring – he's back, in part – but it's not. It feels as if we are looking at each other through the thick ice of a frozen pond.

'He's going up to Oxford, a new golden life. He'll soon forget about you, us, Black Rabbit Hall. You know that, don't you? That this summer will just be an odd blip in his life.'

I bite the inside of my cheek, fighting a fresh flood of tears. If I react now I know all Toby's suspicions will be confirmed. And the end is so close. Toby will soon leave for boarding school, me for London, Lucian for Oxford, our secret left behind at Black Rabbit Hall, sleeping, safe, its heart beating softly, until the Christmas holidays when Lucian and I will return and kiss it back to life once more.

Twenty-Nine

The last day of the summer holidays

At dawn I crawl into Kitty's bed, comforted by the plump sweet lump that is Kitty sleeping. Barney joins us, hot-limbed and restless, using my chest as his pillow. The bed is cramped and stinky but preferable to being alone in my room unable to sleep, torturing myself with Toby's words. Still, by the time the sun shines through the nursery's flowery curtains, I am convinced that Lucian will not only forget about me at Oxford but go on to marry Belinda Bracewell. Of course he won't bother returning to Black Rabbit Hall today to say goodbye! I'm quite certain of this until after lunch when I hear the engine spluttering up the drive. I run to my bedroom window.

Heart in my mouth, I watch Peggy – circular seen from above – bustle down the stone steps and open the passenger door. Caroline emerges, turquoise scarf fluttering at her neck. I wait, and wait. Then . . .

Lucian's brogue lands on the gravel. It is already more exciting than the man stepping on the moon.

I cannot breathe. I've imagined it a million times in the last few hours – running down to greet him, the small secret smile that says, 'I love you', the brush of our fingers as we pass in the hall – but now the moment is here I cannot move, paralysed by the knowledge that I will know immediately what has happened between him and Belinda just from the look in his eyes. If something has, it will be like seeing a body lying dead at the bottom of a pond. So I sit on the edge of my bed, sick with nerves, pinching my cheeks, furiously brushing my hair and desperately wishing I had a pretty dress. After what feels like weeks, my hair brushed out of control, sparking with static, I hear his tread on the stairs, the bump of a bag on the floor.

Three soft raps: our knock.

The moment the wardrobe doors click shut, we fall into the furs, desperate to hold one another. He is so solid, warm, so mine that I cry with relief and happiness. His thigh pushes hard between my legs, breath shredding in my ear. It keeps pushing, a growing, tightening pulse. A seam rips in the crackling heat. I throw my head back and cry out. There are no edges.

We are nuzzling and whispering ourselves back to earth when I hear a snuffling sound, something moving about outside the wardrobe doors. Boris?

'Ssh . . .' I pull back, waiting to hear it again.

'It's nothing,' he says, bending over to kiss me.

It happens so quickly. The bleach of sunlight. Boris barking. Caroline screaming. I grab a fur coat to cover myself, cowering against the hat boxes.

'You little slut!' Caroline shrieks, eyes popping red.

'Christ.' Lucian tries to pull up his trousers.

'Come here!' Before I can do anything, Caroline's arm shoots out, yanking me up and out of the wardrobe, her rings digging into the flesh of my arm. To my horror, she rips the fur coat away. And I am naked before her, skinless, raw, trembling so much my teeth start to chatter. 'Oh, look at you! You stupid, stupid girl.' She starts to shove me back and forth, so that my breasts hurt, like she is possessed. I start to cry, shocked, burning tears.

'Stop!' Lucian shouts, white-faced in the wardrobe, hands gripping the sides, pulling himself out. 'For God's sake, stop. Mother, we're in love.'

'Love?' She stops shaking me, but the reprieve feels fragile, as if she might start up again even more fiercely. 'Stepbrother, stepsister,' she whispers, upper lip curling. 'You cannot *love*. Not like this.'

I bow my head, cross my arms to cover my breasts. The pink dressing room starts to spin, like a nightmare carousel. I taste salt in the back of my throat, tears, blood, fear. Without warning, Caroline leans over and slaps me hard on my cheek. It is such a shock that it doesn't hurt.

Lucian grabs her arm roughly. The room quivers on the edge of violence. 'Don't. Ever. Hit. Her.'

Caroline glances down at her son's hand, back up at him, something changing in her eyes, fury cooling to something more calculated, more deadly. 'You have betrayed me horribly, Lucian.'

'I've fallen in love, that's all.'

She pulls her arm away from his hand, closes her eyes, the lids quivering and twitching, as if tiny insects are running beneath the skin. When she opens them again, there is a determined look in them, a strengthened resolve. 'I'll have to tell you now, won't I?'

'Tell me what?' asks Lucian, warily. His chest is flushed livid red.

I grab the fur coat off the floor, shakily cover myself

again, hear her voice in the blood-pulse of my head, not registering its meaning.

'Alfred was not your father, Lucian.'

'What? What the hell are you talking about?' Lucian steps backwards. A terrible sadness starts to creep across his beautiful face like a shadow, pulling down the corners of his mouth, bruising the hollows of his eyes.

'Have you not wondered where you get your gypsy dark hair? Your height? Your good looks?'

'There is Indian blood on Daddy's side.'

Caroline shakes her head slowly, holding us – the room, time itself – in sickened thrall. 'Hugo is your real father. Hugo *Alton*.'

I hear my own gasp as if it were someone else's. See my father's bloodied name hanging in the knifed hush. Lucian, white, frozen, his lips parted with a silent scream.

'You're lying,' he manages, voice a husk. 'You're lying, Ma.'

'I didn't know I was pregnant when Hugo left me for Nancy all those years ago, my darling.'

'No.' Lucian is fiercely shaking his head, trying to dislodge the words from his ears.

'I married Alfred, and the dear man brought you up as his own. He never knew. No one knew, Lucian.' She lowers her eyes and voice, humbly, a woman in church. 'But now you do.'

A strange noise comes from the back of Lucian's throat. I reach over to clutch his arm, but he doesn't react, seems to look right through me. And I can feel his great spirit shrinking, his heart folding upon itself, smaller and smaller, until it no longer meets my own.

'It's not true, Lucian!' I cry. 'Don't believe her.'

Caroline leans close to her son, pouring her poison into his ear. 'Lucian, you are the rightful heir to Pencraw. And *that* little whore is your sister.'

A crash outside the dressing-room door. The sound of scuffling, heavy breathing. Boris. Let it be Boris.

'Who is it?' Caroline bolts upright, vein pulsing on her forehead. 'I say, who is there?'

Thirty

Caroline tosses Lucian's guitar on to the back seat of the car with his bag of clothes. 'Go!' she shouts, banging the bumper. '*Now*. You cannot remain here another minute. I swear Toby will kill you. Please. Leave now, I beg you, Lucian.'

Lucian looks up at me pressed to the bedroom window. I nod. *Go.*

The car speeds down the drive, roars through the trees. I stand there looking at those trees for some time after he's gone, numb, unable to make sense of what we've been told, knowing only two things for certain: I can't go back and undo my love for Lucian any more than I can go back through time and stop Momma falling off her horse; I must find Toby.

Yes, that's what I'll do. Find Toby. Explain everything. Explain everything so he understands, which is what I should have done weeks ago. If Toby understands, he'll forgive. I'm almost sure of it. And he will not think Caroline's lie true for a moment. So what if Lucian is as dark as Daddy? If there is a similarity in their height and build? We are all fair or redheaded and we are certainly Daddy's children.

Summoning all my courage – I can only imagine the white heat of Toby's fury – I splash water on my face, straighten my messy hair with my fingers and take an unsteady breath, anxious about what awaits me downstairs. Will Caroline have told everyone? Will Peggy know? Oh, please, don't let Peggy know.

But downstairs is unsettlingly ordinary, the world as it was an hour ago. The faint squeak and grind of Annie's mangle. The ginger cat crossing the hall, tail piped. Caroline is nowhere to be seen. Nor Bartlett.

Click click click.

I follow the faint sound of knitting needles to the sunroom. Kitty is contentedly slumped on Peggy's knee, pouring water from a toy teapot into a plastic dolly cup, while Peggy's small, strong fingers twist and tug green yarn over her needles.

'Have you seen Toby?' My voice sounds almost normal. Like it hasn't caught up yet.

Peggy shakes her head, watching the wool knit. 'Dare say he'll be back soon. Rain's on its way. I can feel it. When you do find him, Amber, tell him the blanket for his tree house is coming along nicely, will you?' She holds it up, half finished, in different shades of green: moss, river, leaves. 'He'll be able to use it during the Christmas holidays at least. He won't freeze in the branches.'

Christmas: how will we ever get that far? Even tomorrow feels terrifyingly uncharted now. Like I've fallen off the edge of the map.

Peggy puts the knitting down in her lap, frowns. 'You're pale as curd. What's the matter?'

'Nothing,' I mumble, leaving Peggy wondering, rushing away from further questions.

Outside, the clouds are swollen, the air heavy and damp. I

stop beside the falcons, wondering where to look first. The woods, obviously. Toby will be in the woods. I try to run. But my legs won't work properly, my feet leaden as diver's boots.

Soon the rain starts to fall, splashy warm teardrops, drenching me in seconds. I plough on for a few more minutes, dress sticking unpleasantly to my thighs, before being hit by a bone-aching exhaustion, unable to see through the rain, unable to go on.

I'll wait for Toby in the drawing room, I decide wearily, intercept him the moment he walks into the hall.

So that is what I do, sinking to the rug beside the globe, pushing it with a cold fingertip, spinning it until I can see New York, circled in happier times. And I keep spinning it, searching for the comfort of its honeybee hum. But the globe sounds different today. Less honeybee hive, more a wasps' nest stirring.

'Seen Old Harry?' I look up to see Barney, lolly lump in his cheek, white tennis ball at his bare foot, letting some kind of bug ladder from the finger of one hand to the other. 'I left him running around the hall and he's scarpered. I want to try him in his new travel basket.'

'He never goes far,' I manage, struggling to care about a rabbit on such a day. 'Maybe Kitty's put him in her pram.'

'No. I looked.' He walks towards me, lightly tapping the ball. 'Want to see?' He holds up his hand. The beetle is jewel-purple, like one of Grandma Esme's brooches on the move.

'Pretty.'

'Duh. He's a boy!'

'Fearsome?'

'Yes. Fearsome.' He laughs, flicking the beetle off his wrist into his cupped palm. 'Will you help me look for Old Harry?'

'I can't right this minute. Sorry.'

'When, then?'

'Not now, Barns.' I sigh. 'I've got to . . . to find Toby.'

'The rabbit's more important. I won't go to London without him.' Barney sticks his lolly back into his mouth and dribbles the tennis ball out of the room. Shortly afterwards, I hear the front door slam. Although I know it's probably Barney going out, there's also a small chance it may be Toby coming in, so I pull myself up.

The hall is empty, cooled by a gust of rainy air from the just-opened door. I look up the stairs: nothing. Strain to hear footsteps: nothing. I glance at Big Bertie: almost four. I'll wait a little longer. I still feel so tired, so strange, so heavy. Back in the drawing room, I grab a cushion off a chair, throw it to the rug and lie down, unable to stop the black velvet of my eyelids closing like curtains.

'Anyone for the beach?'

Her voice wakes me, clear as a bell. I rub my gluey eyes. And there she is, feet away: Momma in her green silk dress, perched grasshopper-light on the edge of the pink velvet chair, head cocked, smiling through her copper waves.

'Momma?' Disoriented by joy and sleep, I scrabble across the rug towards her on my knees like a baby, reach up for the hem of the dress. My fingers close and it becomes the tasselled edge of a green cushion. The chair is empty, and yet she is there, outline dispersing slowly, like aeroplane trails in the sky.

I don't know how long I stare at that chair, numb with pins and needles, waiting for Momma to reappear, knowing I must have been half asleep and imagined her, equally certain she was completely real. *Anyone for the beach?* I know what I must do.

'Oh, hello, young lady! I wondered where you'd got to.' Peggy intercepts me in the hall, cradling the fat kitchen cat in the crook of her arms. 'You look half asleep.'

'I . . . I dozed off.'

'That's not like you. You must be coming down with something. You still look terribly pale.'

There's a pause. A breeze swings restlessly over the black and white tiles. How long before she knows? I wonder again. Sees me as someone else entirely, someone shocking and shameful?

Peggy nuzzles the cat's head with her chin, nods at the closed drawing-room door. 'Are the monkeys in there, then?'

'No.' The cat starts to purr loudly. 'I haven't found Toby yet. Barney went off looking for Old Harry.'

'Up hill and down dale after that silly creature! Today of all days. I want Barney and Toby to sit down and get some half-decent food in their bellies before the journey. *I'll* be cooking it. Mrs Alton has a terrible migraine and doesn't want to be disturbed. Sent Bartlett home early she did, saying her services weren't needed.' She can't hide her pleasure at this. 'I should grab Barney. We still need to locate his left shoe and wash bag. Where did he go?'

'Don't know, sorry.'

'When did he leave?'

'Um. About four.'

'Oh, not long, then. I'll give him a little more time.'

I am already through the front door when she calls, 'And where are you off to, looking so furtive?'

'The beach. I think Toby might be there. I'll bring him back.'

'Not if you're poorly, Amber.'

'I was just tired. I'm fine now.'

She looks unconvinced. 'Sure you're packed for tomorrow? You all need to be at the station first thing, you know. No dilly-dallying.'

I dart to the door.

'Be careful,' she calls after me. 'High tide. Don't go and get yourself cut off or anything daft. And you can tell the others it'll be stargazy pie served in the kitchen. Just like old times.'

Thirty-One

'The baby's dead!' Kitty is screaming – eyes wide, electric blue – running up the front steps. 'The baby's dead!'

'What?' I grab her by the shoulders, kneel down on the wet stone. 'Calm down, Kitty. What baby? What are you talking about?'

'In the woods – the woods!' She points with a finger. 'I saw it. By the swing. I did, Amber. I did.'

Peggy and Annie, hearing the commotion, rush out but can't coax sense from Kitty either.

'A baby? Come now, Kitty,' says Annie, shaking her head.

'It was,' sobs Kitty, burying her face in Raggedy Doll.

'Annie, you get Kitty inside,' says Peggy, looking worried all of a sudden.

'Pegs . . .' Annie picks up Kitty, lowering her voice to a whisper '. . . remember the St Mawes foundling last year? You don't think it could be a local girl's little 'un, do you?'

Peggy frowns. 'I don't know.'

'Oh, my giddy aunt! To think of such girls in our village!'

'We shouldn't judge them,' says Peggy. 'We should never judge the desperate.'

'I suppose not,' says Annie, doubtfully. 'But not everyone's so big-hearted, Pegs. It's no wonder the wretched girl's dumped it. Imagine the shame.'

349

'Annie, please be quiet,' says Peggy, irritable now. 'I'm sure it's nothing but I will get a blanket, just in case.' She turns to me, cheeks flushed. 'Amber, you run on ahead. I'll meet you there. Hold it tight to your chest. Keep it warm whatever you do until I arrive.'

Glad to escape them all, I dash off, springier after my sleep, worrying not about a baby – for how can there be a baby in the woods? – but Toby. Where has he gone? What can he be thinking? I stop every few yards, peering through the tree trunks, calling his name. Only the birds call back. No sign of Toby. Or the baby, for that matter.

As I near the tree swing I slow. A few more paces, I stop. Squint.

There *is* something.

I creep closer, heart thumping, trying to make out exactly what it is. What it is not.

The creature is hanging by its feet, fur stripped off, pink, bald and sticky as a newborn.

But it is not a baby. It is a rabbit. Like something hanging in the butcher's window. And beneath the carcass a black pelt hugs the bulging tree roots, bloodless, slit as expertly as dressmaker's cloth. I cover my mouth with my hands. There is only one person I know who can skin an animal like that.

'Poachers?' Peggy pants up behind me, tartan blanket bundled in her arms. 'Some sort of horrible . . .' Her voice trails off. And she knows, as I know beyond doubt, because we have both spotted Great-Grandpa's knife a few feet away, glinting in the wet green heart of a fern.

I recoil, dazed, sickened: in slicing up the rabbit Toby has sliced us all apart, cutting through our sinewy strings and bonds, old loyalties, the soft tissue of our past. He has cut himself completely adrift.

'Good grief,' mutters Peggy, then strains for her competent housekeeper's voice. 'Right. Let's get this poor thing down. We don't want Barney finding it.'

She passes me the blanket, rubs her hands together, as if warming them up for the grisly task, unhooks the rabbit off the tree by its bunched feet. She might have been selecting it for supper if her eyes weren't filled with tears. She hesitates, rabbit swaying from her hand.

'What, Peggy?'

'It's cold. Stiffening. Must have been here some time.' There's a strange look on her face. She rolls the rabbit in the blanket – a pitiful veiny ear pokes out – and glances up at me. 'Amber, love, when did you say Barney left again?'

We stuff the dead bunny into the small, stinky room above the cellars where pheasants hang, a place where Barney would never look. Inside, her back pressed against the closed door, forehead sweaty, Peggy fires dozens of questions – 'Why would Toby do that to the rabbit?'; 'Is this connected to Lucian leaving so abruptly?'; 'Is there something you're not telling me?' – which I meet with stuttering unsustainable protestations of ignorance. I am on the verge of telling Peggy everything when she decides the dead rabbit is starting to smell so we leave, locking the door behind us.

We find Kitty calmer, eating custard creams on Annie's knee in the kitchen. For Kitty's sake, we tell them it was nothing, just a dead squirrel, caught on a branch. But I feel

Kitty's eyes follow us as we leave the room, her child's antennae sensing another story.

Peggy drags me on a search of the house's most obvious places. Toby is not anywhere: no surprise, not after what he's done. But neither is Barney. We get back to the hall, where we started. I feel dizzy now, my mouth dry and tasting oddly of ink. Peggy opens the front door, scans the lawns, glances over her shoulder at Big Bertie. 'Well, it's not yet five. At least Barney's not been gone long.'

'Oh, that clock's been stuck on not-yet-five since me and Kitty got back in,' says Annie, peering over a huge vase of flowers, cracking it down on the marble shelf. 'Big Bertie's started to slow again – have you noticed? Gets jammed just before the hour. So much for that silly man's tinkering! I bet he charged a fortune as well.' She shakes her head, tweaks a tall blue flower. 'Really, all Mrs Alton's clockwatching does is lead to confusion. It's a darn sight simpler to look at the sun here. I always said so.'

Unease curdles in my stomach. It is suddenly far from clear how long Barney's been gone, how long I slept, if he left around four, if he'd had time to find the rabbit. Should he be back by now? Are there unaccountable minutes we're unaware of? Are they important? I cannot think straight. I cannot make out what matters and what doesn't.

'If he was upset he'd come back to the house, wouldn't he? And there's nothing to see in the woods now so we don't need to worry about that,' Peggy mutters to herself.

'I'm going to find him.'

'You are? Wait . . .' Peggy hesitates, a thoughtful frown. 'Don't tell Barney what happened to his rabbit.'

'Pegs, I thought you said it was a squirrel?' says Annie, stepping closer curiously.

'What shall I tell him?' I ask, ignoring Annie.

'Nothing. Just don't hurry back too quickly. I've got a friend in the village who has dozens of rabbits in hutches for pies. I'll pop over there now, find a match for Old Harry.' She unties her striped apron, shoves it into Annie's hands. 'Right, I'm off. I'll make that poor rabbit rise again, if it's the last thing I do.'

I stand on the wet grass, arms crossed, shivering in the sunshine that has broken through the rainclouds. It's so hard to scramble my wits together, push Caroline's words out of my head. I see the raw pink rabbit everywhere I look. But there is no time for self-pity or distraction. I must find Barney. That is all that matters for now.

I take a deep breath, wonder where to start. It occurs to me that Barney might have expected to find the rabbit here on the lawn. Old Harry's got as far before, freezing at the possibility of freedom, shaking at the scent of fox. But Barney did not find Old Harry on the lawn. Could not. So Barney would have gone on. He would have kept looking. Where?

The iron gate at the edge of the woods is ajar. Not much. About the width of a boy. Or did Peggy and I leave it swinging? Quite possibly.

Edgy now, I follow the narrow, twisting path through the trees, quick but silent on my rubber-soled plimsolls, eyes and ears alert for my brothers. The den by the tree swing first, I decide, then upstream to the tree house where, more than likely, at least Toby is hiding.

A few minutes later, I stop. After first searching the ground floor of the house, Barney would go through a back door. The kitchen garden. The vegetable patch. The outbuildings. Why did Peggy and I not think of those places? I will turn back.

But I do not turn back. Because my eye catches on something round and white on the path: a tennis ball, its yellow seam bright against the bark flakes. The tennis ball Barney was kicking in the drawing room earlier?

My heart starts to bang against the buttons of my dress. The tree we found Old Harry hanging from is only a short walk from here. Presuming Barney did find it, where would he run in his blind horror? Where on earth would he go, if not home?

Anyone for the beach? The sound of someone blowing into a glass bottle. A rustle of leaves. *Anyone for the beach?*

It feels like I'm flying then, feet barely touching the ground. And I get to the coast quicker than I ever have before, stitch stabbing my side. But, crushingly, Barney is not on the beach. There is not much beach left, the tide coming in fast. I scrabble back up the rocks and along the stony coast path, calling his name. I check beneath the gorse, part the long grass, the cow parsley and meadow-sweet, shout for him from the top of the stiles, weave through the cattle to the field's hedges. And he is nowhere, absolutely nowhere at all.

How long have I got? The sky is pinking but bright. There is still time. The ledge. Yes, I'll go to the ledge. Nowhere offers a better view of the cliff tops opposite, or the coast path. If Barney or Toby is close, I'll spot him easily enough.

But on the cliff – where that tussock of tough, spiky grass pushes up from a crack in the rock – I hesitate. I don't know why. Maybe it's a sense of foreboding. Maybe it's because Toby is not with me. I have to force myself to dangle my feet off the edge this time. Not look down. Don't look down and you won't fall, Toby always says. Falling is all in the mind.

I don't fall.

I press myself to the cliff face, shade my eyes and scan the green cliff tops. No one. Might Barney have gone back to the house by now? I imagine us running in different directions, paths crossing a few seconds too late, just missing each other. So I sit, breath slowly easing, and start to lose myself in the big pink sky, plans of escape. After all, what loyalties tie me here now?

. . . a huge black bird diving over the cliff into my thoughts, so close its talons might catch in my hair. I instinctively duck in its wing draught, nose meeting the cool skin of my knees. And when I look up my eyes are no longer on the sky but flotsam bobbing on the high tide swell below. No, not flotsam. Something more alive. A dolphin? Or those jellyfish that have been washing up in the cove all week, like a lost cargo of grey glass bowls? Maybe. I lean forward, dipping my face over the edge to get a better view, hair blowing wildly, heart beating faster, sensing something terrible beneath the shimmering surface, not seeing it.

A moment passes. Another.

Then a dark shape rises, breaks the surface. What? An air-filled T-shirt. Hair, black-red curls, seaweed-spread . . .

Clumsy with panic, I scrabble off the ledge, kicking at the cliff face, unable to find my familiar foot holes, skid down rocks, desperate to get to the bottom, wade into the

355

sea and save Toby. But when I drop to the sand he is already out of the water, dripping over a small crumpled figure, on the last bit of beach left by the hungry tide. I blink and blink but it is still Barney and Toby is kissing him, blowing air into his mouth. Water is dribbling out of the corner of Barney's lips. Toby looks at me and starts to sob, sorry sorry sorry, something about the rabbit being for Lucian to find and he didn't know what he was doing until after he did it and he saw the knife was covered in blood and the fur on the ground . . . *Breathe, Barney, breathe!* He is pushing so hard on Barney's chest – pumping, pumping, pumping, making his little body bounce on the sand – that I cannot bear to look, so I just hold his limp wet hand as the sea pulls at our ankles, the patch of sand at the foot of the cliff getting smaller and smaller until we are against the rock face holding Barney out of the water, our hands on his ankles, beneath his armpits, his head lolling back, and suddenly he coughs, spitting water, and he is alive! 'Come, on, Barns!' Toby shouts, but the next moment the cough stops and his body sags in our arms, and everything that ever happened to us draws to that black point, to the disappearing sliver of sand, until the water rushes in and that, too, washes away.

Thirty-Two

I watch them leave Black Rabbit Hall in disbelief, hands spread on the window. Why is no one looking up? Don't they know I'm here? I wave madly, knock on the glass. But Toby's face is buried in his hands as he staggers into Fat Tel's taxi, a boy blinded by grief and guilt, the fight all gone. The putter of the engine soon drowns me out, whisking my poor brother away. A strict boarding school in the north of Scotland, Peggy says, where a frozen winter's night falls shortly after noon. A second taxi, London-bound, shoots off a few moments later, Annie, Kitty and Boris huddled in the back. Daddy's Rolls is nowhere to be seen. Has he left too? Was the silent kiss on my forehead late last night my goodbye?

And where is my dear little brother? Where *is* he? I refuse to believe he is caught forever in those lost minutes, the jamming cogs of a tall-case clock. I refuse to be the big sister who didn't search for his rabbit because she thought it trivial. I cannot be her. And he cannot be dead. For how is it possible to show your sister a beetle on your finger and a few hours later simply not exist at all? I cannot grasp it.

Footsteps. I leap off the bed. Peggy. Let it be Peggy. But as the steps get closer I make out the hard peck of heels. It is not Peggy.

The key twists in the lock. Caroline doesn't look at me,

slides a tray of food – soup, bread, water – across the desk near the door, banging it up against the plate of uneaten toast. I am still in my nightie, but she is immaculately turned out, perfectly made up. I picture her hand dipping a powdery puff into a mirrored glass pot, dragging her chalky-pink lipstick across her mouth, then reaching for the dirty bunch of keys that she is gripping tight in her fist.

'Eat something.' She nods at the tray.

'I'm not hungry.'

'You need to keep your strength up.'

'I need to be with Kitty. Kitty needs me more than ever.' My voice is a whisper, croaked from crying. 'Please let me go with the others.'

She doesn't waver for a moment. 'Impossible.'

'What good am I locked away up here? I cannot bear it.'

'You should have thought of that before you screwed your brother.'

I don't flinch. I don't break her gaze. She's lying, I'm even more sure of it. Toby warned me what she was capable of. I didn't believe him then. I do now. He warned me, too, that a bad thing was going to happen. It wasn't a meteorite. But it has crashed into us just the same.

'And do stop banging on the door like a hooligan. No one can hear you.'

'Peggy will hear me,' I say weakly.

'Peggy knows what has to be done, Amber.' Caroline turns, reaches for the doorknob, draped silk sleeve swinging off her arm.

'I demand to see Daddy.' Not taking my eyes off that doorknob, I wonder how long it will take me to reach it, if I can grapple her away.

'Your father is in a terrible state this morning. Now put him out of your mind. He won't be visiting you for a while. No one will.' Her voice hushes without softness, and her pale eyes seem almost to glow, winter light in cracks of ice. 'Least of all Lucian.'

'Where is he?'

'Oxford. Getting on with his life.'

I ache for him, the pain physical. 'Have you told him?' I swallow. 'Does . . . does he know?'

'Of course not, Amber. This is our little secret. You, me, Peggy, Hugo. No one else must be troubled, not if we want to keep our reputations intact.'

It takes every ounce of strength not to cry. To stand firm as that small, claustrophobic room contracts, squeezing the air from my chest. 'I refuse to be locked away like a criminal. I will escape.'

'Amber,' she warns. 'I don't want to have to break your spirit.'

'You could never do that.'

The keys clink on the ring. 'Don't try me.'

'I hate you. I hate you so much.'

She snorts. 'I dare say you'll grow to hate yourself more.'

I think of Momma, who would always tell us how precious we were, whatever we did, whatever mistakes we made. Then I just think of Momma. Try to will her into the room. It doesn't work. Tears flood my eyes. I try to blink them back but they keep coming.

'Listen, Amber.' Her voice softens a little. 'You are lucky, very lucky, to be kept at home, that your father is such a sentimental man. There are places that girls like you get sent away to and, believe me, they are rather worse than

359

this.' She opens the door a little. The landing light twinkles through the gap. I count the paces. Four? Five? 'And it is not forever.'

She reaches to pick the toast plate off the desk. I edge forward, bare feet soundless on the floor. Her eyes flick up, wondering if I have moved. Grandmother's Footsteps. Not taking her gaze off me now, she grabs the plate quickly, barring the exit with her other arm.

I fly towards that door with everything I have left. It unfolds in slow motion. The shocked hole of her mouth. The smash of the plate. The toast and china scattering across the floor. Caroline only just managing to get out, slamming the door behind her. I rattle the knob fiercely. But she is already twisting the key in the lock. And I hear her breath, loud and relieved. Heels tripping down the stairs. I thump the door, calling Barney's name over and over and over.

I don't know how long I thump and shout but when I stop my hands and throat are sore. The room is kaleidoscope-shattered by tears. But it suddenly feels like Momma is there too, tugging on the sleeve of my nightie, pulling me to a precious place I thought I'd lost – ripped away like the soft fur from the rabbit – and a chilly, sunny spring day, a beach that is still benign, a sandcastle that has taken me and Toby hours and hours to build. The tide is playing at our ankles, bubbling around the bucket battlements, teasing them away. Our shorts are sodden, scratchy with sand. We're hungry, thirsty, blue-toed. Momma is smiling, beckoning us to the shore for ham sandwiches. We ignore her, intent only on proving that this time – unlike all the other countless times – we can beat the tide and our castle will hold. Toby digs frantically with his left hand, me with my right. Sand arcs through the air. We keep rebuilding, buttressing. One tower dissolves. Then another. And it's all starting to go and Barney and Kitty are clapping and giggling on the beach and we are clinging together on the mound, wobbling, teetering, until a furious white wall of foam rushes in, flattening the sand, tumbling us into the freezing froth, stinging salt surging up our noses.

The next morning, we walk across the cliffs to the beach and start to dig another one, the same but bigger.

Thirty-Three

Lorna

'I suspected the moment I saw Amber naked in the dressing room.' The shadow of Mrs Alton's cane lengthens in the evening sunlight falling through the window, like a black line drawn across the wooden floor. 'Her slip of a figure had noticeably filled out. And, of course, there they were, undressed, stinking of each other, and it all . . .' she closes her eyes briefly '. . . started to make a dreadful sense. Amber couldn't possibly have gone back to London.'

What? No, she's heard it wrong. Lorna sinks to the single iron bed, bandaged tightly with white sheets, like something from a wartime field hospital. A faded cloth doll, with black stitches for eyes, a bead dangling off one, rests against the pillow. She picks it up. It lolls forward in her hands, stuffing sprouting from its neck. 'You've lost me. Sorry.'

Mrs Alton leans forward in the wooden chair, touches the powdered tip of her nose lightly with her index finger. 'Oh, I do hope not.'

Puzzled, uneasy, Lorna looks around this plain, monastic room at the top of the east tower – the school desk, the chest of drawers, a row of dog-eared paperbacks along a solitary shelf – and begins to feel the breath of the past blowing icy cold on the back of her neck.

'Of course you're not Endellion's sister, twin or

otherwise,' says Mrs Alton, after a long sigh, hands meeting each other on the top of the cane.

'Sorry? You mean . . . But why would Dill lie?' stutters a disbelieving Lorna.

'Endellion is incapable of subterfuge. She repeats what she's been told, unquestioning thing that she is, quite the opposite from you in every way. And she was told there was a twin.'

Lorna's head starts to thump, her mouth dry. No, she cannot take this in. She must leave. The woman is obviously quite mad.

'Endellion was born six weeks early, a scrap of a thing, two days before you, which was enormously helpful to all concerned.'

'But . . . Peggy . . .' The Ps. She can see those Ps now, marching across the paper. 'Peggy Mary Popple's name is on my birth certificate.'

'Indeed. The doctor was quite happy to fudge that. Old friend of the family. Loyal as a dog. Died never leaking a word. He and Hugo covered their tracks perfectly. Left you quite untraceable, Lucian's and Amber's reputations wholly unblemished.'

Lucian? Lucian and Amber? Lorna's breath is coming fast. She's hyperventilating. No. Not possible. Just not possible. It is too much to believe one thing, then be asked to believe another, to keep ripping up the story of your life and starting again.

'Peggy offered to bring the baby up as her illegitimate baby girl's "twin". We couldn't let her do it, of course, far too risky.' She nods to herself, reaffirming her own conviction. 'But it planted the seed.'

Lorna grips the doll tighter, pressing it to her belly, the pale room darkening at the edges of her vision.

'Don't look so aghast. It was an . . . administrative detail, and it helped everyone enormously. It really did. Peggy was ostracized in the village. She fully expected to be sacked from Pencraw too. Instead we offered her security for life – her and Endellion – and in return she saved the Altons from . . . irreparable disgrace.' She winces, imagining it. 'She also gave the baby – forgive me, you – a half-decent provenance. Obviously, if it had ever got out that it was born of incest . . .'

Lorna clamps her hand to her mouth. 'Oh, God, tell me that was the lie.'

'It was, yes.' Mrs Alton jolts suddenly, bringing her hand to her cheek as if someone has just slapped her. 'I did come clean to Lucian, after Hugo died. But by then it was all too late. Life sets hard as concrete, Lorna. It sets terribly quickly.'

Lorna cradles her head in her hands, lets out a small moan. They sit in silence for a few moments, lost in their own dark worlds, gulls wheeling at the window, the buzz of masonry bees in the ivy.

'Not one of us, but a decent couple, the doctor said, plagued by miscarriage, thrilled with you,' Mrs Alton says eventually, as if trying to add a more cheerful spin. 'The wife promised to bring you back to Cornwall regularly so you had some knowledge of your Cornish roots. Amber drew much comfort from that, I believe. Oh dear. Lorna, I fear I have quite overwhelmed you. Please say something.'

But she cannot. For the disparate parts are coming

together like bits of a space station locking soundlessly in the airless black: the Cornish holidays, the photographs at the bottom of the drive, her mother's absurd insistence on knowing her 'cultural heritage' while not bothering to educate Louise. So her mother had tried. Despite all her anxieties about the adoption she had still tried to do the right thing. Something brittle deep inside Lorna softens and gives. How strange, she thinks, that by finding my birth mother I discover the true nature of my adopted one too.

'Of course, they weren't told you were from Pencraw. Goodness, no. But I fear there was gossip.' She sighs. 'There is always gossip.'

As Lorna sits on those tight white sheets, the bed in which she was born, her mind starts to work backwards, pulling events together, sequencing each stitch, seeing how Mrs Alton's lie is the dark metallic thread running through it all. Her rage starts to rise then, her dark eyes flash. 'Why fabricate such a cruel, cruel thing, Mrs Alton? Why?'

Mrs Alton blinks several times, in quick succession, adjusting to Lorna's anger. 'I thought it would end things between Amber and Lucian definitively and we could all get on with our lives.'

'*Get on?*' she repeats, disbelieving, fury cracking her voice.

'Lorna, you must understand. Pencraw meant everything to Hugo, and its fate was far from certain. Something had to be done. Toby was not capable of inheriting the house. Pencraw would have been safe with Lucian. Hugo knew it too. That's why he didn't ask too many questions. They even look similar! And they got on so well. He *wanted*

365

Lucian to be his.' The shadow of the cane starts to tremble. 'As he lay dying on the terrace – a heart attack, brought on by sheer grief over Barney's death two years before, I'm quite sure of it – I made a solemn promise to keep the house going, whatever happened, and I have honoured that. I have honoured that at least.'

'You shouldn't be here!' shouts Lorna, standing up, railing at the injustice of it all.

'Lorna, I can live here as long as I wish. In the absence of a resident owner, or one of competence, I manage this house. Hugo's will was unambiguous.'

'But Toby is the heir!'

She frowns. 'Yes, and that is the flaw in the system, the reason so many estates have been run into the ground over the years, family fortunes that took centuries to build lost in months by some . . . liability of an eldest son.'

'He was just a messed-up kid! He needed help!'

'You are not a schoolteacher for nothing, I see.'

'How could you? How could you cheat Toby like that?'

'Lucian put Pencraw Hall in Toby's name many years ago, weeks after Hugo died. Toby wasn't cheated, not in the end.'

'Then where *is* Toby?'

Mrs Alton's mouth tightens.

'Where is he?'

Mrs Alton looks away.

Lorna recoils in disgust. 'Well, it's no wonder no one wants to return. You've turned Pencraw into a house of horrors! A house with its heart ripped out! Like – like a piece of taxidermy! Nothing is worth what you've done. *Nothing.*'

Mrs Alton is mushroom-pale. 'My dear, I thought if I explained it, you'd understand.'

'I *do* understand,' she says, the anger turning into something else, something calmer, colder. Her hands stop shaking. Her eyes are dry. She's got what she came for at Black Rabbit Hall: her story, for better and for worse. Yes, the past has dropped over her, like a lobster pot. But she can crawl out from underneath it now. She is free, and very much wishes to go home. 'I have to leave, Mrs Alton. I don't belong here.'

'Oh, but you do!' Her fingers travel to her necklace, swivel the pearls faster and faster until Lorna fears they might fly off and scatter across the floor, like loose teeth. 'Fate has brought you, returned Lucian to me in your form. You are to stay, Lorna. You *must* stay.'

She almost laughs then. '*Stay?* After everything you've done? Are you mad?'

'It's the builder chap, isn't it? Jon? Tom?' gabbles Mrs Alton, spraying panicked spittle. 'The plumber. You can bring him too, if you wish. Have a wing! The whole house! Or would you prefer the estate cottage?'

'Mrs Alton, please . . .' There is something bizarrely childlike in the woman's inability to grasp the effects of her own actions. 'Stop it.'

To Lorna's horror, the old woman's eyes fill with tears.

Outside she hears the sound of a car coming up the drive, hard braking on the gravel. 'I'm sorry to leave you upset,' she says quietly.

Without warning, Mrs Alton lurches forward, jettisoning herself off the chair, hands paddling, a woman drowning. 'But I am your *grandmother*!'

The word, even though she was anticipating it, dreading it, punches with its unique grotesque force. For a moment neither of them speaks. In the horrified hush they hear the sound of footsteps on the stairs, faint, getting louder. They both look to the door, wondering who will burst in. Knowing they haven't long.

Lorna pulls away. 'I had a grandmother, Mrs Alton, the best anyone could ever have. I do not need another.'

'Then just sit with me for a while.' Mrs Alton clutches the back of the chair, making it rattle from leg to leg. 'Please. Hold my hand. No one ever holds my hand.'

Lorna glances down the stairwell, dark as the mouth of a cave. For her own sanity, she must leave this room. Walk away from it, step by step. If she can just get to the bottom of the staircase, where it widens and opens, where there is light.

'Can you forgive me? I beg your forgiveness. I am dying, Lorna.'

Lorna hesitates, hand on the doorknob. Oh, God. What to do? How can she ever forgive this woman? She closes her eyes, heart racing. Tries to think, hears the footsteps pounding up the stairs. What would Nan advise? The most decent person she ever knew. No, she never gave the wrong advice.

'Lorna.' Mrs Alton's voice is a pathetic whimper now. 'Don't leave me shut away in this ghastly place alone.'

Lorna turns and walks back into the room.

Seconds later, there he is, arms spread wide, a giant in the narrow doorframe.

'Jon!' Lorna's flight is visceral, instinctive. She runs into those arms, buries her face in his shirt, her legs almost folding beneath her with relief.

He cups her shoulders, eyes searching hers. 'Are you okay?'

She nods, blinks back her tears, so many different feelings – joy, sadness, emotions that have no name but spread like hot water in a cold bath – tunnelling along their locked gaze. 'A lot's happened,' is all she can mutter, the frenzy of her thoughts stilling beneath the weight of his hands.

'I know.' He picks a strand of hair off her hot cheek.

Mrs Alton coughs, reminding them of her presence. Jon peers over Lorna's head to the pale lady gripping the back of a chair with swollen fingers.

'Mrs Alton?'

She nods, eyes still wide with surprise.

'Are *you* okay?' he asks gently, beginning to sense the conversation that has torn up the air in this strange little room.

'I – I feel rather tired.'

'Come on, love. Let's get you downstairs, shall we?' Jon takes Mrs Alton's trembling thin arm, helps her down the staircase, easy now, one step at a time, settles her into the armchair in the modest living room at the bottom of the east tower, tucks a tartan blanket over her lap and pours a knock-out glass of sherry, all of which she accepts without a murmur of complaint or pulling rank, as if she has been waiting a very long time for a young man to take charge. Her chin drops to her chest, eyes slowly closing. Jon turns to Lorna, who is witnessing Mrs Alton's compliance with growing amazement. 'Now can I get you a drink?' he asks.

It is like the first night they met, the noise and crowd of the party fading away. And she replies, as she did then, 'Yes, please. I'd like that very much.'

Wine appears from the cellars in dusty bottles – swung like rolling pins in Dill's tiny hands – vintages fragrant with honey and blossom from Mediterranean summers long ago. Dill, Alf, Doug and Louise circle them in the drawing room, chirping like excited birds, then seem to spirit away into the rest of the house, leaving Jon and Lorna alone with the wine, potted shrimps, crackers and cake, the sound of Alf's laughter and the dog's excitable bark the only clue that anyone else is in the huge house at all.

Lorna laces her fingers with Jon's. Surprisingly, it is night now, a glossy black sky, pierced by stars, pinholes of light. The temperature has dropped with the sun, and the late August air, billowing through the open window, is spiced faintly with autumn, the sweetness of harvest.

Jon circles his hands around her waist, pulls her towards him. Warm breath circulates in the closing space between their mouths. The moment shivers, raw, hesitant. There is so much to say that Lorna doesn't know where to start. The intensity of the last few hours has left her mute.

'Shall I build a fire?' he whispers.

She nods – he knows what she wants before she knows it herself – and watches, mesmerized, as Jon kneels down and builds a perfect pyramid of logs and kindling in the fire-place. He strikes a match and blows, big bellows breaths that make the flames leap and dance, her heart just the same.

Soon the fire is raging, smoke pooling in the corners of the inky room, the crackle of the flames a primal sound that calms something deep inside Lorna, connects her to a precious place where the present is most alive, the past and future as wispy as dreams. They sit on the rug, Lorna cradled inside his legs, his chin on her head, a perfect fit. And slowly, tentatively at first, Lorna starts to tell Jon what she has been told, threading it all together once more, living it again – but from a safer distance now. When she has finished, they sit quietly, the hush broken only by the spit of the fire and the faint tick of a clock. Jon bends down, kisses the soft baby skin beneath her ear. 'You are extraordinary, Lorna.'

The sweetness of the comment makes her eyes fill with tears. 'I don't feel extraordinary.'

He pulls her closer. 'Well, you are.'

She reaches out, prods a glowing log with the iron poker, showering sparks into the blue dark. 'All this stuff. It's bad, bad stuff. I don't know what to do with it.'

'It's not your stuff. It's not you.'

'But it made me. It's *in* me, Jon.'

'And that's why I'm grateful for it, every death, every screwed-up lie, all of it, Lorna.'

She turns from the fire to look at him. 'You can't mean that.'

'Lorna, I love the woman you are, the woman you will become, the mother you will surely be. All I ever wanted was to know every bit of you, not to be shut out.'

She casts her eyes down. 'I didn't want that bit to – to be part of us. I wanted it to go away.'

'It didn't.'

'No.'

'But I shouldn't have pushed for it. I'm sorry. It wasn't my place to do that.'

She leans her head on his shoulder. 'The funny thing is, in the end it was this house that pushed me into my past, released it. Not me. Not you.'

He gives the smoky room a respectful nod. 'Quite some house.'

'Better with you in it.' She skims his knuckles lightly with her fingers, brings his hand to her lips. 'I can't believe you drove all the way down here.'

'Raced like a nutter, done by a speed camera at least twice.' He pauses. 'Not very sensible, Jon.'

She smiles. 'Not at all.'

He nuzzles her neck. 'Secretly I quite enjoyed it.'

She laughs, and in the release of her laugh, she can hear other laughs, superimposed on one another, tiny echoes. She turns to glance quizzically at Jon, wondering if he has heard them too. But his expression hasn't changed: his attention all on her. And yet it is as if the Alton children – Toby, Amber, Kitty, Barney – are in the room, a playful shimmer in the grey woodsmoke, a leap of blue in a golden flame, just for a strange, beautiful moment or two. Then they're gone.

Thirty-Four

Eight days later, New York City

The diner is dark and caffeinated. Outside on the street, it is bright, windy, the city glittering beneath an absurdly blue sky. Lorna's eyes cannot adjust. Neither can she.

New York. Greenwich Avenue. The centre of that inked circle on Black Rabbit Hall's globe.

Jet lag mixed with a sleepless night – her mind turning over itself, wired by the distinctive sounds of a strange city – has given the morning a surreal blur. She knows it's a cliché, but it's hard not to believe she's in a movie. That someone's not going to run up and bark, 'Cut!' and send them home to Bethnal Green.

'Sure you're okay?' Jon asks, shoving the laminated folded map into the back pocket of his jeans.

'I don't know.' She's unsure whether she's about to start crying or laughing hysterically. Maybe she'll just hail a cab back to JFK. 'My hands are shaking. Actually, I'm a bit of a mess, Jon.'

'You don't look it,' he says softly. His speckled hazel eyes are filled with light.

'Well, that's something.'

'You look beautiful.'

She smiles then, nervously twisting her hair off her neck – how can it still be so hot in September? – and letting it drop, satisfyingly heavy and glassy, thanks to the scalp-scorching blow-dry off Broadway. On Louise's orders she has also treated herself to a mani and pedi (having natural nails in New York is the equivalent of walking Bond Street with hairy wildebeest legs apparently) and an expensive blue dress from a shop in the Meatpacking District. Her red heels – while admittedly not too great for walking – are her lucky shoes, the ones she was wearing when she first met Jon. Her red Dorothy shoes. Click your heels three times. 'Ready,' she says.

'Okay. Just need to get my bearings.' Jon flicks down his Ray-Bans, looks up the street, frowns. 'About three blocks this way, I think.'

'Perhaps we could use the map?'

'I don't need the map. New York is a logical city.'

What is it with men and maps?

He grins. 'We're not in Cornwall now. Don't worry.'

But she can't help it. The idea of being late, of anything going wrong . . .

That nothing has yet gone wrong is miraculous. She hasn't been felled by food poisoning. She hasn't erupted into terrible acne. The plane didn't even fall out of the sky. She is here, in New York, standing improbably on a 'sidewalk', minutes away from the woman who gave birth to her. The thought makes her feel sick with fear and elation, and squeeze closer to Jon. Oh, how she loves this man. She thinks again of the long, magical night they spent in the inky drawing room of Black Rabbit Hall, time suspended in the drifting woodsmoke until dawn kissed the room awake and they stumbled up the stairs to bed.

On their return to London, the rushing city streets ruled

by the clang of Big Ben, everything immediately speeded up. Jon wanted to help Lorna. If she'd let him. What did Lorna want to do? She wanted, yes, she wanted to try to find her birth mother. No, she absolutely wouldn't go to pieces. Jon at her side, she felt strong enough to take the risk, newly grounded, deep-rooted in her own life. Also, she didn't think there was any real chance of finding Amber Alton.

It took a few clicks of a mouse. Lorna went to pieces. Jon had to send the email, make the call she was far too nervous to make, ask the question that Lorna didn't dare voice, would she like to meet?, and when the answer was 'Oh, my God, yes, yes! When?' and the cup of tea slid from Lorna's hand, Jon was the one who pulled it all together, squeezing the trip into these young September days before the new term started, blowing out his zillion-aire clients in Bow, booking tickets in Business – she'd be better rested, it had been a hell of a week – and a room in a cramped but charming hotel on Washington Square, lightly kicking away what had always felt like immovable barriers. Life hadn't set so hard in concrete, after all.

Don't Walk.

Walk.

A taxi honks. They're taking too long to cross. It's the red shoes. They turn into a side-street. She pulls on Jon's hand. Stop. She wants to take it all in, just for a moment: the movie strips of New York lives through the blinds of the brownstone houses; the hot wind splicing through the subway gratings; the way the sheer, soaring scale of this city makes Black Rabbit Hall shrink to such a teeny point of insignificance.

Three blocks. Two. One. 'Jon, I can't do it. I really don't think I can do this.'

Jon has already prepared for this. He has contingency plans. 'Okay. No problem. Let's go back to the hotel.'

'But I can't do that either!'

'We'll just stand here, then.' Jon wraps an arm around her shoulders, hugs her to him. 'Until you're ready.'

'The doll! Bugger. I've forgotten Kitty's doll.' Lorna scrabbles in her handbag.

As soon as Mrs Alton heard from Dill that Lorna was visiting New York – Lorna and Dill having stayed in regular contact – she dispatched her with the doll to London on the train. At Paddington station, Dill's tiny hands pressed it furtively into Lorna's, as if it were some rare smuggled jewel or stolen child, muttering something about Mrs Alton confiscating it many years before.

'No. Yes. I've got it!' She yanks the doll out of her bag, kisses it with relief. No passer-by raises so much as an eyebrow. She likes this city.

Jon holds her face in his hands. The sun is hot on their backs. 'You see? You have everything you need.'

Does she? If it all falls apart – and it well might, she's not silly – what is she left with? Jon, her family, some hard-won self-knowledge. This, she decides, is enough. 'I know.'

'Good. Because we're here.'

'You're joking? Oh. My. God. You're not joking, are you?'

Six steps. A smart black door. A row of three bells on a dulled brass plate. The second bell. Apartment two: 'Amber and Lucian Shawcross.'

Thirty-Five

Amber, the day of Lorna's wedding

It's the clink of a pipe beneath the dressing-room floor that makes me physically jolt, a sound buried so deep inside I'd forgotten it was there, the acoustic version of looking at myself in the mirror and seeing not myself but, for a brief, startling moment that makes me burst out laughing, my mother.

Momma feels so extraordinarily close today, closer than she has in many years. I can't help but picture her stepping in and out of different dresses, asking me over her freckled shoulder to zip her up. Barney, too, under her feet, laughing, Peter Pan, forever six. Toby watching us, slouched against the doorframe. Bonfire head. Left hand to my right.

I sit down on the dressing-room stool, overwhelmed with yearning for the rules of physics to be overturned, just for a few seconds – if it could happen anywhere it could surely happen here – and to see those deeply loved faces reflected back in the mirror, pink, full of life, as they were.

But only my own lived-in face appears in the mottled glass. I stare at it curiously, angling my chin up and down, obsessed with searching for her in my features. And, yes, there she is – in the upper lip, the cut of the jaw – my daughter. My. Daughter. Such words!

It's hard to believe that it's been less than two months: endless phone calls, two visits, one in New York, one in London, each one bulging, over-spilling, the retelling of entire lifetimes squeezed into the brace of days and differing time zones. We are mindful of overloading her. We have tried to be sensitive to our son Barney too, who is thrilled to have a sister but has been used to the kingship of being an only child. Easy does it, Lucian says, batting everyone else off: Aunt Bay, Kitty and her family, Matilda, our stunned friends, the artists at my gallery, Lucian's dumbfounded colleagues at Columbia.

Every morning since Jon first called, I've shaken Lucian awake. Am I dreaming? Are you sure it's real? Has she forgiven me for giving her away? My old fear – that the people I love will vanish or die – bubbling up again. He rubs his eyes, scrabbling for his glasses on the bedside table, and reassures me in the way only Lucian can.

After that little ritual I can allow myself the sweet agony of counting down the days, hours, minutes until I can see or speak to Lorna again, besotted by this wonderful young woman, of me, yet not me, the baby wholly loved, wholly lost, who has forged ahead bravely with her own life, sought out the answers she needed, survived Black Rabbit Hall, her spirit and humour undimmed. Oh dear, I've become quite silly with love.

Lorna. Not the name I'd have chosen. But it suits her, the down-to-earth honesty of it. I was too terrified to call her anything but 'Baby' in case this made me love her too much – futile, I did anyway – because I always knew that I couldn't keep her. After she was taken away – tugged from my arms as I screamed, Caroline, mouth like a paper cut, telling me not to be selfish, do what was best for the child, the hurried flight of the doctor's feet down the stairs – I returned to London, a raw, skinned thing. I told only Matilda – no one else knew, my incarceration explained by illness – and on those precious nights I slept top to tail in Matilda's bed, we'd spend hours talking about Baby, where she was, who she'd become, red-haired like me or dark like Lucian. A few months later, my father, desperate to lift me out of my listless, tearful gloom, finally agreed to let me live with Aunt Bay and go to school in New York for a while, neither of us realizing it would turn into forever. I remember standing at the airport, brown leather suitcase at my feet, Matilda leaning over, glasses askew, whispering in my ear, 'One day, Baby will come and find you, Amber. She will. Swear.' I didn't believe her.

I decided on the plane, staring down at the roof of white clouds, that I would pretend the baby had died, along with the others. That this was the only way I'd ever survive.

Of course, I could never stop wondering, looking at the calendar, thinking, She's three, or First grade, or Sixteen, today. And I did survive. Life is full and busy. New York is crammed with shrinks, work, yoga and art. There were wounds I didn't want to heal – to recover was to forget, and I wanted never to forget – but I had a duty to our Barney not to be a basket case.

A knock on the door. 'Party's starting, honey.' Lucian's voice breaks my thoughts. 'Do you think you might be ready before dawn?'

'Almost done.' I lean towards the mirror, tongue scouting my front teeth for rogue bits of Chanel lipstick, twisting around to check the lines of the dress, feeling a wave of insecurity. Is the long green dress too much? Too green? Will Lorna like it? It's not very mother-of-the-bride. But what is the dress code for long-lost birth mother at a wedding in Cornwall during an unseasonably warm autumn? I have absolutely no idea.

'Barney's already gone down, attached himself to the prettiest girl in the room as usual.' Lucian moves from the left-angled wing of the mirror to the flat centre. He slings his arms around my waist, kisses my bare shoulder, smiling at our reflection from beneath his mop of salt and pepper hair.

I wonder what he sees. The middle-aged married couple we are? Or the teenagers we once were? All I know is that when I look at him, I don't see grey hairs or a softening jaw but Lucian as he was the day we were reunited: snake-hipped, floppy-haired, every inch the bright young scholar pacing nervously beneath the Bridge of Sighs in the honey-eyed Oxford sunshine, unaware I was watching him a few feet away, too scared to leave the shadows of a narrow cobbled alleyway. It was almost two years since I'd seen Lucian, but he still sucked the breath right out of me.

His letter had dropped into Aunt Bay's mailbox only days before, thrillingly Queen-stamped, faintly scented with the familiar inky smell of his fingers. He wrote of how his mother had confessed her lie (proving to me what I had always felt to be true), the baby he was never told about, all I'd suffered alone. Could I ever, ever forgive him? Could we meet? That he knew about the baby and still wanted to see me — Caroline had said I'd ruin his life if I ever told him, that he'd hate me for ever — was such a relief, such a shock, that I sank to the floor and wept. Aunt Bay sprang into action, throwing my prettiest, shortest dresses into a bag, bundling me into a cab for the airport, instructing me to yell, 'Oxford, please!' at the other end.

Stepping from the shadows of that narrow alleyway, I had no idea what would happen next. So much time had passed. I felt weary and battle-scarred, no longer the fresh-faced girl he'd loved. But when Lucian looked up a shaft of sunlight hit the jet glitter-longing in his eyes, and I knew. I just knew that nothing would part us again. Of course, I didn't know how difficult it would be to stay together either, to move from that sweet, sweet kiss to a marriage of twenty-odd years. I'm not sure anyone does.

'Great dress.'

I smile at him in the mirror, glad to be pulled out of my thoughts. 'Not too much?'

'In a good way.'

'Well, too late to change now. Also, I've lost my bag. Have you seen my gold one?'

He puts on his black-framed glasses, looks around the room.

We both spot it at the same time hanging from . . . the wardrobe door.

'Oh, my goodness.' The wooden paws. The fur-muffled cries. The joy. The horror. All that came after. It is here still.

Lucian reaches for my hand.

Another moment passes. Two. We bow our heads, remember those we've lost. Then Lucian picks the handbag off the door and, holding hands a little tighter now, we head downstairs to the party.

*

After a couple of hours, I take refuge at the edge of the woods close to the rabbit holes – still busy, I see. The effusive greetings and hugs of strangers – 'Wow, you look just like Lorna!'; 'Here, Lil, meet Amber Shawcross, yes, *that* Amber Shawcross, all the way from New York' – are touching but exhausting.

Also, I want to spend some time in the company of my own memories. They are in vibrant form this evening. Sitting on this mossy log – just the feel of the velvety green moss peels back decades – my childhood seems more vivid than New York last week. And I can still see them all so clearly. Us, as we were: Momma and Daddy, giggling on the terrace at some unknowable grown-up joke; Kitty determinedly bouncing her toy pram down the stone steps; Barney running across the lawn, slowworm cupped in his hands; Toby beckoning at the edge of the woods, 'Amber, come, look . . .'

But I cannot keep any of my dear ghosts with me long: the past is soon beaten back by the giddy vitality of the present. Black Rabbit Hall has never looked cheerier or more alive, bathed in the warmth of this wonderful Indian summer, festooned with Chinese lanterns, fairy lights, bunting and balloons, the low autumn light winking in its freshly polished windows. Children roll down its sloped lawns. Beautiful young people dance on the terrace, long-legged girls circling my delighted son, taking turns to twirl from his hand. Trays of tiny triangular crab sandwiches and pasties wobble on the palms of teenage locals, shoulder-height through the crowds. ('Too much booze, too little food,' Lucian whispered in my ear approvingly. 'Like all the best weddings.')

I take it all in and marvel at the passing figure of Dill, who has grown into such a facsimile of Peggy that I quite forgot myself and rushed up to hug her on first sighting. Last time I saw her she was the size of a kitten: in those bittersweet days after Lorna was born, Peggy would steal into my room with a tin of cake and we'd sit on my bed trying to suckle our babies.

Lorna says it was her lovely sister Louise and Dill who made this wedding happen, brought it miraculously together at the very last minute. They have both been rushing about for hours, it seems, good-naturedly rescuing old aunts lost in the towers, drunk teenagers from the woods, all the while trailed by a flume of excitable children and the one-boy carnival that is Alf, who keeps making Lucian play the *Toy Story* tune on the grand piano.

Lorna's got a great family: loving, close, blessedly normal, everything I hoped. If Sheila were alive I'd thank her. Lorna says their relationship was never a particularly easy one, but Sheila clearly did something right and for this I must be eternally grateful. And Doug is great. I like Doug a lot. So does Lucian. The two of them – unlikely pair that they are, Doug in a baby blue suit and pink tie, Lucian in his crumpled black Prada – have been sitting on a hay bale for the last hour, laughing, drinking cider and smoking cigarettes, even though they had both given up years ago. Lorna, I can see, is discreetly watching them too, checking how they're getting on.

All the while, Jon's extended family – glamour! noise! sequins! – move through the estate like a shoal of exotic fish. They talk at a million miles an hour in an accent that, after all my years abroad, I struggle to pin down. At the helm of it all is Lorna's mother-in-law, Lorraine, a woman who is somehow always in the field of vision, wearing a leopard-print hat the size of a satellite dish. But even that is dwarfed by Aunt Bay's headpiece, a giant plume of peacock feathers, their fluffy petrol tips shaking above the heads of the crowd as she totters along on Kitty's arm, telling anyone who will listen about her dear late sister, Nancy, who adored a party and cut such a dash in green. Kitty laughs, happy to let Bay take centre stage. Her joy comes from showing her own four children – all Americans, Kitty having joined me in New York aged sixteen, marrying a dear friend of mine and settling in Momma's Maine – that the wild old house she's told them stories about actually exists. And, no, seriously, their cell phones won't work.

I cannot help but wonder what Caroline would make of it all. Would she be happy? Or was she incapable of joy? I don't think we'll ever know. Thankfully, she died in a hospice in Truro last month, gripping Lucian's hand. He somehow found it in his heart to forgive her at the very end. I never will. Like the rest of the universe, I heaved a sigh of relief when she died and asked God what had taken Him so damn long.

'Anything I can get you?' I look up and see Jon, tall and handsome in a navy suit, smiling shyly. 'Another drink?'

'No, I'm good, thank you.' I pat the space on the log next to me. 'I'm being looked after exceptionally well. It's a lovely wedding, Jon.'

He sits down beside me, big boxy knees pulling at the fabric of his trousers. 'A bit weird to be back?'

I laugh. 'A little.'

384

'Lorna was worried it might stir too much stuff up.'

'Ah, don't worry. Black Rabbit Hall lives up here anyway.' I tap my head. 'And, you know, I'm pleased it does, I really am.'

He stares down at his huge feet, radiating the sweet, slightly baffled air that grooms have on their wedding day, that Lucian had in City Hall all those years ago. Nice shoes, I notice. Conker-brown Italian brogues, slightly old-fashioned. Lorna's influence, I suspect. I wish my teachers at school had been half so stylish.

His knee starts to jiggle. 'Mrs –'

'Amber, please!'

'Sorry.' He laughs nervously, knee jiggling faster, before blurting out, 'I spoke to Toby.'

I freeze. 'What? What did you just say?'

'Your brother Toby called me,' he says, more softly now, letting the words sink in.

The ground really does fly from my feet. I steady myself with a hand on the log. 'You *spoke* to Toby on the phone? How . . . Shit. I'm sorry. Forgive me . . . How on earth . . .'

'I sent him a wedding invitation, along with a letter explaining who we were, my details if he wanted to get in touch. I didn't hear back from him, didn't think I ever would, to be honest, but as I was getting out of the shower this morning, mind on other things, obviously, a man called, husky voice, saying it was Toby Alton and he had to know, was this really an invitation to the wedding of Amber's long-lost daughter? He just couldn't believe it. But he sounded so happy when I said that it most definitely was.'

My eyes fill. And I'm flung right back to that feverish

night in London when I couldn't sleep. I'd sat up in bed and scribbled a letter to Toby at his remote boarding school – 'The Prison', he called it – confiding in him about the baby. I'd kept the secret from him for more than a year and could simply hold it in no longer. A week later I got a simple note right back, one I've always treasured: 'I know. I dreamed about her. Be strong, sis. Love, T.'

'Would you like to take a minute, Amber?' Jon asks, as I wipe my eyes. 'I should have warned you. But I didn't want to get any hopes up.'

'No, no, really. I'm fine.' I catch tear-smudged mascara on the edge of my finger and try to smile. 'Please go on. What else did he say?'

'Not much. He couldn't come to the wedding, but he wished us all the best.' Jon drops his eyes. 'There was a crackle, then the line went dead.'

'I – I still don't understand. How did you know where to send the invitation? He phones or writes to me every few years, telling me he's alive and well, but that's it. He never leaves a number, nothing.'

'Dill found his address.'

'*Dill?*' I'm almost too stunned to speak.

'A few days before Caroline died, she handed over a huge damp bundle of old letters, admin and documents – they were tied together with garden twine – the stuff she thought Dill would need to keep things going here. Dill found Toby's details somewhere in that – various addresses over the years, Kenya, Jamaica, Ireland, Scotland, letters from Caroline's solicitor, demanding money for the upkeep of the house, all sorts of things. Not much mail coming back the other way. But still . . .' He pauses as I shake my head in mute disbelief. 'I guess it makes sense that Caroline knew where he was all along. She could manage the estate but never owned it.'

My head is spinning. I don't care about the estate, who owns it, who doesn't. Only one thing matters. 'Where? Where *is* my bloody brother?'

'A smallholding on the Scottish Isle of Arran.'

'Arran! *Arran?* That is *the* most dumb-rabbit stupid – Give me his number, Jon. I'm going to call him right now.'

'I knew you'd want it. But no number came up on my phone when he contacted me. I'm so sorry.'

So he's slipped out of reach again. All I want to do is shake Toby, my selfish, wild, beloved brother, shake him and shake him for his self-imposed exile. By punishing himself for everything that happened, he's punished everyone else, too. But that was the thing about Toby: if he was up, he raised you with him, like a god; if he was down, he dunked you under, too, hand hard on your head. God, I miss him.

'I'm sorry if it's not a good time to tell you,' Jon says, biting his lower lip, 'but it's the first chance I've had all day and I thought you'd want to know. I haven't even told Lorna yet.'

Lorna appears like a vision then, running across the lawns in bare feet, glossy dark hair studded with white flowers, coiled over her shoulder. Alf skips behind, carrying her shoes. I have to scramble myself together. I don't want anything to colour her wedding. It's not about me or Toby.

'We gave up on my heels, didn't we, Alf?' She laughs, sits down beside us in a puff of tulle and cool evening air.

Her elated face is flushed by the sun setting behind the woods, beautifully framed by my mother's white fur cape, slung over her shoulders, diamanté clasp winking. 'Hopeless on grass. Come on, Jon. To the ballroom with you! Dancing!'

Jon stands up rather quickly. 'I'll see you up there.' He shoots me an apologetic smile, takes Alf's hand. 'Come on, Alf.'

'But I am the carrier of the shoes!' Alf protests, wedging himself on to Lorna's knee so that he can't be easily extracted.

'A very serious job.' Lorna wraps her arms around him, smiling up at Jon. 'Do you mind if I come up in a bit? I'll bring Alf. Could do with a break from your uncle Reg, actually.'

'He's not comatose under a tree yet?' He bends down, kisses her. 'Seriously, take as long as you need. Everything's running late anyway. Nobody seems to have noticed.'

We are silent – I'm still reeling about Toby – until Jon is out of earshot. Then, over Alf's head, Lorna leans towards me and whispers, 'Good together, you think?'

I take her hand and squeeze it, probably too intensely. I'd hold her hand all day if I could. 'Lorna, you two are simply wonderful together. Perfect.'

She smiles, kicks out her feet, wiggles her toes into the grass. They are my mother's feet, I notice, the second toe longer than the first. 'I think so, too.'

We sit there companionably, me still not able to say much, her chattering easily with Alf, pointing out the first bats of the evening, the woods, through the trees to the cliffs, a teeny beach where four children loved to play, the ribs of a smuggler's boat poking out of the sand at low tide, dolphins in the deep. Alf is transfixed. But then the sun sinks abruptly, as it does in autumn down here, as if yanked by a puppeteer's string, and it is cold.

Time to go back! Alf jumps up. Time to dance! We walk to the house, Alf stopping every few steps to poke a curious chubby finger into the sugary brown molehills. The terrace is a roar of noise. More people are dancing, even though you can't hear the music. Alf pulls on Lorna's dress, 'Aunt Lor . . .'

Lorna cannot hear him. Uncle Reg is staggering along the balustrade towards her, singing, 'For she's a jolly good fellow!' in a drunken baritone. A woman in canary yellow is pressing glasses of champagne into our hands. A camera flashes. 'Smile!' Another flash. 'And again. One for the grandkids. Lovely!'

'Aunt Lorna,' Alf says, tugging on her sleeve more crossly. 'I want to show you something.'

It is at this exact moment that it starts, the internal twanging, the beep of an old long-forgotten sonar. I look up from the rim of my champagne glass, puzzled, wondering if we're due an electrical storm.

'Aunty Lorna, will you just *look*?'

'Sorry, what, Alf?' Lorna peers down at him, distracted.

'Black rabbits!'

The noise fades, everything fades, as I follow Alf's pointing little finger, past the rabbits hopping out of the burrows, to the edge of the woods where someone – it must be a man, it is a man – is walking up the slope silhouetted against the blood-red sky, his outline sinewy. His head is bent into the wind. His hand on his hat. Walking slowly but purposefully, like a farmer out in his fields at dusk. He short-cuts up the steepest slope, as he always did, and pauses at the top, pushing the rim of his hat up with one finger, gazing at the house from beneath it, just for a fleeting moment, but long enough for the last flare of sun to catch the fire in his beard before it sinks behind the trees.

I call his name, start to run.

Epilogue

My children's foreheads: Toby, tree resin; Amber, a hormonal tang of late; Kitty, milk. Barney is not in the kitchen to kiss or sniff. I check under the turned feet of the table, half expecting to see him there. 'Where's Barns?'

Rabbits, they tell me. Off on one of his capers with Boris.

A moment later, we find the daft old dog skulking behind the door.

Thunder. Peggy stares out of the window, fiddling with that crucifix necklace of hers, muttering unhelpful things about the storm being 'blown in by the devil himself'.

It's certainly a squall. So often the storms that announce themselves early, those mighty black operas rolling in from the sea – keenly spotted by my dear husband on the terrace – disperse before they hit with any force. It's the ones that give no warning and crack across the sky like a shotgun that you have to watch out for. Still, the garden needs the rain.

Where will I find your imp of a brother?

In the den by the swing rope, Amber tells me, flicking up those serious green eyes of hers, squishing cream on to her scone. As my daughter is right about most things, I determine to start looking there.

Toby, my sweet gallant boy, offers to go instead. No, he

must finish his tea. They must all finish their tea, which is terribly late today – that range is such a rogue. Always hungry, the children have shot up like reeds since we were last here, ankles shooting out of the bottom of trousers, long, pale wrists from shirts. Peggy can't cook fast enough.

I leave them chatting, squabbling, walk across the hall, decide against a mackintosh or hat. Crazy, really, but after days of being trapped in London, looped with painkillers, leg up on that damn stool, I'm desperate for a drench of rain. A Cornish storm beats coffee mornings in Fitzrovia.

Knight doesn't share my enthusiasm. He is fussing, twisting back his ears, not himself at all. I mount him, wrap my arms around his neck, murmuring in the silly baby voice he likes best. He calms a little but remains reluctant. I push down in the stirrups. A shooting pain flies up my leg, a reminder of the accident, all those dead city days stuck in that turquoise velvet chair. And I feel a wave of gratitude to Barney for getting me out here, the wind ripping through the trees, thunder crashing, like a wonderful mistuned school orchestra.

Through the gate to the woods – the hinges need oiling, must mention it to Hugo – it is quieter, hard to ride. Some of the trees have come down; branches and twigs are still falling. We pick our way through until I spot the swing rope rocking in the strange yellow storm light, as if a child has just leapt off it. 'Barney?' I shout. 'Tea!'

A giggle. I whip around, trying to spot him in the gloom. 'Barney?'

He springs out of a wigwam of sticks, a laughing, leaping creature, his pale bare soles flashing as he runs. 'Catch me if you can!'

'Oh, for goodness' sake, where are your shoes?' But he isn't listening. He is hopping over fallen logs, glancing over his shoulder to see if I'm on his tail. 'I'm warning you!' I shout, getting mad, even though I was just the same as a child.

He starts to scrabble up a tree, wilfully disobedient, as Hugo will fume later, bare feet curled around the bark like a bear's, higher and higher into the dark canopy, looking down at me, grinning. I think I see my boy exactly as he is then, he me, and we both laugh.

But Knight starts to hoof backwards, agitated by the storm, the thunder rolling through the valley. My blouse rips on a branch and flaps in the wind. And suddenly Barney is gone, swallowed by leaves. I begin to panic. Will he fall? Has he fallen? No, Barney never falls from anything. 'Enough now, Barn . . .'

A flashbulb fork of lightning: Barney's face, silver in the leaves. Knight wants to run. I pull him back hard. My weak leg slips from the stirrup. I really need to get the horse out of the storm now, Barney home. 'Grab my hand!' I shout, reaching up to Barney.

Boom! A clap of thunder so loud it trembles the leaves. Too loud.

Knight snorts, bucks, piston-rises, up, up, up, until there is nothing solid beneath me, no saddle, no stirrup, no hot horse flesh. Only hands outstretched, fingertips touching for a fraction of a moment, a surge of love, white-bright, shooting through the sky like a star.

Acknowledgements

A heartfelt thank you to the talented, passionate teams at Michael Joseph and Putnam, especially my brilliant editors Maxine Hitchcock and Tara Singh Carlson who have made this novel immeasurably better and are such a joy to work with. Louise Moore for the wise advice and encouragement that first got me thinking about this story. My wonderful agents – Lizzy Kremer and Kim Witherspoon – whose unwavering belief in *Black Rabbit Hall* from the outset played a huge part in its creation. Also Harriet Moore, Alice Howe, Allison Hunter, and the rest of the teams at David Higham Associates and InkWell Management. Keeping the home fires burning . . . Mum, as ever. Tess, Emma, Kirsty, Izzy and Flip for being so welcoming since I moved to the manor. My children, little tribe of three: the best lines are all yours. And Ben, for pulling the rabbit out of the hat every time. Thank you.